STRANDS OF WAR

ALSO BY THE AUTHOR

It's Different at Dartmouth: A Memoir

Jean Alexander Kemeny

STRANDS OF WAR

HOUGHTON MIFFLIN COMPANY
Boston 1984

Library of Congress Cataloging in Publication Data

Kemeny, Jean Alexander, date
Strands of war.

1. World War, 1939–1945—Fiction. I. Title.
PS3561.E3984S7 1984 813′.54 84-10494
ISBN 0-395-36176-1

Printed in the United States of America

S 10 9 8 7 6 5 4 3 2 1

For Jenny and Rob

Acknowledgments

For their help: Martha Alexander, John Bogle, Sanborn Brown, Richard Bueschel, Mona and Eddie Chamberlain, Elizabeth Dycus, Bill Eastman, Ruth LaBombard, Becky LaHaye, Peter B. Martin, Arline McCondach, Harry McDade, M.D., Madelaine and Tibor Mikes, Thomas O'Toole, Maurice Rapf, Stuart Russell, M.D., Ethel and Ernst Snapper, James Strickler, M.D., and Judy Wiley.

A special debt to: William P. Davis, Jr., Norwich, Vt.; the team in the Modern Military Branch of the National Archives headed by Robert Wolfe, Washington, D.C.; and the reference staffs at the Howe Library and Dartmouth College's Baker Library, Hanover, N.H.

Grateful thanks to all the people at Houghton Mifflin, including Luise M. Erdmann, who copy-edited with flair. Particular thanks to David Replogle, who wore two hats. As head of General Publishing, he took a chance on a first novelist; as editor, he endured my outbursts, calmly guiding me and the manuscript through the necessary revisions.

To John Kemeny, my husband, love for help beyond words.

Prologue

MARCH 1945

She surfaced off the southern tip of Nova Scotia, breaching like a monstrous whale — save for the superstructure and the guns. The seas streamed from her gray, round sides. Far off to starboard lay Cape Sable — and farther west: the U-boat's rendezvous.

It was an hour after dawn.

The Captain stood on the bridge of the conning tower scanning the sea and the sky. The sea ran only to small chop; it was the sky which gave him pause: a mackerel sky.

He saw storm in the rows of small fleecy clouds. He smelled storm in the damp carried by a breeze that was freshening.

The weather stations on Greenland had been destroyed; the picket weather boats in the North Atlantic were all but gone. He had only his senses to guide him now, but his senses were keener than they had ever been, sharpened by hatred and an almost certain prescience of doom.

His boat could make the coast in thirty-six hours barring catastrophe. Faster without the damned snorkel.

The Captain swore at the sky and cursed his cargo. He thought of those in the Reich who had sent him here. One by one he ticked off names and relegated them to the deep: Adolf Hitler . . . Karl Dönitz . . . Heinrich Himmler . . . The picture of the floundering trio was a tonic and revived him. For a moment he smiled, savoring the image.

And then his face sagged as once more he searched the furrowed sky and found no blue. He turned and hunched his shoulders against a gale that was not there, a wind that was already whistling through his bones.

In the gray light the Captain was an old man, weary and sick at heart. He had seen too much and fought too long.

His name was Steiner and he was twenty-eight.

1936

FROM: REICHSLEITER MARTIN BORMANN
REICH CHANCELLERY
WILHELMSTRASSE, BERLIN

TO: HAUPTSTURMFÜHRER WILHELM SCHMIDT
CENTRAL SECURITY OFFICE SS
PRINZ ALBRECHTSTRASSE, BERLIN

Schmidt:

I always knew that placing you in the Central Security Office SS had great possibilities. From Brownshirt to Blackshirt with a snap of my fingers (and a snip of the scissors!). I shall only bring up the Röhm affair from time to time. Associating with that Putsch-plotter, that pervert! Be glad it is only a painful memory. You could be dead! Rotting alongside Ernst and Schleicher.

But enough of that — for now. You are in a position to know what Himmler and Heydrich are up to. Particularly Heydrich. That weasel has wicked teeth. Who's he going to slash next? I want to know every move they both make. The moves they don't inform me of. What about their intelligence service? What are they hatching there? Are they branching out? How far? Beyond Europe? What of Canaris? Should we infiltrate that dummkopf's network? Shouldn't be hard. The Abwehr fails so much of the time!

As you must be aware, my star is rising. Hitch your wagon to it, dear Willi, and you stay safe and sound. I won't mention that you have little choice in the matter. I have become known as a toiler for the Führer. (Also a toady by the envious.)

My position here is secure. The Führer depends on me. Hess depends on me. Therefore, I wish to branch out under the cover of all this dependency. I want to establish an intelligence service of my own. Known *only* to the two of us. Of course, this idea cannot work without help from within the Reich, but those that you recruit to do the inside work will report only to you, believing that they are part of the SD. I want agents in place *around the world.* Don't cringe, Willi. It is possible, and I will enlighten you in a moment.

I want agents in place to gather information for me *now and in the future.* Whatever information comes in will be scrutinized by you (and me, if it appears earthshaking), and I will decide whether to pass it on to the SD or the Abwehr. Any information given will not appear as a result of my network, of course, but rather as tidbits or morsels which were filtered to the Führer (through *my* office) by persons unidentified. Feeding the SS and Canaris will be like lunch at the Zoo! They will be beholden to me, growl for more, and roll on their backs if they get it.

But these agents you will recruit for service beyond the Reich should be prepared to serve in other capacities later, if the need arises. I have not the slightest idea what that need could be, but I wish to be prepared for *any* contingency.

There is, of course, the matter of funding such a network. At the moment my treasury is small, although much larger than anyone would imagine. I was a most conscientious administrator of the Party Relief Fund. Ask Putzi Hanfstaengl. Impressed him with my diligence. And he's a Harvard man, as he informs me, which, I understand, in America is like being on the right hand of God! So — the foreign press secretary would vouch for my work. What's more, after the dwarf and the drug addict got through filling their pockets, the Relief Fund was in bad shape. Bled it nearly dry, the greedy bastards! Despite the mess Goebbels and Göring left, I came in and made it work. *No one* guesses I skimmed a bit here, a bit there. Not a lot, but enough to start my own discretionary fund. It is a beginning. But I expect more opportunities to open up, and I expect you to keep your eyes peeled and your ears atune on this matter of new monies. If the SS has the pie, I want a piece of it!

Bormann

P.S. Do not forget the alternative method of agent selection. The method which breeds such loyalty. The tie that binds you to me. Utter terror!

Willi,

Good work! To walk one must take the first step. An American, you say? Keep him on ice and let him shiver until we decide when to unfreeze him. No money involved with this one? Just fear? Wonderful! Fear and blackmail work, don't they, Willi!?

Bormann

1937

HANNES
BUSSETT
SUMMER

The library is cool and quiet and clean, the only goddamned place in the whole of this goddamned state that is free of dust. The people aren't in here getting out of the sun and the wind because they're all out scratching the earth and praying for rain. Who reads when the cattle are dropping and the pump just drips.

This place is my real home. It's like a palace with real marble floors. I could be anywhere. I *am* anywhere but in Bussett. The place that God forgot. The place that Roosevelt never heard of — and if he did he'd forget it quick too. The place will die with only the peaks of the roofs sticking up through the dust and the windmills still whirring for nobody, until one by one all the wooden blades are ripped off. There isn't any fight left and our throats are as parched as our fields. That's for sure.

I come here in my stiff overalls with six inches of daylight between the place where they end and the tops of my workshoes. At the front door it seems only right to spend a few minutes whacking and stomping to get rid of the outside. Clouds of crap-colored powder fly off and settle on the porch.

Once inside I clump to the shelves, choose a stack of books, and walk past Miss Mandelbaum, the librarian, who smiles and nods happily. She believes I am a soul worth saving. That's what she says. I think she's right.

I sink down in a soft stuffed chair that is *not* falling apart. I lay out my books on the long table that smells of lemons and try to forget my nightmare, reading about other people's dreams. Uncle Alois, if I don't hear from you soon, I'll choke to death in Bussett!

* * *

I discovered the library because of the lentils. This spring Papa sent me into town to scrounge some. I hitched a ride on the cart with Duncan, who still has a horse that can limp forward. In Bussett — which will be a ghost town soon what with all the foreclosures — I went into the feed store and spent an hour arguing, shouting and finally sweet-talking that tightwad into extending our credit a mite longer. Twenty-five pounds of lentils — which will be our supper and lunch and breakfast for how long? I stole some onions for flavor.

Duncan had long since gone, so I was left to figure out a way back to the farm when for really the first time I noticed the library. In a one-street town that is tumbling down, I spied behind the wrecks a new brick building with white columns set off in a grove of trees. All around, green green grass shiny with drops of water.

Nowhere for a hundred miles round does anything germinate in fields all cracked and bare. Yet here were live growing things! A Garden of Eden!

I forgot that I had to get home. I forgot that I was carrying a heavy sack. I forgot everything I was supposed to do. I walked into the Bussett Town Library and changed my life.

The lady at the desk seemed surprised to see me. No wonder. I was the only customer. I stammered something because I really didn't know why I had come and she was kind and sent me to some shelves and told me to pick what I wanted. That first day I read some Kipling, rousing tales, and asked if I could take a book home. I promised to return it as soon as I could although I wasn't sure how. She said of course and stamped a date in the back. The due date, she said. I had a week! A whole week. I could manage anything in a week!

Back I walked the six miles to the farm and never even noticed the weight. When the bag split open and the book fell out, Papa beat me. But that was usual. He liked to do it every evening just before supper. With his fists, and Mama stirring the soup, not seeing, not hearing. Not caring, I think . . .

It is supposed to be a great day, the day you graduate from high school. It wasn't. There were only ten kids and six of them were girls who wouldn't talk to me anyway. Most of the boys had already quit and gone on to find a better place to scratch if they were lucky. The school stood like an old elephant in a dirt pile and inside we stood in our knickers or feedbag dresses and listened to the principal say a lot of stuff which nobody heard. Other graduating classes had outside speakers. Once one came from Omaha! But who would want to come to Bussett now? Nobody in their right mind, that's for sure!

Mama and Papa came and didn't say one word to anybody because they're so suspicious of the neighbors. There are Germans to the north of us, way far north, and Germans to the east of us — but we are the only ones right here. Which leaves us with no one to talk to.

Once the neighbors tried visiting, tried to be kind. While I hid embarrassed in the barn, Papa would order "you Presbyterian trash" off the land, always screaming in German because English was like a burglar, sneaking up on him. Papa felt better after yelling but I paid for it. For sure I paid for it! The kid who's *different.* The *Henkel* snuck in with all the MacDonalds, Stuarts and MacBains.

Papa likes failing because he can blame it on Nature and shout at God. His God is Lutheran, and nowhere around Bussett or Goucherville or anywhere is there a Lutheran church, so Papa and Mama stay home on Sundays and pray to their God while the rest of the town, the Scotch-Irish, go to church and pray to their God, but nobody's prayers are answered and nobody's God hears.

With graduation over, my schooling has stopped. I use every excuse to get to town and sometimes no excuse at all. I just leave and make a beeline for the library. I stay all the day and come home in time to get whipped, eat a little supper and read the books I've taken out. The summer's gone into July and I've read most the adventure stories and have started on history. European history which doesn't seem important enough to teach in a dead old American town. And, because I was born there, German history, which is full of a lot of states always fighting. A lot of war.

I'm up to Bismarck now and today I brought him and some more onions home. It was a very special day because I think it is the last time Papa will hit me. Mama chopped the onions to put into the lentil soup. (I wish we'd had a pig's knuckle to add to it!) I can still see the onion juice and some little white squares sticking to the knife. Papa grabs me like always. But not like always I grab the knife right out of Mama's hands. Mama stands there gasping like a fish — and Papa's eyes bulge out — and I just stand there and point it at him and nobody says a word. And then Papa sits down at the table like nothing has happened and Mama serves him and I go upstairs and sit on the bed, shaking. I must have sat there for a long time because it got dark and I lit the kerosene lamp to read by but I couldn't keep my mind on the book. All I could think of was would I have stabbed Papa if he had hit me? Could I just push that knife into him? I must have gone to sleep thinking about it because I woke up in the middle of the night trying to wipe blood off my hands — and there wasn't any! I didn't stab Papa and I won't stab anyone else, ever, anytime!

Today I got to talking to Miss Mandelbaum and asked her how come her voice sounded like cool water, which it does. She smiled and said that when she came to Bussett she thought everybody talked like the sound fingernails make scraping down a blackboard. I got goosepimples just thinking about that! I guess I never thought about the way we talk, but after listening to Miss Mandelbaum and then bumping into Mrs. Murray out in the street because I was thinking not looking and her bawling me out to beat the band, well, I sure heard those fingernails!

Miss Mandelbaum was hired by someone who works for Mr. Bussett to come and make this the best little library between the Rockies and the Mississippi. I thought that was great but she said she had failed and then tears started to sprout in her eyes which are a very pretty blue when she takes her glasses off. For a lady that must be as old as thirty she is nice looking with her dark hair and all.

She said she had tried building up the collections. Books were for reading and no one was. So I told her what I thought — that people had too much on their minds nowadays for books.

But then she stuttered out about not fitting in with the people around here and I said I knew what she meant. With a name like Henkel, I didn't either. I told her we were the only two with German names so we were alike. She looked at me for an awful long time and then gave me a funny smile and said she didn't think so.

I guess I wrote that I was different. But I didn't write about the things that happened. I wasn't going to either until I saw Billie Joe Campbell across the street. I thought Billie Joe had gone for good but there he was big as life and twice as mean, looking at me like he used to. I kept on going and he kept on going and I kept on hoping he'd stay on his side which he did. Maybe he didn't recognize me because I've grown a lot in the last year. That's why my ankles get sunburnt because we can't afford a new pair of overalls.

Seeing Billie Joe brought back a lot of awful memories like the time he and a couple of his buddies locked me in the janitor's closet. Probably that doesn't sound too bad except that they grabbed me and tied me up and slammed the door and locked it on a Friday afternoon just after all the kids went home and I stayed there trussed up like a turkey with a gag in my mouth till Monday morning. Saturday Papa called the sheriff because I hadn't slept in my bed, no sir, I hadn't. I was sleeping, if you can call it that, in a tiny space that was filled with mops and pails and cleaning stuff that smelled so awful I thought I was going to suffocate, what with the gag in my mouth — which I was sure I was going to swallow. They looked for me, but they never thought of the janitor's closet, and after a while I must have passed out because I remember waking up feeling little things crawling all over me, and I couldn't whack them off and I tried to scream which only made the gag wetter and bigger. I was so scared I peed in my pants. I had to go and I'd held it in as long as I could but my bladder was near to busting and all it took was me scared right out of my mind. When they found me and took the gag out of my mouth I screamed and screamed and kept whacking at myself to get those crawly things off me. Only mice they told me. Only mice! I think they were rats — and if I hadn't smelled like a pisspot they'd have nibbled me to death for sure!

Today all hell broke loose because of the water tank.

I guess I never connected the library's trees and lawn and the geraniums that are blooming now with the water tank out back. Growing things need water, need to be hosed down and it hasn't rained since God knows when. Forever!

Old Mr. Bussett who named this town, who *owns* this town, said that the water tank should always be filled come hell or high water. We have the first. I've never seen the second! Well — Mr. Bussett who lives high now on all the millions he made squeezing farmers, who left when clouds were still bringing rain, still brings it. Three times a week, the train stops at Bussett and usually the only thing that is off-loaded is water! Water from the east to fill the tank to water the flowers at the *Bussett* Town Library. Twenty men come on the train hauling that water in five-gallon jugs, climbing up the ladder of the library tank and pouring it in. Back and forth they go — sometimes takes all day. Mr. Bussett must pay a lot to keep that train waiting. So that's how come the library blooms and nothing else does.

I was inside, reading as usual when I heard a murmur. Sounded like a truck with a bad transmission. Then I knew it wasn't when the noise got to be a roar.

Miss Mandelbaum was shaking and I was scared too. All the men in the world seemed to be out there yelling. Some had pickaxes and some had shovels or crowbars and a lot of ladders. Every ladder had a man on it climbing fast. And they pounded on that tank and the boards screamed as they got torn apart. Pretty soon water began to dribble out from the holes. The men kept chopping and the water kept coming. Streams of water, a river of water and everybody cheering. That water was a flood now and it swept down the main street but it couldn't sink into the dirt because the earth was like concrete so it rolled on carrying a load of dust on top and ran right out of town. That water tank probably didn't hold enough water to wet one farmer's land, but that wasn't the point.

Long afterward the farmers laughed and slapped each other and told the story of the water tank over and over again. Even Papa who almost couldn't remember how smiled a little bit.

Cousin Alois lives in Chicago where we did once. It's because of Cousin Alois that we are here in America. He sponsored us when Germany was in awful straits and gave Papa a job in one of his hardware stores. I was only a year old when we came over and I don't remember Chicago at all because Papa hated it, the job. He said he was a farmer which wasn't exactly right. He helped harvest grapes in the Rhineland. Papa insisted he wanted to make it on his own, to get back digging into the soil, so that's why we left Chicago to come here.

The first couple of years were OK, I guess, but then the dust started and when it did it didn't stop. The winds that brought the blizzards began bringing gray powder from Kansas, red dust from Oklahoma, and when it swirled westerly, brown shit from Colorado.

It piled up and covered everything, monster clouds of suffocating powder soft sometimes as talcum. We wore homemade dust masks to school. The dust was under the blankets and in our underwear. It was on our lips and in our eyes. We breathed dust, we ate dust, we slept in it and shat it. Did and still do.

Everyone around here struggles, everybody around here is poor. But Papa just couldn't believe it was happening to him. He'd go out and chop furrows in cement and drop in the seed. And then he'd wait for the rain that never came. Every year the seed dried up and every year Papa died a little. But he didn't go easily. He yelled at the sky and when that didn't work he took it out on Mama and me. All Mama did was pull everything inside and stop speaking. That's when he began hitting me. We three were trying to make it in a broken-down farmhouse in a dead place and we were dying inside.

Sometimes Papa would get out the old book of photographs and colored postcards and he and Mama would forget the day and look backward. The Germany they had left behind seemed bright to them now. And the pictures showed pretty towns, neat and clean and maybe prosperous. And there were hills, green hills and a great blue river, all the water in the world, curving so sweet through those hills. And forests, black-green forests. So many trees.

But when I look out at this land it goes on and on. In every direction, not one tree. There's nothing to love and nothing to look forward to.

Which is how Cousin Alois came back into the picture. I wrote to him. I wrote a letter telling him how awful everything was and I wasn't too proud to do it. Papa would have killed me if he had found out, but I kept the letter secret and asked Cousin Alois if he answered not to mention who wrote first.

Back lickety-split came a letter. To Papa and Mama. Not to me. And in it Cousin Alois asked how we were and were we interested in a group he belonged to that took native Germans back to Germany where they could start all over again. Cousin Alois wrote that Germany was different. New, and real exciting. Everybody had automobiles and the roads were wide and straight and with a new leader the Fatherland would lead the way. We had heard of Adolf Hitler but only what the newspapers said about him — which wasn't too favorable. But pretty soon a bundle of magazines came with pictures of smiling people farming and dancing, pictures of people with stars in their eyes, listening to the Führer, for that is what he is called. And pictures of young people, as young as me, wearing uniforms, looking strong and healthy and oh so happy!

The three of us talked far into the night. We *talked.* Mama came out of her shell that night and Papa's face got red with excitement and Mama giggled and I, well I took it all in and grew two inches. At least I felt like I had!

We all slept late the next morning which for farmers is like getting up at sunset. But who cared! There were no real farm chores to do. No cattle to milk or feed. They were dead. No crops to harvest. They'd never been born. No water to haul. The pump, the well, the land was dry. So we got up and had grits with sugar syrup which Mama had been saving for a special occasion and she said she was afraid that nothing special would happen and the mice would get the sugar before we did. But it has!

I was so excited that today I practically flew into town to get to the library. I told Miss Mandelbaum I wanted to read *everything.* I didn't tell her why yet, that I want to be really educated when we go to Germany, because it's bad luck to tell a secret until it comes true. But I was bursting to.

Miss Mandelbaum says my vocabulary is limited is what she says. And that I should read the words of great writers and learn from them how to speak and write better.

She's marked with stars what she calls the great fiction writers of the twentieth century. I've tried some and here's what I think and I'll have to say right here I'm not too impressed.

Kafka is like going into a haunted house all alone.

Hemingway uses easy words but he likes to kill. He really does. Everything from bulls in Spain to bull elephants in Africa. And people too.

Woolf who's a lady is all tied up in word pictures and goes on and ON until I can't breathe!

Faulkner must live in a dusty town too.

Lewis. I don't want to read about small towns anymore. I know enough about them already!

So I told Miss Mandelbaum and she said in time I might change my mind. I haven't got the time!

Miss Mandelbaum figures since I've done a lot of history and tried some of *her* fiction (I didn't mention that I liked *my* kind of fiction. *The Three Musketeers* was great!) how about something difficult but worthwhile — philosophy.

I felt foolish asking what was philosophy. She didn't blink an eye (her eyes are sort of almond-shaped now that I think of it which goes with her name — almond tree — Mandelbaum) and went right on telling me that philosophy contains the thoughts of great men who seek the truth. She pointed me toward the Philosophy Shelf and told me to read until someone hits me and things become clear.

I started with A. Aquinas. I guess the Catholics think he's something. I don't, seeing as God ignores those of us in trouble, so I put him back and went on reading from left to right. Not much hit me, I can tell you!

I came to H and pulled out Hume. Name sounded sort of Saxon. Wasn't. A friggin Scot, that's who. Hume went back fast. Hegel came after Hume when he should have come before. I thought maybe Hegel was a German but I spotted Kant and I *know* he's a German so I plowed along. Maybe he's smart and maybe somewhere he says something but he takes too long to say it. I gave up on Kant.

Back to Hegel. I wasted a lot of time but I found him. Seeing pictures of MY Germany being born again makes everything that Hegel says important right now! It's as though he was sitting down beside me, clearing up all the mess in my life, all the mess in the whole world. Democratic (so called!) governments aren't strong enough to take care of their people. Just look around here! But Hegel has the answers and he gives those answers to Germany and Germany will show everybody!

It's September and it just gets hotter. The sky is like metal and nothing moves but the wind. The leaves on the library's trees are hanging down begging for water and the lawn could be an ashfield. I'm as sad as the trees, thinking about everything that could go wrong because Papa is so stupid!

OCTOBER

We are going back! We are going to Germany and we leave in November! I almost thought that Papa had ruined our chances. When he heard from Cousin Alois that the resettlement program called for families to go to Upper Silesia and maybe farther east if necessary, he broke two chairs (which leaves us only one) and stomped around and yelled that he wouldn't be caught dead in Upper Silesia — too full of Slavs and coal dust and who knows what all. He knew vineyards and he wasn't ever going to try to grow fields of rye or wheat or anything that had to be started from seed. He wanted to go to the Mosel or stay here and dry up.

Cousin Alois saved the day! He must have powerful friends. He knows the head of the Bund and he's pretty high up in the Kameradeschaft, the group that gets people out of here — so — he wrote us a letter that made Papa smile as though he had eaten three helpings of sauerbraten and new potatoes. OK, said Cousin Alois, we'll make an exception in your case. A village, a cottage on the Mosel, a job harvesting grapes, and — AND — for Hannes — a place in the Hitler Youth which will strengthen his mind and body! (as soon as he passes some easy tests).

We didn't have any more sugar syrup. We didn't need any. I didn't know how to celebrate so I broke the last chair, and then the three of us sat down plunk on the floor laughing and crying.

NOVEMBER

We leave tomorrow! I had to say goodbye to Miss Mandelbaum because I was so happy. I told her so fast that the words all ran together and maybe that's why she looked strange not understanding that I was going *back* to Germany. I tried to tell her that I would write about all the great things I would be doing and I'd send her a picture of me in uniform. I guess she didn't hear me.

HENRY

CAPE CHARLOTTE

AUTUMN

I record the whole sordid business. In the event that these notes are ever discovered, perhaps I shall not be blamed.

I have decided upon a hiding place: on the top shelf in a hollowed-out novel by Henry James. *The Sacred Fount,* possibly. Evelyn cannot abide Henry James. She is convinced his characters are hollow; and feels he is pompously philosophical and preachy. Furthermore, she abhors ladders.

I do not have to worry about Alvira. Never, in my memory, has she dusted *anything* above her nose.

Conceivably, the affair has been forgotten, lost in the system, misplaced, misfiled. Yet I have that prickly feeling, almost a vestigial awareness, that I am being toyed with.

It was a glorious two weeks, the beginning. A bit of negotiation for the firm in Hamburg and then the chance to be part of history in Berlin. The Games. The Olympics. The pinnacle of Sport. I was euphoric. Everyone was. Such excitement as each country marched in. And then came the Americans, jaunty in their straw boaters. I felt such pride I wanted to shout "Huzza!" Of course I didn't. But I wanted to.

Evelyn didn't wish to come. She detests sports and she loathes Germans. I have little fondness for the Germans, either, but I have to hand it to the Nazis. They know how to put on a show: the color, the trumpets, the measured tread of marching men, even the rigid salutes. I was caught up with the crowd and found myself roaring with them, thrusting out my arm with them as the swastika was unfurled.

With the Games' conclusion, my euphoric bubble burst and I was left with only the mist of memory. Tourists were leaving in droves. Berlin again became a gray and inhospitable city: a strange and grim place.

I had chosen my humble little hotel purposely. I detest extravagance and feel that spending outrageous sums on one's person is a wickedness. I carry on that code of ethics which my family has followed faithfully from time immemorial. I feel the better for it.

It seemed a small thing at the time. An added fillip to an extraordinary adventure: a reservation for one at the Hotel Adlon. Dinner in the Grand Hotel. The maître d' took my name and address via telephone on a Thursday for the following Monday, two days before my departure.

By Sunday, I felt my spirits lowering; I felt unwanted and decidedly lonely. Several times I reached for the phone to cancel dinner, but each time an insidious selfish voice told me to cease this nonsense, that I had only this one chance to experience greatness. Indeed, I was almost salivating by Monday afternoon. You see, I had only partaken of tea in anticipation of the gourmet meal.

I felt rather provincial upon entering the lobby of the Adlon. I believe I half-expected to spy Garbo, the ballerina, and Barrymore, the thief, reclining amid the plush interior. Indeed, a *Grand Hotel!*

Milling about the lobby were stunning women in satin and furs escorted by Hitler's military clothed in black and silver, gray and red. Jewels flashed and swords glittered and eyes sparkled. At that moment I would have given anything to have a lovely woman on my arm, to be my dinner companion. To talk to me of trivia. Just to talk to me.

Alas, there was no one. And the wish was fleeting.

I was ushered to my table by a dainty waiter. Definitely dainty. With a flourish he pulled out a chair and seated me. The room was exquisite, though I could see little of it, placed as I was in a corner, up against a pillar.

I ignored the empty chair opposite by attempting to decipher a menu larger than the *Times.*

The gaiety of the lobby carried over to the diners. Laughter, toasts and the tinkling of crystal. Tantalizing aromas swirled and mixed and wafted towards me. Beef and perfume and just a hint of garlic, I believe.

I ordered with impunity: an ovoid goose liver with two large nuggets of truffles imbedded therein; venison steak so tender it might have been sliced from a fawn; and a wine in actuality quite palatable, though, of course, it was *not* the most expensive burgundy.

The dinner lifted my spirits; the wine burned away my loneliness. The group at the next table raised their glasses to me and I responded.

These companionable gestures were repeated for a lengthy time, as I recall, until, to my chagrin, I found I had emptied the bottle! I, an inhibited Yankee, was becoming tiddly at the Adlon —

So it seemed the most natural of things to accept their kind offers of fellowship and join them. More wine flowed as I remember, much of it into me. And oh, how warm and soothing was the grape.

My comrades thought me amusing, hilariously so. Businessmen, I surmised: dressed drably when compared to the bright uniforms that abounded. When they suggested a nightcap at a less public place, I acceded at once. There was a bit of a flap concerning the check, but I insisted. A matter of pride which cost me a packet. Honor can be costly. Indeed, the bill's total (not including wine!) added up to more than two weeks' worth of Berlin's boiled beef, a dish which, I am loath to admit, is vastly superior to that of Boston. It is the addition of marrow bone and a touch of claret, I am told.

The city, which had been so cold, was warm and inviting now. I believe we linked arms and sang raucously as we stumbled down dark wet streets. The small bar was dimly lit and very Bavarian, with steins of every size and color shelved against the walls. I gazed in awe at buxom barmaids, really unbelievably buxom, who radiated glowing friendliness.

Our table reverberated with song: German lieder, so sweet, so sad; the Harvard Fight Song, which I taught them; and various stirring marches which raised the spirits. The bottle of schnapps which danced on the table was replaced with another which seemed to polka. I was beyond the high and happy stage. I was becoming exceedingly drunk. The last I remember before the awful awakening was being escorted back to my bed. And then the room went round and a swirl of nausea engulfed me . . .

Awakening was agony. Inside my head a blacksmith was hammering iron on his anvil and sparks flew wildly, exploding in my eyeballs.

I knew at once that I was in the throes of a hangover, a monstrous one. Every awful symptom about which I had read was present. Parched and trembling, I would soon shatter.

A putrid odor assaulted me. Immediately I suspected the worst: I had fouled the bed, and waves of childhood guilt o'ercame me. Nurse smacking my red, wet bottom.

But — how shall I put this? — when the truth was revealed, I felt, for an instant only I hasten to say, a kind of relief.

I dreaded the moment when I would have to face the daylight; I wished to burrow into the soft dark of forgetfulness and sleep away the pain.

Yet the sparks of light grew harsher, insistent; and with great effort I opened my eyes.

Men in gray were milling about the room: shadowy figures gesturing, muttering.

I attempted a query, but my tongue was covered with moss and immobile. I attempted to move, but great weights held me fast.

And then an unseen hand drew the draperies. All the light of a brilliant sun pinpointed the scene on the bed. I was not alone in the tangle of comforters.

Two indescribably dirty urchins shared my space. Two naked boys clung to each other and sprawled grotesquely on my legs. They seemed to have groveled in a mud bath and now globs of it soiled my sheets.

I was outraged at the brazen behavior. I ordered the filthy little beasts to leave, get out, in a voice I hoped was authoritarian, but feared was only a squeak. They did not obey. They did not even move.

And then there came a rumble, low and building. Laughter from the side. From the men in gray, uniformed men, whom I had forgotten momentarily.

I will never forget them — ever. They became my constant companions in the dim room where I was forcibly taken.

Their faces changed, but they remained the same: my warders, my interrogators.

I shall remember the accusations as though they were engraved upon granite: a barrage of vileness!

"See the knife caked with the blood of two innocents. In a frenzy you stabbed them repeatedly. And here — photographs. Is that not you, stuporous, still clutching the knife with your victims draped over your knees? We have people who will testify that you begged for two boys. We have your procurers."

Throughout the day, the night, if it was night, I suffered an inquisition of such an unholy nature that even a saint would have begged forgiveness.

I whispered to a familiar face: "We had such a jolly evening. Tell them I was a good companion. Tell them I am innocent!"

The face betrayed me. Appalling lies poured out as easily as syrup.

I wished myself away from horror. The thought of gulping down sweet water from some crystalline stream o'erwhelmed me. I *must* drink or, like a parched dry leaf, shrivel up and crumble.

Finally, it was not the thoughts of prison or even the threats to my good name which weakened my resolve. Rather it was ravaging thirst. I affixed my signature to a confession of heinous crimes. I sold my soul to Satan for the promise of freedom — and one cool glass of milk.

HANNES
HAMBURG
DECEMBER

So much has happened I can't believe it! We left Bussett with only the things we could carry. The rest — the posthole digger and the milk cans, the beds — went to auction, and what that brought in went to Mr. Bussett's bank along with the buildings and the land which he owns already. Mr Bussett's got time to sit there holding on to the land till Nature calms down and the soil is sweet again. And then he'll sell it and maybe make a killing. It's the poor who can't wait. The rich win every time!

I remember an awful long train trip and then the boat. And somewhere down in the guts of the boat was a tiny room for the three of us. I was scared of that place. Walls covered with metal. No room to move, no windows. No air! Steerage, they called it. It was the janitor's closet all over again. I tried to stay out of it because I would start to shake and sweat and think I was choking if the light was off. I told Mama and Papa not to worry if I wasn't in my bunk. I would be sleeping somewhere OK. I took my blankets and tried the lifeboats for a couple of days but I nearly froze even covered up. Then I found a sofa in the saloon but a sailor found me. So I gave up but I didn't get much sleep in that bunk. If I was awake I shook and if I got to sleep I had awful dreams. Was I glad to get off that boat!

We've landed at Hamburg. In Germany! I'm scared all over again. We are all German citizens but it's like going to a foreign place where you wonder if they will understand you. I wonder if I have an American accent. I haven't said a word for two days which is as long as we have been on German soil. Papa's done all the talking which is probably why everything is taking so long. I thought we'd land and whip straight to the village. Instead we make out papers and take them from one office to another office and in between we sit and wait while Papa waves the letters from Cousin Alois and yells as usual. Almost everybody here wears a smart uniform and the only sounds besides Papa are clicking heels and noisy typewriters.

If only I could write German. I'm ashamed not knowing how. Funny to be able to speak pretty well but not being able to write a word. I'll just have to start at the beginning and work like hell!

We've been put up in a little hotel. The view is something! A stone building next door, three feet away from my hand if I reach — and no sky. But the food *is* something! I ate schnitzel for breakfast! I asked the lady who cooks and she said why not! (The first time I opened my mouth and she understood me!)

"Everything is in order." That's what they said today. We're off on a train to our new home in Zellheim, and I can't wait!

BORMANN
BERLIN

Ah Willi — so you continue to find the method used on the American to bear fruit? I thought you would. Pick and choose each victim carefully. Tourists from North and South America (including Mexico) and England. Possibly Syria, Iraq. Wine and dine (particularly wine!) each and then set up your little drama. I expect to see that expenses for drugs and film have risen rapidly.

As long as the Reich is a mecca for tourists, as long as the aura of the Games hangs on, and even afterwards, we should have a bumper crop to select from. The world comes to gawk at the new Germany. The word spreads of the phoenix rising from the ashes of shame and tyranny. See the New Order in action and while you're about it fill up on dark beer, blood sausages and expert women who spread their legs with joy. Splash in a spa, spend those marks, see the SS drill in ranks so perfect they could be the legions of Rome! I am a fucking travel poster!

A network based on fear can be strong — unbreakable — if the terror is enough. And for those who give outstanding service, we can sweeten their pots from treasury funds.

Children? You can always round up Jew kids. They won't be missed. Jew kids are always disappearing nowadays. Children will scare the hell out of most — although I'm not so sure of the Wogs. Arabs use boys all the time, I hear. Prefer them. So how the shit does the race continue I'd like to know! The blood that goes along with the frame-up should do the trick — or think up a "special" for our Arab friends. I've got it! Snap one kissing a piglet!

I want to make the best use of tourists while we can. It could be that the influx of visitors will be curtailed by events.

Bormann

Willi,

What do we call our agents in the field? How will we designate them? How will they contact us and vice versa? Details, I know — but I like details. And this whole endeavor is like raising children. I am like the Papa who wants to know when the babies talked and walked — and the names of the little ones!

Bormann

Marvelous, Willi! The simpler the idea, the less chance to get hung up in confusion.

We take a neutral country — let's say Spain — and use the capital's name as the code name for control. (All controls lead to Berlin, of course.) Each agent's code name within a network sphere will be a town in Spain beginning with the same letter as the capital. Right so far?

Spain = The country of the network

Madrid = The control

Murcia, Majorca, Málaga, etc. = Agents

And in an emergency, the words "the capital of Spain" (or Turkey or whatever) included in an otherwise meaningless sentence mean "get the fuck to the drop fast!"

Everybody in the same orbit all wrapped up in a nice parcel. Very neat.

Agents in the USA will have to be spics!

A question. I'm puzzled. If each agent uses a book as the key coding tool and they speak *different languages,* how the fuck are you, at control, going to translate the Spanish, the Arabic, the English, etc.?

Bormann

Willi,

She speaks and writes *nine languages?* What's the world coming to when broads stop being hausfraus? Jesus, I want them spread-eagled, not educated! So she's got brains. Is she built? Anything I'd like? Tell me she's *not* a Jew! I don't want to have to play little games to keep her healthy.

Bormann

1938

HANNES
ZELLHEIM ON THE MOSEL
APRIL

I am still writing this in English but I work hard at learning German script. My tests were *not* as easy as Cousin Alois said, but I talked my way through the math and science and believe it or not questions on the philosophy of the Third Reich!

About the philosophy. I guess they think I've missed a lot, living in America. But old Hegel came and got me out of a hole. I just closed my eyes and pretended I was back in Bussett (not the town! — the library) reading him again. I spouted phrases like: "Germany's hour has come" and "Heroes must lead a supreme state" and "The State has the supreme right against the individual." Stuff like that. I think my professor is a Hegel fan. What he doesn't know was that *all* I knew was some Hegel and not much else of anybody!

So — he thinks I will be a credit to the Hitler Youth! I forgot to mention my birthday. 18! A man — almost.

MAY

We went to Koblenz to be inducted. Koblenz is better than Hamburg which smelled like the sea and rotten fish.

The ceremony was something. Standard-bearers with flags and eagles sitting on top of the poles and a band and all of us singing and our hands placed on our daggers just so, "Faithful Unto Death" they say on the hilt.

We swore on the knights of the Holy Germanic Empire, our ancestors, to help our German brothers, to defend women and children, to dedicate ourselves to the German cause. We swore unto death to be faithful to our leaders, our country and our Führer, Adolf Hitler.

And somewhere in there was the Horst Wessel song and "Deutschland über alles." I have almost memorized the words.

I was so proud that day to be a member of the Hitler Jugend, ready to do anything, yelling all those slogans and raising my arm to the Führer, to the sky — I guess I thought that day was the beginning and things would get better and better. But it's been downhill all the way since.

Where are all the hikes and games and yodeling and maneuvers and campfires? Where is all that stuff that was in the pictures?

And why do I have to live with my parents! Zellheim's a pretty town and the slaty hills are green and the grapes will swell and ripen and there's all the water I can drink and all the food I want to eat.

But Mama and Papa. Where did their smiles go? Papa's like he was in Bussett and Mama's not, so the two of them go at it all the time. They never stop yelling. They never stop complaining. The cottage isn't big enough. The wages aren't either. Papa's knee hurts and he doesn't think he'll be able to harvest when they're ready to pick (although he sure straightens up when he walks down to the beer hall). Mama says there isn't enough white veal in the market and she wants an electric sewing machine and they both want one of those autos that looks like a June bug. Nothing is good enough!

I pictured saying farewell to Mama and Papa and swinging down the road with comrades off to climb a mountain. OFF anyway!

I thought the HJ would be Boy Scouts and parties. Some party! Just *The Party.*

I can't concentrate on the things I *have* to learn because our professor is so boring! I think his brain stopped ten years ago. And it wasn't too big to start with!

We have drill and I don't mean marching. *All the time.*The Party says we have to study, study, study. I thought I was through with all that. More than fifty hours a week of stuff I've already had like math. Here's a problem I copied out of our textbook:

> A Stuka on takeoff carries twelve dozen bombs, each weighing ten kilos. The aircraft makes for Warsaw, the center of international Jewry. It bombs the town. On takeoff with all bombs on board and a fuel tank containing 1,500 kilos of fuel, the aircraft weighs about eight tons. When it returns from the crusade, there are 230 kilos of fuel left. What is the weight of the aircraft when empty?

In Bussett High School we had a math question that used a freight train going from Chicago to Denver. Instead of bombs we had bushels of corn. And the fuel was coal.

Same problem. Different language, that's all.

And then, on top of the fifty hours we have six hours of political instruction plus two hours of racial theory, which leaves me practically no time to think!

We hardly have a chance to say anything, which is good because they're throwing all sorts of theories at me — about racial purity and the Communist-Jewish conspiracy and the just plain Jewish conspiracy.

We learn what Dietrich says and what Streicher says. Boy, *he* sure hates the Jews! He has a newspaper, *Der Stürmer,* which is required reading with cartoons of awful-looking people which they say are Jews doing this and that and generally being horrible.

The only Jews I've seen so far don't look at all like the cartoons. They look pretty ordinary as far as I can tell. Except of course they wear a yellow cloth star. That's the law.

And the political instruction is just a rehash of all the fuss about the Versailles Treaty, which I already knew from the Bussett Town Library. It sure wasn't fair, that treaty, but God! they go on and on and on about it!

At least I don't have to spend much time with Mama and Papa. Be thankful for small mercies they say. I would be more thankful if I wasn't here!

I only say so in this diary, but the flag of the Reich does not inspire me. The red background stands for the people and the white circle for the purity of the cause. But then there's that swastika smack dab in the middle. It gives me a creepy crawly feeling like a black spider moving, always turning. I can't help it, it does. If the Führer saw it in a vision then so did a lot of other people because the Kaiser had a little one on his baggage and old German rulers had it engraved on stone pillars and such. Rolf says that it was a symbol of Christianity that the Greeks sort of disguised. It's not very Christian now.

I wish I felt more patriotic about the flag. If I designed one for the Third Reich I'd keep the red and the white, yes, but right in the middle I'd put the biggest gold eagle, really shiny. And that eagle would be soaring!

In Hamburg I saw all those people in uniform and they moved as though what they were doing and where they were going was the most important thing in the world.

Well I thought I knew where I was going. But I don't even have a real uniform like I thought I would. I don't have a cap with a visor and some gold braid. And I don't have *boots!* I *do* have short pants which makes me look like a baby!

I think what I want most in the world is a pair of black leather boots, reaching up to the knee. Soft but heavy enough so they'd click on floors. If I could have a pair I would rub and buff and polish them within an inch of their lives. They would live! I would make them gleam like two columns of black glass. If I could have them!

JUNE

Maybe I'd better wait for the boots. For a while anyway. They have us marching around doing the goosestep. The soldiers do it so we do it. I don't know why *anybody* does it! You stick one leg out and up, and then just as you're ready to fall flat you stick up the other one. Everybody looks ridiculous, and I started to laugh until I tried it. The upshot is that my rear is black and blue.

BORMANN
BERCHTESGADEN

A slow day at the Berghof, Willi. A slow day means paying bills and going over the accounts, and I have seen the view so damned often, I don't even notice the mountains anymore. (With the Anschluss, the Führer, on the other hand, beams every time he looks toward Salzburg. But then, he is an Austrian and I'm not!)

Trying to liven up a dull day, I pulled out an Atlas. Big heavy bugger! And following your idea for designating agents and control, checked Ireland. Dublin plus Drogheda, Dunlavin, Dun Laoghaire, Dunleer, Dundealgan — Jesus! Ireland has a bucketful of Ds!

Buried as I was, trying to make out the print which is so fine I was squinting, I didn't hear the Führer stroll in with his tootsie. Snuffed out the cigarette between my fingers! Christ, it hurt! And raised my arm in salute to my Führer. A wavering Heil because I was trying to waltz the smoke away. He noticed nothing — but Eva, the little tart, *did.* I could tell by her smirk. That conniving bitch in heat will be sure to mention the cigarette. You can bet your boots on that! Can't stand her and vice versa. Looks so innocent, so blond and sweet. When she spies me, looks could kill!

I thought that the Führer had only come to the office for an allotment of cash, which I dole out when he asks for it. Today was "jewelry day" for Fräulein Braun. (I keep a tray of geegaws at my fingertips for such "selection days.") The Führer noticed the Atlas, open — Thank the Merciful God! — to Europe. Asked why I was perusing it. What an agile mind! I told him I was about to calculate how much territory we could be handed without going to war. The Führer was delighted and went into an extremely long discourse on Lebensraum — AGAIN!

Bormann

Willi,

The royalties from the Führer's likeness on postal issues do not bring in as much as I would like. These stamps are issued for charity, and charity does not begin at home! So the amount I can dip out is negligible.

However, if the Reichsmarschall is able to acquire works of art and other baubles from German and Austrian Jewry, I want to be in on the selection process. You notice I do not use the word "take." "Acquire" has a more civilized connotation, don't you think? I don't see why we have to be so prissy, come to think of it. The Jews have no rights to *anything!* So, let Göring keep his round ladies — Rubens, or whoever. Give me gems, any day!

Hess is always in his dreamy state, with wide mood swings. Which gives me great leeway in running the Office of Secretary.

Continue your most successful activities re recruitment. And, as I have mentioned frequently, but it bears repeating, use whatever means necessary to *win* converts to our little endeavor.

Also, have you thought about a roving agent, one who could keep our people in line? Sort of a Sturmführer. One with brains, stamina, and enough ruthlessness to scare the shit out of anyone who wavers.

Think about it.

Bormann

EMMA
CAPE CHARLOTTE
SEPTEMBER

MY DAIRY
EMMA

THIS IS MY DAIRY. I AM IN THE SECOND GRADE. ANNS DOG PEENUTS HAD PUPPYS.

DECEMBER

IT SNOWED AND I AM 7 YEARS OLD. I HAD A BIRTHDAY. THE SEA IS BIG TODAY AND I AM BIGGA THAN I WAS YESTADAY!

BUFFY

CAPE CHARLOTTE

SEPTEMBER

Dear Meg,

What Ho! Your roommate writes after only 17 years! So I'm not the most conscientious correspondent in the world. Makes each letter infinitely more valuable.

I knew you'd nearly croak when you opened that invitation to my wedding. "The girl most likely to fend off Valentino" or something analogous. My love, you know damned well I would have gotten into Valentino's pants before he got into mine, sand or no sand. But — beggars can't be choosers. Let's face it! I was big and clumsy and plain. While all you gals were whipping up to Dartmouth, ready for the big fight on the football field and the bigger tussle in the frats, I stayed home in the dorm, aloof. Well, baby, I cried my eyes out. I would have given both of them for one good screw!

Money does one thing. It gives you a chance. I took Manhattan and all the salons, too. "Mademoiselle, let us emphasize your good points . . ."

"Find one," I said.

". . . And," they added, "we'll minimize the others."

Oh, to be minimized to five feet four. Of course, it would have meant the loss of both legs up to the calf!

At one of those dreadful parties where everyone slinks around in satin, smoking Turkish, and slumping, I met a real live one. Well, almost alive. Anyway, he's mine and it has actually lasted six years.

No kids. Maternal, I'm not. And Pudge doesn't seem to miss them.

So OK, he's not the world's greatest lover. But we coexist, and Daddy thinks he can add something (I'm not sure what!) to the business, so everything is nice and cozy.

I know I haven't thanked you yet for the handsome wedding present. Meg, be thanked most heartily. I haven't broken a single goblet, which is unlike me!

You *will* hear from me again. I promise within the next decade. Semper fidelis and all that,

Buffy

P.S. Really Meg, how can you possibly exist in that superficial, artificial nouveau sprawl called Los Angeles? I hear rats nest in the palm trees!

HANNES
BAVARIA
SEPTEMBER

They said it would be a vacation, a summer camp for the Hitler Youth. Troops from all over. And the place *was* beautiful, near a lake with the mountain peaks still white with snow even in August. We did have singing around the campfire and pretend combat with real rifles and some games BUT—I guess I have just enough strength to sketch in some of the wonderful highlights. Ha! Very funny.

Why do we have to have lectures on a vacation? Why do we have to listen to more stuff on racial purity?! It's like being forced to eat so many Brussels sprouts that you're full to busting and may puke. And then they keep shoving them down your gullet until you burst. I may stop believing in racial purity very soon!

SS Bannführer Hesse is a lot older—maybe thirty-five. And he likes to hurt. As soon as he found out about me—where I'd come from and that I was new in the HJ—he really shoved it to me. More than that, I think he'd liked to have killed me if it could look accidental.

I guess it all began because of the letter to Miss Mandelbaum. I put it in the camp mailbox with enough stamps so that it would go by aeroplane.

Pretty soon in stomped SS Bannführer Hesse, waving an envelope at me and hollering why the hell was I writing a Jew. I told him she was not a Jew! She was a special person and a friend. With that name? he yelled, and then his voice got low, which was even scarier. Quit having friends like that, he spit out, or you'll find yourself in a camp splitting boulders till you fall dead!

So I tore up the letter to Miss Mandelbaum. I'm sorry because I promised to let her know what's happening to me, but if she's really a Jew there's no way I can keep in contact. I don't want to get black marks and lose points. And I don't plan to whack rocks till I drop!

Funny, Miss Mandelbaum doesn't look like a Jew. Or talk like one. Or act like one. Maybe there are a few good ones in every barrel.

The little brats, the Pimfe and the Jungvolk, who'll grow up to be big rats like Hesse, were running all over the campgrounds causing trouble. They were playing war and trying to act like grown-up storm troopers. Hesse gave them a speech. He never gives a short speech. He can't say anything in five minutes if he's got fifteen or thirty. Anyway, he gives them a lecture about looking for traitors and informing on traitors and asks for volunteers to learn the why's and the how's, what to look for and who to tattle on and who to tell then.

I felt a little sick when I saw all those hands rise up. All those kids wanting to know how's the best way to sneak around and listen at doors and find out if Mutti or grandfather or the neighbor downstairs is saying something dangerous to the State. The sly little beasts are so eager to turn in someone, they'll stop an old woman on the street and order her to prove she's not a Jew or grab another and yell at her to prove she hung the swastika out the window last week on the anniversary of the day the French surrendered at Sedan. In 1870, for God's Sake!

I agree we need some people to be on the lookout for dissidents and real traitors, so maybe we need some watchers. But do we need a country of watchers? And midget stoolies?

Hell Walk. Something old Hesse fixed up. He only sends the Youth he wants to humiliate and hurt on Hell Walk. I'd heard about it in whispers, never out loud. People didn't want to talk about it really. I can see why. If you didn't finish to Hesse's satisfaction you got whipped. He made a special thing out of the whipping. At night with torches and everybody sitting around in a circle watching some poor kid tied to a post and Hesse swinging away. Now I know why Kurt is embarrassed to take off his undershirt. He's got the marks for all time. The marks to prove he didn't finish.

He got me, friggin Hesse. Picked me out of the crowd when we were listening to the five hundredth lecture on pollution of the races. I don't remember what. I was sound asleep.

In front of everybody he said something about testing my manhood. And strength and courage. And I said Oh Shit, and Rolf said Oh Jesus, and someone else said God be with you, you poor bastard.

A hike said Hesse. A walk of 3 kilometers. From here to Lizard Rock. Named because the thing looks like a crouching lizard perched up on the high hill. You can see it from camp.

There are rules, of course, said Hesse. You must follow the trail — which is blazed by stakes or red ribbons. Never deviate from the course. Stay within the stakes and ribbons. An obstacle is to be climbed or forded or hacked away. Time is of the essence. You will be clocked. No matter what is in your path you must stay within the marked boundaries. If you trip and fall it must be within these boundaries. A toe outside, a little finger outside the markers, and you are finished. You will be monitored! Now off!

Not even a whistle to start. Just a wicked push from Hesse.

I remember a crowd of boys not saying anything now, just watching as I took off, and then I forgot them and everything. My mind was on the course.

I had my dagger and not much else. What I knew about woods you could have put in a thimble and have room left over to add mountains and rivers.

A meter at most, the trail was. And it led to an old quarry that hadn't been worked for years it looked like. The stakes went down into it and up out of it. So did I, slipping on gravel, banging my knees, and almost drowning in a deep pool of water that had collected at the bottom.

Through sharp brambles and undergrowth that was like piles of barbed wire, I hacked away and bled away and wished my short pants were heavy knickers.

I heard a cough. Old Hesse must be near. And watching.

Now I was on a spongy forest floor and no light shone through the trees. The ground went down and I don't mean gently. It almost fell it was so steep. And I almost did too. Almost tripped over moss-covered logs that were soft and rotting.

Out into the sun. The stakes went across a roaring river. An ocean of white water. I was supposed to ford the river just a few inches before a waterfall, tall as a windmill. It made a hell of a noise. Like a screaming animal. I started across trying not to look down at the sharp rocks waiting to get me. The water sucked at my legs and I was sure I'd go over. Those damn stakes just stood there like iron. They *were* iron and hammered in so hard ten floods wouldn't have knocked them down. Oh God — the water was so cold my legs were dead and my balls were freezing off. I couldn't feel my feet except to know that under them were lots of rocks, slippery slimy buggers. And then I was over and I could almost see Lizard Rock, except there was a stinking tree in the way.

The reason it was in the way was because it was supposed to be. A pine or some damn thing with needles. The trail narrowed and there wasn't room to slip around either side of the trunk.

I was trying to figure out what to do when there was a shout from the woods. Old Hesse yelling "Over it you crud! Over it!"

I was so mad I was crying and I couldn't breathe and I went up that tree like a monkey with ants in its pants. Up and up and up I went and the tree just seemed to grow higher. The needles hit my face and the blood was streaming down and I had to stop sometimes to wipe it off but I knew that if I stopped too long I'd give up for sure so I kept climbing. And then all of a sudden I was near the top and I could see for miles and then I saw nothing. The top was so tiny it couldn't have supported a bee. It didn't support me. I went right over the top and down the other side. I heard an awful crack as I landed. I knew I was done for sure. And then I looked down from the branch I was caught on and I laughed and then I cried and then I got hysterical. I had fallen straight down and I could see the trail marked right below me. I had fallen right on course! Not a toe out of line. How's that you bastard?!

From then on I floated. Right up to Lizard Rock. The trail ended at the bottom but I felt so good I climbed him. I climbed to the top and sat on his head and said To hell with you, Bannführer Hesse!

When I got back to camp the kids pounded my back and called me Old Shatterhand and said I had run the Gauntlet and I was a hero and boy had I shown old Hesse what I was made of.

I ached for three days and my cuts stung. But I *was* a hero. I really was. And I know I can survive whatever they put in front of me!

It's great to be a hero! I think I'll try it more often. The boys call me comrade and ask my advice on everything. Because I came from America and *finished* Hell Walk makes me wise and sort of mysterious.

They think America has golden shores and is full of Indians riding around and whooping. I'm going to let them have their dreams. It would be mean (and maybe wouldn't make me so mysterious) if I told them the truth — that Karl May wrote what he never saw. He made it all up. America may have golden shores but she sure doesn't spread it around to the Plains! I've seen real Indians — groups off the reservation — Cheyenne, Sioux, Arapaho, and they aren't wearing war paint and feather bonnets whooping it up on fast horses. They aren't strong and dignified. They aren't anything but pitiful and sad.

BUFFY
CAPE CHARLOTTE
DECEMBER

OK Meg — I cannot stand your pitious pleas, hence the filler for what you defame as "my sparse outline." I thought my letter was concise. Pithy and succinct. Pithy, anyway.

Onward. I left all you mooning, engaged gals and hiked myself to Boston, which to a hick like me was the Big City. I soon learned that a Smith education does not a secretary make. So two years of Katy Gibbs, white gloves and all. Now I was prepared!

For a stint in a little prestigious publishing house, you know the kind: thin novels by wan writers; verse from poets who can't. I began to imagine the world as a paneled office inhabited by dried-out old editors who had had their larynges removed. The place was that hushed.

So I scuttled out of there. This time I latched on to a job with *Vogue* — as a fashion writer of all things! Disaster! There is no fashion in Boston. I thought up a short piece about Beacon Hill ladies, a tongue-in-cheek thing, about their choice of style. Style they ain't got, which was the point, unless you call tweedy butt-sprung rumps "stylish." God, Meg. They even wear wool in July!

Well, I wrote it . . . about all the rich frumps who, at the dot of four, leave their charming brick townhouses with the violet bow windows and cluck down to the Ritz for tea.

Tried *Vanity Fair.* Turned down. And it was good. To hell with Boston! Make way, New York!

That's when I hit the beauty salons. Had my hair dyed titian. Then with résumés, resolve and a red marcel I hit the larger publishing houses. Hired as editor in a famous arty one. And oh God! What has happened to Art? Swipe paint on canvas and the critics swoon. Throw words randomly and the critics have orgasms. Poetry arranged like broken ladders or seesaws out of kilter. No beginning. No end. No sense. NONSENSE.

I began to write marginalia: "I think this would make better sense in a circle"; then, "I can't understand what you are getting at, or is it your purpose to confuse?" The end came when I crossed out the entire page and wrote "CRAP!"

Back to hoofing it. On Madison Avenue. The home of Greed, Exaggeration and Downright Lies. I speak of advertising, in case you have not recognized the breed. While there I became "the indomitable Miss Sinclair, a tough broad with a man's mind." And my hair changed to mahogany.

During that time I began a series of one-night stands, usually culminating a sloshy evening. Actually, the stands weren't a culmination of anything. The men were faceless, forgettable. After one tumble, there was no request for a rematch.

And then I met Pudge at one of those evening soirees. He seemed out of place — so proper. Too damned proper. A walking, breathing Puritan. But I wanted him. For security, if you must know. I landed him in '32, three years after we met. You ask what took so long? He did, the twerp! Fought almost all the way. But I held the rod *and* a baited hook and he finally bit.

The market going bust had something to do with it, to be honest. We still thrived and he . . . well . . . I had him investigated (Shut up!) and found that Black October had diminished his family to the point of no returns. Genteel poverty. Succulent bait, that's me. I know and I don't care! He's only an old-fashioned Yankee who wouldn't admit, even to himself, that money is the root of all *stable* marriages. "Stable" meaning he doesn't stray. Doesn't dare!

So, here we are back at Cape Charlotte. I love the old house on Porpoise Point, my birthplace, my birthright. I love the gleam of the floors and the ruggedness of the stone and the pieces from Asia that remind me of my ancestors' voyages to the mysterious East. I even love that damned lighthouse which blinks in my eyes each night. It is *not* true, contrary to rumors that abound, that I placed the maids' room facing it! Grandfather fought the government for years over the placement of that thing. They took the tip of his land by right of "eminent domain" for a beacon "to guide all ships at sea and guarantee to them safe passage . . ." In other words: "Steer clear. Reefs!" Well, Porpoise Point Light has been there for years with two Coastguardsmen manning it. I never see them.

Sometimes I admit to a certain restlessness. Being a housewife with a house full of servants is not particularly taxing. Pudge is not demanding — in anything! So I will mull on what has not yet become a problem.

Good Lord! You have the story of my life — IN FULL. This should hold you. This *will* hold you. I am exhausted. Forever!

Love,
Buffy

P.S. I just have the strength for one last word. Important. There's going to be a War. I know it! There just *was* a War. I mean it was still on when we were freshmen. And we aren't *that* old! Everybody (but me, it seems) sits calmly and smiles complacently and lets the

Germans arm and bluster and take over. I can see those bloody Nazis goosestepping across the whole of Europe and nobody will do one damned thing about it!

Shit!

1939

EMMA
CAPE CHARLOTTE
JANUARY

I HAVE A BIOLET DRESS. IT IS OGANDY. IT IS MY FAVARIT CULA. IT GOT WARSHED AND MUMMY SAID IT IS NOW GRAY. IT IS NOT. IT IS GRAYBIOLET. IT IS STIL MY BEST DRESS.

JUNE

I AM AT NANAS AND BUMPASS. YESTADAY WE WENT ON THE FERY BOAT AND TODAY WE WENT TO THE MOVIES. WE SAW SHIRLY TEMPUL IN LITTLE MISS BRAWDWAY AND I CLIMBED A TREE AND MY TUTH FELL OUT. I AM LEARNING THE LITLE LETERRS BUT I CANT PUT THEM IN YET UNTIL I DO K RIGHT. I AM NOT SURE WHEN TO PUT THE BIG LETERRS EXCEPT AT THE BEGINNING. THIS IS A PICTURE OF ME WITH MY TUTH OUT.

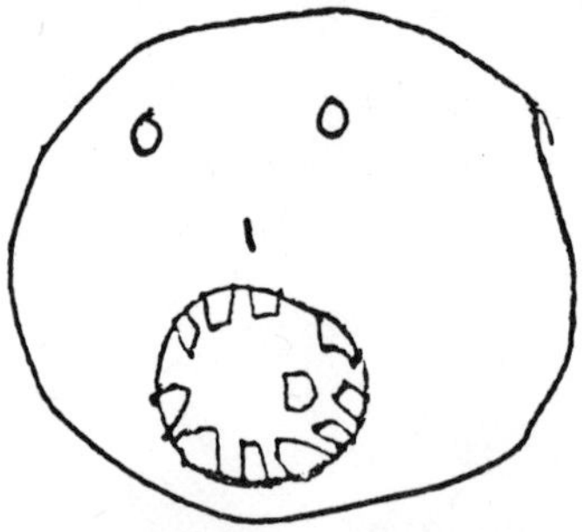

SEPTEMBER

WE ARE IN NEW YORK TODAY. WE WENT TO THE WORLDS FAIR. I SAW A PANDA WHO LIKED ME. MUMMY BOUGHT A WOODEN BOWL WITH FLOWERS ON IT. SHE LOOKED AT IT AND SAID POOR POLAND. WE ARE STAYING AT THE HOTEL COMODOOR.

NOVEMBER

There is a war across the ocean and I live on the ocean with big rocks. My town is called Cape Charlotte which is halfway between Bostin which is a big city with the customshousetowa and Bahaba which is sort of an iland with a pretty mountin on it. November is a brown time every year except when it snows which it doesnt do usually.

BORMANN
BERLIN

Willi!

Get on the stick fast! The "events" I mentioned several years ago are about to unfold. Within a month. Poland.

We'll set the Poles up with an "incident" involving the murder of Silesians. That we have to kill our own is all for the Greater Cause. With luck, the English and the French will cluck "shame" and sit on their asses — again.

But this action will mean our supply of visitors dries up — just like that — so mount your final offensive and grab any promising lingerers. "Blitzkrieg" is the operative word. And what about our top agent? Dig one up — NOW.

Hess becomes more weird. Sees visions, or something.

On the other hand, the Führer *is* a visionary. He is absolutely brilliant!

Heil Hitler!
Bormann

Parties are my downfall. I go to one with every intention of remaining a true husband to Gerda and a loyal lover to Manja, and then along come all those lovely ladies twitching their asses at me. Life is too short not to taste new delicacies.

I almost had a tasty morsel last night when you interrupted me. Conspiracy over champagne and caviar is a pisser, Schmidt! You mumble with your mouth full. Chew first, you clod! I was so busy dodging fish eggs I couldn't tell whether the news was good or bad.

I don't want to see your stupid face in a public place again! If I do, I will personally stuff a sturgeon down your gullet. *Understood?*

I want the data in a memo, not the eye!

Bormann

* * *

According to your interminable memo, Willi, I am to gather that you latched on to a real find in the Café Margarete — by chance. The Führer would call it destiny. I call it blind luck!

And all because of your intense need to gulp down some Haselnuss-schnitten, for which the Café is justly proud. (About the only thing the Hapsburg Empire can be proud of! I resent that I've had to curtail my intake of those delectables. Pastries cause my uniforms to shrink — particularly at the neck.)

You asshole! You play spy in the office and are oblivious to the best-known secret west of the Oder — that the Café Margarete is *the* liaison point for free-lancers, a place teeming with intrigue and agents-for-hire!

The Café is crowded, noisy. Everyone is dressed in mufti — the shiny blue suits of the unsuccessful traveling man — nosing about like hounds on the scent. Spies for sale being looked over by the SD, the Abwehr, the Gestapo. But not our Schmidt. He is dressed in the full uniform of an SS Captain standing out like an emblem and his mongrel nose twitches only for Haselnuss-schnitten. You shit!

Taking an empty seat opposite a dapper little man, you do not notice his apoplexy until he spills Kaffe mit Schlag all over your breeches. He pats you dry, apologizing profusely all the while. It is only when he wipes his sweating brow with the sodden napkin, leaving swaths of coffee streaks, that your tiny mind makes the connection: The uniform of a Hauptsturmführer SS has, shall we say, unnerved him. He leaves hurriedly, and using your few aimless brain cells you become the great actor, Schmidt. Ah, what a drama. Out you stomp in simulated rage, have him followed, picked up and questioned. The agent-for-hire is hired.

Schmidt, the bumbler, falls over a gold mine!

So our man now thinks he is working for the Security Service SS. I wager that terror will keep this linkman honest, knowing that the tentacles of the Sicherheitsdienst section reach far — and are viciously barbed.

But they won't scratch me!

Bormann

Willi,

The longer I look over our man's dossier, the more I like him — mind brimming with schemes. At first I was taken aback by his photo, wondering whether a cherub could command obedience — crack the whip — but his fascist record in the Romanian Iron Guard speaks for itself. The dregs of humanity slither in that group. Pogroms, beatings, torture: specialties of the house.

So he'll cost a king's ransom. Christ, Willi! Pay him! He could be invaluable. Make him King Midas for all I care.

Just keep him out of the clutches of the Security Service and the Abwehr. They'd drool over such an agent!

Oh, while you're about it, get me some more ethnic jokes.

"Romania: The land of bilk and money" — and — "Bribe a Romanian enough and he will skin his own mother alive; double the amount and he will serve her up as a roast." Gut-busters!

Bormann

P.S. Yes, make him "Midas." Toyed with the idea of calling him "Father Christmas." Puking thought, right?

The New Year comes and with it the visions of the Führer become reality. If only that vile Festival of Christmas didn't exist! I have forbidden its celebration at home, but it is still held at Berchtesgaden. My six little mewlers are too spoiled there.

HANNES
ZELLHEIM ON THE MOSEL
MARCH

I think I have outgrown the HJ. I have outgrown Mama and Papa for sure! They question my every move. Like who was that girl I was talking to on the street and was she pure? I don't know whether they meant racially or sexually! (I didn't talk! I bumped into her and was embarrassed and she thought I was stupid, so that went NOWHERE!) Am I learning everything the Führer wants me to? Am I progressing fast enough to get somewhere fast? I sure want to get out of here *fast* and I will. I'm due to go into Labor Service in two weeks. And in four I will be nineteen!

BAVARIA
MAY

Guess what? I'm a farmer. Just what I always wanted to be! God, we are planting furrows a mile long and every time I put in a seed I think of Papa. At least the earth turns easily. It rains here!

JUNE

Things are looking up and I mean way up! It was time to hay — the first cut — and the grass was sweet and all of a sudden who came to help scythe but a whole mess of girls! The League of German Maidens — the Bund Deutscher Maedel. Their camp is only a short romp from ours. Maybe it was put there deliberately because mixing is encouraged. I am taking every opportunity to mix closely!

Two years ago I didn't dare talk to a girl — in Bussett — only two years ago? I hadn't ever even kissed one! But I wanted to. I wanted to so much, but I wasn't worth a wink. But this is Germany and I am somebody and my goal has grown. To love a different girl in every haystack. The field is immense!!

JULY

I've grown some more. I am almost two meters high. Well, not quite. But I am over six feet!

I've decided one thing I will not be and that's a farmer. Diggers of the soil are so engrossed in looking down, so absorbed in small things they live a very dull and simple life. And they're at the mercy of the weather. Nothing they can do can change it. I want to look up. I want a chance to change the world — at least a bit!

AUGUST

I've been hoeing beets all day in the sun and the sweat was running off so hard I must have watered half a row. Don't think beets like salt water. Good! I hate beets.

All I could think of was that poster in the Munich station, the one for tourists advertising the spa. It's near here, the spa, and while I was hoeing and my back was hurting I could picture the rich lolling in the mudbaths and hot mineral springs. "Come to beautiful Dachau, the spa of southern Germany."

AUGUST

Danzig is in the news every day. The Polish Corridor. The talk of war is everywhere. Will we go to war over it? It's hard to tell. The Führer has gained a lot of territory by blustering and bluffing. A good poker player takes the pot, so Kurt says and he ought to know. He wins all the time! Which is not fair — I taught him how to play in the first place!

The army is a possibility. If I join now, soon — it would look good on my record and a war would give me a chance to prove myself.

NOVEMBER

I remember seeing marching men in a parade last year — black greatcoats and boots, helmets and rifles held just so. They seemed so proud to be the Führer's honor guard, his Leibstandarte SS.

I can hardly believe that less than two years later I am one of them!

I owe it all to Rolf who gave me some advice. Hold out for the SS, he told me. Don't wait to be drafted by the Wehrmacht.

How right he was! The Wehrmacht is ruled by the Junker class. Junkers are born, not made. They say who will rise and who will die — who will ride in the command car and who will draw the cart.

I am the son of a farmer and I will always be classed that way by them. The Wehrmacht is a gray army of followers, of peasants — and the leaders are always the nobles.

So — I chose the other road. They examined me from mind to toes, from heritage way back to the Hitler Youth. And I was in!

A private in the combat arm of the SS, the Waffen SS. I have a future! Class doesn't count here. Determination and deeds do.

I may be a private now but to reach the top you have to start on the first rung of a ladder. I'm standing on it!

Already the Poles have given up! Capitulated to use a better word. They fought our panzers as though this action was a hundred years ago — with cavalry! Stupid men charging our armor with bayonets.

I am not through with my training and the war is over! It was too late to go to Poland and now the armies sit and do nothing.

I can fire a rifle and hit the target — not the middle but a couple of the outer rings. I can dig a hole fast with a bayonet and jump inside. Most of me fits. I have marched and run and marched and run over half of Germany with a full pack. I can squirm on my belly while live ammunition is being fired and *not* lift my head like that stupid sod next to me did. Blown to smithereens! I can cut through barbed wire and crawl through metal pipes and climb a barricade. The other day three of us had to jump into a very shallow hole and let a tank roar over us! He probably hoped he could squash us. Well, he didn't.

I was not chosen for panzers. I mean tanks, not armored cars. Tanks. I don't know what I would have done if they had decided I would be a good bet to be a tank crew member. I went down into one and started to shake and sweat and the oil smell made me sick. I don't like being closed around with metal. Well, I didn't have to worry! The Leibstandarte doesn't *have* panzers!

1940

HENRY
CAPE CHARLOTTE
APRIL

Why do I continue to brood? No word from Germany. Not a peep. Berlin has more important things on its mind than a middle-aged man (am I really that?) who is not a hero. Norway and Denmark, for instance.

I have but one confidant: this paper, which in all truth gives me little comfort. Evelyn? Would that I could share this burden with her. But I am plainly *not* in a position to do so. In her mind I am still on trial and my performance lacks a certain flair, as she is fond of telling me. While she might forgive me the mess I find myself mired in, she *could* not, she *would* not tolerate the slightest tinge of scandal touching the firm. Sullying the name of that venerable institution is tantamount to treason.

MAY

It has happened.

The Nazis have dropped from the sky on Holland and they saved one to drop in on me.

An unlikely looking parachutist. He appeared in the office with a bona fide appointment made a fortnight ago. Ginny swallowed a story and marked it on my calendar. Who questions a Mr. Lowell re import-export?

I do. He has a Mittel European accent that oozes, then flows s's. Thick saliva-smacking s's. Mr. Lowell, indeed! Try Lowenstein. Looks like one of that ilk. On the other hand, Mister Hitler and his followers choose *not* to mingle with the chosen people. Whatever, his name is not Lowell and never will be!

His dress. No Lowell would be caught in a casket clothed thusly: a foppish, dove-gray suit so supple it seemed to be fashioned of doeskin. The buttons: large, pearl. And spats! Really! I gave them up a number of years ago, as did all my friends. He carried a tightly furled umbrella (black, I am happy to note) which he twirled or thumped. At times he pointed it at me like a foil.

He did not waste time on amenities. I do not think he has the breeding to know of these things. He came abruptly to the point, his little pink face glowing with excitement. I was fascinated with his mustache, white and full and waxed on the tips: it quivered as he spoke. I could not take my eyes from it even as he discussed the business at hand: a very glossy print of gore in Berlin which was flapping in his hand. Oh, what ghastly memories that photo resurrected!

Pointedly, nearly stabbing me in the eye with the tip of his umbrella, he outlined services which I am to perform in exchange for "these things." You may keep this one. We have others.

Others! How many *others?* Ten? A hundred?

Disposal of the photo was uppermost in my mind, hence I missed a part of his instructions. Furious at having to repeat himself, his round pink face turned puce.

He spoke; I tried to take the orders in, for that is what the words were: orders. I could be most helpful by providing useful information about the port and its activities. Useful to whom? I queried. The Nazis? To our *friends,* he replied with a smile. Movement of convoys. Rendezvous points et cetera.

He looked at me intently, his eyes berry brown, piercing me on a pin: another small, squirming bug for his collection.

And to pass the information? Coded messages, he answered. A simple and almost foolproof way. A book known only to the parties involved. Page numbers, paragraph numbers, word place within the sentence.

I tried to digest his instructions and could only focus on my stomach, which was *not* digesting. I can empathize with those whose stress causes churning in the abdominal area.

The drop: I beg your pardon, Mr. Lowell, but what is a "drop"? Those eyes again. I was now a mindless bug. A "drop," Mein Herr, is the designated place where you will hand over your messages.

I learned that the place so designated is an Italian grocery in the East End of Jamesport, a section which I have had no cause to visit in the past. Although I have always liked Italians, they can be unrelievedly demonstrative.

I felt like a child on the first day of the first grade, attempting to learn the entire alphabet in one morning.

Whom do I see at the grocery?

That is not your worry. They will notice you.

Oh, God. Already known. Perhaps whispered about . . .

Your control will be *Madrid.* Your code name is *Majorca.*

But that is not what I would have chosen, I exclaimed without thinking, and continued: It's a frivolous place! What about something more cultured, something from opera . . . Wagner . . . Tristan! He thumped his umbrella so brutally it left a scar in the parquet. NO WAGNER!

Ah ha! A large blunder on my part. Mister Hitler is an aficionado. No, Wagner was *not* a good example.

His voice had a freezing quality now: Any message from us will contain the word *Madrid.* If we need something urgently, you may even be contacted in person. A key sentence in the conversation will contain the phrase "the capital of Spain." Upon hearing this phrase, you will go immediately to the drop and pick up your instructions.

And now the book. Use only this edition. *No other.* Guard it carefully.

The book; I suspected as much. A sprawling history written only to titillate the masses. At least it has enough pages. Possibly, I will be able to locate the correct word somewhere within!

And then, without so much as a leave-taking, Mr. Lowell disappeared — there one moment and gone the next.

I merely sat, quite immobile, hardly feeling. In a state of trauma, I expect.

Thankfully I remembered the photo. Rid myself of it immediately; hence I burned it in the ashtray placed conveniently on the desk for guests who feel they must smoke, although I frown on the practice myself. It burned rapidly and gave off an acrid odor. The ashes smelled vile, not at all resembling even a cheap cigar, which was the story I had prepared for Ginny, should she question the residue. Quickly, I raised the window, fanning the air, and then raced to the loo where I flushed the horrid stuff down the toilet. Or tried to. I have complained incessantly about the lack of water pressure in my lavatory. A good operating toilet has a sucking vortex. Mine mades a weak circle that goes round and round but rarely down. I was frantic when I heard the outer door open, for a disgusting gray ring still remained. Rapidly, I removed it and reappeared, trying not to sniff the air noticeably. The smoky pollution was no longer present and Ginny was so intent on lowering the window and muttering that May was not spring in New England, she failed to notice my palsied hands.

JUNE

Today I reconnoitered the East End. No wonder I had never visited the area before. It is another world, grimy and cold, even in June. Tenements colored in dreadful pastels, dying green, pitiful peach, rise four stories. Wooden, old sagging porches. What could ever possess one to live here? You would think any right-thinking family would eschew this place for one more sunny . . . and with a view of the ocean.

Many of these buildings have first floors given over to various small businesses. I noted a dry cleaning establishment, a notions shop which seemed to have little for sale but a few button cards and some cheap lace on a roll. It was difficult to ascertain, for the windows were coated with ancient film. And there *is* an Italian grocery, one which advertises itself as the inventor of the "Submarine," whatever that may be. I dare not imagine. Fly-specked, in any case, I suspect.

I did not go in. I do not want to go in. But I am stiffening the sinews for that initial visit when I push open the door and some damnable bell tinkles my arrival.

I sat at my desk today and contemplated the art of spying. What little I know of the genre comes from the pen of John Buchan, who portrays most sympathetically the plight of men caught in the web of intrigue.

A most curious spy am I, clad in somber suit, with my grandfather's watch chain looped across my waistcoat. A Phi Beta Kappa key would add a civilizing touch, I think, but alas, I do not possess one. Missed it by an eyelash. "Granny" Gransome and I differed on my interpretation as to the extent to which the Italian period was influential on Chaucer's writings. Hence a lower mark than I deserved, and, as a consequence, the Society passed me by.

I do not care for the label "spy." It connotes slyness, deceitfulness. If I must, I shall be a "secret agent," which has a more dashing ring. I have a nasty feeling I shall not be good at this line of work. I loathe intrigue. And I never dash!

At gatherings, I have always managed to utter a few meaningful phrases — here and there. But for the last few weeks I have been unusually close-mouthed. Indeed, I have been the Great Stone

Face, for I am terrified of blurting out something regarding the Iberian Peninsula, which sticks in my mind like a white hippopotamus. Blurting and then having an acquaintance, perhaps, chatter back blah, blah, blah . . . the capital of Spain . . . blah, blah! What do I do then? Leave in a flurry? Saunter out insouciantly? Or stay and become so overwrought that the glass of sherry slips from my hand. Spanish sherry! Oh Mercy!

The only person who is not in league with *them* is Evelyn. Under no circumstances would she find herself in such a horrid position — spying for "those bastards" (I quote her exactly) — and — she would never discuss "the capital of Spain." She would say "Madrid," conferring idiot status on anyone who was ignorant of its position.

BORMANN
BERLIN

Schmidt!

A friendly little bird chirped out the news that you were seen last Friday at an affair in the Propaganda Ministry — deep in a conversation with Heydrich!

If the discussion went any deeper than weather or women, I would have to assume that you were no longer loyal to those who rescued you from slaughter — namely me!

Heydrich is a comet, rising fast. Chief creator of that multiheaded monster — the Reichsicherheitshauptamt — in which you labor so diligently. Its branches include everything inside Reich Security and snake farther out, sending agents abroad without interference from the Foreign Office. He's a Hydra, that Heydrich — not bad, eh Schmidt? Cut off one head (or is it an arm?) and two regenerate! RSHA powers are immense!

So choose your conversational partners carefully, you cretin! Picture a dossier linking you to Röhm in *so* many ways appearing as if by magic on — let's say — the desk of SS Obergruppenführer Reinhard Heydrich!

To avoid such unpleasantness, I would suggest that in future you stay *anonymous.* (You have a good start already. "Wilhelm Schmidt" is such a forgettable name. Keep it so.)

You are not to talk to Party bigwigs under any circumstances, unless silence could be taken for intentional rudeness. *You are not* to ingratiate yourself to the higher-ups through work done or ideas suggested. *You are not* to do any job assigned to you *brilliantly.* Your performance must *never be better than adequate! You are not* to draw attention to yourself in any way. Is this clear? *Very clear?*

Sadly, there are no promotions on the horizon. You will remain a petty Party functionary for the rest of your life. But that is the price for life, Willi.

Now to more pleasant matters. Very soon, maybe early next year, the Führer's image will be on the regular postage issues, which means that the *Reichsmarks roll in.* Since *I* am the bookkeeper, I see my little fund growing by leaps and bounds!

So Midas has made a number of journeys already? Our go-between was a good choice, eh Willi?

Bormann

P.S. Summer. A lovely season — particularly when it includes France!

What the hell, Willi! You mean we are minus our only British agent? So the pansy couldn't take the thought of his beloved England bombed to a shitpile? Suicide is for cowards. I hope the bastard is floating out there in the smoke, watching us flatten London! Isn't it just like an Englander to shoot himself in his dahlia garden?

But that puts us at a disadvantage, doesn't it? No agent, and no chance of recruiting an expatriate in Spain, Portugal?

On this one you were stupid, Willi — but with luck and good weather, we will not need an agent in a country that could be ours in weeks!

Bormann

P.S. Delighted that Midas has found a confederate in conspiracy within the Mexican Embassy in Washington. Diplomatic pouches to the Continent, but more immediate: Radio to Lisbon, on to you, and thence to me with the speed of light!

BUFFY
CAPE CHARLOTTE
AUGUST

Dear Meg,

It's me after less than two years and I can see you falling over. Well, I did, literally. A shock! Can you believe it? Me, hearty as a horse and sometimes resembling one (have all my teeth), experienced what is euphemistically called a "small stroke." Probably won't happen again for years, if at all, they say. Small comfort. Here I am on the sexy side of forty and suddenly my mouth turns down in a sneer, my left side doesn't belong to me anymore, and I slur like I've had tee martoonis too many.

Spent a couple of days in the hospital being stuck and photographed and generally bothered at all times of day and night. They have me in toto on paper and film; I, on the other hand, have crossed hospitals off my list of restful places!

Recovery began after a couple of weeks and now I am almost there. At least the speech. And the mouth smiles on both sides now — when I feel like grinning. Which I don't. BECAUSE — I have to walk with a cane. Lean on it. Hate it, the damn thing!

Daddy's been wonderful. After all those years when he ignored me, he's had a change of heart and shows some. What the hell, maybe he feels guilty, sorry for me. Who cares why. Anyway, he's teaching me the business and I'm still good at it. Wasn't such a slouch in the old days! Daddy let me sit on the Board, first as an observer, now as a *full member.* Guess who shines with brilliance, who outshines most of those old geezers? ME!

Think Pudge is jealous — or something. Probably jealous. He only works for the company thanks to Daddy. And he has never, *ever* sat in on a meeting of the Board. At least I think that's why he's so cranky lately. Come to think of it, he's been grouchy for months now. For example: a small thing, but typical. I was limping around the library feeling blue when I thought of reading something that I could plunge into — anything. Pulled out *Gone With the Wind.* Hadn't reread it since the movie. Figured I'd study Scarlett. Get a few pointers. Jesus, that Vivien Leigh is gorgeous! So — I pulled the book out.

Anyway, there I was engrossed when Pudge burst into my bedroom, *trembling.* Now Pudge never trembles, let alone twitch. And he has *never* burst into my bedroom. Oh, sad truth! *GWTW* was the reason, not me! Snatched the book right out of my hands. And marched right out muttering he had to finish it! My book! How dare he!

Keep your fingers crossed that the leg gets better and that Pudge becomes a mouse again. I liked him better when he squeaked.

À bientôt,
Buffy

P.S. They wouldn't believe me, they wouldn't believe me! Now Paris is crawling with vermin. The whole damned continent, maybe England, bless her spirit, will feel the boot.

HANNES
THE WESTERN FRONT
FEBRUARY

I haven't been chosen for anything! I am just a plain soldier. I guess the Waffen SS needs *some* but I thought we were the elite and nobody was a plain nobody! Maybe we are. The Waffen SS isn't even an official name. Maybe we don't exist at all! We just sit around and play cards. Rummy. And listen to the Victrola. And eat at the canteen. And sometimes have maneuvers. It's boring.

MARCH

They sit behind the Maginot Line and we are back of our Seigfried Line and we can see each other's laundry flapping and nobody does a damn thing! We just sit! What a way to fight a war! A stinking Sitzkrieg!

This Schutze will go crazy if nothing happens soon. March is a rotten month. The snow melts and the fogs come up and the sky is gray and I'm sick of cards and I *won't* take my leave at home and I miss girls and my "brothers" are stupid louts and I've heard the same old records over and over and nobody's thought up a new card game since the Middle Ages!

And the food kitchen has gone way downhill. Think they set all the pots in the snow before they serve us. Haven't seen anything steaming since November except the coffee, which isn't!

APRIL

Way back. It seems years ago, when we were burning some undesirable books like we were ordered to, I grabbed one out of the fire. Kept it. An American (English, I guess) dictionary. It was a little charred around the edges but it says it has 50,000 words in it. Paper so thin it feels like Bible paper. I wonder how many I *do* know? For sure not fifty thousand! And since I haven't anything better to do, I'm going to learn them! All of them. I keep writing when I can but I write worse now than in Bussett. Maybe because I haven't spoken English out loud now for a dog's age — and I'm almost twenty! It would be a plus for me to know *both* languages well, like a man.

Something's happening. Up in Norway and Denmark. I think we've got them both. But you wouldn't know it from our outfit. We're perching but no one's given the order to swoop!

MAY

Just a bit here to say we went. Did we go! Code word "Danzig" flashed and over the border. I should say around. Up and around. We just ignored the Line, the Maginot. From Switzerland to Luxembourg the stupid French built this border fortress above and below ground. OK. But then they just stopped the damned thing near Belgium. It's like a cattle farmer putting in a tough link fence to keep in the animals but not enclosing them. Even dumb things like cows will wander to the end, see open plains and walk out! You'd think the Frogs would learn from the first War. The Kaiser did the same maneuver! And way back the Romans did too. But nobody says the French have much up there. I'll write when I can. I don't know when. Anyway, we are now *officially* the Waffen SS! And I am Schutze Hannes Henkel, Leibstandarte Adolf Hitler SS!!!

I need a breather. For three or is it four days we have raced around Holland like shit through a goose and I have done it all on my fucking feet! An infantryman. The lowest of the low. This elite type has sore feet, bloody feet. I am attached to a motorized division but *very* loosely. We walk, we run behind. When lucky, I attach myself to the side of a truck. Usually, I am not lucky. This is called a lightning war, a Blitzkrieg. So we are blitzing. I do not blitz, I slog. At bivouac I drop in my tracks and dream of promotion to a lorry driver. Oh and "motorized" does *not* mean armor. The Leibstandarte AH has none. We aren't even up to division strength and we're reinforcing the Ninth Panzer. They have tanks, half-tracks, armored cars. The real machines of war.

We haul.

Why the hell haven't we gotten rid of the horses? Slow, stupid beasts! There's a bloody lot of motorized equipment here that whinnies, I can tell you! Napoleon was right. An army does travel on its stomach. Horses' stomachs! Oats and hay and grain and water. We drag tons of stuff to keep them going instead of artillery and seats for the infantry! I'd like to slaughter the whole lot of them and send them back for soap. I could use some. I stink!

The damned Panzers get the credit! Tank commanders, arrogant sunburnt sons of bitches get their pictures taken looking all dusty from battle with their sungoggles hanging like medals around their necks.

* * *

The people run. They don't know where they're going, only that they've got to get away from the fighting. Which means they clog the highways which means the enemy gets stalled. Try to weave an armored division through broken-down, steaming Peugeots and thousands of terrified refugees. Can't be done.

I was on a hill eating a lousy ration when two divebombers came in and cut a path right through the people. A mower through wheat. They fell all over the road. Some ran into ditches. Seemed like little bugs. Dead bugs. Didn't get up. Two more passes. Those that hid under the Peugeots were damned sorry if they felt anything exploding into a fireball.

It's funny. I didn't feel a thing, watching. Nothing. No excitement or sadness or anything.

The people keep coming pushing baby carriages full of stuff. Families. The children walk fast trying to keep up. The old people hold hands and lag far behind. There are fewer automobiles. One has a mattress lashed to the top and on that an upside-down table. Must be precious. Looks like a dead animal, all four legs sticking up and stiff. First the refugees run out of food and then they run out of water. But that they can get. All along the way nice Frenchmen have set up stands with lots of water — for a price. Those greedy Frogs charge their own people! Many francs for a sip. Life savings for a liter!!

We're pouncing down on the British-French forces. I don't pounce. I want to crawl. I'd give my soul to be a courier. He has a motorcycle!

I've been in three countries in how many days? Not many. Or hundreds? I don't remember anything except the tracks I follow. When we crossed the first border I said: Now you're going to see windmills. You couldn't prove it by me that Holland has any!

Borders mean nothing. Rivers we cross on pontoons if the bridges are blasted. Villages, faces, all the same. What's real? Water that tastes like metal from my canteen. Stukas screaming. The smell of cordite. The white pebbles that hurt because I'm sitting on them. And the warm sun on my back feeling good.

Rushed in to help the 7th Panzer commanded by Rommel. Heavy attack from British and French tanks. There was talk of panic among the Death's Head Division SS and parts of the regular army. Anyway, the French attacks got weaker and finally stopped. The Wehrmacht has the panzers but we have the guts! And we saved Rommel's skin! People say Rommel is a tactical genius. Say he learned tactics studying the Battle of Gettysburg. Even visited the battlefield. All I remember about that time was three days of blood. Pickett's Charge. And something about the South trying to outflank the North. Outflank on both sides? What the hell did Rommel learn from that?

Forced march to the coast. We have the British and bits of the French and Belgian Armies bottled up. There are only the beaches of a place called Dunkirk and the sea ahead of them. We've got them! And we're squeezing the noose tighter by the hour.

Who in God's name ordered a halt!! Not Dietrich, our commander. Not him. Some goddamned general of the Wehrmacht, that's who. The Führer will be furious. We'll probably never find out who made the blunder. We never find out anything!

We just heard that Sepp Dietrich has been rescued by an assault team from our Third Battalion. He lay in the oil and the mud for hours after his reconnaissance car turned over. They are heroes, those guys who got him out. I won't get a chance to be a hero or even a corporal at this rate.

JUNE

Well, we didn't get the prize, but I got one, sort of. The dimwits who command the Luftwaffe and the regular army let the BEF just float away on little boats pretty as you please. Let 'em go, for Christ's Sake! A couple of hundred thousand of them right across the Channel!

But — I am now a SEATED Schutze! Some poor bastard got himself shot right off his cycle so now I have it. And I'm supposed to ride it, that's the problem. No one here has time to teach me what to do when the thing skids, which it does all the time, particularly in the mud. I'll teach myself if I don't break my neck in the trying. After all, I am now a COURIER!

Oberschutze Henkel is a courier. A private first class, which doesn't make me feel as good as it should since I know that the guy blown off his cycle was a corporal. Well you can't have everything.

I can't even have the new BMW cycle which is supposed to perform in mud. It'll arrive just after my final spill, that's when.

So what's a courier's mission in life? To carry messages, right? Wrong. A courier's mission is to carry to his colonels and whoever whatever his colonels and whoever want him to. Sometimes that actually includes a teletype message from headquarters.

First I check out the signals shed. Usually they don't have much if anything for me. And they won't have anything at all if they don't camouflage better. Not that there are many allied planes flying around, but from the air, branches with dead leaves stick out like a sore thumb. Then I make the important visit, the one to the supply house. The stuff in that barn is for Very Important Types like Colonels. I hand the guy in charge a requisition, get the stuff and zip off, good and sure that my branches are new and my helmet's covered with fresh green leaves. In my sidecar is my dispatch case and inside that are a couple of bottles of Schnapps and usually a ham. Guess the grease is good for the leather. Once I nearly went off the road smelling a ham. I closed my eyes and pretended to tear it apart and was chewing happily when whoosh! I was in the ditch. That day I was carrying two bottles of champagne — and damned if the things didn't get bounced around so much the corks just burst. Well I couldn't just sit there watching all that good bubbly get wasted so I helped myself. Better down me than into the earth! Had some explaining to do at the front. Not really the front. These guys don't go that close.

Then there was the time my whole sidecar was a ladies' department store. Silk and lace underthings like you've never dreamed of. For who, dammit? They get girls at the front and we don't have one!

It sort of spoils my image of the SS, this black market dealing. Maybe it's the spoils of war, but we're still fighting and things are *not* equal!

I am a *hero* and it happened just in time! Would you believe just five days before the surrender! I am sitting in the field hospital hurting like hell and feeling great. My battalion commander has put me in for the Iron Cross (2nd Class) and I get a promotion to Corporal! SS Sturmann Henkel — about time!

Maybe it was luck or maybe I was destined to be there. Whatever, I *was* there at the right time.

I was tootling along actually carrying a message when way up ahead of me there was this tank, this Panzer PK-IV, 35 tons of her barreling along so that the earth was shaking and sending up clouds of dust that nearly knocked me off my cycle. Then out of nowhere came a shell, I heard the whistle, and then a ka*room!* The cycle went head over teakettle and I went onto the road hard. I got up feeling around to see if I was still in one piece and then looked down the road. That monster had stopped grinding. She was hurt, that I could tell, and everything was oh so quiet. Just me and a dying tank. And then all at once she blew oily smoke and then from way inside awful squealing like porkers frying. I ran closer and there was someone hanging out of the turret, maybe the commander — and he had to be dead. Besides the fact that his clothes were almost blown off him, his head was too. Hanging a foot from his neck by a few shiny strings. Gristle. Well, I didn't think. If I had stopped to I wouldn't have climbed up and heaved him off. I'm *sure* I wouldn't have gone down inside and pulled three madmen out. But that's what I did. One by one I threw them over the side. They were hollering and gasping and black with soot and I was telling them the shit to shut up and I was blind and burning up — but somehow I got the three of them away before that dinosaur exploded. Well that's when they found me and the three guys I'd saved. And I remember before I passed out to say I had an urgent message which must be delivered. Well it could have been urgent. Pretty quick thinking on my part. And I *am* a hero!!

EMMA
CAPE CHARLOTTE
JANUARY

I lost my old pencil box so I got a new one that has three drawers! It has pencils and a pencil sharpener and a big rubber erasa and a ruler and a round thing that is like a ruler for something and a lot of nibs for my pen and a pen wiper that is very soft for wiping pens. It has another thing with a point on it to make circles with if I have to make circles.

MARCH

I spit up 31 times today. I have the whooping couff. Mummy hasn't any more clean sheets and she says she can't wash anymore so

I am sleeping on the funny papers which we can throw away after I read them which I am trying to do fast before I spit up all over them. I make a lot of noise when I spit up.

JUNE

We made a map of Italy today. You mix salt and flour and water and put it on cardboard and try to make it look like Italy. Miss Harmon said mine was the best. Mummy and Daddy told me at supper that many solders were saved by little boats that came from England to save them. I can't remember the name of the place but the soldiers had to sleep on the beach a long time. Rodney cut off a piece of his little finger with the paper cutter.

HENRY

JAMESPORT

AUGUST

I admit to a certain state of tenseness, for today I entered the grocery with my first message. As I expected, a harsh tinkle upon opening the door. On such a lovely warm day, the door was closed. Obviously: the odors emanating from within would fell the populace!

I did little work for the firm yesterday because I was laboring to code and could not concentrate. Outside, the familiar noises of construction seemed magnified to an intolerable degree.

Finally I finished my crumb of information: the manifest of one merchant ship, Brazilian registry. Since the entire cargo was oil and the destination unknown (because I could not find out), the message itself was short. However, searching for the correct (or nearly correct) word took an immense amount of time and effort.

Inside, the shop was empty of customers but crammed with every kind of indigestible victual: barrels of gray, crinkled objects which I assumed were a strange breed of olive, swimming in brine; pickles — and peppers, the deadly kind which destroy the nasal passages; cheeses in the open air prey to every species of germ; and swaying under a dilatory fan — blades encrusted with eons of grease and grime — hung long sausages of varying colors and heft. A haven for bacteria. Braids of onions and garlic were displayed. Such an amount of garlic should be outlawed. A hint is fine; a hank is dreadful. Creeps out the pores for days on end.

And over all hung the corpses of flies, or the soon-to-be corpses, still struggling senselessly, all stuck on sticky yellow strands of curling flypaper. Many, however, had not yet met their Fate and were settling comfortably, twitching their feelers, testing the cheese.

I stared at the strange mixtures resting (they did appear tired) in trays behind a glass window. Next to the trays, behind a sign which read: "Meats — Custom cut," were slabs of anonymous flesh. Where was the "Submarine" of which the shop so proudly boasts? Could it be in one of those covered barrels? A cigar-shaped object, submerged in brine?

Happily, I note here that, as yet, I have not lost my wit.

And then from behind the back drapery a bulky man appeared wearing a splattered apron. Insolently, he asked what I wanted in an accent decidedly Italian.

In a quandary, not prepared to purchase *anything,* I pointed to one of the hanging sausages. My choice was severed with the sweep of a knife. "Dat'll be one fifty-nine."

I retrieved two dollars, and here I am not too humble to state, thought quickly, slipping my message *between* the two bills.

My offering was received without so much as an eyelid twitch. The cash register rang, the money was placed within, and I was handed loose change, the sausage — and a small manila envelope.

"Next time pay for it with a large bill." And he glided back behind the drapery. How can such a large man glide? I thought, and then remembered what I held in my hands.

Since no one was about, I unsealed the manila envelope and cautiously peered inside. Another one! Another photo from Berlin!

Needless to say, I left hurriedly, the sausage tucked under an arm. I tore the envelope to shreds and popped it into the first available rubbish bin. I almost heaved the sausage also before prudence intervened. After all, I had paid for it.

Of course! It is now clear. The two one-dollar bills were adequate for my purposes. But, in turn he has envelopes to give to me. From them. Therefore, his request for a *large* bill ensures that my change will be at least two bills of smaller denominations. And concealed between them — my reward.

The sausage sits in my desk drawer, more odorous than ever. I believe I will take it home. And I will show it to Evelyn. Seeing the long, slimy thing will drive her to distraction. Bother her no end. So unlike me. Quite unlike me. But then, I am not me, am I?

OCTOBER

I came with the sole purpose of passing another message, but curious, I asked to see a "Submarine." The large man asked how would I like it. Having no idea how, I answered "the usual." If "the usual" is what was handed to me, I dare not think of what a "deluxe" might consist. A sandwich of sorts, a "Submarine." Between a doughy roll is crammed all manner of sliced meats, cheeses, gray olives, pickles, hot peppers, tomatoes and dried herbs. And then over all vinegar is sprinkled and olive oil poured with no restraint. The result is a sloppy handful.

It was wrapped fairly securely. Only a bit of oil seeped through, unfortunately staining my waistcoat. The only resemblance between this submarine and an undersea craft is, I suppose, its shape: elliptical.

The day was clear and bracing and I had time, hence I entered the park established for the citizens of Jamesport by Sumner Pugh. I knew old Pugh's son, Wellington, a worthy fellow. Well's father, however, was a robber and a thief, but — I suppose one could say in all truth — a self-made man.

October is my favorite month, a time when the leaves are on fire but the air is frosty. The park was nearly deserted. A bit cool for old bones and there were no children. School keeps. I like to come here to watch the geese as they rest on their trek south. Canada geese. I enjoy feeding them scraps.

I sat on a bench near the pond and soon a few old-timers waddled up, honking hunger. For a moment I was in despair. I had brought nothing — and then I remembered my "Submarine." With greasy fingers I tore off bits, which to my great surprise caused a stampede. One determined fellow practically sat in my lap, begging for more. Of course, I fed him. But then I wondered what all the fuss was about, and gingerly took a bite. Lo and behold! The concoction is delicious. Just the right blend of ingredients!

Wait 'til I bring one home to Evelyn. She will think I *have* gone mad!

EMMA

LOON LAKE

AUGUST

Dear Daddy. I HATE camp!!!! Please can I come home. Im scared of swimming and I couldnt think of what animal to be so one of the cownselers made me a turtle. I had to crawl around the floor all night at talent night and when they did a play of Winny the poo I was the tallest so I had to be Cristofer Robin when I wanted to be Eeaw. I cry every night and my polar bear is getting dirty and I want to come home.

Love,
Emma

CAPE CHARLOTTE
DECEMBER

I got a five year diary for my birthday from Nana and Bumpa. They are my grandmother and grandfather which are Daddys Mummy and Daddy. Mummy doesn't have any. I mean she did but they aren't here anymore. They died. You can put in five years of the same day on one page.

The 5 year diary isnt big enough. I tried skrunching up the words and I didnt say much but they still went down into 1942. Maybe if I write and tell them they will send me a 1 year diary.

They *did* send me a new one but now I have to copy all the old days into it. My NEW DIARY has a lock on it so people can't open it unless they have the key which I have hiden so they can't find it. HAHA!

This is not a page in my diary. This is written as almost anybody can tell on school paper because I cant find the key to my diary. I have looked and looked.

I thought I found the key to my diary but I didn't. I'll never find it and it is lost forever unless I rememba where I hid it before Im old and gray and die. I am writing in my diary because I cut the strap off so now I can open it and *so can everybody else.* But I don't think Id better hide the diary!

Mummy and Daddy gave me a dictionary which I can look up words in when I want to spell better except that I don't know how to if I'm not sure how to spell the word in the first place. I am going to look up every big word after I write it and if it isn't there then I'll know I wrote it wrong, I guess. I can't ask Daddy and Mummy because this is a SECRET diary!

HANNES
FRANCE
AUGUST

Being a hero oils the way for sure! Zip! down a greased pole into OCS. SS Officers' Candidate School. Truly! Deeds *are* rewarded in the Schutzstaffel! So what that I haven't gone through six years of the Adolf Hitler Schools. Who cares if I'm not enrolled in a Nazi Political Training School. I've *proved* I can take it with the best of them.

I leave for Berlin in two weeks for assignment to cadet school. I am almost healed. The rest on a *real* bed helped and the food was *hot*. The nurses weren't. They were antiseptically pure! I had my eye on the night nurse, lean Lili with braids coiled round her head. She had a "touch-me-not" look so one night when she bent over me, I touched her. Right on her breast. Couldn't feel much through the starch. Could feel the slap she gave me — right on my poor bandaged hand! My burned hand!

Have used this healing time to study my dictionary. Every day ten new words to memorize, to learn how to use. Synonyms important too. Perhaps (not maybe) I'll attempt (not try) to write more flowing prose (not better) and not use *stuff* or *they say* (who says?) or THAT'S FOR SURE again! Doing a rough calculation, it occurs to me that 50,000 words will take me close to fifteen years — not allowing time out for wars, screwing and leaves!

Just had the formal ceremony. My battalion commander came to the hospital and I was standing beside the bed dressed in my only good uniform. Salutes and a couple of photographs and a short speech and that was it. The Iron Cross Second Class was pinned to my tunic along with the Silver Badge for wounds suffered in action. I suppose it was action, though I never saw the enemy. Heard him. Felt him sure as Hell's Fire!

BERLIN

Berliners are snots with chips on their shoulders. The dialect is rough enough to make me think of Bussett!

The capital of the civilized world is not impressive. Berlin's even grayer than Hamburg. I expected what? A new Rome? I wanted edifices (new word) of white marble with tall columns lining the boulevards. Some of the streets *are* wide with trees and much is going up — buildings. Maybe Berlin will look like Rome when they're done. But the Chancellery is very ordinary. Some guards and flags. It's supposed to carry great mystique (two). I stood and waited for my spirits to overflow or something. Here is the seat of power. Here is the office of our Führer. There is his balcony. Nothing happened. Maybe there's magnificence (three. I'm showing off!) inside. Hope so. There *are* antiaircraft guns on the roof.

Oh, and my first day was a first. The bloody British bombed us last night! They actually had enough planes to come right over the heart of Berlin. Little damage, I guess. BUT that fat man who runs the air show around here said it couldn't happen. It has.

I leave for OCS tomorrow, so used today for more wanderings. Got off the streets and into the back alleys. A couple of painted whores stopped me and practically got my pants off before I could get the two of them off me. I'm not that desperate! Yet.

A sign intrigued me. Went in and browsed. Old books. Used books. Books I think are deleterious (now that's a *good* one!) to our health according to edict.

Behind some pamphlets was a small book of paintings. Not real. Pictures of paintings. I've never been to a museum, but this was a museum all wrapped up in one little book. The colors! Colors of sun and fog! A French church at different times of the day. Water lilies and ponds and snow scenes and bridges that jump out at you slowly through the smoke. The shopkeeper told me that Monet is decadent. The dictionary says "decadence" can mean a decay in art. Well I'll take decadence anytime over the posters that are all over. Fierce fighters clenching their teeth and stabbing the enemy. Every bayonet drips blood. Oh, and I bought something else — a grammar book from America! "Property of Harrisburg, Penn. Schools." Wonder how it got all the way to Berlin? Pretty dirty, inkstains and foodstains all over. Maybe the second time around I'll understand English grammar!

BAD TÖLZ
OCTOBER

Back to Bavaria! And did I laugh. I am enrolled in Junkerschule! Me who didn't want to mix with Junkers anytime, anyplace and here I am. There's one big difference. It's an *SS* Junkerschule. A big difference. The barracks, the school, is the oldest of its kind — AND — isn't too far from my old Hitler Youth camp. Same high snowy mountains. Same damn Isar with its waterfalls!

Black boots. I have them! I love them! And the uniform. And the visored cap. The cap doesn't have gold on it. Instead the braid is silver. Nicer. With a silver skull they call a Death's Head. A skull resting on bones, but I think they look like angel's wings. "Death's Head" sounds classier than skull. The uniform really fits me. Black tunic and breeches and the famous two lightning streaks. The double Runic S — from an ancient mystical alphabet.

I wrote Mama and Papa *after* the medal pinning. I didn't want them messing up the ceremony! I only told them I had a decoration and a wound and I was going to OCS school. Not what kind — or where.

On leave I should drop in on them. Bang at the door. Order them to open up. There stands the Black and Silver. It'd scare the hell out of them!

The grammar book doesn't like dashes much. It loves colons. Henceforth :s. When I remember. I'm staying away from "Who" and "Whom." Period!

Same kind of ceremony as HJ induction. Swear new motto — "My honor is loyalty." We all swear obedience unto death to the Führer, so help us God.

NOVEMBER

Oh God, I AM SO TIRED!

Outside: Up mountains, down mountains, through rivers, through mud, around and around the parade ground. Goosestep *perfectly.* March a white line *perfectly.* Present arms *perfectly.* Basic training was a breeze compared to this!

Inside: Salute. Snap! Salute. Snap! Even at meals. Salute. Snap! Perfectly!

Lectures on strategy: Old battles refought.

Field exercises: I've been in the field!

Sport: Win a badge. Jump high, climb higher, run faster!

Recreation: Skiing. I'm pretty good!

History: Of the SS.

Racial theory: Four times as much is spent on political indoctrination as on engineering and three times more than on troop duty. Only tactics is equal!!

DECEMBER

As an SS officer candidate I must have and maintain: integrity, chivalry, good fellowship, helpfulness, honor, obedience, and fearlessness. Also, I must develop a family spirit! (Not with mine, by God!) Oh, and I must show irreproachable conduct in public! (Where? We've been to one concert and a museum. A total of one day out of prison.)

Think my diary is safe from prying eyes. I still write in English because I can express my thoughts better *and* most anyone picking it up is *not* an English expert. But about the prying eyes part. The rules are rough: "Offenses against fellow comrades (THEFT) are severely punished — usually by *expulsion.*" So I think they'll keep their greasy little paws off my things.

1941

BORMANN
BERLIN

Willi!

Hess is insane! Flew right off his rocker in a stolen Messerschmitt-110, and had to parachute down in Scotland. Served him right, finding himself on the wrong end of a Scottish pitchfork! Wish that farmer had skewered him!

I had *nothing whatsoever* to do with this plan! I was not involved in any way, much to the sorrow of those who wish to be rid of me.

The Führer showed me his complete trust and devotion. As of this date, I am Chief Executive Officer of the Party Chancellery, responsible *only* to Adolf Hitler himself. In effect, the *real* Deputy Führer (although I don't, as yet, have the title). You may, in the near distant future, be corresponding with the #2 man in the Greater Reich!

The Führer was understandably shaken, at first, by what seemed to be a traitorous act by Hess. But it is clear that in his warped mind, Herr Hess intended to begin a dialogue with the English. I do not care what his motive was. What *does* matter is his absence. I will fill it willingly and ably.

Whether Hess' flight was the trigger, I cannot tell, but on the day after, the Führer issued two tough, *very* hush-hush decrees (involving our fat neighbor to the East — the one with whom we are on talking terms for the moment — but that moment, I tell you, will last only a month or so longer. You did *not* hear of the coming squabble through me!). The decrees state that *all* civilians taking arms against the *occupying* Wehrmacht forces be shot immediately. No trial. *And* — here's the ballbreaker: that the to-be-occupied eastern territories be "cleansed" of Jews and other troublemakers. Heydrich takes on this task with glee. Einsatzgruppen: Special Action Assassins. Have you gotten wind of this Group over there?

While I have your close attention, Schmidt, I want you to pursue a thought I had and use Midas to gather more Americans. Yes, I know they are not in plentiful supply here — but — there are plenty of German-Americans in the middle of the United States. Some belong to the Bund. Others are quietly cheering for the Reich.

Have Midas check out the area and be ready with a report this year.

Bormann

HENRY
CAPE CHARLOTTE
AUGUST

Utter tedium this: locating the exact words for my ciphers! However, I *am* spared some valuable time since "latitude" and "longitude" are designations frequently essential to my messages. With amusement, I note that within the tome's text two words are used with utmost regularity: North and South!

NOVEMBER

They have exploded eastward and threaten the very gates of Moscow. I believe Mister Hitler expects to do that at which Mister Bonaparte (with an "e" unsilent of course. Attempting to make the world forget his Wop origins, Napoleon took the French pronunciation) yes . . . at which Mister Bonaparte failed miserably.

I have *not* failed. Following the instructions of Lowell, divining fact from the blather of colleagues, I now possess a bonanza! First crumbs, then crusts, now an entire loaf!

Eight freighters and tankers of British, Canadian and Free Poland registry will sail from Jamesport in four days' time to rendezvous with ten merchant ships from Halifax. Rendezvous point is 53 miles due south of the western tip of Sable Island. The convoy carries oil, wheat, aircraft parts and antiaircraft guns. Only two escort vessels are scheduled to shepherd them.

I must and will divorce myself from the consequences of my actions. I liken myself to the general who devises a battle plan on paper or to the bombardier who plots the wind direction and drift of metal eggs. There is a curious non-involvement here, for none of us will see the actual carnage.

Even without my information, that convoy might, quite possibly may be, intercepted by a prowling wolfpack. I take heart in this possibility.

BORMANN
BERLIN

Dear Willi!

Isn't this an American song? "Merrily we roll along, roll along . . . beyond the Black Sea shores!" The last is mine! And the Führer's! And the German people's! My God! What an Army!

So our American on the coast — "Majorca"? — has come through with a big one, finally? Convoy rendezvous point.

No, you shitting ass! We do *not* give it to Canaris! We will never give *anything* to the Abwehr! That numbskull bastard is a traitor. I know it in my bones!

Send the information on to Dönitz. The Grand Admiral will radio all undersea craft and — Poof! No convoy. And, in the process, the U-boat king will owe me one. I won't let him forget the debt, if and when the time comes. You can bet your boots on that!

Reward Majorca. Give him *several* prints of his indiscretion this time.

Bormann

HANNES
BAD TÖLZ
JANUARY

Rolf's coming!! He's got a leave and he's taking part of it to see me. I haven't seen him in God knows how long. Bet we'll look changed to each other. He went another way. Through the Party Political School and now he's in one of these Order Castles — Ordensburgen.

Well, he came and went and I'm not sorry but I'll come to that in a minute. Rolf had everybody drooling (except me) about his castle — his big stone Schloss. Said it belonged to some Graf and he (Rolf) had everybody believing that he was there watching them throw out the blubbering Graf and the Gräfin in tears. I know he made up that part about the Count and Countess because the SS had that castle *long* before Rolf got there!

Then he looks around at the dormitory and sort of sniffs and describes "my Schloss." Describes the great stone blocks and the slit windows and the enormous hall and the grand staircase. There's a banquet table he swears can sit *sixty* with heavy carved chairs all around and a fireplace high enough and wide enough for six men to walk in side by side. When he mentions the wild boar with a vicious snout on the wall I notice he doesn't mention roast boar! About the walls. They are covered with coats of arms and great stag heads and banners bloody from ancient battles, the blood all rusty now. And there are lances and Saxon shields and suits of armor in the corners and great candles flickering.

He says he and his comrades all feel like Teutonic knights. We *are* Teutonic knights, he says, and his voice gets wavery and his eyes get watery.

So I say, isn't the whole place pretty Spartan (from Greece) and damn cold at night and he looks like he'd like to kill me. Those eyes of his that used to crinkle up when he laughed could bore through a pillbox now. And he hasn't laughed once. Not once. And he used to be a cutup! Maybe he's the elite of the elite but he's hard. Hard. He's changed and not for the better. If I didn't know him I'd say that he was nuts. A real fanatic. A real Hesse, that's what he is. My God! Bannführer Hesse all over again. I don't know Rolf anymore and the barracks looks pretty good right now.

FEBRUARY

We healthy Nordic types are supposed to digest everything that Goebbels spouts. *We* will inherit the earth and wipe out all the non-Aryan polluters of the human race. "Subhuman Slavs" is *out* at the moment. For how long? For as long as the pact with Russia holds, that's how long. We're always having to readjust our thinking. Getting back to Goebbels — he says there are certain races "more closely allied to monkeys and apes." Anybody with half an eye looks at Goebbels and says, But you're a midget clubfoot with a monkey face! But the little monkey is all ready. He digs up some professor who works with bones to say Goebbels is the one exception — "a dwarflike German who grew dark"!

Well, I'm not going to point that out. Let someone else try. Let someone else take the heat. I'll just get good grades, memorize and spout out what they want to hear. I'll toe the mark and stop worrying about things that don't make sense. The "deviant" doesn't get where I've gotten. I know what it's like to be different. And it isn't roses!

* * *

Everyone is writing "journals," so it didn't seem strange for me to work on my diary. Only difference is the language. And maybe the thinking. Probably the thinking.

The other night it was almost lights-out when in marched the Sergeant Major. We were all scribbling. "OK, lads," he says, looking very pleased with himself, "let's hear some of these pure thoughts you've been putting down. Dedicated lads like you must have something instructive to tell us all." And with that the journals went CLAP and we all shrunk down in our bunks. So the Sgt. Major orders Koch out of bed. Up ramrod stiff is Koch. "Read turd!" yells the Sergeant Major. "Give us an excerpt *here*" — and the Sgt. Major opens the journal in the middle and points with his eyes closed. Koch salutes and swallows a couple of times and reads all about a girl he's been screwing! He squeaks out that part and then he adds something like he was doing it for the Fatherland to make a little SS baby. I'm damn sure that wasn't in the journal!

Meanwhile I'm dying. If he gets to me I know I can't fake it. And what is in my diary will get me kicked around from here to kingdom come and back again. So I look very pleased with Koch's reading and I'm *not* chosen. But that's not the whole story.

I've got to write a NEW diary in one night! So I hide my regular diary pages in "Tactics" and take a blank notebook and go to the latrine. And for eight hours I sit on the can and write like a fool. My butt hurts and there'll be a nice red ring on it for days and I can hardly see even with the flashlight. But the worst part is knowing when to groan and moan and when to dip my water cup in the can and dribble and splash the water back in to sound like I have the shitters. I save that for when the cadets come calling to pee and I tell them to get the hell out, I'm dying.

Well I write and dribble and write and groan and splash some more and finally I've got one — a NEW DIARY. Not thoughts for every day but maybe enough to fool the Sgt. Major, I hope!

For example: I remember the *exact* date we climbed that mountain. Ice-climbed a sheer face! We were all so scared we nearly pissed in our pants and I was swearing under my breath a lot of things I shouldn't have, so I wrote them down the night of the climb. In my NEW diary I said: "Today we climbed a difficult piece. With every ounce of my body I reveled in the hurt of exertion for I knew I was hardening myself for the Führer. With each whack of the ice-hammer on piton I praised the Party and all it stands for." That ought to hold the Sgt. Major!

And then I worked on that notebook, bending it, breaking the spine until it opened every time to "my page." By God, two nights later, who should the Sgt. Major point to but me. Up I went ramrod stiff. Snap! Salute perfect. Bang! It worked! The Sgt. Major had no control over my notebook. He stood there with it opened to "my page"! So I swallowed and tried to look embarrassed and I read. I read with such feeling the Sgt. Major had to peek down to check if I was faking. But there it was in black and white. *I'm* his fair-haired boy now, by God! He took the whole thing — hook, line and sinker.

MARCH

Rosenberg's back in favor. "Subhuman Slavs" is back in the curriculum — and how! And our instructors are in fine form. They love to hissssss the terrible words. It's hard to hiss "Juden" so they're having fun frothing at the mouth now. "Slawische Untermenschen" is a good spitting phrase. There's a hurry-up feeling here. Something's up!

NEAR LEIPZIG

I'm gone! Off in a flurry of dust to a place outside of Leipzig called the Frontier Police School. And I haven't got my brevets yet! I'm a Goddamned hero, I've saved three guys from burning up, I've been in combat in three countries, I have two medals and I'm almost tops in my class, and what do they do with a few months left to go to graduation but pull me out. This had better be a step up!

What did I say? This place is two, maybe three steps up. I really must have conned the Sgt. Major because this is *not* your ordinary SS Junker OCS. This is a "leadership" school. Tear your heart out, Rolf. I'll be elite but really before you can shit again! Because I'm *with* the elite. This place is full of really bright people. I mean professors and lawyers. There's even a parson and an opera singer! We're from the Waffen SS, the SS Secret State Police which is called the Gestapo, and the regular Kriminal Police. One Kripo, name of Schwoermer, is a dud and a boot-licker. I think he wants to lick mine. Always hanging around me. But he must have tasted a lot of boots because he's a major and I'm . . . I'm almost commissioned, I think! I'll play it easy and stay out of his way.

APRIL

I'm a man. Really a man. Yesterday was my birthday. 21! And in response to a letter telling Mama and Papa my address and hinting that I was going places, I got a couple of presents. Typical. From Mama a poppyseed strudel with a tiny note warning me not to eat it all at once because (not because I might get a bellyache — oh, no!) because butter and sugar are scarce!! Papa sends a photograph of himself as a private (is that all?) for the Kaiser. He looks dumpy, ridiculous. Maybe it's the helmet. Papa writes that I am part of a great movement and much is expected of me and not to bring shame on him and Mama! Jesus! Mama scrawls "Love" at the end which is very untypical. I will not answer them. Let them read about *me* someday!!!

We're training for "special action." That's what this school is all about. I don't know exactly what the "special" is yet. But I will soon.

I'm with a really good group of people. They're different, not schoolboys or cadets. These men, most of them, are older — and brilliant. No other word for it. Brilliant. And they're not fanatics like Rolf. Their eyes are kind. Many have university degrees. They know culture — art and music. And law. We have a lot who know about justice. They are refined and sophisticated (except for Schwoermer, who thinks culture has something to do with calisthenics!). I want to learn from them. I've never had a chance to learn from a lot of really educated people.

Waldi, who has a wonderful singing voice, so full, is teaching me about opera. I don't call him Waldi to his face because he's an officer, but I bet he wouldn't mind. I think he said he's performed in the Vienna Opera House. Well maybe the Volksopera. Whatever, he's always singing Wagner, who seems to be the most popular composer around. I like the love music from *Tristan.* Now that is sexy music! But we're in intensive training now. NO LEAVES. NO LADIES!

We're playing hide-and-seek. Honest to God! And I have to laugh inside watching my intellectuals (good word!) huffing and puffing and getting all red in the face as they run. Some are so fat that when they try to hide behind a tree trunk, both sides stick out. But what I want to know is, who hides and who seeks?

MAY

I know all the secrets now. Who hides? The Jews. Who will seek? We will.

Maybe my friends here knew it all the time. I didn't. But now I do and at first I had some trouble with it. So I asked for a copy of Hegel which made me look good and I sat down in my bunk and I read him all the way through and thought hard. And it came to me. If I substitute the word "Jews" in place of some of his general words, look what happens. "Moral claims (of the Jews) which are irrelevant must not be in collision with world historical deeds" and "War (against the Jews) is a great purifier" and "(The State) must trample down many an innocent flower (the Jews) — *crush to pieces* many an object (Jew) in its path . . ." With my insertions, Hegel says do it for the good of Germany and the whole world! Ride with it Hannes and keep YOUR MOUTH SHUT and just believe what they say — it's a lot easier and they know more than you do!

The Einsatzgruppen. That's what we are. Special Action Squads. To be mobile. Very mobile. The elite of the elite of the elite, Rolf! I thought the Leibstandarte SS was the Praetorian Guard! They're not even a division. Only a beefed-up (with a few motors) infantry! WE are the Praetorians!

JUNE

Things are coming thick and fast! Operation Barbarossa soon. Great name! Whoever makes up these names must have a time for himself! Barbarossa was Friedrich I of Germany who had a red (get it — RUSSIA) beard. And he is supposed to sit at a stone table with his knights waiting to give Germany the highest place in all the world. He's waiting. And we're raring to go!

OK. I think the Führer along with Hegel has hit on the perfect solution. Get rid of the Jews, who almost everybody hates for good or bad reasons. Maybe even jealousy. Who cares WHY. But dispose of them and what have you got? A united front against *something*. And that's what you need to persuade everybody to your thinking. It's genius, that's what it is! Somebody has to pay to make this a better world. Somebody's always paid and I guess it's the Jews' turn this time. Too bad — but that's the way it is.

We have split up into subgroups for greater mobility. I'm in Einsatzkommando B 8c. There are only about 3000 of us in the whole Einsatzgruppen and in B there are about 750, which includes radiomen and some female secretaries. Tough titties!

They sure do things fast in this man's outfit! My commission just came through! Whoosh — an Untersturmführer! About time. I've been working my ass off while those cadets were reading bedtime stories to the Sgt. Major. Three silver pips on my collar badge, gleaming!

DUBEN

A long day. But a day I'll never forget. I met *Heydrich!* We were trucked nearly 100 kilometers to Duben and assembled to hear from the man who thought up the Einsatzgruppen. I looked terrific! An officer!

Heydrich. I can't explain what happened exactly. I listened to him give us a speech which was pretty good, not sensational. He was very correct. A good Nordic type. I know he plays the violin and is very cultured. I know his boss is Himmler. Why I don't know, because we all called Himmler "Chicken Shit." Of course I have never met Himmler. I've never met *anybody* until today. But some of the cadets had, and said old Himmler has chicken shit around the edges. A bit of the chicken farmer sticking to him still, I guess. But about Heydrich. He's young and looks like he'll last a thousand years and he's what the SS is all about. There we were assembled, and after the speech Reinhard Heydrich inspected us and he stopped right in front of me. Stopped and looked at me. Those eyes! It was like being hit by lightning, having electricity pour through you, glowing like a sparkler or — I can't explain it. I was lit up, that's for sure. And at that moment if Heydrich had asked me to hack my foot off and hand it to him, I would have. I would have hacked away and been glad to. It was weird and wonderful!

EMMA
CAPE CHARLOTTE
JANUARY

The men put in a new furnace today which is pretty nice because it is an oil furnace! Which means it doesn't burn coal which is awfully dirty sitting there in a big black pile on the floor and gets all over you. And Daddy doesn't have to shovel it in and then shovel it out. The ashes I mean. Sometimes he had to go down in the middle of the night and shovel in his pajamas because the fire had burned up and it was VERY COLD UPSTAIRS. Our new furnace burns oil which you don't even see because it comes from a tank or something.

FEBRUARY

I don't think our new furnace is doing much better because even when it is running it is STILL COLD UPSTAIRS! I think I am going down in the cellar and kick it. Sometimes people act better after they've been whomped.

I whomped the furnace and when I did it burped sort of. Anyway I think it needed it because it is still pretty cold upstairs BUT the bathroom is VERY COZY NOW!

JUNE

I said goodbye to our icebox yesterday but I wasn't really as sad as I pretended because we now have a REFRIGERATOR. It has a little cave inside like an igloo with frost on it. That's where we put two trays of water which quicker than a flash go to work and make ice squares which we are supposed to call ice cubes. I will miss the great big iceman but I like ice squares better!

JULY

I am pretty tired. First Mummy said that the Germans were almost running through Russia and the Russians were burning everything so the Germans couldn't get it and everybody is rooting for the Russians. She showed me Russia on the map and it is pretty big and it will take a lot of running people to capture it. And then we played capture the flag until it got dark which was pretty late but it was lots of fun.

HANNES
ON THE POLISH-SOVIET BORDER
JUNE

Just when I think something is hopeless, along comes Lady Luck and smiles on me. I was giving up on my English grammar and the damned dictionary when who should take an interest in me — but a PROFESSOR of English. That was his specialty at the University. And when he found out, and I thought I had kept it pretty quiet, that I had spent some time in America, he suggested we talk to each other — in English. In fact, he is trying to organize a small class, but I am his first pupil!

I know we will be pretty busy during the day. They have described our mop-up duties, but that always leaves the nights for learning!

In case anyone is wondering about where we get women, we sure won't get them from the secretaries that will travel with us! I wouldn't touch them with a ten-foot pole. Talk about tough titties! They're hard, like Rolf. Waldi, the singer, calls one Brünhilde although she's really Hanni. She's big, like a man, and I can see her with one of those Valkyrie helmets on, the one with horns, bellowing from a stage. She bellows from anywhere as far as I can tell. She ought to be in the unit as a fighting man. She'd be good at mopping up and I don't mean with a wet mop, either. She's aching to pop some Jews, talks about it all the time. Give her a rifle and she'd go nuts, popping away. Maybe she has nuts! I wouldn't be surprised at *anything*, nowadays.

Operation BARBAROSSA! To the east sit 5 million Jews just waiting for us. "Proceed ruthlessly," they tell us. The army goes and we're standing on tiptoes, ready to follow on their heels. This will make France look like a picnic! Russia, here we come!

RUSSIA
JULY-NOVEMBER

We're off! Right behind the Wehrmacht. Almost hitting their heels! They cut — and do they cut — I've never seen such an Army. There never *has* been such an Army! They cut and we reap. That's what we're here for. To separate the wheat from the chaff. The chaff will just be blown away.

When I talk about the Wehrmacht now I don't just mean the regular army. I have to include all the Waffen SS divisions because the Wehrmacht means those too. I hope the Junker generals aren't all up there pulling the strings.

I wonder where my Leibstandarte SS is now? Heard awhile back they were in the Balkans — Jugoslavia or Greece — helping the Italians. The Eyties need all the help they can get! Suppose the Leibstandarte is in on this push? Do they have more motors? Or even panzers? God! I wish I hadn't been hurt being a hero. I missed the Leibstandarte Victory Parade last July in Berlin. Missed being there and in it by a month!

I can't breathe, we're going so fast! I knew when we crossed the border into Russia! At least I think I knew when because the churches that were still standing in Poland, the Catholic ones with their steeples pointing straight up to God (they hope), have changed to steeples with onions on top! Must think God loves little onions! Where I came from he didn't even spit on sets of them!

I think an operation is about to commence. Our group, Einsatzgruppe B, is heading for Belorussia. We'll hit Mother Russia right in her white gut!

The operation was minor, the first for kommando unit 8c. We were told that the pickings will improve as the Army moves ever forward. The operation: we flushed out a covey of Jews from a town. Told where they were by a peasant. We don't need scouting parties of our own. The Ukrainians will do it for us! Anyway, we herded them to an open pit which a couple of our men had started and which our guests finished. A motley group, about fifty, wailing softly, arms about each other. Then quiet. They waited for the volley which came, as sure as the wind. Dropped and most were dead except for a few who twitched. Another round and they were finished. I was not squeamish. This is a job. A necessary one, says Heydrich and the Führer. My friends, my educated comrades. They all agree. The whole thing reminds me of France and the clogged roads of people running. But then and now I am distant. Then and now people become just moving figures. Livestock — or less.

That figure, five million Jews, has shrunk, according to people who should know. They ran — east. But that still leaves three and a half for us. That's over 1000 per man — at least. But we have to find them. They won't walk up and say, "Need some more for your quota?" But there's an interesting point: These Russian Jews have been cut off from the rest of the world — a lot of them, anyway. They don't know our methods in Poland — or Germany for that matter. To them, we are a hell of a lot better than the Czar. They still remember him and his Cossacks, thundering into a village and swiping off heads and whatnot.

In one month our armies have penetrated *300 miles.* And the Red Army retreats all along the front from the Baltic to the Black Sea! But in their wake they leave a wasteland. Rather than leave us a billet or a grain of wheat or a piece of usable machinery, they have torched what they could — down to the black earth! In the face of defeat, they have taken the time to sweep up whole areas of useful industry and carry them along. Presumably hoping to set them up again out of harm's way. Beyond the Urals? In Central Mongolia? There is no place to hide, for in the end we will carry the war to Asia! Alexander the Great is about to be displaced by Adolf Hitler!

After hours, when we have had a good day and things are quiet, I have a lesson with Friedrich. He likes to wind down by playing teacher, which he does well. And I am a good student. He makes me talk, he makes me read poetry by Englishmen *out loud.* He makes me write essays and criticizes my wording and sentence structure. Friedrich sounds like an Englishman because he studied at some university there before the War. And he looks like one in the movies . . . Leslie Howard, that's who! Imagine Leslie Howard in an SS uniform and that's Friedrich. I am learning so much! (He says, besides my other problems, I use too many exclamation points!) So I will endeavor to cut down.

The Bolsheviks have not wasted everything. The pickings are still good. They did not take their Jews along for some reason.

While our main job is disposal of certain elements, we can kill two birds with one torch. Why waste ammunition when a single match can do the trick? When we discover an untouched church of the onion variety, we save it and assemble our daily cache of Jews. Into the house of a Russian Orthodox God are pushed the unbelievers, the damned. Does the God of the Russians cry out in horror at the defaming of his House of Worship? We *do* hope so. The doors are locked to keep the Devil out. But the Devil seeps in, licking at the timbers. The roar of the inferno muffles most of the shrieks. And when all is still and charred, the remains are crushed to particles and ground into the earth.

We are, however, running out of churches. Which leaves us with the other method: pits.

Christ! Lady Luck went whoring and left me with Schwoermer as the unit commander for a while! Friedrich's off with another unit and I don't know where Waldi is, so I'm stuck!

Schwoermer, who plays one role during working hours, adds a twist at night. I don't know that I can write about the nights now. It's too humiliating.

During daylight hours Schwoermer has me, orders me, into a field gray uniform, devoid of decoration. Nothing that smacks of the SS.

The people group in anxious knots. Bareheaded I go from one to another, herding them in a line without seeming to. I calm their fears, ruffle the hair of the children. And the Judas goat shall lead them.

Your belongings will be returned to you soon. Notice, please, they are tagged and ready to accompany you on transport. Nakedness is not shameful. It is as God made us. The pit? The pit makes delousing more convenient. Cleanliness is next to Godliness, is it not so? Follow me and in a short while you will be free of vermin, which flourish in the crowded conditions you have endured. For this inconvenience, we apologize. How sad — an old one just fell. A moment while I help her. It is better that you huddle together in the pit. That way the time of spraying will be lessened. The soldiers who appear on the rim? They only wait to observe the ritual. Rifles? So they do. All soldiers carry arms in time of war. This is war. War uproots. War imposes harsh conditions. But do not concern yourself with war, for soon you will be far from the fighting. Do not fear us. We are here to help you. Think only of the train that will carry you away from destruction. Think of the good times you will have together. No more filth. New housing. Resettlement with your loved ones. Food to nourish the body. Laughter to uplift the spirit. Picture your new life and hold the children close. Tell them they are playing a game. If they close their eyes *very* tightly and wish hard, they will get a special present. Everyone will close their eyes now, for the spray could injure the membranes. Now wait for the spraying machines.

Wait.

Wait for the silent signal.

Wait for the arm to drop.

Wait for the spraying machine guns.

No more waiting. They drop in clusters. Families cling to each other. They fall in hordes, neighbors and strangers. They become a mass of white flesh, one atop the other. Screams dissolve into moans. Wails become whimpers. Writhing almost ceases.

It is Schwoermer's moment of glory. The pit is his stage and he strides in, puffed up with importance. All eyes are on the lead actor whose reputation has preceded him. He never fails to please the crowd. His audience waits in hushed silence, knowing the next scene by heart. Schwoermer delivers the coup de grâce methodically. One shot per in the nape of the neck. He wades through the dead as a hunter would slog through a swamp. Bodies are only decomposing logs now, to be heaved aside. White limbs flop, bounce, quiver. The blood coats his boots but he does not care. They will be cleaned thoroughly tonight by a subaltern.

Schwoermer searches untiringly. Under the piles a malingerer may be still alive, stifling screams into the earth. Schwoermer always roots them out. A kick in the teeth. A bullet in the brain. Schwoermer always wins.

The play is over for today. There is no applause as the audience disperses. The curtain descends. Lime and earth fill in the pit. The players are covered.

But the play will have a sequel and a sequel to the sequel. For there are always other Jews who can be persuaded to appear in crowd scenes.

Our kommando unit is a machine, well oiled, which functions smoothly. But we hear our kill ratio is lower than those of the groups to the North and South. We may have to go back and do another sweep.

I'll *never* outrank Schwoermer! Luck is still a bitch, deserting me. I'll always be under that bastard's boot. He not only holds a whip over me, he holds the pen. The pen that writes my record of obedience — of subservience. I'm a slave by day and a stud (and worse) by night. I can take my pit job. It isn't pretty but it works. It's what happens after dark that gets me. Schwoermer the fanatic in daylight becomes Schwoermer the madman at night. After hours we are encouraged to have recreation time. I work overtime on Schwoermer's recreation!

Schwoermer's off my back. Away! For two weeks, maybe more, and Waldi's now in charge. Schwoermer's inspecting the methods of Einsatzgruppe A in the north and also C, SE of us. He knows a thing about methods! We do the best we can with what we've got.

With S. away, I have used the evenings for fun and education. More lessons with Friedrich, who's back. He's pleased with my progress. And Waldi asked to borrow my Monet book. Thinks Monet put music on canvas. Waldi put on a record of Debussy's called "Clouds." Those two, Debussy and Monet, say the same beautiful things each in his own way.

Also — I have learned to play bridge. A good game. A thinking man's game. Not trivial like Whist.

Why did I dream? Why the nightmare?! It is early September and the weather holds. Schwoermer's still away, the work proceeds well, if not record-setting, and I have had the most fulfilling, educating time I have had in my life. Why the horror? It obviously had to do with that time in July, but why does that time disturb my night now?

It was a small operation as operations go. We came upon an unexpected cache: about thirty-five Jews hiding in a small copse. It was deemed prudent to dispatch them quickly, without fuss. So they were marched to a ditch next to the roadside. Mostly women and children. Unlike some previous groups, this one seemed to understand its Fate, for the mothers crooned lullabys and caressed the children. They did so until the band reached the ditch and then there was a strange turn of events. Mothers pushed the little ones away, pointing with fervor, urging the young ones AWAY from them to the edge of the grass. And the children, laughing as though they had spotted a prize, did so, scrambling to be the first to the sides. The women grouped together and the children were scattered, bent over, engrossed in whatever they had found. And so did not notice the rifles.

An arm dropped; the rifles rang out. The mop-up began. The usual blood, pools at the bottom, garnet droplets around the children. But among those droplets, ones of a different hue — scarlet. When the bodies of the little ones were tossed on their backs, most had the same scarlet smeared on their lips.

Garnet blood. Scarlet strawberries. Tiny wild strawberries.

A child's dream: berrying.

A mother's diversion. The last one.

The nightmare repeats now: children with huge bellies vomit all over my boots. Blood pours from their mouths, but the gush becomes an endless flow of half-digested strawberries. Perhaps my inner self rebels at the death of children. This would be quite natural. I do find shooting youngsters under the age of — let's say — eight to be distasteful.

I have read over the above piece and am rather pleased at its wording. I think I have expressed myself well. I will have to show it to Friedrich for comment.

I have had it with Schwoermer! He's back and has decided to join our little group. For a time he is playing our game — BRIDGE! And he cannot play like a gentleman. His outbursts have gone beyond the bounds. He has no sense of fair play. He has no sense of play at all. Just what you would expect of a former Kripo. A dunce who cannot bid, cannot count tricks, cannot bluff a hand. What in the fuck did he do in the Kriminal Police? Specialize in torture, which seems to be the sport of bully-boy ignoramuses? When he upended the bridge table and I was playing six no-trump, that was it! A dummy giving me directions when he bid me into the mess in the first place!

I have mentioned to both Friedrich and Waldi that Schwoermer is ordering me to do unspeakable things. Not what. And also that S. holds my career in his hands. They have some pull and maybe I will get out from under S.'s jurisdiction. I cannot tell them *the what.* I cannot tell anyone. It is a blot on my conscience. But at least I have the courage to ask for help in this matter.

I could refrain from writing of those nights. I could bury them in a recess of my mind and clamp a lid tight and never speak of them. Ever. But I have always told the truth in this, my journal, and I will write of those times. For they are over. F. and W. have requested a transfer for Schwoermer, citing his exceptional regard for duty, and Schwoermer will just have to recruit a new companion! The transfer is on its way. Unless some bloody bureaucrat loses it! God be with me!

It seems like a dream now. But it was real. And it happened again and again. At least a dozen performances we gave, maybe more.

We are two actors in a play, Schwoermer and I. We write it and set the stage. It is always the same play. Only the ingénues change. As my superior, Schwoermer is the lead actor. I am the supporting one.

My role has many facets. I am procurer, pimp and stud. Schwoermer is always onstage and he will have the ingénue first.

Have I ever described Schwoermer? Think of a pig. Pig eyes. Gross white body. Hair, pale and bristly. He ruts like a pig, snorting and snuffling.

I know when acquiescence is necessary, for I need Schwoermer's good will. So I am his comrade. I root and rut in his garbage pail.

I take the girls from a large selection. A few Jews, but mainly peasants from the area. Who cares as long as they are round and blond and young. Schwoermer's preference.

The set is essential. Schwoermer feels his quarters are too utilitarian, not romantic enough. He likes the coziness of a peasant's cottage as long as it is not too shabby. So I get time off to search for plump beds and painted furniture and dainty curtains at the window. I roust the owners and requisition their cottage for as long as we plan to be in the vicinity.

The curtain rises on Schwoermer. He sits in a shadowed corner, watching, waiting for me to appear with the girl who is dressed for a party in fetching dirndl and embroidered blouse.

I make love to her as Schwoermer the voyeur stares. I caress her neck, kiss her trembling lips, fondle her breasts and talk to her of love. While I slowly disrobe her, Schwoermer's excitement builds. I turn her around for inspection. Lovely, he sighs. His breeches are around his knees now and he flicks his upright cock occasionally in anticipation. Not too much, or he would pop off too soon and the moment would be lost.

The girl is naked now. She shivers as I rub her belly low down with my cock. She puts my hand between her legs and moans with abandon as I play and tease her there. She clings to me, hot and ready.

Schwoermer climbs clumsily out of his breeches and pushes me aside. He and the girl fall on the bed. She cannot tell one from the other, as Schwoermer is well aware. She fucks Schwoermer and she thinks of me. Schwoermer is noisy as he screws. He labors at it, sweating his pig smell, and glistening pink. He finishes and collapses.

The girl is mine now and I must take her or Schwoermer will feel I am not playing my part. The first glow of desire has left her body, and I take her with little spirit. I come, but with no satisfaction, for I know the ending of the play.

Schwoermer will have her once more before he shoots her.

The good weather has passed. Winter is setting in, and with it come deep frosts. It becomes more difficult to dig the pits. So scouting parties look for ones already dug — unused, of course. Also abandoned quarries or gravel pits.

EMMA
CAPE CHARLOTTE
SEPTEMBER

I am going to learn all the swear words there are and every single one is going right in here. I know so far

GOD
DAM
HOLY MOSES
JESUS
CHRIST AND
SHIT

There's one I heard Mr. Maxwell say but I don't know how to spell it exactly. I know it was a swear word because Mr. Maxwell saw me and got all red. It sounded like fukin. Daddy says Godam sometimes and Mummy says Jesus Christ in the Foothills and Hells Bells and Panther Tracks. I am going into the 5th grade!

OCTOBER

My kitty Tortoise almost caught a chipmunk today which I spanked him for. The chipmunk should have been asleep for the winter in the stone wall but he probably has a very big family and was getting a little more food for the table when Tortoise pounced. Well that chipmunk stood right up on his hind legs and BIT Tortoise on the nose and he was so surprised he just stood there and the chipmunk squeaked like he was very mad and jerked his tail and ran like Hell under the stone wall. Tortoise usually doesn't go hunting. I think he would rather lie down. He is called Tortoise which

Mummy made up because his fur looks like a turtle's shell but prettier and shinier and darker like a tortoise shell which is a relative of the turtle. Maybe an uncle. He is really a very nice cat.

DECEMBER

Today we went to Jamesport to hear the Messiah, and when we came out they said the Japs had bombed Pearl Harbor. Daddy says we will be in the war. He says the Germans are worse than the Japs and he hopes we will fight them too. I am glad they didn't bomb on my birthday which is tomorrow.

I was ten years old yesterday and I got five dollars and some maple caramels from Fanny Farmer. My birthday was sort of squashed in between December 7th and today when President Roosevelt declared war on everybody and said December 7th would live in infamy which is pretty awful.

HANNES
RUSSIA
DECEMBER

Certain kommandos, particularly in the low ranks, have complained of stomach problems. It cannot be the food. For example, last night we had fricassee of hare. Chunks of light meat swimming in a deliciously seasoned gravy. We had come in from a day of exceptionally tedious work. Hard to bury bodies when the earth is like iron. And then from the kitchen, that aroma from Heaven!

We are at war with the USA! The Japs have bombed the hell out of the fleet at a place called Pearl Harbor in Hawaii and are moving on all fronts in the Pacific. With the Axis in full gear, America can't rearm in time. My God! Think of it. An America under the Reich! We'll give the West Coast to the Japs.

Leave. Finally. In Warsaw. I'll write after it's over. I just want to immerse myself in culture and evenings of pleasure. Will buy some patent leather dress shoes in the city. Sure to be parties at Christmastime.

Schwoermer's leaving. Should be gone before I get back! God (and Friedrich) worked wonders!

POLAND

The leave is almost over and I sit on my bed with a bottle and contemplate life.

Warsaw is the end of the earth. Some of it is smashed; some is a haven for Jews. Right in the heart of the city sits a ghetto behind a wall almost as tall as two men, topped with barbed wire. And inside this protected area live thousands — I don't know how many — Jews. Still alive. What goes in is restricted. Not much food, I hear. And the corpses do pile up: starvation and cold.

Children sneak in and out of the ghetto carrying loot. Right under the noses of the guards, these kids operate. There's the problem. The guards are *not* German. Not Aryan. They are from the east — Lithuania or someplace. Poles too. You can't trust Poles to do a thorough job of anything!

I am blabbering because I have nothing else to do but get pissing drunk. About Jews, I'm blabbering. Why don't we just march in and shoot the whole lot — NOW?

Haven't met a decent woman! The SS brothel is full of them, but they're all blowsy and blond and I never want to touch that type again.

Wore my patent shoes just once. Just once! And the food wasn't worth it. And the company was boring. Warsaw is depressing and the only good time I had was a small shopping spree and the discovery that the Poles do one thing right. They make Slivowitz. Slivowitz warms the belly and soothes the brain. Slivowitz calms the nerves and makes all things bearable. Enough of it, that is. I have had almost enough now but not quite because I am writing a song and I must put it on paper before the pen slips out of my hands and I pass out — which will be quite soon . . .

Beautiful Slivowitz,
Plums from the tree,
Fermented in casks,
To rescue me.

RUSSIA

Back from the Warsaw leave a little the worse for wear. Brought along a whole case of Slivowitz. Some for Friedrich and Waldi, a *lot* for me, and one bottle for Schwoermer, in case he's still around. He isn't. Also brought back two black leatherbound, blank-paged books, which I shall use for journals. Had the shop put a gold double Runic S on the corner of each. Very discreet and handsome. The pages are thin, tough. And ink does not bleed through. When bored, I may copy over my entire diary. Much work, but my words going back to '37 are on twenty different kinds of paper, and the ink is not permanent, and I want a record of my life. A clean copy. I shall not change a word of the early entries, even if they make me cringe at the naiveté.

The last parcel contains Beethoven recordings. Heavy. Three symphonies: the Third, the Seventh and the Ninth. I have not listened yet, but Waldi assures me that the odd-numbered symphonies are superior to the even-numbered ones.

Schwoermer has gone, but not where he should have. He has not reported to his new kommando unit. What the hell is he doing? Holed up screwing some new girl — to death?

Ah! Schwoermer, you went too far. Missed me, you did. Pimped for yourself, you did. And died for it.

No more wading through dead meat. No more fucking doomed girls.

It must have been unpleasant, your dying — which pleases me. An act of vengeance.

Which girl was it whose death triggered yours? They all looked alike. How stupid of me! I don't *know* her. I was in Warsaw! I had no connection to your last fling. I am clean and that's why I still live. You had to have a young one, so you rooted alone. But she had kinfolk — a father, brothers, perhaps. Peasants. Slavic justice can be brutal, can't it, Schwoermer. Drawn out and exquisitely painful.

I can feel the knife, thin and sharp, and hear you plead as they sliced your cock to cutlets. One thin slice at a time. And was it then, or before, when they gouged out your eyes — first one and then the other — replaced by your nuts. Sockets that once held your pig eyes now bulge with your balls. Did you feel your eyes pop out? Did you remember your new eyes, your nut eyes? Did you scream for mercy, Schwoermer? Did you scream?

The wind blows and never stops. The snow is blinding and we keep hunting.

Tonight the soup was pink! Warm and soothing. Asked what it was and was told "Borscht." Meant nothing, so I continued probing. Seems we have a new cook, a White Russian, who has given us a number of tips about hidden Jews. Rewarded him with a job in the kitchen. He wants nothing more than to cook for the SS — and maybe be a kommando. He'll lose his job, maybe his life, if I ever so much as breathe that soup again. BEET SOUP! GODDAMNED BEETS!

The Leibstandarte Adolf Hitler fights brilliantly. I miss fighting a real war. I miss my old comrades. Six were horribly mutilated by the Red Secret Police near Rostov recently. Sepp Dietrich took firm measures. 4000 Russian soldiers met their Valhalla. So they were prisoners. Innocent. War is tough on innocents.

Long nights, short days. Ground concrete. Digging impossible. We are desperate for any kind of hollow, however shallow. For the first time in ages, we have a backlog due for "special cleansing" and no place to put them!

I am now sure that the Skull of our Corps, the Death's Head, sprouts a pair of angel's wings. Which makes us what we are: Angels of Death.

1942

EMMA
CAPE CHARLOTTE
JANUARY

Janice and Buddy and Elwood and I went tabogoning. The dictionary says that should be TOBOGGANING, which isn't fair because we all say TA! Anyway, it's Elwood's TOBOGGAN and he told everybody he wanted to steer so that nothing would happen to it. If a little scratch gets on the varnish he gets mad. We took it over to the hill above Mussel Cove and did we go! There was a crust of ice on top of the snow and down we went and we couldn't stop, and we bumped off one pine tree and then bumped off another, back and forth bumping off of trees and going like the wind. And the only reason we didn't go right into the ocean was because we hit some rocks right on the beach! We all fell out screeching and laughing so hard that it really hurt. Elwood had such a great time he didn't even notice a really long slice in the bottom of his toboggan. And I didn't tell him!

FEBRUARY

We got blackout curtains for all the windows. And the car lights have to have a black half moon painted on them. The blackout curtains are scratchy and not very nice to look at, but we have to have them because we live on the coast. I don't know what they are made of, but Mummy says it's worse than muslin. The white part is on the inside if you put them inside and the black part is on the outside. They sort of snap together so no light can get out and show a German submarine where we live. The curtains look like a quilt and are stuffed with stuff.

* * *

MARCH

I've been singing along all this time the song I call the cereal song. Hot soft Ralston and a really raw, raw bowl of, bowl of suet. Well, I thought they should mention Purina instead of suet for breakfast because raw suet and milk and a banana if you can get one is not my idea of a great breakfast. I'm glad I didn't tell anybody about the cereal song because it isn't!!! It's a crazy language song about a boy and a girl and a dream and a stream and I forget what else and I can't understand the Andrews sisters half the time anyway!

HANNES
RUSSIA
FEBRUARY

On and off we have tried the gassing vans. I hear they will be given another chance in Poland, but personally, I find them too slow. Of course, they are mobile in months without snow (which I am beginning to believe do not occur in Russia!), but Jesus, those vans can only hold a handful and death takes awhile. Too long. Wasted time. Also rather noisy. Those beating fists, drumming. A bullet is surer and quicker, all in all.

A tiring day. Row upon row were machine-gunned into the ditch. The operation went faster this way. But there was a complication. Instead of flopping into a compact mass, the bodies, in the bitter cold, stiffened and overflowed the space. So we worked far into the night, snapping legs and arms until the pile was reduced to a reasonable size. Have only a thin layer of gravel to spread on top. A very thin layer. The earth is rock and snaps our spades. Will ration the gravel and depend on Russian snows.

That Carole Lombard is a saucy bitch. My type. The men enjoyed the movie, laughing and shouting good-natured obscenities. A new record: the film projector only broke down three times!

We were not satisfied with the thin layer of gravel to cover our day's output. So I suggested a new method which was enthusiastically received. Consequently we were granted two flame-throwers which have eased our burden immensely. There are no mounds around now which can decompose in a thaw and cause disease. The thrust of the flame is powerful and does the job quickly and efficiently. I note that the fat from the bodies, when raised to a sufficient temperature, sizzles and sputters in the burning process. But this does not last long and soon all is ash.

The weather is too foul for target practice. Bitter, and spitting snow again. Frostbite has become insidious. It creeps in without warning and strikes the men as they sit and wait on the edge of the pit. They are impatient, waiting for the next batch, fingering their weapons. Against orders, they throw away their gloves, the better to feel the trigger. The transport is late. Fingers grow numb, then freeze so solid that they snap off like brittle chicken bones.

BUFFY
CAPE CHARLOTTE
MARCH

Meg,

Not so good this time. Another stroke. A doozy. Why me? Why does that Great Stinker in the Sky have to send down lightning bolts with my name on them?!!

The legs are gone — completely. Two things attached to me which don't belong to me — useless as two hanks of ribbon! So I wheel around in a contraption, furiously. I *am* furious. I'm mad as hell! For a while I wanted to scream and rant and all that came out was a gargle. I wanted to wave my arms and only one waggled.

I waited for some improvement before letting you know. Couldn't weep all over the letter. Had to be the old Buffy, the tough gal again. Can't have you weeping over the husk.

Where am I? Confined but coherent. Mind still sharp. Maybe sharper. More focus. Ideas flow. I see the solution before the others have even grasped the plan. It was sticky for a while, trying to learn to talk all over again. Honestly — for a bit, my grandiose (but damn good) schemes were presented with a lot of ahs and grunts and baby gurgles! But I am a certified miracle attested to by the medical profession. And now the speech, the voice, is reminiscent of a tipsy Tallulah, seductive in its timbre. Who needs limbs when one can think and make things happen? And sound like Bankhead!

Daddy's bad — cancer of the liver which doesn't cheer me — but when he learned about it, instead of curling up and crying, he became an infernal machine. Busy, busy. Putting affairs in order.

Signing over a lot of shares to me. Company shares. Teaching me more than the business. Teaching me *how to run it!* (A strong signal to the Board!) Daddy has faith I'll outlive him, although after my latest episode and his determination, I wonder whether he'll bury a daughter.

No, by God! I'll live to run this company and do a hell of a job! And since the Board SITS at its meetings, what's another chair, even if it does have wheels?

I am indomitably yours,
Buffy (and I'm not being a martyr!)

P.S. Pudge? Solicitous but not THERE. I can't explain the feeling I get when I watch him without his knowing. His mind is far away; I can tell by his eyes. It's as though he's bobbing all alone on an endless sea. He looks right through me, even when we talk — which isn't often. Sometimes I could wish for a small token of what? Affection? But he does not offer and I *will not* beg!

EMMA
CAPE CHARLOTTE
APRIL

Everybody is a little scared. We aren't winning the War so most all of Daddy's and Mummy's friends bought fancy rifles with telescopes to hit German parachutists. They say remember Holland and Crete. They're practicing skeet shooting, but since they hardly ever smash the clay pidgeons I don't think they'll do very well against real live people. But I was very good and didn't mention it. I am having trouble with fractions.

NOTHING happened today and it is a terrible day and I have a stomachache and I HATE FRACTIONS!!!

My desk is pretty messy inside and outside. Inside it has a lot of papers and books and crumbs from my lunchbox and other things. Outside it has marks and initials and inkspots all over. Today I opened the top and hit the inkwell that I had taken out to fill, and it rolled right off and splattered my socks. I guess it wasn't quite empty. Anyway, the desktop has more spots on it now and I'm never ever going to fill the inkwell again unless it is sitting in its hole!

* * *

MAY

Mummy was pretty serious so I turned off "I Love a Mystery." She said all of us, the family, the neighbors, everybody had to prepare for a siege. I asked what a siege was and she said she would explain it later. So we are stocking up on Crisco and B and M Baked Beans and peanut butter and dried onion flakes, and candles and other things. The only place we can hide this stuff is in an empty hole under the bottom drawer in the kitchen. I wanted to add a jar of Marshmellow Fluff, but everybody said no, that wasn't a staple. So I said it was one of my staples. But I guess we're going to have a siege without Marshmellow Fluff because the hole isn't big enough.

America needs tinfoil to win the War, so I have started a ball. I went around to all the neighbors and told them please to save their cigarette packages when they are empty and all the kids to save their gum wrappers. Everybody smokes cigarettes so that's easy. But the kids keep forgetting and I can't chew that much, so I remind them again and again. What I do is pull off the tinfoil and add it to my ball. It worked fine when the ball was as big as an egg, but it doesn't do so well now because the ball is pretty heavy and bigger than Daddy's head. The tinfoil just won't stick and it peels off. I think I'll have to pull the whole thing apart and have a lot of little eggs. It rained today, a lot, and then the sun came out and then it rained again and the wind blew, and then it stopped and then the sun almost came out and now it's foggy. Somebody can't make up his mind.

JUNE

School is almost out and I have my own ration book! I had to sign my name on it and how old I was and the color of my hair and eyes and how much I weighed. I don't weigh so much so I added five pounds!

We can't go and play at Fort MacAllister anymore. Because of the War. We used to go over when I was littler and they'd play Taps and then we'd watch all the soldiers stand up straight while the flag came down. They marched back and forth and folded the flag better than we did at camp and they played Taps better too.

I don't know what's so secret. I know everything about that Fort. There are grassy hills that are really hollow. Bunkers, they call them, to store ammunition in. And I've climbed over every gun they have. Great big things that stick out to sea. The guns have been painted so many times I don't think the wheels would move them, so what good are they? We'd play hide and seek under them because they sit in big round holes with a lot of machinery which I bet doesn't work either. Once I thought of a great hiding place so I tried to wiggle down the end — the place where the bullet comes out. That wasn't so hot because I got stuck and some soldiers had to come and pull me out. But it's fun to holler down the hole. The echo sounded like a monster's voice!

The Fort and James Head light are right next to each other. Every night the light goes on in the lighthouse. It's not a very big light, but it shines on a pile of glass and it gets magnified a million times. Well, not a million, but a lot! And the light moves around in a circle to keep boats way out to sea off the rocks. The only time you can't see the beam very well is when it's snowing cats and dogs and blankets. I won't miss going to the lighthouse because the stairs up to the top are scary. They go round and round and up and up and they don't have any backs on them, so I thought I was going to fall and I threw up.

JULY

Daddy is a plane spotter. And I guess he's supposed to be on the lookout for fire bombs too. Daddy wears a tin hat and sits on top of the bank building in Jamesport every two weeks for eight hours at a crack. He takes coffee in a thermos bottle (to keep him awake) and says that he would rather have a scotch and soda, but that would make him sleepy so he doesn't. Mummy makes him some sandwiches and he takes his silhouette (I had to look that up and I would *never* have found it except there was a silhouette of a man next to the word. Who would know there's an h in there!) cards of German bombers and fighters and sits in the dark. How can he tell what silhouette is what in the dark?!

I know a Stuka silhouette. But I am collecting American plane cards. War ones. I had *two* B-25 bombers which nobody wanted to trade for *until* they were used to bomb Tokyo! Now everybody is calling me up and I'm waiting for the right offer. In April Jimmy Doolittle took those bombers and he sailed right off the Hornet for Japan. Everybody knew that big bombers can't take off from an aircraft carrier — except Jimmy Doolittle. The trouble was, most of them couldn't come back. They didn't have enough gasoline.

Buddy just called me up. For *one* of my B-25s he will give me a P-40, a P-47 Thunderbolt, a P-51 Mustang and a Dauntless! I said OK as though I wasn't dying to have them. Sort of bored like.

AUGUST

Mummy says she is helping the War Effort, but she isn't helping me. She makes soap on the stove and stirs it with a long wooden spoon. I think she puts in some fat and some stuff that burns people — ly or something — and it cooks for a while and is supposed to come out soap. It comes out a brown gooey mess and it doesn't smell like soap and I can't get any bubbles!

SEPTEMBER

I saw a moose today. All by myself at the bustop I saw a moose! Nobody believed me, but they did when some people saw it swimming across Loch Cove. The moose was not at all surprised to see me and was very nice. It was too tall to pat and had antlers as big as a living room. I wish I'd had some sugar lumps.

BORMANN
BERLIN
JUNE

Two great pieces of news, Schmidt!

Heydrich, who wanted territorial power, got some. And is he sorry! The big frog in a small Slovak pond is wasting away. At this moment, I am awaiting news of his demise. I shall drink to that! And to whoever did the deed. It is assumed that the ambush was carried out by Czech terrorists using grenades and other weapons dropped by the British. But — there are rumors — and I repeat, they are *only* rumors — that the SS was involved, and the blame put on those naturally expected to react to Heydrich, Butcher of Prague. He *did* love to reign with terror. There will be many in Berlin besides myself who will be drinking in delight today — hopefully today!

The other tidbit is that we have finally found a way to dispose of Jews in quantity! We will phase out the large-scale "Open-air policy." The pits were too public; the vans too small. Last month the genius of chemists finally bore fruit. Namely: they have come up with a method which is foolproof and airtight. (Not bad — "Airtight!") A violet-blue crystal of hydrogen cyanide, I think. I don't know the fuck about chemistry. But it works exceptionally well. IG Farben had the patent and two firms, one in Hamburg, one in Dessau, refined it. An airtight chamber, a pack of Jews. The crystals are poured into vents to become deadly gas. The gas disperses and in a matter of minutes — thirty at the most, when the mass has stopped writhing — disposal begins.

Over a thousand in *one day* at Auschwitz — and this is just the beginning! There is a frenzied war on among German businessmen to be the winner in the contracts for crematoria. They are falling over each other to come up with the latest designs for quicker burning. And one firm, seeking a contract, cited the furnaces it had built for Dachau and Lublin, mentioning how "they have given full satisfaction in practice." Companies like to keep their workers busy. And full employment is good for business. So the race is on.

It is this matter of increasing numbers which interests me. Many have gold bridgework which is yanked out — from the living, the dead — or raked up in the ashes. Whatever the method, the result is *gold.* More important, there is jewelry, gems, spectacle frames, and Reichsmarks — bags full. Multiply each person's worldly goods, the convertible ones, which he carries on his destination to nowhere, by *millions* (which is our goal), and the sums are staggering.

The "Final Solution" is the answer. As I have mentioned, gems — cut or uncut — torn out of necklaces or rings, liberated from workshops, are my special interest. Diamonds, particularly.

Diamonds fascinate me. What the hell is happening in Antwerp, Amsterdam? I hear Asscher's diamond works in Amsterdam is still operating. For whose benefit? I want some — a lot! — of those diamonds! In fact, I want my own little factory someday — cutting away just for me.

Start doing some research. And keep your eyes open for a way to siphon off some of the booty from the camps — particularly Auschwitz, which is on its way to becoming tops in its field. A booming concern. The treasures from there will be flooding the market!

The latest: At a party the other evening, a couple of SS from RSHA, but not your section, IV-B-4 they were from, swapped recipes! Two black-clad killers, jabbering just like hausfraus! They were trying to come up with the perfect solution for leftovers. Soap, they were making. The end result was: "Take 6 pounds of Jewish fat, 5 quarts of water, and 4 ounces to 1/2 pound of caustic soda, boil for three hours, and then cool." Disgusting! Right during the meat course!

Bormann

HANNES
RUSSIA
MAY–AUGUST

Weather still bad. So we had the men clean the billets to pass the time. Two new comedies in. They will help, for there is an increase in stomach cramps. We cannot blame them on the food since the cramping seems to attack only those who do the actual shooting.

Weather improving but with spring come the mud and the rain. Rain makes the killings more tricky. Water and blood and wet earth combined into a sticky mess. Several of the men slipped on the bodies, and one required hospital care for a sprained ankle.

Weather ideal for disposal but there was a large roll at sick call. Everything from migraines to continual nausea. Also, we are hearing reports of nightmares. Screams in the dark. It was to be expected. We were warned that this could happen. So — I will have a little talk with the troubled ones.

Believe my talk helped. I showed sympathy for those who have problems with the disposal. Told them that they were thinking in the wrong vein. Of course the duty is unpleasant, but as long as they see *people* in the pits, *people's* bodies piled, they will have difficulties. I asked them to liken what they do to that which is done in a stockyard every day. Livestock are killed and there is no fuss, no guilt. Henceforth, they are to think of all as livestock — pigs, sheep, steer, whatever — their choice. Just meat. And I reminded them that when they've seen one squirming pig, they've seen them all.

I have to tell myself over and over that I, and the SS, are dedicated to Blood and Soil. And that Germany's backbone is the peasant. A letter came today from two peasants — my parents — a shit-list of complaints and whines: They don't have enough soap, and God ranks high he who is cleanly. (Save me from the religious!) The sugar allotment is too small and why can't I as a Party member get it raised?! Papa feels he is too old to pick and needs time off. End of letter. Not a word about how I am or what I'm doing!

There they squat, out in the country where butter and eggs are still available; where ducks and piglets are slaughtered illegally; where hills are green and bombs don't fall!

* * *

On the heels of this letter came a cablegram. From Mama. It seems that Papa now *does* have time off. All the time in the universe. The cart he was driving caught its wheel in a rut and overturned, killing him instantly. His blood must have mingled with the whites and yolks from several gross of crushed eggs, freshly laid. What a waste! What a mess!

Over Mama's wails, I have ordered cremation and no service. She can have him near her, however. His ashes will rest in an urn of Carrara marble which she can show off to the neighbors.

The Ukrainian militia operates with dispatch. Our sharks. Whip them up with a bit of histrionics and they're ready to initiate a pogrom! We use them as kommando units to beef up ours. And they can do a lot of the dirty work. They are adept and anxious for these jobs. Feel they are fulfilling ancient enmities — which they are doing with alacrity. Anti-Semitism is rife here. They have no qualms about exterminating children, for example. Do it handily and happily. And all their salaries come from Jewish coffers. Serendipity!

It took till now — late spring — for me to figure out the mystery of the injuries. I have solved it by good detective work. During the cold, a number of the men were limping into the field hospital with severe bone bruises on both heels. Since there was neither chafing nor blisters accompanying the injuries, I ruled out ill-fitting boots. The bruises began to show up in November, and *only on those who had disposal duty.* The bruises disappeared with the coming of spring.

A rifleman, gun cradled and ready, sits on the edge of a pit as the roundup strips for the final time to be moved into the death line. It is cold, the rifleman is bored. He has done this fifty times and he tires of waiting. The edge of the pit is full of frost and iron hard. The rifleman's legs hang over the side, becoming bloated from gravity and numb with cold. He has to stay alert, wary of any untoward movement. And he must shoot with speed and precision. But his legs are dying on him. And his feet will fall off — unless — he pounds circulation into them. And that is what he does. He drums those feet against the pit's sides, legs swinging back and forth incessantly. And the heels take the blows!

* * *

Heydrich, Reichprotector, has been *ambushed, wounded* in Prague! Czech terrorists most likely. The word is good. He will recover!

Heydrich is dead. *Dead!* My God, I cannot believe it. His spine was shattered. Because of this I expect thousands of lives will be shattered!

They have been. Immediately, the Gestapo executed over a thousand Czechs. One hundred and twenty resisters besieged in the Karl Borromaeus Church. Dead to the last man. And Lidice. A town no longer. All men and teenage boys shot. Most of the women carted off to Ravensbrück. The children dispersed — "lost." No trace remains. Yet that spot now becomes a monument to the memory of Reinhard Heydrich.

Now that he is gone, there is *no one* to replace him. No one. Himmler does not inspire blind loyalty. Not from me. He doesn't inspire even a pfennig's worth of a fart. Soft, that's what he is. Soft. Ordered the execution of a hundred Jews late last summer. On a whim. Wanted to watch. Got to him, it did. Hysterical, nearly fainted. That's why we got the gassing vans. More humane. Who cares. Killing is killing. Dead is dead. Why does the method matter? Why is Heydrich dead? Why do the good die young?!!

The summer is here and for a brief period, very brief, we will relax. The earth is soft again. The pits are quickly dug and the naked do not shiver in the summer sun.

Mama broke her hip, I am informed. Slipped on a newly washed floor. Obsessed with cleanliness. I'm sure she had already washed the floor twice that day.

We have a problem. Even in death the corpses cause trouble. The men who knock out the teeth have been stealing some of the gold. That gold belongs *only* to the treasury of the Schutzstaffel!

I have given away the Ninth Symphony. I cannot bear to listen to it. Sgt. Braun was most grateful.

* * *

Friedrich looks ill. He does not sleep. I have heard him pacing. His face is gray. Perhaps he has the dysentery. He should see a doctor.

I copy my journal on nights when we do not play bridge, which is happening more frequently. In fact, bridge games are rare with Friedrich absent so often.

Friedrich woke up everyone with his screaming. He was in shambles, frothing at the mouth, and hiding whenever anyone approached. We contacted the field hospital, which sent several medics with a restrainer. We all watched in silence as Friedrich was taken off, tied up like a parcel, and shrieking of Divine Retribution — at least that was one Private's opinion. To me, his shrieks were indecipherable.

EMMA
CAPE CHARLOTTE
NOVEMBER

Today we landed in North Africa and tomorrow we are going duck hunting! Daddy is going to take me to Quaker Meeting Bay all by myself. I have to go to bed early now because we have to get up very, very early.

I'm too tired to write about duck hunting. I'm too cold and too wet and I'm still shivering and I'm going to bed right now!

Duck hunting isn't so exciting. You have to get up way before the sun does and then you have to drive a very long way still in the dark so you can be there before the ducks wake up. You put on sweaters over sweaters and waders which come up to your waist and are hard to move around in. Then you sit in a swampy place and wait for the sun to rise which it didn't because it was raining. And you can't talk very loud because the ducks might hear you, if there are any ducks. So you wait some more and you get hungry and you chew a tuna fish sandwich which is a lunch sandwich and tastes funny because you are eating it at breakfasttime, if you were home which you aren't. There isn't anything interesting to do while you wait, so you watch a bug crawl up a piece of tall grass and then crawl down again because the grass stalk wasn't so interesting for the bug, either.

Then Daddy takes out a silvery bottle and swallows something which he lets me taste on the end of my finger. He says to think of licorice, which I do. But this stuff is greenish and VERY GOOD. It makes a nice warm roll all the way to my stomach which a licorice stick doesn't.

And then along come some black specks and Daddy whispers for me to stay still which I have been doing *all day,* and he stands up and Whoom! The specks really don't seem alive or anything until one falls, and then I know it is a duck and it's probably hurt and I don't like duck hunting after all. Daddy wades out a very far way and I can see the duck flopping in the water and I'm glad I didn't shoot it! Daddy has to break its neck because the poor thing is very hurt, so he whirls the duck around by the head which is supposed to do the trick. Well, it did alright because all of a sudden the body goes sailing into the bay, and all we had to show Mummy for the whole day was one duck head!

DECEMBER

There was an awful fire in Boston a couple of days ago. They're still trying to find out how many people died, but they think almost five hundred!! Five hundred people died in a club of coconuts and they couldn't get out and they couldn't breathe. They were screaming and piling on top of each other. I never heard of so many people being burned up!

BUFFY

CAPE CHARLOTTE

NOVEMBER

Oh Meg —

Daddy's dead. I never knew how much I needed him — to lean on, to learn from. He went quickly — by choice. And in dignity. If dying is dignified. It's rotten, that's what. He couldn't stand the thought of living only for morphine, of being mindless after it, so three nights ago he crawled out of bed, literally dragged himself into the study and shot himself. Even did that right. Up through the mouth. How many times do I remember his anger at friends who botched the job. "The temple's not sure," he'd fume. "The damned fool wanted to leave a grieving widow and he's left her grieving all right — over a blinded vegetable!"

Just back from the funeral, which is why I'm in a black mood. Very simple, very Episcopalian. Too simple. Not one mention of the deceased — at his own service. When I go, Meg, will you — and I'm asking you, not Pudge — will you, you don't even have to come, but will you ask whoever does the service to please have a lot of rousing singing and say that *I lived?*

Ye Gods! How much do you charge for your ear? I feel better. Really do!

I must retool. Speaking of which, we — the company — must retool. There's a war on and we can contribute, but not in the state we're in. I've thought about this and think we can get ready within four months. If everybody works — and they will, I promise you.

Because — because! I am about to be named PRESIDENT of Sinclair and Sons, shipbuilders extraordinaire! So there! (Being majority stockholder had nothing whatsoever to do with this honor, you understand. REALLY!)

From the Atlantic to the Pacific — oceans of love,

Buffy

HANNES
RUSSIA
SEPTEMBER–DECEMBER

The summer sun sinks earlier each evening and winter approaches. And with it comes a new distraction. By day we exterminate. By night we listen. The Reds, those remaining communists who have not died with the Jews, have formed roving bands. They call themselves "Partisans" and try to disrupt our communications and ambush lone couriers. As a result, we have had to curtail any nighttime activity. Being a mobile action squad helps, for we do not stay in any one place for an extended period. Our length of stay is regulated by the availability of the harvest. When the pickings are poor, we move on to riper areas.

I have been notified that Mama has suffered a cerebral embolism. Immobility produces clots. She hangs on, unable to move or speak. The prognosis: no improvement. Mama is a vegetable.

Friedrich has gone around the bend and will not be back. His ravings unsettled some of the newer recruits, and it is time for another uplifting speech. I would have wagered a year's pay that

Friedrich would never crack. But it goes to show that instability lies just beneath the surface. Perhaps intellectuals are more prone.

New speech. Made it up on the spur of the moment. Had them enthralled. Likened Jews and other undesirables to colonies of termites eating away at the structure of the Thousand-Year Reich. Sapping the strength of her underpinnings. Destroying the structure. Munching, always munching, insatiable for more. Think of yourselves as the exterminators, I told them, the saviors of the Reich. Think of yourselves as the *only* group who can rid the Fatherland of those who could destroy it. Exterminate all! Had them panting by the end. They were raring to go and clean out the pests!

Mama hangs on. A turnip. She hangs on to a bed that could be better used for a brave and wounded soldier. I shall not give the order, but there are rules for who shall live and who shall die. Euthanasia is practiced frequently. And on those less ill than my mother. The retarded, the blind, the deviants.

Winter is here — with a vengeance. And it will stay for eons! Our haul today: 2 Gypsies, 1 Russian Army officer, 196 Jewish men, 77 Jewish women, children — uncounted, 1 criminal and 17 suspected communists. A diverse bonanza. It was a shooting paradise for the ranks.

I cannot complain about the men's behavior now. It is exemplary. They carry out all orders with precision and speed, and even joke about the job. Humor always leavens unpleasantness.

SS Sgt. Frank released to be with his girlfriend. Their baby is due at any moment. I certainly expect marriage from him.

Mama died two days ago, slipping from a contained void into an immense one. How she died is of no interest. She was, of course, already gone. It is strange to remain unmoved at the thought that I am now technically an orphan. I have been one all my life.

In the winter nights, which stretch forever, I copy into my journal. I have two tasks: to record the present and recopy the past. As for the latter, I am up to August 1940!

I can look into the future. A distant future. Fifty years hence, I see a large stone house, beautiful, sturdy, permanent, standing on a high hill outside Munich. Green lawns roll down and out of sight to be hidden by the fog of the valleys. On clear days one can glimpse the Tyrol and the Obersalzberg. In this house I see a man still vigorous, still bursting with ideas as he sits in a paneled library, books to the ceiling — the ribbons, the medals, the testament of his life spread round. Comfortable as a cat, his memories warmed by a glowing fire, he leafs through two battered journals. He smiles as he reads the ramblings of a boy, the heartaches, the wistful dreams, the fierce determination to succeed. For a moment he glances at the photographs on the wall of a hundred smiling faces — the powerful, the distinguished, who asked only for the honor to pose with him.

He raises a glass to toast the boy who has turned dreams to reality, who has succeeded beyond the bounds of imagination. I see him clearly, this man who is me.

While we make Germany safe from all her enemies, the armies get the glory. I notice their propaganda units are not filming any of our exploits for public consumption or posterity! The Wehrmacht's hands are dirty. They pretend absolute innocence about our actions. Yet who supplies us? Where do our rations, our gasoline, our quarters, come from? The Wehrmacht! Those haughty, well-bred Junkers with their long thin noses cannot smell murder? They need us. They want us. They just hold their noses, the bastards! So the "Final Solution" is a phrase not to be bandied about. Stuff your mouths, clog your ears, blind your eyes, you monkeys! Know no evil!

Why the hell haven't we been supplied with any new comedies? The men know all the words — and they need *new* ones! The Black Corps' spirit needs uplifting. Some crazy antics to drown out the howl of a Siberian winter.

Sgt. Braun has six hours to dispose of the Ninth Symphony! If that Beethoven record is not smashed, I have informed him that it will be melted down and he will eat the black residue for dinner. Music is manipulative and I cannot bear hearing the "Ode to Joy" again. There is an underlying theme which few hear. It is a dirge. A Dirge of Despair.

What else in the depths of winter? New orders: rid the countryside of "partisan activity." Which means a war with sharp-toothed ferrets. No more confining ourselves to the cushy job of rubbing out rabbits.

1943

HENRY
CAPE CHARLOTTE
JANUARY

Saw old Widge today. I should say "Captain" Widgery. He'll make Admiral, I'll say that for him. Had him for dinner. Rather fortunate. I was running out of pertinent information when Widge shows up attached to the Naval Air Station just up the coast, not more than 10 miles NE of here.

Can't say I was too fond of him at Harvard, but he's mellowed a bit. Surprised to find him in the Navy. Wouldn't have thought that zipping in and out of Marblehead on that tippy craft he called a sailboat would have made such an impression. But then, of course, there was his barnstorming period. Combine the two and what do you have? An idiot in the United States Naval Air Corps! What the man sees in flimsy craft afloat, aloft, I cannot fathom! But there it is. And there he was, going on and on — garrulously so. I was a capacious sponge. Evelyn, as usual, became bored early, and delightedly I watched her take her leave. I wanted Widge all to myself. The fact that Widgery is Navy (or somewhat Navy) makes absolutely no impression on Evelyn. I am convinced that she cannot stand men who weren't born in a boat. Can't stand Harvard men, either. Me, she tolerates — barely. Harvard, she says, is greatly overrated, living off an ancient image of scholarship. Jealousy, no doubt. Harvard is *above* women!

I fixed her. We had Indian Pudding for dessert! And although she shot daggers at me through coffee, even Evelyn cannot break the barriers of good behavior to shout at her spouse before guests!

You see, Evelyn was not brought up to consider Indian Pudding a true culinary delight. She calls it "Redman's Mush." I, however, could dine on it every day. So I made a foray into the kitchen as soon as Evelyn had left this morning and had a short chat with Cook, assuring her that Evelyn had changed her mind regarding the menu. Thus *my* dessert was served — properly: with a dollop of chilled whipped cream. The warmth of the pudding created rivulets, then pools of cream, reposing in the crevices. The contrast in temperature and taste was simply heavenly.

With a bit of cognac under his belt, Widge became a gabby old fool. Wouldn't believe for an instant that a fellow classmate, a wearer of the old club tie, would betray his confidence. If I'd told him all the information would be coded and sent forthwith to the enemy, Captain (soon to be Vice or is it Rear Admiral?) would've laughed heartily, swearing that my sense of humor had improved with age.

How many PBY's, Widge? How many torpedo dive-bombers? How many short-range scouts? Thank you very much, Captain, Sir. And how's Margery? And the children? Do you expect a carrier soon? Two retrievers? Golden? How splendid. The Fleet, Widge. *Where is it?* Grouse? No, I prefer pheasant, myself. Magnificent fowl, don't you agree?

Captain Widgery's knowledge is limited; and one can endure his company just so long. A single evening was much too lengthy! He does not deal in submarine nets or the movement of the Atlantic Fleet. I'll have him introduce me to one who does. A Porcellian, perchance?

BORMANN
BERLIN

Willi,

Canaris can't pick 'em! I told you so! The master spy uses precious U-boats to transport so-called saboteurs to America. Sods! Two boatloads captured. Executed, most of them. The Abwehr's spy network in America is not so strong, eh Willi?

Which brings me to my point: You say the Bund was disbanded and known sympathizers watched. Sure. But those agents of Canaris' had help in the States. And those helpers can't all be known! There must be more! Unknown now, but ready to come to the fore if necessary. *When* necessary. And the funds keep rolling in here, ready to keep them happy there!

Tell Midas to be a bird dog. Find me some good *U.S.* Germans that are under *no* suspicion. He can do it, given enough incentive.

Give him a bonus for every new worker he recruits.

The Mexican connection, I see, is performing up to snuff.

I can outdo Canaris any day!

The news is not good re the Russian sector around Stalingrad. The foul weather had hindered us and the Bolsheviks care nothing for casualties!

And *when* do I get a diamond man of my own?

Bormann

HANNES

RUSSIA

JANUARY–MARCH

The fortress that was Stalingrad is crumbling, reduced to a pocket of wounded and dead, and still they fight. The dead cannot be buried; the wounded have no place to lie. Bad news is an express train; good news is a local.

Meanwhile we have our hands full with the animals who call themselves "partisans." They use the forest like weasels, slinking in and out, attacking our flanks and backsides, nipping, slashing, then slithering back to disappear into their holes.

What manner of unearthly beings are we fighting? How can they outwit Nature so easily? They hide in snowdrifts for half a day and emerge with all parts operating. Warm, with blood still coursing through their bodies. Fingers and toes intact!

Snared one. The prisoner has not enlightened us with the magic of surviving a Russian winter. Will only say that getting frostbite in the Army of the Bolsheviks is a court-martial offense!

What the retreating Reds were not able to carry in '41 is fodder for the partisans. We were told that they were random starving bands. We believed the shit that poured from Berlin: "Eliminate these roving nuisances." A sideline when not engaged in the "Final Solution." These roving "nuisances" are well organized, well equipped. On a tip we discovered one of their camps, empty of life. There was evidence that they had pulled out hastily, leaving food and a small cache of weapons to wave under our noses. "See, we don't need this. Help yourselves!"

They scavenge abandoned supply dumps and have an ample supply of automatic weapons and ammunition.

They use the night, the fog, the snow. They creep up silently on skis, clothed in white, attack and disappear in the swirling snow. Two Waffen SS groups have been massacred by white phantoms. Ghosts who show no mercy!

Our quota of Jews is depressingly low. Einsatzgruppe B will dispose of no more than 100,000 — if we are lucky.

Stalingrad gone. The Sixth Army — gone.
Von Paulus surrenders. God has deserted us.

I cannot believe that anyone but the Devil created Russia. This vast foul place is unfit for normal men. I have cursed the brief summer, when insects breed in the swamps and emerge in clouds to devour us. But then when winter rolls in from Siberia on winds that howl like tortured demons, and my frozen bones ache so awfully for sun, I would gladly give up an arm to be sucked dry of blood if only I could feel the warmth of another summer.

And then there is the mud. Year-round mud. Stinking, sucking, squirting, slurping mud. It is here in spring; it is here in autumn. One rain in summer turns dry ruts to quicksand. One thaw in winter turns hard earth to quagmires.

The major railways are constantly under attack. Hit and run. Hit and run. They loot our moving trains and make off with our latest equipment: from weapons to binoculars, telescopes — even the newest radio sets!

The cordon was tight. We torched every tree. It was impossible to break out. Yet they did. One by one, man by man, they slipped through somehow, to disappear, God knows how. Christ, no! God has nothing to do with this. Satan is their savior. It is witchcraft, this disappearing act. Once I scoffed at the "subhuman Slav" rhetoric. I was so wrong. They are *not* human!

What day is it? What year? I have been in the East for centuries. Partisans roam the countryside almost at will. Tracks, tunnels, bridges — demolished. They wait. They wait with great patience and then they pounce. A sniper blows off the head of a noncom. Several officers in a staff car are ambushed. A platoon disappears to be found a week later, stripped of flesh. Eaten by starving dogs or peasants. A climate of fear is upon us. We are shooting at demons in the dark.

BUFFY
CAPE CHARLOTTE
FEBRUARY

Hey Dearie!

We're off and running, gearing up for great things. Can't wait until the first baby slides down and hits the water. I'll be there to smack her backside with only the best — French, of course. It has to be la crème de la crème in case the wallop showers me. New York State has never passed my lips, and besides, my first ship deserves the best!

Oh, Meg, I have never felt so good, so much in command of *me,* not to mention the Yard. I pore over blueprints. We're bringing in marine engineers, construction crews, welders, riveters, the works. Jobs. Jamesport is booming. New housing needed. We're financing a small development out near Cape Charlotte High School — small Capes — and a bus service to and from the Yard. Three eight-hour shifts. Around the clock. You couldn't tell midnight from noon. Blazing lights, welders' sparks. Bustle and noise. Marvelous!

I am so het up I have changed my image to fit the mood. At least a veneer. A violet veneer. Really! Do you remember that rock Mummy gave me God knows how long ago? The oval amethyst as big as a jumbo egg? Well, extra large, anyway. Had the thing reset to wear on my bosom. Sometimes as a brooch, sometimes dangling from a gold rope chain.

That began the metamorphosis. In order to create a TOTAL image I ordered dozens of nifty outfits in the purple range from mauve to gentian. Glorious violets, lovely lilacs, understated lavenders. Guess lavender is understated anyway. Stay away from magenta and fuschia. Too tarty. And only old bags wear grape and plum. Since the legs look wizened, *are* wizened — no muscle — I have glorious lap robes. You have to see my panne velvet creation — royal purple. Feel like a queen.

Remember the hair? Remember how I ran the gamut between carrot and strawberry, with more subtle shades in between? Go back before, to Smith. What was I then? A kind description was mousy brown. A brutally honest one was mole-colored. Well, I hadn't seen my old head for God knows how long, and I wanted to. Guess I wanted to discover a glorious misty gray under all that red paint. Took a hell of a long time to get back to au naturel. Au naturel, if you must know because I will tell you, was hair a skunk would be ashamed to show in public! Even a hyena would hang his head! There I was as God intended me — I told you he was the Great

Stinker! — striped!! Patches of mole, patches of parchment yellow. Not even speckled. STRIPED! Looking at me in the mirror was a ninety-year-old hag — a freak!

I carried on in my usual subdued manner. Scared the hell out of my hairdresser, who finally calmed me down with fairy tales. About artistry and such. Twern't fairy tales. Actuality.

Let me describe the phenomenal transformation. My face is now surrounded by an angel's aureole — a halo of vivacious violet-gray. NOT blue! Vivacious, because I had the verve (or the nerve) to have it streaked platinum. I am a bloody frosted iris!

But it works. Always wearing the rock, which beams like a lighthouse, I careen about in shades of purple — never anything else. Violet is my signature — my statement (as the world of fashion trills). Heads turn; men listen.

Even Pudge has reentered my orbit. Somewhat. He perks — a little. Writes little essays for himself, so he informs me. Has begun to make up puzzles. Crosswords. Why, I haven't the faintest. They bore me to tears. But he seems enthralled.

What's more, we're entertaining a bit. Some of the mucky-mucks from the military who diddle around, checking up on our port capabilities and harbor defenses or whatever. And, when they are passing through, we even see some of Pudge's old school chums who are in oh so secret positions. Haven't changed an iota. Still oh so social snobs. After dinner, I excuse myself as quickly as possible. There is nothing worse than two Harvard men reminiscing, unless it is three or four. Utterly beyond belief. Pitiful and passé. The times are changing and the class of old Porcellians is out-of-date and rather sad.

Have to rush and give menu to Cook, then into town with Alfred.

In haste,

Buf

STEINER

OFF SOUTH AMERICA

MARCH

My dearest Ilse,

I ache for you. I want to put my head in your lap and cry. I can hear you say, "Is this my Rudi, my brave strong sailor who never had a moment's fear? Does he shirk his duty?"

Ilse, I am *afraid*. And my "duty" is to kill as often and as painfully as possible.

Please let me tell you what happened, why everything is wrong.

I wish I could pour it out to you with our arms around each other. Instead, I'll do it clumsily in this letter, which I will have hand-delivered when we reach port. I'll talk to you and try to pretend that there aren't thousands of miles of ocean between us.

In the beginning, and for several years after, the tracking, the hunting, was good sport. You know how proud I was on leave, how I would regale you with our exploits and feel like a man. A superman. You said I was, particularly in bed, if I remember!

You should have seen us on the boat after we demolished a convoy. The crew and I slapping each other and jumping around like schoolboys.

It took one touch of a button to fire a fan of torpedoes out like a fusillade of mammoth bullets, to send sluggish toy ships to the bottom.

I never surfaced to watch the end. It was not squeamishness. I just felt no exhilaration, no need to be in on the death throes. I was an anomaly among my fellow commanders, most of whom were loath to leave the scene of triumph.

Mainly, I went into the cold layers of the sea for safety. How many times did we lie there in awful silence as vengeful escort vessels tried to find us? How many times did we survive, to surface in jubilation ready to strike out again, and add more tonnage to our monthly total of kills?

Please bear with me. What I'm about to write is not pretty, but I shall go out of my mind if I cannot share with you the awfulness of what I have witnessed.

We were cruising the southern Caribbean. The crew was up on deck collecting the dry laundry, or soaking up the sun, and the war was far away. The air smelled of blossoms, though we were many miles from the nearest land. And the breeze — the breeze was gentle, soft like a down feather brushing the skin. For a little while we were mindless of war.

And then suddenly on the horizon a lone tanker appeared. She was out of Aruba, most likely, low in the water, heavy with oil. No need to dive. I barked orders in my most authoritarian voice, and my crew, half-naked and sunburnt, jumped to action stations.

It was never a contest. Our deck guns hit her square amidships, and she went up in a series of explosions.

For the first time I watched from the bridge of the conning tower. I stood there and watched what I had done, and couldn't move. First the heat hit me, and then waves of sound roared past like a gigantic train. The ship broke in half, and bow and stern rose together like the crushing jaws of a crocodile. Farts of fire and oily black smoke poured upward and then, like a shot, she went straight down in a hissing cloud of steam. Bow and stern locked forever in death.

But it was not over. Across the water came the shrieking sounds. Little specks, insects, with antennae gone wild, became men with flashing arms, swimming in a sea of fire. Swimming to nowhere. The fire engulfed them and the shrieking ceased . . . except inside me.

I have chalked in a new column next to "Tonnage." It reads "Lives lost?"

I love you more than life,

Rudi

BUFFY
CAPE CHARLOTTE
APRIL

Meg love,

Who is Alfred? You ask as though I toss his name off to tantalize you! A deep dark secret that I have held back until it is no longer possible to hide his existence.

Alfred. Alfred. The name conjures up a heroic image, doesn't it? Old English kings and whatnot.

Meg, dear. As much as I would adore to adorn Alfred with lusty qualities and have you imagine the worst (or best?), the truth is that while Alfred *is* English *and* while Alfred *carries* me in his arms *and* that while Alfred *is* my chauffeur — Don't say Aha! Wait! Alfred is sixty-two; a fainthearted snob with just enough strength to move me from here to there; and passion has *never* grabbed him, poor man.

Alfred's goal in life is to buttle. But since I do not include a butler on my list of necessities, Alfred is resigned to being a houseman rarely and a chauffeur often. Although he tries to prove to me that buttling is in his blood by periodically polishing the silver within an inch of its life, I disappoint my poor Alfred by persuading him that polishing the Packard *is* and *will be* a large portion of his life.

He was nonplused when I had her repainted. Basic black was his idea of what a limousine should be. For the upper, upper class (which is the only class Alfred really feels comfortable with) understated black, no other. Ignoring his tut-tuts, and using a bit of pull, I sent her in for a facelift. The lift was really for me. To enhance my image. The "Lavender Lady" chose burgundy. Blends well with purples. Imagine, if you will, a claret Super Packard. Imagine the interior — sumptuous deep velvet, redone with the warmth and glow of a fine French wine, Nuit St. Georges, perhaps, or — blood — if you are sanguine. Imagine Alfred blending in, wearing burgundy livery which he hates and which is too much and I don't care!

So there!
Buffy

EMMA
CAPE CHARLOTTE
JANUARY

It was so cold out today that the sea was steaming and the sun rose and shone through so we had pink sea smoke! So cold I wore my skipants into school! No skirt, just skipants. WELL, Miss Olsen is sick so we have a substitute who's *awful* anyway and she said — "Go home and change, Emma. You're not allowed to come into school wearing pants!" Just like that. So I called Mummy and she called Daddy who had the car and home I went. I didn't want to go back, but Mummy said I had to so I did. But was I mad! It's a stupid rule because if you wear skirts to school you have to wear skipants under them anyway to keep your legs from falling off and the skirt hangs out so it won't wrinkle and then you have to wear a long enough coat to hang down to cover the skirt. I wonder if they'll ever make skirts so they don't wrinkle so maybe I can tuck them into my skipants. They'll make a bigger bottom, but I don't have any anyway, so who cares.

MARCH

I nearly got *run over* by the school bus yesterday! We had to wait for the buses on a little hill just outside the school door. Well, whenever it rains and then freezes there's always ice on that hill. Well, I slipped on that ice and I fell, and boy did I slide down fast right at the Star Farm Road bus that was just leaving. I almost went under the front end and would I have been squashed! But somehow I stuck my legs out and pushed on the front wheels just a little, which shoved me up the hill a tiny bit. Then I slid down again, and the back wheels almost got me! But I shoved on them and up the hill I went again, and by the time I slid down again the bus had gone! So

I didn't get squashed but my lunchbox did!!! Am I glad. I was the only one in my grade who had to take a big black lunchbox to school like the shipyard workers do. Now Mummy says I can have a new *square* lunchbox with Bambi and Flower and Dumbo on it!

APRIL

I can't get the loops in Penmanship! Miss Olsen does them on the blackboard *very quickly,* and when she's done she's made a round tunnel with no light showing through. She calls them graceful loops and says motion from the shoulders. Well, I do motion from the shoulders and Miss Olsen tells me to stop making coils of barbed wire!

MAY

Mummy was so mad today she sizzled. I thought I had done something, but Daddy said no, the Blue Point Inn had done something. It all has to do with Jews and I said I didn't know what Jews were and Mummy stopped sizzling for a minute and said yes you do. Dr. Goldstein and his wife (who was Mummy's roommate. *Mrs.* Goldstein was) are Jews. So I said I didn't know that and Mummy said why should you. Why should anybody care who is and who isn't? So I asked why she's so mad, and she told me that she had called the Blue Point Inn to make sure they would have room for old friends and they said sure, they were practically empty because the season hadn't really started yet. So Mummy called her roommate, the college one, the one I know, and said there's room at the Inn, so the Goldsteins wrote for reservations and got back a letter fast saying fine, so up the Goldsteins came only to be told that there was a mistake and they were sorry but they hadn't a room left.

And then Mummy really got furious, spitting about wasps and I thought she meant a swarm of yellow jackets and she was saying how wasps breed gingerly and I could see why with their stingers in the way, and then Mummy said they give birth with difficulty because of their tight cunts and small pelvises. And their blood waters down and in each generation the children grow up with thinner noses and longer faces and fewer brains. That's just the way she said it. So I could see all those black and yellow thin bodies laying eggs that would grow up to have pink blood and long, long noses and be pretty stupid and sting people. But she wasn't talking about yellow jackets. She was talking about people we know. She was talking about us! We're wasps. (That is supposed to be capitalized!) Well, not exactly. Mummy doesn't have a narrow pelvis. At least she's always complaining about her hips. And she and Daddy read all the time and know a lot so they've got brains. And my nose turns up — a little bit anyway. Daddy and Mummy said we'll have to have a talk about this soon. I'll learn all about wasps, no, WASPS! and Jews and hotels and things.

It's hard to understand and Mummy tried to explain it to me today. About the Jews. Somehow I thought they were another kind of people who lived across the sea and wore shawls like Mary and carried jugs on their heads and lived mostly in the land of Canaan. And then some of them moved to other countries and Hitler hurt them awfully. I didn't know that all the time I knew some and they aren't different. They're like everybody else except when they give their names out. And then something happens. They become different, just like that! I guess what is scary is that if the Goldsteins lived in Germany or Poland or almost anywhere over there, they would be running and hiding and maybe dead. What Mummy wants me to know is that it isn't just the people at the Blue Point Inn, that other people I know and like wouldn't ever kill Jews with a gun. Instead they use words to kill their insides.

HENRY
CAPE CHARLOTTE
JUNE

I have always believed that it is utterly wrong to mix two unlike species. I am discussing, of course, marriage and the begetting of children. The issue from two people of quite different backgrounds — class and culture — and race, need I add — could, *would* be a mongrel, not belonging to either world and, therefore, become alien to all of society. Perhaps a menace.

It has been proven that marriage between two people of different religions dilutes belief and, indeed, that dilution weakens the very foundation of our Christian country.

The less one class or race mixes with another, the less chance there is for foolish young things to meet and become besotted with one another.

Our clubs, our inns, should have the right to discriminate. Discrimination is the mark of the well-bred.

Mrs. Pickering, on the other hand, has cast an odorous pall on the practice. I speak, of course, of the matter pertaining to the Blue

Point Inn, an establishment of quality and commitment to its clientele.

She has, in effect, challenged the right of the management to choose who shall enter and who shall not.

A small incident set her off: I believe the Inn refused, most graciously, of course, to honor reservations that acquaintances of Mrs. Pickering had made by mail. It *was,* and *is,* the policy of the Blue Point not to admit those of the Hebrew persuasion. Mrs. Pickering should have been acutely aware of this practice. The Blue Point Inn is only seven miles down the coast, after all!

It was unfortunate that the refusal had to be done in person. The name "Goldstein" should have rung alarum bells, but obviously the reservation clerk had not been trained properly!

I gather from the waves of gossip surrounding the unpleasantness that Mrs. Goldstein had been Mrs. Pickering's college roommate. *Never* would I have found myself in a similar position; my roommates were screened most carefully.

Well, the incident will blow over soon, I expect. Imagine Mrs. Pickering's gall, nay, her vulgarity, in calling the manager a "Nazi"! Dear God, we do not dispose of Hebrews. This is a free and open country. Each of us free to do that which is right and proper.

HANNES
RUSSIA
APRIL–JULY

Destroy one group and two rise out of the ashes to vanish in the vastness of this wretched land. What manner of people are these who torture and kill with such delight? As babes, they must have suckled at thick brown tits that gushed not milk, but venom.

The village was picked clean of life, or so it seemed until we flushed a group of partisans from a barn on the outskirts. A ragged band, evil-smelling, cut off, I presume, from a larger group. Two grandfathers, one male adolescent and three solid women. Oh, how they despised us! Manacled, they still spat. The spit became drool as each was shot in the belly and strung up to choke slowly. We have been hanging them high, out of the reach of the dogpacks which slink in from the forest to feast. Obersturmführer Brandt has the scene on film, which he showed to a visiting group of SS officers. Some were visibly shaken by the famished hounds lurching futilely at legs which were still kicking feebly. Still alive. Franz has suggested lowering the gallows, to feed the dogs and increase the agony. The suggestion has merit. Terror used correctly is a deterrent.

It appears that news of the film was leaked to Himmler. It has been confiscated. But no order has come down to discontinue the practice. Therefore, the gallows will be lowered.

The Jews come only in trickles now. On the other hand, the partisans have become a flood. We chase them through the backcountry on roads barely fit for carts. Only our ski troops could maneuver the terrain in winter, and now with the spring rains, the roads are impassable. *Mud!* Motorized vehicles wallow, sink, and die in it. We use carts to chase the carts. Whose horses are the faster? Whose horses have the stamina to unloose hooves held in the death grip of muck! Overtake a cart and what do you find? Two small babushkas, innocent and shawled. Two grandmothers who are likely to be holding machine guns under the wrappings. *No one* is innocent in this vile place!

Despite incredible losses, the Soviet Army has seen a resurgence. We fight an enemy to whom life means nothing. Victory is all to them and death has no meaning.

I have not been feeling well these last weeks. Even the summer and the sun have not been of help. At night I dream, perhaps in fever. I must be feverish, for the dreams are horrible. Hallucinations. Horror.

The nightmares vary. I have had several of the strawberry-vomit variety. But last night there was such a one that I was driven from my bunk to cower in a corner. Franz found me and shook me awake, but even then I stayed in the throes of terror for a day and could not go out hunting.

I shall write of it, and in doing so perhaps cleanse my subconscious. I cannot give in to weakness of the mind.

In the dream everything is ice. I am ice, an iceball that spins to the horizon and then on to the next horizon. Spinning, always spinning, the iceball. Finally it rolls to a stop before a field of withered corn. But the stalks change, grow ripe and become rows of naked sexless beings. They stand immobile, and then as one they march toward me, spitting fire. Long red tongues of flame lash out, enveloping me. And the iceball that is me dissolves into minute droplets which spread and freeze. And roll in all directions to infinity.

The sexless stalks wither, drop, and all is quiet. And then I rise, whole again, untouched. And I am alone on a frozen landscape save for a great mound beside me. The mound is covered by earth, yet I can see through the covering earth to the bodies below as through thick glass. They seem to squirm; in slow motion they writhe: Men sheltering women. Children embraced by mothers. Lovers coupling in a last frenzy.

And then I hear it. A howl of death. But not from the pit. For the motion there is quite silent. Across the ice it lopes, making straight for the mound. A hound of hell scratching, tearing at the glass, crazed with the smell of freshly slaughtered meat. The carcasses taunt. And the beast claws wildly. But futilely. The glass is steel and will not shatter. In its fury the hound turns on me. It leaps at my throat and I stab it. I slash over and over. Blood gushes from its wounds, flooding the earth, freezing like hot syrup on snow. But the thing will not die. It only gathers lust from the smell of its own blood and lunges at me. The demon dog pushes my head into the blood and I lap up the clots. My tongue freezes to the ground, and each time I try to pull it free, the sound of tearing membranes crackles cross the void.

I am becoming ice again. My body hardens quickly; my sweat is rivulets of crystal. I can no longer move. And now the hellhound begins to feast. The feet go first . . . I cannot write this!

I am ill. By night I sweat and scream. Demons pursue me. By day I shiver in the heat and cannot keep much food down. What goes in comes out rapidly as bloody, brown water. I shrink in size. I am drying to a husk. The fever is with me always. And the pain. Oh, God! I cannot stand the slightest touch . . .

EMMA
CAPE CHARLOTTE
JULY

I hate my feet which are too big and my legs which are too long. Nothing does what it's supposed to. I can bounce from rock to rock on the beach barefoot, but I always trip in the jump rope and *everybody* can jump rope! Amy tried to teach me to jitterbug and gave up. I can't tell when to wiggle my bottom and when to wiggle my feet, and my arms get tangled when I try to whirl under. Maybe if I went barefoot all the time I would do better. But then I would have to have tetanus shots all the time instead of only the times when I step on rusty nails, which is pretty often. The time one went right through my foot I thought I would get lockjaw, particularly when my mouth shut tight and wouldn't open. But Mummy told me it was all in my mind. It wasn't just there, it was in my jaw and it hurt, but it went away when we had Floating Island.

AUGUST

Mummy made a great sacrifice. She dug up all the hybrid tea roses and delphiniums and columbine and planted a Victory Garden. Actually, Daddy did most of the gardening. Mummy did the canning. This has been a busy summer! We had to find jars with snaps that weren't rusty, and that took time, and then we had to find rubber seals with lips, which took even longer because there's a rubber shortage. I am an expert shucker of peas and snapper of beans. And I can pull off corn husks faster than I can tell you about it. The corn silk takes awhile longer. Anyway, we practically lived in the kitchen and it was hot! Steam burped out of the pressure cooker and ran down the walls and our faces. Mummy said it had to be good for the complexion or why do English ladies have such soft peaches and cream complexions? I think it's because of the rain *outdoors* in England!!

Yesterday something happened to the pressure cooker and stewed tomatoes are all over. Even the ceiling is red. So yesterday and today we didn't can. We cleaned.

SEPTEMBER

I was almost going to sleep when there was a scratching on my window, which is just above the garage. So I opened the blackout curtains and there was a big fat raccoon just standing up and looking at me. He seemed sort of sad so I told him to wait, and I went down in the kitchen and got a piece of bread. The raccoon waited right where I told him to, and when I got back in the room I handed him (I was a little scared he might bite me) the bread, but he took it *very gently* in his paw-hands. And he watched me with very interested black eyes as he chewed every crumb. Well, not quite. About halfway through eating he decided he was bored watching me, so he watched the stars for a while. I told him that was all the food I had, but I don't think he heard me because he kept standing up and looking very lonesome. Well, I was very fierce and closed the window and pulled the blackout curtains and I'm going to sleep!

The raccoon is back! And my window is very dirty. I think the raccoon must have stood up all night *leaning on my window!!* This time I got a sugar cookie from the kitchen, and boy did he like that!! That's enough, raccoon! Go find some crabs or something. I wonder what a good name would be for a raccoon? I think Robin Hood might be good. Robin Hood was a bandit, but he gave to the poor. I'm not sure my raccoon would share his sugar cookie.

Robin Hood has been missing a week. I hope he's OK.

Robin Hood is back . . . with four little raccoons!!! Robin Hood is a LADY raccoon, but I can't change her name. Robin and the four little hoods. Now I need five sugar cookies!!!

I think I'm going to like the seventh grade *much* better than the sixth grade. First of all, we are through with fractions. I hope I never see them again! Decimals are much easier and I almost never get the points wrong. And — tra la! — we are through with diagramming sentences! The subject and the verb were easy, but then Miss Olsen would give us a *very long* sentence with clauses that modified other clauses, and everything was strung out all over the page and there wasn't any room. So I didn't learn a thing! A couple of months ago we landed on Sicily, which I forgot to put on my old map of Italy, the flour and salt and water one. But that's OK because we have landed in Italy now.

NOVEMBER

It has been an awful week, mostly because of Carolyn. All of it because of Carolyn if you want to know! In September Carolyn wasn't too bad and I tried to like her. But maybe because she's fat, which is too bad but didn't make any difference to me, she began to tell lies. She's always tattling about somebody to Miss Butterfield, but Miss Butterfield who's no dumb bunny usually doesn't pay any attention. Which makes Carolyn mad. She was grouchy anyway because she likes Brad and Brad likes Sally, so he doesn't even look at Carolyn. Well, on Monday at recess I was sitting in the john in the girls' room and I pulled up my pants and opened the door and then remembered to flush. So that's how I caught Carolyn writing on the wall. She didn't know anybody was in the john, so she was busily writing until I flushed and then she stopped for a minute and I didn't say anything, so she went right on and then she gave me an "I hate you" look and I went out, but not before I saw what she was writing. "Miss Butterfield is a cunt." Now that word is one which I still don't know and I've been meaning to ask Mummy who used it once when she was spitting about WASPS. Well, after lunch Miss Butterfield looked very cross and asked the girls who had written the sentence. For a while nobody said anything, and then Carolyn raised her hand and in her sweetest voice said, "Miss Butterfield, I was in the girls' room and it was EMMA." I couldn't believe it, and I got all red and my mouth was so dry I couldn't say "You rat, Carolyn!" which I wanted to yell. I couldn't even say *I didn't do it!* Everybody was looking at me so hard and I couldn't say anything. And then Miss Butterfield stared at me and I felt so awful, I started to feel as though I *had* written it. I hadn't! But I couldn't help feeling as though I had! Maybe I was dreaming when I watched Carolyn. Maybe I was guilty, but then I knew I wasn't when I looked at Carolyn's face and it looked the same way as it had when she stole most of the kids' ice cream cups. I saw *that* and I wasn't dreaming and I didn't tell that time, which I should have! I started to cry and Miss Butterfield said, "We'll discuss this later." Well, all day in school I thought everybody was saying to themselves, Boy, will Emma get it. All I could think about was Miss Butterfield's face and how she probably thought I was an awful person when I'm not, and how am I going to prove I didn't write on the girls' room wall when I did once. A long time ago I wrote "shit" behind the top of the john just to see what it looked like. It was in very small letters, but it wouldn't come off because the ink is permanent. It is very permanent. I rubbed and rubbed it and finally smudged it enough so unless you really knew what was there you couldn't guess what the word was except that it had four letters. So maybe that's why I feel so bad. Because I did write on the girls' room wall even though it was in May. I have used up four days of my diary writing this!

Well, I went home with a terrible pain in my stomach. And I had supper, which didn't taste so good. So then I told Mummy and Daddy about the whole awful day and said I wasn't going back to school EVER! And they said I really had to and don't worry — everything will turn out alright. And I said it wouldn't and I wouldn't and I started to scream and cough, and then I got the hiccups which wouldn't stop, and my tears rolled down and tried to drown me. All because of stinky Carolyn! Mummy said Carolyn wasn't worth all this noise. So I stopped. But I was so tired from all the howling and everything I went right to sleep. I didn't even read. And I didn't dream about sneaky rotten Carolyn at ALL!

So the next day I went to school because although I had prayed we'd have a blizzard and the roads would be closed, all God would give me was little drizzle, which wasn't very helpful. Then Miss Butterfield asked to see me at recess, so all the kids went out looking over their shoulders to see if they could catch Miss Butterfield bawling me out or something. But she didn't. She just listened without saying a word while I told her what I saw. And I told her about Carolyn and the ice cream, too! All she said was "Thank you, Emma." And she told me to go out and play. There wasn't much time left and I had to go to the bathroom quick, so that's what I did instead.

Well, the kids know I'm not guilty now because! Carolyn can't go out for recess. Carolyn can't go out during lunch and she has to eat all alone! Carolyn has to stay after school and I don't know what she does, but I know she has to do it for a *whole month!*

Brad still likes Sally and Carolyn has lost all her friends except for David — meow! They whisper all the time. He believes anything she tells him. Who cares. They're both drips!!

Carolyn, that's
THE END

BORMANN
BERLIN

Willi!

So most of the diamond cutters are out of Holland and into Bergen-Belsen? Not all, Schmidt! It appears that a Jew group was routed straight through to the ovens of Auschwitz "accidentally"! No one will take responsibility. Typical!

While I am not an expert on production, I DO know that diamond cutters don't grow on trees. I DO know that industrial diamonds are *essential* for the tools that fashion our great war machine!

I blame that snob, Speer! Artist, architect, he calls himself. I call him a leech, sucking up to the Führer! Speer, Minister of Armaments, doesn't want to know what's going on. Doesn't want to know where his labor force is from. Doesn't wish to discuss extermination camps. Leaves the minute they come up in conversation so that his tender sensibilities are not bruised! Speer goes right on drawing his pictures, huddling with the Führer, his nose in the air when he sees us. But — his feet are right in step with the Führer's. Tagging along like an obedient puppy waiting for a pat. Good boy! Sit! Stand! Good dog! Fine fellow! The shit!

Do you know that that swine talks about me behind my back? Calls me a philandering pig, a boozer. Worse.

Speer wants me out. He tries to take my place of trust. Tries to usurp my warm relationship with the Führer. But I won't give an inch! Mark my words. Speer will fall!

Back to Bergen-Belsen. Let's get a Jew diamond cutter out — before the lot of them vanish! Get the best, Willi! — the best! Then transfer him to a smaller camp, an out-of-the-way place. And by the sea? I am not up on the camps. I leave that junk to Himmler. Uncle Heinrich could tell you the daily output of Treblinka at the drop of a hat and he's always looking for hats. I trust that you will *not* explain the purpose of our little transfer to RSHA. Let the SS think the order came through channels.

And, Willi. Remember the little worker needs the tools of his trade. (I don't know what the fuck they are. You find out!) Cutting through the red tape is your worry. For your sake, I hope the tools and the Jew end up at the same place. Where's a diamond cutter without cutting tools, eh? Up a dry creek, that's where! With you, Willi, if you fail my little request!

Bormann

Also, enlighten me about the supply of gems our man will play with. Tell me a bedtime story about your searching, sticky fingers.

HENRY
CAPE CHARLOTTE
OCTOBER

Once I agonized over the impossibility of gathering information. Now I am overwhelmed with a mass of detail.

What in the past seemed irrelevant has, with time and expertise, become pieces of a pattern, easily recognized.

My situation, of course, is ideal. Being associated as I am with such a patriotic endeavor ensures that no suspicion falls upon me, yet gives me access to privileged information which otherwise would be decidedly difficult to obtain.

My one failure so far has been with the Navy. Except for Widge, any attempt to elicit information from high-ranking officers in that service has come to naught. They seem to discourage snooping. Indeed, they are extremely close-mouthed. Prissy types, Navy. But I shall not give up the ship. Rather good, that!

Aside from this singular difficulty which I shall overcome, I have experienced an interesting few weeks.

First, I gave myself a stern talking-to. A change in demeanor was necessary. Haughty Henry (I am, and cannot help it) must become Hearty Henry. A good fellow. All men are created equal, I kept repeating, even as I know that phrase, slipped in by our Founding Fathers, to be patently false.

I practiced when Evelyn was not about. In front of a mirror. At first the performance was wooden, even embarrassing, but after the first few attempts, I began to catch a glimpse of heartiness. Not too much, you understand. But a bit of warmth crept in and I continued the charade. I placed a chair next to me. The chair, a rather good example of Hitchcock, was suitable. Bare lines, no upholstery. The chair, you see, represented a denizen of the docks. And on it I practiced jovial greetings, even a slap-on-the-back-how-are-you-old-boy type of address. The chair, of course, did not answer, just as I expected a tight-lipped wharf inhabitant would react to my cheery conversation — at first.

And, as I expected, my initial live contact did not produce great rapport. But I persisted, and gradually they o'ercame their suspicions and allowed me to join them in their daily tasks.

As lead actor in this playlet I should win not only plaudits, but a sustained, standing ovation. I was superb. Not only did I take extraordinary interest in the fishing fleet and the daily catch, I fondled same! The latter, of course. Imagine, if you will, great masses of squirming bodies giving off odors too nauseating to describe. Imagine, me, Henry, wading in, wearing wellingtons, handling selected items of the haul. I exclaimed with awe and those fishermen took me to their heart. I could not bear to sit *too* close. But we conversed in companionable tones. The lack of a suitable vocabulary, the dialect, is appalling! So I injected a question here, a question there, listened, and tried to fathom answers which were gibberish at first. Like hearing Middle English for the first time, until suddenly, by the tenth lecture, the rhythm of the words, the words themselves, are clear.

My trips to the docks have paid off handsomely. Not so the warnings on posters which abound: "Loose lips sink ships." Indeed, they do.

DECEMBER

My communing with the common man has confounded Evelyn. She is well aware of my aversion to chatting with the lower classes.

But I have anticipated her queries by inventing a tale which should keep her in check.

The tale has possibilities, which, when first suggested to her, were far from the truth. But on reflection, these trips to the docks will bring down two fowl with one blast. The first, needless to say, is to gather information from the source. These people hear and see things which I cannot. But now, as newfound friends, they impart their knowledge to me willingly, with no hesitation. Fulsome gossip of the wharfs. Invaluable!

The second result is a surprise to me. And is the tale I told Evelyn. I find the entire area to be most fascinating in itself. That which is abhorrent can also hold fascination. Evelyn believes I plan to write a history of the waterfront. And, forsooth, I shall!

The idea came to me the other day after a nasty blow: a wind of such force that the timbers of the house shook as in pain. The sea seemed intent on destroying. Spray lashed the windows. It was a nasty, freezing rain. I'm afraid my roses are gone.

I left as usual for the office, but instead of proceeding there immediately, I parked the auto, a dull brown Studebaker of which I am most fond, on Water Street, and made notes as I walked, focusing with intensity. I have always driven through, never noticing the surroundings. Trying, in fact, to blur them from my vision.

The cobblestones, slippery, glistened with the damp. They have been in place for as much as a century and a half, I would hazard. On the western side of the street is a row of brick buildings with a view beyond the wharfs, beyond to the channel and the open sea. Buildings, run-down now, faded and forlorn in their neglect. Across the façade of one is painted the legend: "Dr. Sam's Sure-Cure Elixir." Who knows what it was sure to cure?

Cafés, saloons, a ship's chandler, used-clothing stores, occupy the row on street level. Who lives above? Fisherfolk, deadbeats, females of ill repute?

Once this brick row was elegant. Townhouses of the wealthy with manicured lawns running down to the moorings. And the view was of commerce and clipper ships, I imagine. The owners of the houses owned the ships which ran the trade. Bustling docks and billowing sails dealt in luxuries and in lives. Ivory and silk, rum and slaves: the currency of the age.

The brick is dripping dry mortar. The row will collapse. A pity. Restored, this row could be charming once again. Perhaps my monograph will cause favorable comment and the city fathers will look into the feasibility of such a project.

Across the street, still active, is Commercial Wharf, an ancient building of loose clapboards and shredding paint. The wharf lists to port — rather dangerously, I think. In the aftermath of the storm, small boats below are still bobbing. At first glance, these fishing boats appear to be coated with hot paraffin, then sprinkled with a mammoth salt shaker. On closer examination, this is only an illusion created by layers of frozen spray: two weeks' worth.

The ocean of the waterfront is far from fresh, stagnating, never joining or mingling with the rest of the sea. Thus its surface is a disgusting mélange of oil patches, rubber fragments, angular ice chunks and sodden orange peelings.

Sitting on lobster pots is a small knot of fishermen munching sandwiches. Some are gutting fish. Knives flash and silver bodies fly to flop atop their kin. The barrels fill up rapidly. Over the side of the dock go the entrails, to float with the flotsam.

There are legends of a historical nature to be uncovered on the waterfront. The docks and all who live and work here are a community unto itself. I shall attempt to research the past and the present, and give to Jamesport a record of its harbor.

HANNES
BERLIN
NOVEMBER

It is November and I have lived through amoebic dysentery and arsenical compounds. It is November and I am not in Russia. I am NOT IN RUSSIA. At some point I was rushed to the field hospital and from there transported west and west and west again. Away from the human crap that gave me this — in the food, the water — in the air? Away from the East and all its evil. Soon I shall gain back my strength and be fit for active service again. But I have been promised a posting in less harsh climes.

For the moment I do desk work. And what I have come across is shameful, criminal! In October our leader, our Reichsführer SS Heinrich Himmler, gave his usual pep talk at Posen. He is always pepping up in Posen. This time it was to SS generals and police generals. I will quote a passage about the extermination of the Jewish race: "Among ourselves it should be mentioned quite frankly, and yet we will never speak of it publicly . . . Most of you know what it means when 100 corpses are lying side by side, or 500, or 1000. To have stuck it out and — apart from exceptions caused by human weakness — to have remained decent fellows, that has hardened us. This is a page of glory in our history *which has never been written and is never to be written.*"

The emphasis is mine! Never, never, he says! What the shit! We work like dogs doing our duty. We are responsible soldiers of the SS, of the Reich. We were *chosen.* We were the elite of the elite. How many times were we told this? The Einsatzgruppen, the Special Action Groups. The Special Tasks Groups. The Special Shoot-you-in-the-mouths, you shits, Groups! The MOP-UP, DISPOSAL, ELIMINATION, EXTERMINATION GROUPS. With one short sentence, Himmler wants us to disappear, vanish, with a pat on the head. For more than two lousy, stinking years of our lives trying to operate in a lousy, stinking, pissing country that nobody in his right mind should have tried to take, for who the hell wants it or needs it? We get nothing! Nothing!

The medals given out are few. I came across the "Eyes Only" list. Some high officers were awarded the War Cross of Merit. Einsatzgruppen officers. But there were penciled notations after their names: "Secret Reich Matter — for psychological discomfort!" That's code for "special merit in the technique of mass extermination." I had no notation because I had no medal! Because I am not worth anything but a ribbon, a tiny bar that says by the colors, if you look closely: He served on the Eastern Front!

Fuck them, those cowards! Hiding behind code words. We did their dirty work. We found *very* final solutions to their problems. But only a handful will ever know of our deeds!

BUFFY
CAPE CHARLOTTE
NOVEMBER

Dear Meg,

Just in case, I have installed ramps all over the house, even up to the front door, because while I still have hope about the legs—some improvement, that is—there ain't none yet. BUT I can build ships faster than any shipyard in the whole US of A. We're an assembly line of ships. Liberty ships. Nice name, that. A lifeline to Europe.

My ships (and they *are* mine, every blessed welder's seam of every lovely lady is etched in my mind) seem to slide down the ramp weekly, dripping bubbly from the keels. OK, they aren't lovely on the outside—no sleek lines or slim prows—but on the inside—in their souls they have spirit and beauty. They're tubs if you want to know. Marvelous tubs that never complain! Just plow the seas, lugging the goods. The merchant fleet is damn lucky to have them. The meat and potatoes of the service, that's what they are.

From gestation to birth I've had my hand in. But I can't name the children. It just isn't fair! Instead, some office in Washington does it. Some meek little bureaucrat who couldn't possibly beget anything names my babies! And *he* names them all "hes." Ships are *shes,* dammit!

Wonder how much patronage comes in here? Do you suppose there is covert competition among certain types to have their names out there on the bounding main? I can see every ward boss from Jersey City to Kansas City vying for the honor! Sure I'm cynical. I'm the mother!!!

I bless the day my great-grandfather decided to come in from the sea (leaving the poor sperm whales alone!) to start life ashore as a ship's chandler. From a small marine supply house to an elitist boatyard specializing in custom boats for loaded (not drunk—monied!) customers. Every teak board, every brass fitting, perfect—and expensive. Yachts for weekend gentlemen sailors.

We have survived and prospered to become a sprawling, bustling GIANT of a yard. Hurrah for capitalism!

What is Pudge doing? Spending more time at the office. Seems to have taken a real interest in the Yard—all aspects—and is chummy with everybody on the docks. This is *not* my old Pudge. In times past he wouldn't have been caught dead chatting to an employee. Now he even chews the fat with fishermen!

Sweetie, you sound divinely happy with your brood. My lot seems to be a breeder of ships!

Fondly,
Buffy

P.S. I do hope the War will be of limited duration. Not only for humanity's sake, but for mine. I cannot guarantee the lifetime of my ships. A Thirty-Year War might give the Yard a bad name!

EMMA
CAPE CHARLOTTE
DECEMBER

I'm 12, but I have to stay in bed for my birthday because I have the grippe! I'm sick and tired of modeling clay! The ears of my elephant won't stick. They flopped off, and what's an elephant without ears! And the trunk that curled up goes down a little every day. So I have decided to carve a rabbit from Mummy's soap. She says OK if I don't mess up the bed, save the shavings and be VERY CAREFUL with the jackknife. I am always very careful!

I'm not going to carve in soap anymore and it is hard to write this. I tried to smooth the rabbit's tummy and the knife slipped and cut my thumb, and I had to have six stitches!

It's getting near Christmas and I hope it snows! I hope it covers all the brown and the gray and the dead stuff. I hope it snows so much that we will be snowed in for a week. But please don't turn off the furnace! I helped Mummy wrap presents for the soldiers and sailors. They will get them when they go through the train station. Mummy belongs to the Travelers' Aid, and she and other ladies stand in the cold station and hand them out. They get lots of presents — a razor and a toothbrush and some toothpaste and a nail file, a comb, a package of Chesterfields — and a Milky Way. I ate one Milky Way and we didn't come out even.

Today Daddy and I went skating on the Blue Heron River, which isn't blue but neither is the Great Blue Heron. They're both gray. It isn't easy to skate in the winter. If the snow comes too early, then it will melt, and then the river will decide to freeze. So there you are with frozen slush-mush all bumpy, and you might as well give up on skating for the whole winter. But, if it gets very cold in December and it *doesn't* snow — well then, the skating is PERFECT. Smooth, smooth, thick, thick ice on a river that goes on forever down to the sea! Once in a while you might hear a great rumble under all that black ice. If you see a *moving* crack you skate like mad for the shore! Daddy is the only father for miles around who has figure skates.

Everybody else has great big clunky ones. They are called hockey skates, which is a game that big men play in Boston, but I've never seen hockey. Anyway, Daddy has taught me to skate backwards in a circle! I can't skate on one leg yet. I tried putting one out in front of me and I went whomp! on my bottom!

1944

HENRY
CAPE CHARLOTTE
JANUARY

I do miss the Newtonian. Now there's a place where a gentleman may find peace and fellowship among others with whom he can feel instantly comfortable. We all value the same virtues. We all grew to manhood in the same milieu — that is to say: Groton, St. Mark's, St. Paul's, possibly Exeter. And, of course, we all, or practically all, entered Harvard. I hold nothing against a man who did not finish the College. Once a Harvard man, always a Harvard man.

There are, perhaps, half a dozen Elis, a second-class school. I note that the few who have been accepted as members here rarely mention the Old Blue Tie. And they *never* wear one inside the door.

At night, I long for the calm, the tranquillity of the Newtonian. I need the comfort of the Club, to be once again in the bosom of a family, for I consider all who enter its hallowed halls as extensions of my family — even the staff, those silent servants who anticipate our every need. How I long for the warmth, friendship and easy companionship that one can only have with another man. Oh Boston — how I miss The Cradle of Liberty, where there is no doubt *who* is *whom.*

The Newtonian: No nameplate designates it; one *knows* the address. A view of the Common with lanterns twinkling — or my favorite sight: a row of chimney pots silhouetted 'gainst the ripening moon. Happiness is: a light supper of bubble and squeak, a glass of port, a crackling fire, the murmur of content — and chimney pots. What more in life is there?

FEBRUARY

At times I forget that the purpose of this clandestine life is the reinstatement of my good name. I am reminded of the latter only when receiving payment for goods delivered. It has become habit to tear the payment to shreds and dispose of the vile photos as rapidly as I am able. But once this action is over, a strange emotion takes hold.

What began with foreboding, nay, fear, has become with the passage of time a facet of life I knew not existed: thrilling, sparkling excitement!

This new dimension, this double life, has delivered me from dreariness. I see in the glass a twin, cleaved from the same egg, symmetric in all things save one. There is the proper, morally upstanding, somewhat colorless Henry. The other half lives by his wits, outwitting. Adroit, most persuasive. Amoral? Possibly. A dullard? Decidedly not!

A coup today! I have secured the exact location of the antisubmarine net which stretches across the channel, that narrow neck that leads to the body of the harbor and Baleen Bay. Inside, one U-boat bent on destruction could have a field day popping off an anchored Fleet. Dare I use a cliché? Sitting ducks in a shooting gallery?

The coup, however, is not quite complete. The Navy still keeps closed-mouth re the opening and closing of said net. I am not sure when and how this occurs. Also, I do not know its depth. Does its opening depend on the draft of a surface vessel, and if so, what is the maximum depth of that draft? If I could glean this information, then a lurking U-boat could follow the vessel, right on the stern, and pass through unnoticed. I doubt that radar — or sonar — would detect the combined length in time. This maneuver might be termed a "suicide mission"; nonetheless, sinking a goodly portion of the Fleet would be a glorious reward: death with distinction!

While the Navy is recalcitrant, the Army is not! By diligent and, I must say, clever and subtle digging, I have a goodly collection of data. It went off today. I saved it up so that Madrid would receive a *large* amount of information. Perhaps this will make them see clear to rewarding me with more than photos. I need negatives *and* the confession. I deserve them! I have been a true laborer in foreign vineyards and have gathered a goodly crop.

Madrid will have at its fingertips the following: the seacoast radar installation at Fort MacAllister. Arc of Detection: 17 miles. Five other installations are pinpointed, completing the defense of Jamesport harbor and Baleen Bay. Each arc overlaps the other, making a tight radar ring.

Coastal artillery: batteries number 13. Ten are 90mm and the remaining three are 3″. I have located each and have given coordinates. Primary assignment of said artillery: defense against motor torpedo attack/landings. Secondary: as antiaircraft battalions. Heaviest concentration of artillery fire is at Fort MacAllister, which oversees channel entrance: one long-range 16″ and two medium-range 6″ gun batteries, plus one AA battalion. Seacoast searchlights are attached to all battalions and groups.

Have pinpointed location of floating mines outside channel entrance. Was placing them on a grid overlay when Evelyn rolled in. Turned over coastal survey map swiftly. Answered Evelyn's query: am working at a particularly difficult crossword. She bit again. Frankly, I amaze myself at the ease with which I am able to extricate myself from untidy situations.

HANNES

BERLIN

JANUARY–JUNE

Ah! They remembered me. Again, as an afterthought. Promotion to that position I once saw on the horizon. I am there: SS Obersturmführer Henkel.

The bombs fall continually now. Cities lie in ruins. Soldiers die by the thousands and the Russians occupy what once was our killing ground.

Physically, I'm strong. But I cannot sleep. I'm due for leave and I'm taking it now before I go berserk!

OBERGURGL, AUSTRIA

The parish is high and still. I climbed the Hohe Mut, a Wildspitze, but smaller, skis strapped to my back. From the top, a sweeping glacier, and Italy to the south. No war. No sound. Just sun and a ptarmigan in the snow. One run down through unbroken powder. Flying through purity. Mulled wine and feather beds and sleep, unbroken. I need three years' worth of sleep! The hotel is almost empty and my leave is nearly up.

BERLIN

Back to the city. Tried some whores. They are like Berlin — gray, emaciated, sullen, spirit broken. I need laughter, wine and warmth!

Had a marvelous thought. I *will* outrank Schwoermer! I go on and he molders. Cheered me up the entire day.

O Blessed Spirit Who watches over me! You are kind and giving! I am posted to France! Maybe Paris? France is a plum of a posting. The French may be decadent, but I am ready and willing to experience a dose. Hail to Hedonism!

LYON

Shit! *Not Paris.* Just once I wanted to be an officer and enjoy the benefits. Instead, some city called Lyon, some backwater out in the provinces. My assignment? What else — hunting partisans. That experience I have had. Up to my eyes! The French call themselves "The Resistance." Crawling with Reds, it is.

A nightmare — and I was *never there!* The lines go on and on through swirling snow. Bundles of gray rags shuffle silently, bending low to escape a deadly wind. Its howl the only sound except the rasp of breathing. Long ago, these gray-clad figures threw away their snowshoes; and the skis are lost. The sleds still haul the heavy equipment, but the armor is useless, for the guns cannot fire. Oil and blood congeal in this white cold. The horses' breath is a labored roar. And with each breath, carbon dioxide lies like a frozen fog over everything. Men freeze solid where they stand, mouths gaping wide. The horses fall and are hacked to pieces before they die. Horse meat becomes broth, and those lucky enough huddle around the boiling pot to catch the brief warmth of rising steam. All eyes stare westward. The dead mean nothing except delay. To move a dead man out of the way is like dragging a ton of timber. Heat and energy wasted. But this is the only track. To deviate means certain doom in snowdrifts up to the neck. One by one, the rifles are dropped by the wayside; the artillery is jettisoned. The halftracks are tipped over and abandoned — an offense punishable by death, but no one shoots, for the sleds are free now, piled high with dying men. They ride until the horses move no longer. They ride if the traces are slashed and men become horses. The line stretches forward and backward, ten, a hundred miles — thousands and thousands of beaten, freezing men trying to get home, trying to crawl from the enemy hard on their heels.

Somehow the window had blown open.

I awoke in bitter cold and perspiration had poured forth. The linen was drenched with ice water. I was cold; I dreamt. Of Stalingrad? Or have I leapt in time, foretelling the future?

Lyon: bourgeois; commercial. Center, however, for hunters — and the hunted: the Resistance movement. Chief hunter: SS Hauptsturmführer Barbie. Head of the Gestapo for the sector. Head sadist. Schwoermer, you and he are kindred spirits.

At least, I am billeted in a small chateau, charming and comfortable. And spring is in the air. I think more of sap rising than I do about the little cells of resistance that pop up: patriots out of hibernation. The weather is sensual. The smell of blossoms can turn one into a romantic. There was never a sweet odor in the East. The women here are as sensual as the weather. Not fat cows: chic. How, after four years of war, do they manage to retain that certain flair that German women could never capture, even in peacetime? French ladies can make hats out of newspaper seem sexy!

The Bolsheviks have crossed into Poland! 200 miles to Warsaw! What in hell has happened? The priorities are *not* with the Wehrmacht. Trains trundle out of here, out of every junction on the Continent, laden *not* with supplies and ammunition for the front — but with fodder for the ovens. The "Final Solution" is top priority. Soldiers of the Reich starve and die so that the remaining Jews can burn.

I see as little of Barbie as I can. I hunt; he plucks the catch. At Gestapo Headquarters or down in the depths of Montluc, he is in his element. At his invitation, I went to the prison once to watch. He kicks the belly, boots the kidneys, injects acid in the bladder, drowns in ice water — and enjoys the show. I have not gone back for an encore.

I do what I am good at — tracking. But I do not go beyond the capture. What occurs afterward is not my concern. It is out of my hands.

I roam the countryside with my SS, a seasoned partisan fighter, flushing out the bands. The Maquis is riddled through with Reds and rotting from a lack of unified purpose. The diverse groups cannot overcome their hatreds. They quarrel incessantly and jealously guard their turf. Left hates Right. The Center cannot hold them. We are not the enemy of France. Frenchmen are!

My territory is a vast hunting preserve. Within, all's fair. They hit; we hunt. They vanish; we track. Someone screams a little and we learn.

What a marvel to motor back after a day's search and relax at a glittering soiree at the chateau!

Barbie keeps sending Jews to ovens, tying up the trains! All tracks in Europe lead to the camps! Munitions and food pile up because there is no rolling stock available to transport them east. And the Reds sweep on!

The cattle cars trundle day and night now — from the Balkans, Romania — from Western Europe and the East. There are so many trains, so tightly packed, that the dispatchers are having nervous breakdowns. One car was shunted to a siding by some insane fool. It waited on a spur for an engine that never came. In time it was forgotten, for no one heard the cries. Bloated bodies produce a foul gas which, in sufficient quantity, has a mighty force. The explosion was heard for miles. What a waste! How many other cars are uselessly sitting somewhere in transit — forgotten? Those cattle cars are needed for the Wehrmacht! Now!

At least I have a job that keeps me in the open air and moving. Good exercise for the body. I can picture the camp commandants sitting on their butts, totaling, always totaling. Their butts grow fat, their bellies, paunchy. A dull job, theirs, waiting for the next transport. It pours through the gates. Left: life; right: death. Or is it the other way around? Minor decisions. Shovel in; shovel out. A job for the witless.

It isn't as though the camps really contribute to the war effort — those that live to work. Their output is a joke:

Mathausen: Stones, heavy.
Dachau: Porcelain.
Stutthof: Mattresses, hair.
Auschwitz? Auschwitz: Soap.

* * *

I've met a girl! A lovely thing: Gisèle. Gisèle: a lovely name. She haunts my days and I cannot wait for night.

So young, so fair, so innocent, so fine. Her green eyes glow with infinite depth. Her legs are as long as a foal's. Hair of honey, tied back with yarn. I gave her a satin ribbon but she will not wear it. Too grand, she says.

Gisèle. My gazelle. Pert and cautious; sleek and supple. I long to feel those soft sinews moving under me; hear you cry my name. You must not run.

Swiftly, the block was cordoned off. The building was surrounded; all apartments emptied with dispatch. The inhabitants huddled together, still groggy with sleep. Room by room, we searched and found nothing. No Maquisards, no meeting room, no transmitter. Nothing. A bogus tip.

But I found Gisèle. A slip of a thing in a sexless flannel nightdress. I spoke to her and she turned away. I offered to escort her back and she refused. At first, I thought that it was my execrable French, but of course it was not that. She was terrified of the conqueror wearing the insignia: SS.

She clung to the hand of a tiny woman. A mother, bent and withered, yet still dignified. Each seemed to give strength and calm to the other.

I bowed courteously and most correctly. I told them not to fear. Forcefully but gently, I maneuvered the elder woman across the street, through the heavy door, into the courtyard and up the stairs. Gisèle held on to her mother and had to follow. The hallways were wide and dark and musty. But the rooms of the apartment had an elegant air, despite the peeling paint. The damp of spring seeped through the shuttered windows, and I felt terribly young and inarticulate. More than anything at that moment, I wanted to be a simple Frenchman in baggy corduroys and beret. Obersturmführer Henkel did his best. Courtly, I kissed the old one's hand, smiled at Gisèle, and left.

I've met her three times now. Each time away from the apartment. She swings down the street to our rendezvous at the café. And I watch this girl, who is skin and bones, dressed in shiny blue serge, with white ruffled collar, and my heart ceases. It actually pauses a beat. I am whirling with wonder. I am in love with a witch!

* * *

I want to clothe her in velvet. Feed her until her cheeks pop and become rosy with health. Throw away those ugly wooden clogs that pass for shoes and buy her boots of Spanish leather. She will have none of it.

I am old at twenty-four; I am young and sixteen! I am in love. In love! Who cares about the Maquisards when one can make love! Let the Resistance resist, just so long as my girl does not! Let the French have France. Just give me Gisèle to take home.

I come for her in mufti. No uniform for courting. Black is out this year. But her mother sees beyond the plain gray suit. I am German, and the lady's few words spit with hate. I cannot cure her wounds. And hers do not heal. A husband dead since '38 from lungs ravaged by the gas of the Great War. A son, now part of the earth near Dunkirk. Their faces stare at me from the table. My gifts of food stay untouched. All efforts of conciliation are rebuffed.

Up the funicular to the basilica of Notre-Dame-de-Fourvière. A massive thing with yet another tower above it pointing toward her God. She ran up the steps to the top (hundreds!) lightly, without pause. Not to be outdone I followed, but she had wings! She seemed an angel in some soft white dress that made her look like a child at her first Communion. Perhaps she wore it then. But she is *not* a child and I wanted to kiss her badly. Yet all I could do was bend over and pant! A romantic lover outdone by a girl!

High above the city we stood. The day was golden, clear and sweet — a sauterne kind of a day. Nothing in the air but light.

Half a circle and two hundred miles of France were ours. To the east, Mont Blanc soaring sharp and white, and Switzerland just beyond. To the west, the Puy de Dôme, a round volcano rising almost 5000 feet from the lunar landscape of the Auvergne.

She saw beauty in the mountains and marveled at the clarity of air which brought the rugged land of peaks and puys within our grasp. We could reach out and hold them.

But the awesome sight held dangers she could not dream of. For westward, within the Massif Central and its volcanic domes, and east and south, hidden in the high plateau land of the Haute Savoie and Alpine Massif, massed Maquisards, pockets of Resistance. Pockets of *pus*. Beyond her vision I could see them. Burrowing. Waiting. From the tower I could blot them out with two hands.

Wipe them from the face of the earth — from the tower, I could.

Back down she pulled me — to the Chapel — and there she knelt before the Virgin, murmuring and crossing herself endlessly.

Such kinship with the Virgin! Christ! If I don't do something soon to change her status, there'll be a second Immaculate Conception!

Today we had a picnic, Gisèle and I. The day was fresh and full of promise. The new grass was our bed, and the bursting willows bending down to the river, our canopy.

Sancerre, cold chicken and the cheese of Langres. Gisèle ate gustily, forgetting her inner vows. She smiled at me and crinkled up her eyes in the spring sun. They are as green as the buds on the willows! We kissed and she responded — gingerly at first, then thirstily. I tried to loosen her hair, which she had bound tight in one long plait. We tussled and laughed, and I threw her clogs into the river. They floated quickly out of sight around a bend. For a while we were lovers yearning for each other. And then she collected herself, carefully buttoning the blouse that I had so surreptitiously undone.

How many women have I taken? How many forcibly? How many without desire? I desire her above all things, and I cannot do it!

She gazed toward the river and remarked that once the water had been full of wild fowl. Now there were none. All eaten. Food for a defeated people.

The spring day grew chill and the gay mood was gone. I took her back. My night was hell!

I tell her that I work at a desk. That I am a lowly subaltern — a paymaster for the district who happened to be passing by that night. I don't know if she believes me.

Yesterday there were landings on the coast of Normandy. A beachhead may have been established. Has a Second Front begun? Where are the all-powerful secret weapons we have been promised? The Vengeance weapons that will turn the tide?

All hell breaks out in the Vercors. The FFI, the Free French Forces of the Interior, a grand name for squabbling groups, attempts great deeds of derring-do. French are flocking to join. Suddenly. And not out of patriotism, I think. The Resistance is an escape from forced labor.

My mind should be involved with putting down insurrection, but the spirit is lacking. If I had to choose right now between the decimation of the FFI and the bedding of Gisèle, there could only be one choice: I must find a bed!

She did not come to the restaurant. I waited till midnight, and the supper grew cold. I brought the food and had it cooked specially — and she never saw it. I will call when it is light. Maybe she is ill.

She is not ill. SHE IS NOT ILL. But soon she will scream for illness, for release, for death! While I was pining away at the restaurant, my Gisèle was languishing in Montluc, three blocks away. Picked up on suspicion as she came to meet me. My prim little virgin is *a courier for the FFI* and she was carrying a message for them tucked next to her luscious bosom!

I do not know her. I watch them break her slowly and I give no sign of recognition. She sees me and will not beg. She has a strength that seems to cover the awful wounds of her body with a cloak of numbness. The body before me is not the fantasy of my longing. It is bloated and bleeding.

She does not talk. She will not talk. She is pulp. Except for those eyes. Those great pools have lost their luster, but not their power over me. She sees me. She sees me! But she will not ask for mercy. If she would only beg forgiveness! I cannot watch more . . .

So be it. The bitch is dead. Long live the fool! There is some mercy in the fool. I had her shot before dawn. They had to tie her up. She could not stand. She did not scream for God or me. Just before the fusillade, I thought I heard a tinkle of laughter. It could only have been in my mind — the faint remembrance of times past. She is gone, blotted out, forgotten . . .

We bloodied the streets of Brantôme, hanged them high in Nîmes, mowed them down in Oradour! We've massacred the face of France and still they resist!

I do not care anymore. I loathe Lyon and need to be . . . somewhere . . . far away. I have the adjutant's cycle. Much larger and more powerful than the pitiful thing I had . . . so long ago. I shall take it out for a spin in the rain and see if it can outrace the wind.

EMMA
CAPE CHARLOTTE
JANUARY

I have to wait 11 months to be a teenager! I am trying to figure out when to change paragraphs. When the thought changes. But — I don't always have room on the diary page.

I will indent for a paragraph here because it's about Amy and she sure is a different thought. Amy was bragging yesterday, so what's new? This time she said she had more dolls than anyone else in the class. But who cares? Anyway, I think she was hoping to make me jealous and *green with envy* and mad and whatever. So I told her *I* had more of something than she had, and wow, did that get her. She pestered me all day, but I just smiled and said "Guess." When the bell rang she was still going crazy trying to guess, so I gave her a little hint. "Words," I said. I have more "words" than you do. But even that didn't help much, because Amy can't put two and two together and even come up with five. Four she'd never think of. So today she followed me all around hollering "Tell me!" I couldn't stand her any longer, so I finally told her. "Books," I said as proudly as you please. "I've got more books than you do!" The only books in her house are her Nancy Drews and maybe ten more that belong to her parents. Well, Amy said who cares about books and she gave me a bronze cheer, which is *not* like Amy because usually she's *so* ladylike. So here's Amy blowing away, her lips bouncing up and down to beat the band making burping noises. I don't care if Amy doesn't think having books is so great. I do. Anyway, we aren't talking. The Russians are starting to chase the Germans and we've taken a lot of little islands away from the Japs that I've never heard of. But there are a lot of islands left.

FEBRUARY

Daddy came home tonight and yelled "Those bastards!" I have another swear word. Daddy is head of the OPA in Jamesport. But he doesn't get paid for it. The OPA is the Office of Price Administration and does all sorts of things like making sure prices don't go up or down, but stay put. They also have something to do with ration books and they look for cheaters. Cheaters get lots of butter and meat and rubber tires and gasoline and cigarettes. Then they hide all this stuff and then they sell it for lots and lots of money in a big dark barn called a Black Market. They also have those car stickers you put on your windshield to say how much gasoline you can buy. "A" stickers say you can't buy much. Not even enough to go out in the country in your car and have a picnic at the lake. "B" stickers give you a little more gas. Daddy has a "B" sticker because he sells insurance and he sure couldn't sell any sitting in a chair! "C" stickers say you can have all the gas you need and then some. Cheaters sell "C" stickers.

Whenever I think about my winter coat I want to puke. Not spit up! PUKE! That winter coat belonged to my cousin, Ellen. Mummy says that Ellen outgrew it. I know for a fact that Ellen hated it and I know why! Mummy says the coat is the color of new-mown hay. *It is not!* It's a mixture of cow meadow muffins and chewed-up grass, that's the color!

And when am I going to get loafers? I want shiny loafers the color of horse chestnuts so much! I'd polish them every day. If I could have them!

Today is Mummy's birthday. She says the 40th year is obscene. 40 years old is very old, but she doesn't have too many wrinkles yet that I can see. I gave her a garbage can for her birthday, which was very hard to find because of the metal shortage. Almost all the garbage cans are becoming planes. After the birthday party was over, she said sort of quietly with tears in her eyes that she guessed it wasn't the time for a black lace nightgown or perfume. I know the tears were happy ones because I know how much she hated the old garbage can.

MARCH

Amy showed me her diary today. We're talking again. For a while, anyway. She showed me her diary, but she didn't let me read it. Which didn't bother me at all because I couldn't care less what junk she writes! All she showed me were her little stars, which she says are a code for KISSES! Every time a boy kisses her she puts a star in. She flipped through the diary kind of fast and I swear there were stars on almost every page. Nobody could be kissed that much!!

I don't have to flip through my diary because I don't have ONE STAR! I am 12 and one quarter years old and I have been kissed exactly two times, which don't count because it was Spin the Bottle.

Both times Jimmy got me and he smacked me near my nose. Jimmy doesn't count, anyway. Once when I was 8, Eddie and I went under the porch and I thought he wanted to kiss me, but instead he said, "Let's take off all our clothes." Well we did, even though it was cold and rainy. We took off all our clothes and looked at our things. His thing was pretty little and my thing was even littler, and it was awfully dark under there so we didn't see much.

APRIL

Mummy and Daddy took me to see the movie about the battle at Stalingrad last week. I didn't want to write about it for a while. When I think about it, I have to get into bed and put on my socks because I get cold and start shivering. The faces all seemed frozen. The live faces and the dead faces, and sometimes I couldn't tell who was dead and who was just sleeping in the snow. Maybe they were all dead, except those people who wore rags around their heads and were running and shooting. The horses were dead. They were all stiff and covered with snow. Everybody's eyes looked like they had been sucked way back in their heads, and all the houses were piles of stones and it looked like nobody had any place to sleep. Little children came out of holes looking for something to eat. I think rats looked pretty good to them about then. I am glad we still have some food hidden under the kitchen drawers just in case of a siege. Stalingrad was a battle and a siege. I am glad the Germans lost at Stalingrad. I didn't write about the movie that night because my stomach hurt. It hurts again tonight.

Amy is my best friend and sometimes she's my worst friend. It all depends. She has long blond hair which she says someone told her looked like corn silk. I bet nobody told her that! She is so proud of her damned hair and her mother curls it every day in a pageboy (which I could have if Mummy would let me cut off my braids and have a permanent, which she won't!). Corn silk! Boy, you ought to see it when it's dirty. Looks like dead corn silk! I don't want to waste space talking about Amy's hair except there is a reason. She told me that the people who make the Norden bombsight, which is still *very very* secret, need blond hairs for the crosshairs. So Amy sent them a sample — or her mother did. I didn't think I could live with Amy if they said that her hair was so special it would win the war or something. BUT — I don't think I have to worry. Amy hasn't peeped about her hair for two whole months!

MAY

I am sitting under the juniper tree on the knoll down in front of my house thinking up reasons not to do my homework. Way out on the horizon I can just make out the shapes of two Navy planes in formation coming in from submarine patrol. They are so far away I can't hear their motors yet. Every morning since the beginning of the War — which was gosh, two and a half years ago — they have left at dawn, flying in wide circles, farther and farther out to sea. They look like crazy dragonflies hunting for a bug. I wonder what it feels like to be up so high. I wonder what it feels like to be a submarine trying to hide in the open ocean. The planes are near enough now so I can hear the droning . . .

I'm back. That was silly. I pretended to be a submarine and I flattened out in the bayberry, hoping they wouldn't see me and bomb me. I'm cold and goosepimply. Probably the sea breeze. Maybe I was a little scared for a minute. It's a scary feeling, being hunted, hiding.

It's OK now. Here come some seagulls flying one on top of the other, their wings almost touching. They're squawking away as if they own the whole beach.

That was pretty funny the time way back at the beginning of the War when Daddy woke up and saw two planes against the sun, diving in formation right at the house! Before the machine guns could open up, Daddy knocked Mummy right off the bed and they hid underneath it. At breakfast Daddy said the sun was in his eyes and they really looked like two dive-bombers and he couldn't help it if two dumb seagulls had begun to imitate the patrol planes.

Today Daddy and I started to clean out the garage. But all we did was move things around a little. When we began to heave out the boxes of beach glass that Mummy has collected and has taken the best colors out of, she said "STOP! I might find some use for the glass someday." So then we started to throw out the mountains of old newspapers and she rushed out and said that they had the news of the whole War in them and they *couldn't* go in the rubbish. Then she pointed around and said, "Why don't you throw out that and that and that?" Well, Daddy said that and that and that are boxes of lead weights and a couple of ponchos that only have a few tears in them, and a lot of rope that washed up on the beach and you never know when you might need rope . . . So that stuff didn't go either. Practically everything had to stay, so there wasn't any room for the car, which was the reason for cleaning the garage in the first place.

The car still sits outside and gets older and older, faster and faster. It wasn't new when we got it, which was before the War. I think it was Navy blue then. Now it's sort of blotchy. Mummy says it's the salt air. Daddy says the paint job was poor. Sometimes the car looks like it wants a nice cozy place to sleep, but it's not going to get one!

JUNE

We landed on the coast of France yesterday. And we're crawling up the leg of Italy and punching the Germans in the stomach and the Russians are pounding them on the back. The War should be over *very* soon!

But something else happened today, which is D-Day plus 1. I found a cave! A secret hiding place kind of cave! I was sitting on the knoll in my thinking place under the old juniper, just watching the lazy waves wrap themselves around the rocks and thinking how nice it was to feel just as lazy, when all of a sudden a wasp landed on my arm. Well, I HATE wasps, so I ran to the cliff edge of the knoll and hung as far as I could over the side waving my arm. Well, the wasp didn't like that so he went somewhere else, Thank Goodness — but — my hand whacked the cliff and went right into a hole!

You see, the knoll is actually one big enormous hunk of rock with a lot of dirt and bayberry and grass and my twisted juniper on top. I took the easy path to the beach and went around and looked up, but I couldn't see the hole, which was funny. It was invisible from down there because the cliff goes *in* near the top. All I could see were teeny potmarks in the cliff made from millions of years of sandpaper spray slapping it. You can only see the hole from the top if you hang *way over* and know *exactly* where to look. It is really secret!

When I put my hand in the next time I was *very careful.* Something might live there and not like a human girl bothering him. But I didn't get bitten. The hole has a shelf like a long spoon at the bottom of it that goes way back deep into the cliff. There's a lot of room there. And it's a cave, not a hole.

I'm going to put my best treasures into it. I'm going to collect all summer and then, just before school starts, I'm going to take them all out and look at them, and then I'll put them back. I hope they'll be OK over the winter. At least the floor of the cave is dry, so I don't think the sea gets in.

* * *

Every nice day I go all along the beaches and collect things. Daddy calls me his Beachcomber. But you can find lots of interesting things tangled up in the tidelines of kelp (besides sand fleas!).

I have a tiny piece of bleached driftwood that looks like a silver seal. I have a beaded fan of some kind of seaweed that looks more like coral and when it dried out it became light violet. I looked and looked for a perfect skimmer. Over at Cockleshell Cove I got the roundest flattest black one you ever saw crossed with white quartz lines. I save only the best beach glass. And it has to be smooth, with no sharp edges. I have lavender, the teal green you see on duck feathers, and a blue so blue you wouldn't believe it.

I have a pink rock from Easter Egg Cove that is a perfect Easter Egg. I found a mussel shell, dark blue-purple, all lacy platinum on the inside. I have a small stiff starfish, some Chinamen's caps and a sea urchin. And none of them have chips! I have decided to put in some of my best marbles, my special purees with the little bubbles floating forever in the glass.

I don't think I will add the piece of the lifejacket and the Merchant Marine cap.

JULY

I think I found Daphne today! I looked for her for two days last summer. She was only a little white mouse, but I loved her! I even went under the house calling her. I still don't see how she got out of her cage. And now all that's left is a tiny skeleton. I buried her under some stones on the beach, which is pretty stony anyway, and I sang to her and said some things. I told Mummy about it, and she laughed and said it sounded like a pagan ritual. Well, I've never been to a Congregationalist funeral!

I have just finished *The Snow Goose,* and I was crying so hard I almost couldn't see to finish it and I had tear spots all over the sheet. It made me think of Dunkirk again, which I haven't thought about for a long time — not since *Mrs. Miniver* anyway. But reading *The Snow Goose* made me remember something that happened in the spring of 1941, before we were in the War, but the English were, and fighting very hard. I was too little to really understand, so now I'm going to tell the story.

Jamesport is a port, naturally, so when the English needed stuff like food and tanks from America, they sent boats over here and some came to Jamesport. Daddy and Mummy invited two people from an English boat for dinner. So we had a real English dinner with roast beef and gravy and Yorkshire Pudding, which is like popovers. Puffy but flatter. We had apple pie and Mummy's pie crust was good! Sometimes it isn't.

A Captain and a First Mate came. The Captain's name was Bytheway — really! He had a pink face and no hair. The First Mate was very funny, but he looked like a monkey with bad teeth. Mummy said it was a lack of vitamins and too much tea. We had a grand time, and just before I had to go to bed they invited us to visit their ship! After I went to bed everybody did a lot of singing. So the next day I asked Daddy what they were singing and he said Body songs. Well, I didn't know any except "When a body meets a body" and they weren't singing that one.

So when we went down to the docks and up on their ship, which was a freighter, the Captain apologized because she was all rusty and dark. He said she was once bright and pretty, but now she looked awful to try and fool the U-boats.

Mummy brought them lots of sugar and dried onions as a present, and they used up some of their precious food to give us tea and sweet cakes. And the crew gave me a little sailboat that some of them had carved.

The next day was *really* special! The First Mate telephoned Mummy and said that if I wanted to see something interesting, I should go down on the rocks with a white towel. So I did. I waited and waited, and then I saw it. The freighter! It was moving out slowly to meet a convoy. All big boats follow the Pilot Boat out through the channel because the Pilot Boat knows every rock and reef. When the big boat is safe, it is on its own and it toots "Thank you and goodbye" three times. Well, do you know that after the English freighter did its three toots, it didn't stop tooting. It tooted and tooted and tooted all the way to the horizon! It must have tooted a hundred times to *me!* I waved my towel like mad until my arms wanted to fall off, but I wouldn't quit because they wouldn't quit. I wished them good luck and everything else good I could think of — and it didn't work. IT DIDN'T WORK! They were torpedoed! The Captain wrote that he and the First Mate and a couple of other crewmen had been picked up, but that the old ship was gone — down to the bottom of the sea! So I'm crying thinking about all those sailors who had made me a sailboat. And there are tear spots all over this page!

STEINER
IN THE ATLANTIC
MAY

Ilse, Ilse,

My God I miss you.

I have become an automaton and my crew are the walking dead. I command by rote, out of habit and learned experience. I have no room in my brain, no spirit left anywhere, to innovate.

The men stare ahead and see nothing but home. And there is fear in their eyes that while they are so far away, home has been obliterated in a firestorm. They see their families engulfed in flames, screaming as those sailors did in the sea of oil.

Retribution? We all feel its hand. Retribution for a New Order which brought not life, but death, to everything it touched and touches.

Am I the immediate cause of this awful malaise which eats away at all of us? Do the men see beyond my lifeless eyes into whatever passes for the kernel of being? Do they see that I hate this War, that I despise what I have done in its name? Do they see that I loathe not only our leaders but the common man, the good German who took up the cudgel in the name of the Reich and became a monster?

I don't know who first said: "My country, right or wrong." He was wrong. So awfully wrong.

I became a little god. A sailor who loved the sea commanding a killer machine. And I knew it. I stayed out of politics and played the obedient naval officer, who only did what he was trained and ordered to do. I sank ships and severed supply lines . . . and then, one day, I saw what I had done.

Even now, there are still some Siegfrieds of the sea. My peers, my so-called comrades, who play the deadly game with enthusiasm. They are like vicious little boys who revel in the gory tales of blond Norse pagans. They dream of mass murder and then a decoration to salute their deeds. They hear the blare of trumpets as our great leader marches toward them, his sacred arms raised high to place the ribbons round their necks. And as they feel the touch of Adolf Hitler, they are forever blessed by God. The Godless God.

Konrad Vogel, my Chief Torpedo Mate, went mad this morning. He has been with me since the beginning. In port, he learned that his wife and young son had been crushed beneath the rubble of their apartment. Their bodies were pulled out — in pieces. For three long weeks, Konrad held his anguish in check. It burst out this morning. He bashed his skull against the bulkhead until it cracked. He lies in my bunk, babbling. Blood pours from his nose, and we are far from help.

Promise me. Promise me that you will go to the Ötztaler! The mountains have to be safer. Take Elsbeth and go. Get out of the city!

I expect Vogel will die. I hope he will. He is like a squashed pumpkin that no longer feels the awful pain of loss, of love. I hope he will die soon. Better here than in our compassionate country where idiots die by fiat.

Go to the Kellers'. They will take you in. Let me picture you and Elsbeth snuggled under eiderdown, breathing the pure air of the Obergurgl peaks, away from the bombs. I want to come back to you, and to my child, who will hardly recognize me. So much I want to.

Someday, you and I will climb to the upland meadow and look down at a toy village and the tiny white church bright with murals. We will eat goat's cheese and warm bread amid brown cows, and the only sound will be the sweet tinkling of their bells. We will sip Riesling and become giddy in the sun. And we will sleep in the shepherd's hut and make love in new-mown hay, and you will complain that you prefer linen to fresh-cut grass. But I will caress away the tiny welts from your round rump, and we will love again so hard, you will swear the grass is satin.

Ah, Ilse, it will happen. I know it. Bear with me. Wait for me.

I love you so,
Rudi

BUFFY
CAPE CHARLOTTE
JUNE

Oh Meg,

The goddamned legs are *never* going to work. Ever! I know the doctors told me this. But I wanted miracles. I believed in mind over matter, and boy did I work on the matter. All this time I have willed feeling and strength, and I don't know what all, into these useless things. It wasn't strong enough, all this will. So maybe I'll have them off. OFF. And get some substitutes. And prance around — well, not prance — but move vertically!

Have you ever noticed how styles of walking and posture have changed? In our short lifetime — well, it's short compared to the age of the earth — here's change for you.

As children. Shoulders back. Tummy in. Chin up. Glide and watch that head. Glide as though there's a dictionary up there. Don't drop it and DON'T SLUMP.

As gay young things. Slump. Slump! The pelvis must arrive before the rest of you. Hipbones (I never discovered mine) first. Head brings up the rear. (The rear follows the pelvis. Am I confusing you?)

As mature types. Be proud of the prow. Point your bazooms. Let everything else follow in stately measure.

Me (now). Lead off with feet, then knobbly knees. The rest rolls silently behind on rubber wheels.

I read over this letter and find it is bathos — at least the last part. Maybe because it is a beautiful day and the sea sparkles and the air sparkles and I can see for miles — almost to the end of the earth if I set my mind to it. I hate sunny days! They are at odds with my mood. Give me a bitch of a storm, with the foghorns crying and the ocean seething, and I am content. All of nature is in tune with my anger!

All done. Feel better. Thanks, love.

Buffy

JULY

Meg, my friend,

The mind races. It seems the more I do, the more I think I have to do. I'm not manic, you understand. Just prolific.

I sleep less and wake up at an unGodly hour. There's something intolerable about beating the sun. Those couple of hours before dawn are graveyard hours. They say the time from 3 AM to 5 is the dying time — that more people pass on during that period than any other. Something about the heartbeat slowing to nothing or some such. Personally, I think the whole thing is bull!

At those hours I am wide awake, and my pulse is beating in double time, but since the rest of the world is NOT at work (except the night shift, and they aren't my best people), I can't call my top foreman or managers and send them hopping.

So I stew with nothing to do *unless* I think up a new project. OK, I have thought one up, something to fill in these dead hours. I'm going to try my hand at writing. Not pretty poems, you ninny! A book. A real, honest-to-God book, pages and pages from my imagination. A book full of damsels in distress, and forbidding great stone houses perched on lonely cliffs, with waves crashing and lightning flashing — Whew! Something full of romance and mystery and stuff. Yes, Brontë wrote *Jane Eyre* and Daphne has done *Rebecca.* I'm going *much* farther. Explicit SEX, dammit! Lots of it. Censors shall not set my standards!

So I'm not an expert in these matters. I can dream, can't I? I can fantasize for all those poor housebound women, those readers of *Insipid Romance,* who dream their secret dreams of the tall, dark, marvelously mysterious male who lusts for their inner selves, who sees beauty in their souls. Who lusts!

I'll write a hell of a story for all them ladies, who will then heave those rotten magazines and drown themselves in prose, not pap. (I'll write it for me too!)

Speaking of sex — I was, wasn't I? I do dwell on it at times. Quite a lot of the time, actually. I have a copy of *Lady Chatterley's Lover,* still banned by the pure here, who are not quite sure there really is a penis, or what it does, or if it is an appendage like the appendix. Anyway, just before she died, Mummy smuggled it in from France. The smuggling was so simple because the book was done up to look like a purse from Morocco. When I'm feeling bored and would like to start a fuss, I leave it lying around, particularly at parties — secretly (not *so* secretly) hoping some saintly type will open it, die from shock, and rise right up to Heaven. No luck so far.

The other night I thought I might titillate Pudge into paying me a visit, so I left *LCL* with a *very large* marker stuck at *the* passage and put the thing on his bedside table, right next to the cocoa. He couldn't miss it. (Or would he think it was a purse!?) He didn't miss it.

Meanwhile, I got all gussied up and waited. Ah-ha! A light tap on my door. "Come in, dear," I said in a low throaty voice.

Enter Pudge, the book under his arm, looking almost handsome in the maroon velvet bathrobe I gave him last Christmas and which I have not seen him wear till now. If you want the truth, I can't remember when I last saw Pudge in *any* bathrobe. Since God knows when, that's when.

Propped up against silken pillows, I beam seductive beams.

Pudge perches on the edge of the bed, the book in his hands. (I wish he'd put it down and use them!)

And then . . . And THEN! I am given a *discourse on Lawrence!* In particular, my husband's horror at a coupling between two people so separated by class!

My aim was true. The book hit Pudge square on the nose and he scurried out, yelping softly. I hope it hurt like hell. All night!!

So I shall write my own book. And I'll make up everything!

Will let you know of progress, and scream at you when I'm blocked.

Much love from the literary world,
Buffy

P.S. Don't read the banned Henry Miller's. I did and said, "So what. Who cares!" I'd ban him on account of boredom.

SEPTEMBER

Meg!

Have I told you about my elevator and my aerie? Got a special dispensation (or do you only get that from the Pope?). Anyway, I got something, a permit, to have wrought several marvelous additions to the House. With my being incapacitated, the authorities waived the usual rules against building additions during wartime.

First the elevator. I resented having to be carried upstairs. Particularly by Alfred, who, as I have mentioned before, pants all the way up, loudly, and quite unpassionately. (Pudge couldn't budge a flea!) Since Gable isn't around, I detested the whole operation. If Gable *was* around, it would be quite a different matter! Got an architect. He hasn't had a commission in years. Not knowing how to design a tank or a submarine or a Quonset Hut, his genius has lain dormant since Pearl.

In the olden days a dumbwaiter trundled up to what was then the salon on the second floor. My grandmother tried to pretend she was in Athens (or Boston) and held gatherings of culture there. If she caught a professor of whatever, she was in Heaven. Unfortunately, there were few to snare, and she had to settle for a discussion by ordinary mortals on the metamorphosis of the luna moth, or why magnolias do not grow on Cape Charlotte.

We tore out the dumbwaiter and in its place installed the elevator with space for one only! *My space.* With a push of a button I rise like Venus to the second floor, the wrought-iron gates part silently and voilà! I am in my bedroom. (I appropriated the salon. I like a lot of space to wheel back and forth. I think well while wheeling!)

Now — my other addition. When I was little I always wanted a place to escape to. I tried to persuade Daddy to add a turret so I could be a princess in a tower room, but he thought my heart's desire silly. I can hear Daddy growling, but I ignore him. A 21st-century aerie has been created! And my elevator soars upward to it. Oh, Meg, it is fantastic! Three walls are glass, several layers' worth. I behold a luminescent sea, white breakers, two lighthouses bravely beaming, and the Lightship sending a comforting steady signal, miles out.

I am on top of the world! I'm above everything, including Porpoise Light. In daylight, I can see forever in three directions. I am perched on the edge, hanging in space. Poised over the rocks and reefs, I can almost spit on Snaggletooth. I *can* spit in the surf.

The wind up here screams and I love it. Pudge came up once and went right down. Hates heights. Hates surf. Hates the ocean. Hates the foghorn. Hates the lighthouse. Hates anything that isn't anchored to the ground. His idea of comfort is to spend his life within a three-block area of the Common. Snob!

Love,
Buffy

P.S. How could I forget to mention my "E." Well, *our* "E." We, the Yard, join an exclusive club which normally I would *not* join. I do not believe in exclusivity. Nice word, that. Elitist clubs are anathemas — hangouts for insecure types. The "E," my sweet, is for EXCELLENCE. Awarded by the government for a job well done, no, extremely well done! We have a marvelous large flag with an "E" emblazoned thereupon. We fly it high and proudly.

P.P.S. Paris is free of vermin! Hope they all are exterminated — those louses — and bloody soon!

OCTOBER

Meg,

I'm up in my aerie and dawn is just breaking and the waves are smashing and I'm pounding away.

Thought I'd give you a taste. There's this tall dark mysterious man with curly dark hair and dark eyes, pools of lust. He lives in a dark gloomy house. He has a dark past, and goes out on strange outings with his dark hound in the dark of night, dressed in dark velvet. He broods and scowls, darkly. Generally, he is dark and dangerous — absolutely fascinating.

How do you like it so far?

The first sentence is the key to the whole thing. One just came. How about: "It was dark and . . ." No?

How about changing the whole color scheme? "It was a gray and beastly afternoon." What? OK. Both go. I'll begin anew.

Bye!
Buffy

BORMANN
BERLIN
OCTOBER

Schmidt!

Having received your umpteenth memo on the difficulty of obtaining *one* Jew who happens to cut diamonds, I belted two secretaries. Usually I only whack their rumps! Being so damn busy — I work like a draft horse bearing everybody's burdens, and my own — I never let off steam. Sixteen hours a day do I labor. If I hadn't been so exhausted, I damn well would have marched into Amt III and throttled you right in your own office!

But you redeem yourself just in time. You've got him, yes? Nicely ensconced, surrounded by protective wire. And the diamonds pour in for him to play with. So — Willi. Have you someone there to make sure he keeps his nose to the grindstone? I don't want our Jew to think he is really one of the "chosen people." He's "chosen" only by us and he's to *work* for a living. "Work makes you free." The slogan of the camps, prominently displayed upon entering. What a joke. It can't have been Himmler's. He hasn't laughed, truly laughed, since he was tickled as a brat!

It's been hell around here for the months since the Second Front and the dastardly attack on the Führer's life at Rastenberg. I was there at the Wolfsschance when it happened and the Führer emerged, black with soot, his clothes hanging in shreds. By all rights, he should have been mangled by the blast in a concrete bunker without windows. But a true miracle occurred and He was saved. He is watched over by ancient gods. The Gods of War!

The "Officers' Plot" failed miserably and we are again on a winning course, freed from the machinations of traitors.

The high and mighty — The Admiral (I am speaking of Canaris, that son of a bitch who was implicated and who will die — DIE. Who told you first he was not to be trusted?!). The generals are dead!

Beck and Stülpnagel tried hard to shoot themselves and failed miserably. It took Beck two times — in the head! — and still he couldn't manage it. Rommel was given a choice. The coward took poison. Eight other officers, stripped of their uniforms and wearing oversized trousers (with no belts! A nice touch, that. Demeaning) were brought before the tribunal and then executed slowly. Meathooks and piano wire. Nasty combination. Their frenzied twitchings were filmed. The Führer loved the movie!

All in all, there are 5000 less godless traitors around now.

Suddenly there is a new spirit here. Things are moving — perhaps westward? Late next month, or perhaps December? Let's say I wouldn't take a shooting vacation in the Ardennes then, Willi. There may be a surplus of hunters around.

Of course, I have to be prepared for any contingency and I have prepared the children well. They blab to their schoolmates that just in case, all of us will fly off to Japan and safety. What shit! I wouldn't live with those slant-eyes even if they made me Emperor!

Bormann

HANNES
BERLIN
OCTOBER

My night ride from Lyon ended in disaster. I did not die.

In the darkness, with only the headlight, the narrow road, slick from the summer rain, seemed to be a ribbon of black ice. I skated on it. I flew and swerved and could not skid. The cycle held the pavement, machine outwitting man. The lines of trees rushed by, tall and tapered, all alike, an endless row of them. Far ahead, I picked my spot. The cycle charged, gunned to the limit. And as it smashed the tree, I prayed for death.

I have not written for many months. For many months I did not care. I still do not care. The head healed slowly; the fractures bound together. But there are wounds that will never heal. She does not leave me.

I'm nearly mended, according to my doctors, who pride themselves on their great accomplishment: reconstructing a head. I want to tell them to erase the memories. But that they cannot do.

* * *

It seems I am fit for service. Somewhere. Sometime, someone will come and announce the "somewhere." And I will go and perform again. I can perform, sleepwalking. And that may be my state.

My orders are here. I am to be part of an operation not yet formed, but one which has potential. I see Skorzeny today.

Colonel Skorzeny: SS Kommando. Rescuer of Mussolini. Doer of the impossible.

An offensive of mammoth proportions is in the works! Designed to drive the Allied forces back to the Channel, into the Channel. A surprise offensive which may just overwhelm them.

And my role? Help to organize Operation Greif. The griffin is a mythical winged beast, part eagle, part lion. Is this operation only fantasy?

FRIEDENTHAL, GERMANY
NOVEMBER

Operation Griffin may never get off the ground! Not with what we have to work with!

I was chosen partly for my war record, but mainly because of fluency in English. American-English.

What a motley group! All volunteers. All supposedly fluent. All *curds!* Where is the cream? In all the Reich are these the best they can assemble? If so, we will fail in seconds.

Jesus! I am supposed to turn these turds into American GIs! Capable of fooling the real McCoy. Most have one English word in their repertoire, and that is "Yesssss!" The hiss has got to go — or I shall order them all to be deaf-mutes!

I can't understand *why* this bloody operation is so poorly manned! The Führer approved it wholeheartedly! Those that *can* speak a bit of English think all GIs talk like gangsters.

I am retrieving all I can from days so far back, I'm not sure I remember. The recruits say my American is fine. No German accent. How the hell would they know?

What do Americans talk of these days? Probably what German soldiers talk of — women, home, food. And sports! God, yes. Americans live for sports! Baseball: I remember the Cubs — from Chicago — who always lost!

Who are the stars of the latest movies? What are the plots of recent ones? We haven't seen any recent movies!

Food: Apple pie, that's American. And hot dogs. But I am not an expert on hot dogs. I ate only two in my 16 years as an exile in America. And those were in New York, just before the boat sailed. I remember two limp fingers in wet rolls.

The Stalags are the places to gather information. POW chatter would be useful. But we have little time.

I tried today. Teaching them just one sentence, short and sweet. Ask a GI for a cigarette: "Got a butt, buddy?" It comes back to me: "I say, Butt, a Buddy, if you please"!!

EMMA
CAPE CHARLOTTE
AUGUST

I went over to Amy's house yesterday to borrow one of her Nancy Drews. The latest one. I get to read it when she's finished, IF she's talking to me. When I know she's in the middle of one, I try to act extra nice, which is *hard.* I told Mummy what I did and she said the word was "hypocrite." Well, people who *aren't* hypocrites don't get to read the latest Nancy Drew. I can't be perfect all the time!

I hate to go to Amy's house. The worst part is the library. Besides the fact that it isn't one, because there aren't any books, are the heads of two deer. Mr. Brewster shot them. One is a stag and one is a doe. I know they are dead and stuffed. I know that their eyes are glass, but there they hang, one above the fireplace and the other across the room. Honestly, they seem to be staring at each other and their eyes are sad. They look like they'd like to rub noses once more and they can't, ever again.

The Fleet's come in! And it was some parade! Not everybody can watch a parade like this from their front porch. A front row seat! They came in early, just as the sun rose. Daddy woke me up to see. They just kept coming. First the minesweepers, the frigates, and the destroyers. Then three big ones — cruisers, I think — light or heavy. Next to last, a battleship. But the last — Jeesum! An aircraft carrier. The *Yorktown*? We don't know. It was a sight I won't forget. They were strung out all the way to the horizon. Mummy sat right down and wrote a poem (she is always writing). The poem said that the parade was a bridal procession and which ship was which person. I can't remember all of it, but the destroyers were the ushers, the minesweepers were the flower girls, and the bride naturally was the aircraft carrier. I think the mother of the bride was the PBY that buzzed around overhead, but I'm not sure. I like the poem. Mummy says, "Lousy metaphor!"

Paris is free! Everybody is crying and they haven't even *been* there. I know all the words to "The Last Time I Saw Paris." I can even make the taxi beeps!

I met an awfully nice boy down on the beach today. He's a lot older than I am — almost four years. He is going to be a SENIOR! His name is Peter Trefethen and his father is a fisherman. His mother does what all mothers do. She cooks and cleans house. Peter doesn't have any brothers or sisters, either! Sometimes Peter helps his father and goes out on the dragger or mends nets or paints the boat. He can't go out to sea during school because the fishing fleet stays away, sometimes two weeks. I really met Peter because this crazy dog came bouncing along and knocked me over and started to lick my skin off. It turns out the nutty dog is Peter's and he was walking him, which he is allowed to do if he's done his chores. The dog's name is Apricot and he's a Chesapeake Bay Retriever, which Peter told me is an expensive dog, but there was a runt in the litter and some nice man gave him to Peter. Now a Chesapeake Bay is *not* apricot color. It's a dirty peachy color, so I asked how come Apricot? Peter told me that one night they were having canned apricots for dessert and the dog stood up on his hind legs and slurped up *every* apricot in the bowl! I told you he was a crazy dog!

I saw Peter today. We threw sticks for Apricot and he brought them back — almost every time. Once in a while he was bad and went the other way with them. Peter is very nice!

I didn't see Peter today. I waited and waited on the beach, but I guess he had something else to do. School starts in a week. Poop! I'll be in eighth grade. We had baked beans and fishballs for dinner. We always have baked beans and fishballs on Saturday nights. I'm glad I like them!

I'm going to wait on the knoll under my juniper. It's higher up there than on the beach. The beach has too many rocks and stones and my bottom gets sore if I sit down too long. Besides, I can see a longer way from the knoll. I can see Apricot coming, and Peter — if he ever comes back again.

SEPTEMBER

Peter came back on the beach even though school's started! And today we put up a Tarzan swing. The fathers did most of it. Mr. Thurston, who's a tall man, sort of quiet, got us an enormously long rope from the wharf. It's thick as my wrist, which isn't too big for a wrist, but it's big for a rope.

The men climbed up high in an oak tree back of Amy's house and made sure it was tied tight to a branch. Peter showed them a bowline. Daddy thought Peter was very helpful and *very nice!* The other end of the rope is tied around a stick. You climb into a notch of the tree with the stick and put it under your bottom and then grab the rope for dear life. Whoosh! Out you go! Screeching like Tarzan and *flying!*

In a year I will be in ninth grade in HIGH SCHOOL in a building that's just a school! I've been forever in this place that has four grades in three rooms in the top of the Town Hall!

Next year think of all the things I'll have which I have never had! I'll have a locker, and a home room, and Phys. Ed. and a hot lunch in a *Cafeteria* so I won't have to take my lunchbox anymore. We won't have to eat at our desks, which is very good since now most of my lunch seems to end up *in* my desk. Drops in all by itself. If there's an awful smell, Miss Munroe always pulls up the top of my desk first.

Recess is so dumb! We go out and do nothing. There's nothing to do, that's why! The Town Hall sits on a lot of dirt. Sometimes we play catch with a stone or hang upside down on the railings near the big door where the Fire Engine comes out. When it pours we walk in the hall, which is old and dark. If we can find a squeaky board we bounce up and down on it. It's very boring!

Downstairs beside the Fire Engine is the Town Clerk's Office. I don't know what she does exactly. Then there is a big old smelly room they use for Town Meeting. Miss Butterfield took us last year and said we were watching democracy. Well, I was watching a lot of people get up and holler.

Next door is the Chief of Police, but he isn't there very often. He is our only policeman, but we call him Chief because he likes it. Usually he's a garbageman.

Next year I'm taking Latin and Algebra and Civics and General Science. And I think we will read *Ivanhoe.* Every subject is in its own room. We will move from room to room!

I wish Peter wasn't a SENIOR now!

Peter's been coming pretty regularly to the beach with Apricot. We throw sticks and we talk about all sorts of things — school, animals, the beach, the War. But I think there's a big part of him that he doesn't talk about.

Today Peter and I walked along the beach looking. After a storm, which we had the other day, you can find all sorts of things. A lot of big logs washed up and Peter said they were timbers from a ship that had been wrecked or torpedoed. They had big rusty spikes sticking out and I was very careful. I've had too many holes in my sneakers and my feet!

We found a greasy piece of paper about lifeboats and how to survive in the sea. I couldn't make out all of it. I hope it just fell overboard. I hope it didn't come from a lifeboat in the middle of the ocean.

Peter brought along a map of the coast around here and gave it to me. He said if I lived on the coast I ought to know the names of all the coves and reefs and ledges and islands. So I'm going to study hard and then I'm going to make a map with my own special places on it.

I decided to show him my secret cave. He thought it was neat and promised never to tell a living soul about it. I even took out my treasures. He liked the silver seal best. He'll be 17 very soon. He's the only person I have told about my cave. Even Mummy and Daddy don't know.

I have a new kitty! I miss Tortoise who died. Tortoise was the nicest cat. I think I told about him and the chipmunk. Well, he got old and one day he just didn't get up. We buried him down under a little juniper — not the one I sit under, but a nice one. And we made a marker that said,

"TORTOISE"
A good cat.

My new kitty isn't Tortoise. He's very different! He's all black and shiny and lively and slippery and knocks things down. Then he sits on the floor and looks up at me and says, "Who Me?" So that's his name. He doesn't have a cat's voice. Mummy says he sounds like a banshee. I think his meow is more like a crow's squawk. He follows me all over the beach, yowling. Wait till he meets Apricot!

Who Me sleeps in my bed now, because he shrieked all night that he was lonesome in the kitchen. He sleeps on my head and treads his claws in my hair. Sometimes, when he's really feeling cozy, he sucks a piece of my hair and purrs like a motorcycle. I couldn't live very long without a kitty!

Yesterday was Peter's 17th birthday! And today when he came on the beach I gave him a present all wrapped up. All I could find was some Christmas paper. Thank heavens, Mummy saves every scrap. Some of the paper has been going for years. I don't think Peter minded having Santa Claus pictures on a birthday present because it was the little silver seal out of driftwood. He was very pleased and he *hugged* me! Then he told me that a lobsterman who is a friend of his father's had quite a scare yesterday. He was out hauling pots, which can be very dangerous because your feet can get tangled up in the rope, and you can fall overboard and drown because there's nobody to hear you screaming.

Well, he was pulling in some pots and suddenly the boat was clear out of the water. Just high and dry. At first he thought he was sitting on a huge rock, which he was pretty sure shouldn't be there, but before he could think anymore the ROCK MOVED. It moved sort of slowly and the boat went right along on top. And then the rock sank a little and disappeared, and the boat was back sitting in the water. And then, in a minute or two, an enormous humpback blew off the starboard side and did tricks like jumping out of the water and belly-flopping. The whale made all kinds of circles around the boat, whistling and such, but it didn't try to hurt the boat at all. I think it did tricks because it was embarrassed, scaring the lobsterman.

I forgot to talk about the pins. Mummy has a big map of Europe and every school morning we listen to the War news and then Mummy moves the pins, if anything happens like a big battle. The Germans are red and the Russians are white. Mummy says that the Russians are really red, but the Germans already had those pins. We are green. For a long time the only pins that moved were red. They moved all over. But now the white pins are running, gobbling up the red pins on one side, and our green pins are doing the same on the other side. It's easier to think about War with pins.

This morning after the news Mummy moved some white pins to Belgrade in Yugoslavia. The Russians have taken it back. I always eat my breakfast fast, because when the radio plays the "Muskrat Ramble" after the news, it's time to run, not ramble. (Ha!) But today he forgot to play it so I kept on eating — and I missed the bus!!

I told Peter I liked his new mackinaw, which is a *very* bright yellow plaid. And he said thank you as though he was surprised that I liked it. But he was pleased, I could tell.

I looked up the plaid in our book of tartans. We have it because both Mummy and Daddy are very proud that their ancestors came from Scotland. Now I can tell Peter that his mackinaw is the Barclay Dress plaid.

Peter was on Kala Nag rock, so I ran along the beach to meet him, but I tripped because my dungarees are too long and my boots are too big. My dungarees are sailor pants because they have bell-bottoms and they belonged to a brother of Susan's. She can't wear them because she has hips. But I don't. Neither do sailors, I guess. Somebody told me the Navy would be furious if they knew a girl was wearing their pants. But what they don't know won't hurt them!

Anyway, the bell-bottoms are always tangling up in my boots, which were Mummy's. They are Bean's hunting shoes (which are really boots!). So, when I got untangled, I told Peter the name of his plaid and he said he felt better about the mackinaw, which his mother had made out of a heavy horse blanket. He didn't want to wear it because it was so bright — not quiet red and black checks. But he didn't want to hurt her feelings. And now that I liked it, he'd wear it all the time. That made me feel good and funny all at the same time, and Peter didn't even mention that I tripped and fell flat!

Peter has brown hair that's not straight and not curly. He has eyes that are gray or blue or green depending on what the sea color is. He's *much* taller than I am. Practically the only boy who is! And he smiles and is nice and he talks to me and doesn't make me feel I'm too little.

BORMANN
BERLIN
DECEMBER

Soon, Schmidt — soon — the forest maneuvers which could turn out to be more than puny war games! That's for sure!

On another topic dear to my heart. I had a recent conversation with a gemologist, certified. Inserted the right questions in a bored, lackadaisical manner and got glittering, gleaming — most *stimulating* answers.

Dwell on the following: A small matchboxful of 1 carat *flawless* diamonds is worth several *million* Reichsmarks. The amount, naturally, depends on the grade of the stones, the market and the means of disposal. I am not fool enough to believe that all our stones will be tops — but think, Schmidt! if one matchboxful is worth even a million, what would a kilo of stones bring? Portability, dear Willi. Portability! Imagine: millions upon millions of paper currency reduced to that which can be carried, unseen, on the person of one man!

Which brings me to your idea — on which I shall expand. Up to now you have been using SS camp guards to provide us with stones. Scratch them. I have a better plan.

Had a conversation with Himmler in which he was expounding on the efficiency of the camps, a topic close to his heart, of which you are aware — of which *I* am always aware — since he has little else to gab about. This time, however, his efficiency report was not of extermination but rather the ingenious method of policing the prisoners. Even in the largest camps — Auschwitz-Birkenau — the number of SS is minimal. Perhaps 3000 at most. Because — much of the labor is done by thugs called Kapos. They run things and do the dirty work. They are cocks of the walk until their number comes up — which it always does — eventually.

So bypass the SS. Bribe the Kapos. And use currency. I am swimming in currency. The royalties from the Führer's portrait on postage stamps are flowing in, flooding me! To keep from drowning in Reichsmarks, I *must* siphon off the overflow.

Therefore — what to do with all this currency? The answer is, of course, EXCHANGE it.

Pay the Kapos in Reichsmarks. And in exchange, they are to hand over to your people *all* the diamonds they can twist off, cut off, hide, hoard, swallow. Walking that tightrope — one slip to death — will make the scum fight like the savages they are for the honor of providing us with an excellent exchange rate. Enough Reichsmarks buy protection — even life.

Tidy, eh? Multiply the output of stones flowing down our pipe by twenty, even ten camps and there'll be a hell of a lot of homeless matches!

I want a favorable report on this — soonest!

Bormann

P.S. I repeat an earlier order, just in case you have lost it in that cavern you call a mind! Not all the stones go with our yet-to-be-chosen courier! I want a delectable selection delivered to me, personally. Let's say, 500 grams. And not over two carats. To dribble through my fingers. To play with.

Just filtered in — lousy news! That son of a bitch cow is stopping the gassing! At least in some of the camps! Get the stones!

Next thing you know, Uncle Heinrich will open the gates and a million skeletons will roam the Reich! Dirty coward!

Get *cracking!* Bring me fingers if you have to!

IZAAK
STUTTHOF
DECEMBER

At last I have paper. And the stub of a pencil. They expected me to draw designs in the air? It took several weeks, but what can you expect from such meticulous types? The request for paper caused a furor. A prisoner asking? Not begging? Upset the entire order of things. The pencil took longer. Find your own ink! Now, I could have slashed my finger and finger-painted. But I have bled for them too long. And I have little blood left. Slops do not build up the corpuscles. Today, a stub arrived, the only solid piece of material in my soup plate. But no matter. I have it, and *that's* what matters.

I do as they ask. Design the facets. Polish the stones.

But this I could do in my head. I see the finished gem before I even begin.

The writing materials are for another purpose. I start a chronicle. So much to remember, so much to say. My writing resembles that of a schoolboy, cramped and sloping. I waste paper on unimportant observations!

Where to hide this chronicle. This record of existence. My tiny room, in a drafty annex, was not built with secret niches. The SS would frown upon one of their inmates recording the days. Is it my great ego that impels me to write? Probably. But is it such a terrible sin of pride to want to leave behind — something — tangible? I am a foolish old man to even hope for this, for the boards of the bunk will rot. And somewhere under the weight of decaying wood, a packet of paper will curl in the damp, and rot too. So be it.

I am Izaak Broekman, Jew, diamond polisher, formerly of Amsterdam, and more recently a reluctant transient. I know the guest quarters of Westerbork in Holland, Bergen-Belsen in Germany, and, at the moment, Stutthof on the Baltic.

I prefer my own bed in Amsterdam.

My means of conveyance from one camp to another was not my first choice. I would have preferred the Calais Coach. Cattle cars are for cattle. The coaches had no amenities. Lacking seats, we stood. Lacking windows, we breathed each other's air, which grew fouler day by day. Lacking heat, we froze. Lacking food and water, we died. The dead were not laid out with dignity. They stayed upright, stiffening into logs. There was no room on the floor for the dead. There was no room for the living.

It was May of 1943 when the raid came. We knew it was only a matter of time, and when the SS finally rousted us out of the cutting rooms, the roundup came, perversely, almost as relief. We knew it had to come. For three years we had lived, seeing the ax teeter. Lived quietly, oh so quietly, trying not to be noticed. Always wearing the yellow star. On time to work. The only sound, that of wheels humming. Walking the streets to home, eyes down. Walking to home rapidly — but not too rapidly. Home and alive and free — for another day.

Westerbork: Holland, my Holland had its own camp. What is the world coming to? Then we were moved to a much larger facility: Bergen-Belsen. Spacious it was. Comfortable it wasn't. But we worked. Our wheels followed us. So did the diamonds. In work there was forgetfulness.

Slowly, my circle of friends shrank. One day they were working; the next morning they were gone. We were told how "valuable" we were. Valuable for the skills we possessed. So why did they take my friends?

Rumor had it — we fed on rumor — that a large group of Jewish diamond workers was supposed to be transferred to Bergen-Belsen. They did not arrive. Our reliable source informed us that the group had been rerouted "accidentally" to that place in Poland — Auschwitz.

I was singled out. Left Bergen-Belsen for where? Why me? The trip was long and uncomfortable. At the termination, I knew I had reached the sea. The smell of salt air. A resort, perhaps? This place does not deserve one star. I shall not recommend it to my friends.

I now reside in Stutthof. My place of dwelling has no number on the door. To find me, travel to Poland's Baltic Sea. Look for Danzig and then turn east. After thirty-odd kilometers, you will run into barbed wire. Notice the housing: a number of long, low buildings, one after the other. They all look alike. The architecture here lacks creative flair.

The Baltic air is harsh, harsher than the Zuiderzee — or perhaps I am a bit weaker. For it is winter. It is always winter here.

I want to think of home. After winter comes the spring. At home. Spring bursting out in the fields with such colors that even the finest painters cannot capture the essence. Think of colors: purple iris, celadon sea, scarlet tulips, golden ripples on the canals. Remember gabled houses, old and quaint, secure in their age, providing security for generations. But the locks gave way to rifle butts. Don't think of this!

Hetty's eyes were blue, so blue that people on the street stared at them in wonder. I called them "my sapphires" and she said all I did was think of stones! The two of us — just the two of us. She screamed for me when she was pushed into the transport. "Izaak!" she screamed, and I tried to climb up and was beaten back. It was not yet my time. She called for help, and I couldn't save her. Hetty, who used to wrap her arms around me, rocking me like a child. We clung together so often, laughing and loving. Ah, Hetty, if you live — somewhere — I would know and fight to live also. But there is no will, for you are dead.

They can't seem to make up their minds whether to starve me or bloat me. Yesterday I had the usual slop. Today the stew was rich, with brown gravy, potatoes and turnips — and large pieces of marvelously greasy meat. Pork. Jew bait.

I shall not enlighten them on my religious preferences, or rather the lack of them. I shall not announce that I am no Zealot with a Masada complex; that I renounced the Great Jehovah long ago, along with all the trappings: the shawls, the ambiguous Talmud, the dietary laws, so outdated. Religion is no comfort. It is slop! The Great Jehovah tortured Job. Now he revels in torturing all us Jobs.

It is now becoming very clear why I am kept in solitude. I do clandestine work. Unauthorized work. Someone very greedy, perhaps very high up, wants his private diamond polisher. I see no one except my keeper, the guard who escorts me to the workroom and back — and his superior: the one who checks the progress, who counts the stones and makes notations. He counts carefully to make sure I have not swallowed some.

I know little of what transpires at this camp except what I see when I am prodded to and from work. There do seem to be a disproportionate number of women here. At least, I think they are women. All camp inmates look alike. They have the same stare, and the outlines of the skull are quite visible.

My workroom is across the compound, bolted and padlocked. I would think that all that iron would pique the curiosity of the Kapos and the lower-echelon SS.

The working conditions are not ideal. The generator goes dead at odd moments, shutting off my wheel. I would prefer to move it by treadle, if I had the strength. But with the loss of power goes my lamp, the lone light they have allowed me. There is a window, almost a skylight, high up, higher than I can reach even standing on my chair, but it is grimy, and little light comes in. I have asked repeatedly that it be cleaned, but no one bothers to.

If there is heat here, it doesn't touch me. Probably whatever there is rises to warm the flies in the eaves.

It is exceedingly difficult to facet a diamond when you can barely see it. I shall probably chip some. These stones are good. Better than good. They are extra fine. A fortune in diamonds I am working on here.

I used to pride myself that I could find the soul of any diamond deep within the lump of grayish matrix. Now I know they have no soul. They are only lumps with which to barter — barter for the souls of men. Catalysts of murder.

Well, Izaak, you are still alive. Passably. The hair has come out in clumps now, and you've spit out some teeth, but you're hanging on.

For what? To please your masters, that's what. You do your expert work as though you were still in Amsterdam. "Polisher." Sounds like a jeweler with a chamois. But once it meant "cutter extraordinaire." The one who really fashioned the stone that had been crudely begun. But you were *more* than a polisher. You could take a small mass of mineral that even a child would toss away, and transform that stone into a gem worthy of a maharajah. You were the anomaly. You could mark and groove and cleave on the plane. You could girdle on the dop and facet exactly. You could do it all. You *were* the best!

You are not in Amsterdam, you egotistical fool! You are in a hole called Stutthof and you are working feverishly for filth!

The floor of my room is au naturel, which is to say "earthen." The walls are pine — rough boards which have been pile-driven, it appears, into said earth. One wall is a partition, adjacent to the office of the guards. Sometimes I can hear their voices, but so far I have not tried. The German language offends me.

I tried to think of home today. I tried to live out one whole day in Amsterdam. I thought of my Hetty. I thought of Puccini at the opera. I thought of my brothers, my comrades, and the time we had at the café. I thought of food and love and fellowship and kindnesses, and then I grew sick and cried. I thought of all the things in life I have not done and will never do. The books to be read, the songs to be sung. What a waste one makes of life. Even when we are middle-aged and we are dying, all of us, how many million minutes do we let go, wasted?

I have a visitor! A visitor as cold as I. As hungry as I. And, I confess, as frightened as I. It seeks protection! What can I give you, little brown mouse, who squeezed through a crack no wider than an eyelash? Crumbs from a torn gray loaf? Warmth? My body gives off little heat, but you are welcome to share it. A bed? Make a nest in the pallet, but please do not chew the papers hidden therein. I have not finished my chronicle.

Brown Mouse has decided to stay. She (I am assuming, of course) runs up my trouser leg and sits in my lap. She knows I cannot resist the twitching whiskers. I offer crumbs in my palm, and she makes herself at home there, devouring every particle, but neatly. Then she does a bit of washing, a bit of scratching, and wiggles her nose like a tiny rabbit. I stroke her and she shudders once, and then relaxes. I believe I shall adopt her. She deserves all my care.

I have noticed a small flaw in the pine paneling. When one has no windows, one tends to stare at the walls. In this rustic annex there is one knot in the board — that is loose! It could be a window on the world if I were to push it. But doing so from the inside will cause the round knot to fall outside. I must devise a way to pull it inward.

Brown Mouse *is* a lady. And a mother! My straw pallet is now a nursery. I feel like the papa and cannot in all honesty say that my children are handsome. Truthfully, they are pink embryos, rather ugly, squirming things. But Brown Mouse seems to feel maternal, so I will follow her example and try to love them also.

HANNES
NEAR THE BELGIAN BORDER
DECEMBER

We go soon to infiltrate, disrupt. But we are not ready! So well equipped are we! We have:

Two dozen American Jeeps.

A few U.S. trucks.

Some German Fords painted American shit color.

The large shipment of captured American field jackets was returned — with oaths! Each now had a very visible POW triangle on the back!

We have *no* ammunition for captured American field artillery and only *half* the brigade has American rifles.

We own exactly two Sherman tanks. The rest are German Panthers, hastily camouflaged. Skorzeny is most positive on this aspect. Says they might *fool very young Americans — seeing them very far away — at night!*

I shall operate on my own. And take the best that I can scrounge.

The plan: The Panzers will drive a wedge through the Ardennes and split the British and American Armies. Then on to Antwerp and the sea. Our brigade, such as it is, will follow on the heels of the armor, spreading confusion, blowing up bridges and ammo dumps, cutting telephone wires, switching road signs, snarling up troop movements, harassing — and generally raising havoc. God help those in the brigade who open their mouths!

I sit and write in this eerie, predawn light. We wait in the woods for the signal. This time there is armor ahead of us. A massive war machine, shrouded in tatters of fog, seems to groan and grumble with impatience. Panthers and Tigers, about to be uncaged, strain to be let loose. This is like the old days! And the commander of the Sixth Panzer Army is Sepp Dietrich, once *my* commander. We are all here. The Leibstandarte SS. All of us. I feel a new spirit. I am starting out again not fifty miles from where I was born!

Dawn is about to break. It is ghostly here, and weird, this waiting in the woods. All is hushed now, even the throb of the engines is muffled by the cloak of fog.

It comes. The signal! A barrage of fire to split the eardrums! We move! And historians will say that at 5 AM, on the morning of 16 December, a massive counterattack was launched from the forest of the Ardennes — an offensive that broke the backs and the spirit of the invader!

God! The Tigers are monsters. 70 tons. Too heavy. Too slow! The roads are clogged, almost impassible. The roads were not built for tanks this size and the continual thaw bogs them down, mired in mud. Yet we push the enemy back!

Fuel! We are desperate for fuel. If we had enough we could plow to the sea! The fog is a blessing and a curse. Night attacks, shrouded in fog. Visibility nearly zero. Allied air force grounded. No air strikes.

The snow decays; clouds of steam rise. And muck is left. I have lived in muck for years!

Peiper, that arrogant son of a bitch, commands a battle group which includes the Leibstandarte Panzer. I, who was with them from their inception in the Waffen SS, who remembers the hell we had even *getting* transport, watch Peiper race for the Meuse with *two hundred* Panthers!

My small kommando group has acquitted itself well. We have been living off the land and our wits for almost ten days now — behind enemy lines — with no backup!

We laid a number of mines and blew up one small ammo dump. Could not liberate any fuel tanks. But the greatest coup occurred early on. We ran smack into two American companies. I screamed that they (and we!) were almost isolated by the "Krauts" who were advancing on both sides. They bought my story and withdrew in panic!

Ran into enemy fire and my second-in-command shot. Drove hellbent for Peiper's group and have just reached the German lines. It is Christmas Eve.

Peiper, with your medals flashing! Where were you, Peiper, while I was battling in Russia? You get the Cross of Merit. And I? What do I have? Another job well done. Skorzeny had better come through for me this time!

The Battle of the Ardennes is over. Finished. Kaput. The great counteroffensive fizzled when the sun came out. What happens next? What do we have left to make a happening?

EMMA
CAPE CHARLOTTE
NOVEMBER

This is the time my sinuses begin to act up. Today they started and really hurt and I am running a temperature and I feel crappy and *crabby!* Breathing in a cold breeze is like eating vanilla ice cream when you have a big cavity in your tooth! Sometimes I think the bones in my face will burst, they hurt so. They throb harder than my heart.

Mummy says dogs don't get sinuses because their heads hang down and they drip naturally. So I'm spending a lot of time sniffing in Vick's and steam, and a lot more time crouching in a doggie position.

My sinuses are a little better and the sun was out today, so I went down on the beach and waited and waited for Peter. He didn't come. I kept hoping I'd spot that yellow mackinaw, but I didn't. Maybe he has to help his father.

Anyway, it was dead low tide, so I hopped along the narrow path of shale that's uncovered when the sea is out, and I climbed Kala Nag, which is my favorite rock and looks like an elephant in *The*

Jungle Book, so that's its name. Sitting on top of him is like sitting in the prow of a ship, because the waves swirl in and then part on each side, and you really feel like you're sailing. Today I forgot to wait until the last second before the path gets covered and I can scoot back to the beach. I got interested in a black thing that was bobbing up and down. It looked like a porcupine. I wondered if it was a mine, all bristly with detonators. I think I got hypnotized watching it and wondering, because when I looked back, the beach path was all covered with deep water! I was stuck there for *hours* and I got a little sunburn on my face, which may help the sinuses, but won't help me if Daddy and Mummy find out. I didn't get caught in the clutches of the undertow and nothing blew up, so I think I won't mention it.

President Roosevelt beat Dewey last night. I'm glad. I would hate to have Dewey as president because he looks like a minister and not a president. He reminds me of Mr. Davey, who teaches us religious education. Mummy voted for Norman Thomas again.

Peter told me a secret and I won't tell except here. I think his father knows, but nobody else. Peter is building a hut. He's building it out at the end of the channel on an island called Pig's Knuckle, which is almost in the wide-open ocean!

On nice days when he can get away, he fills the dory with scrap lumber and other stuff and rows to the island, which is about a mile out from his beach. He lives near Fort MacAllister. He says bit by bit he's going to have a nice hut where he can go all by himself when he wants to think. I know what he means. It's nice to have a special place that's all yours and nobody else's to think in. I wish he liked my juniper tree instead of an old island way off. I'd give him half of the juniper tree!

I've only been to one island on the other side of the channel and that's the big one, Bottlenose. Peter says someday when the hut's all finished he'll row me out there to see his island. But first he's got to get me to stop being scared of boats!! And that's going to take a lot of doing!! The currents are wicked around here and I hate boats!!!

Peter started to build his hut about two years ago and the Coast Guard ignored him, so he thinks they don't really care, although Pig's Knuckle belongs to the government. I guess as long as he doesn't show a light at night, it's OK. At the moment he's looking for long metal spikes — big things that he can drive down into the rock so he can tie ropes to them and then the corners of the hut. To hold it tight so it won't take off in big storms and high winds.

I looked for Pig's Knuckle with the binoculars before it got dark. I think I found it, but it looked just like a little lump. A little lump all green with lichen. Sort of alone in a great big sea. But he likes it.

DECEMBER

I hope when Apricot gets older he'll still need to run, because if he doesn't, maybe Peter won't come so far along the beach! It's funny but I don't remember him on the school bus, and he takes it most every day. But of course grade school kids don't talk to SENIORS and SENIORS don't ever notice kids! Particularly on the bus. Maybe that's why he talked to me on the beach. Nobody was there to see him. I hope it was more than that! I bet he thinks I'm a tomboy and I am, I guess. I can run faster than the boys and I can hit a softball a mile. But I don't want to be a tomboy forever!!

Every time I wait for Peter now I get sick to my stomach. Maybe it's the intestinal flu, but why does the bug start messing around the minute I go down to the knoll?

I AM A TEENAGER TODAY. I AM 13!!! I wish I looked 15! Braids are OK for kids, but I'm too old. And I'm not a kid!

Peter gave me a birthday present!!! A shark's tooth!! I put it in my secret cave, but I took it out again and decided to put it under my pillow. I think I'll keep it there for a while.

When I'm with Peter I talk too much. I just can't seem to stop. Amy would smile and giggle and wiggle and smile and giggle some more. I tried giggling and I sounded like a turkey gobbling. I didn't even dare to try wiggling after that.

I'm not allowed to wear makeup. Mummy says next year when I'm in high school I can wear lipstick. Lipstick is supposed to make your lips delectable and luscious, so I went into Jamesport last Saturday and bought the kind that looks pale in the tube, but when you put it on it makes your lips look nice and pink. I wore it today and when I saw Peter coming I pinched my cheeks, too. You know what he said? He said, "Tuck your shirt in."!!!

* * *

The Battle of the Bulge is what they call it. The Germans are really fighting with every tank they've got and we can't bomb them because the weather's awful. I think what the general who was surrounded with a lot of his men said when the Germans ordered him to surrender was neat — it was "NUTS!"

Daddy gave Mummy a pretty silver cigarette lighter for Christmas. You need to put some gas in it to make it go. Daddy and Mummy smoke and so do Nana and Bumpa. I won't ever!! Smoke makes me sick to my stomach, and when I was little I ate part of a cigarette and I upchucked all over the couch.

Peter sent me a Christmas card!

It's Christmas vacation and this is tonight, just before I go to sleep. I have tried a big experiment and I hope I can sleep. I put my head down on the pillow to test and every pin stuck into me. The pins are bobby pins. I have curled my whole head!! It took me almost two hours to wind little pieces of hair around my finger, but I did it. I couldn't find anything like hair set, so I mixed up some lemon jello. It seemed to be just the right stickiness and the color should make my hair a little blonder, which might look nice.

This was an *awful* day!! It was Saturday and Mummy and Daddy slept late, so I got out of bed to check my hair. I was so excited I could hardly stand it, so I pulled those pins out faster than anything. And then I looked in the mirror. And there were all those curls sitting tight against my head, but they were GREEN — really GREEN!! So I brushed and brushed and all that happened was that my hair stayed green, but now it stuck out in all directions like kinky wires!

I went down on the knoll to wait for Peter, but before I left I tied a bandanna around my head to hide everything. I never know when Peter will come, and today I kind of hoped he wouldn't, but at the same time I hoped he would, because I would hate to miss him.

Well, he came and the first thing he noticed was my bandanna. And he said right off what are you hiding and I said not much and he said come on show me. I didn't want to! So I tried to change the subject, but he laughed and pulled off the bandanna, and then he really laughed. He laughed and laughed until the tears were running down his cheeks, and then the tears began to run down mine, but I was crying, not laughing!

Well, Peter felt bad that he had made me miserable. So he apologized and said he couldn't help it, that I looked like a walking electrical charge. Well, I didn't think that was so funny either, and I swatted him and started to cry again. And then I wailed that I had done it all up to look nice for him, which I had not meant to tell. That made my face get hot and I knew I was blushing, so I went away and sat down on a rock with my back to him so he couldn't see.

Peter came over all quiet and serious and told me to keep my braids — that they made me look pretty. Which means, I guess, that he wants me to stay a little kid. I wish I knew what to do!

I washed my hair as soon as I got home. It took five shampoos, but the green is out! Lemon jello was a lousy idea!

Emma Pickering. Emma Pickering. What an ordinary name! I don't even have a middle one. And Frankie loves to make me mad and call me "Enema!" which is pretty stinking. Sometimes he yells "Enema Pickled Herring!" which is worse, and I yell back, but I haven't thought up a horrible enough name for him yet!

Peter thinks my name is nice and to stop worrying about awful nicknames. He thinks Emma Pickering has a nice ring to it. Well, it does have a ring at the end.

I like Peter an awful lot. This is the first time I have *ever ever* written this down. When Peter asked what boy I liked in my class, I couldn't say anything. I would rather die than tell him who I like. I follow him around like a puppy. I know I do and I can't help it. He must be completely dense not to know that I LOVE HIM!!

JANUARY-FEBRUARY 1945

BUFFY
CAPE CHARLOTTE
JANUARY

Meggy,

I write. I write! A novel. Don't ask me how one does a novel. I have not the faintest. I just do it, and when the characters become *people,* people I can care about — or *hate,* when they begin to do things that I have no control over, even though I have *created them,* given them *life,* then perhaps these fingers do *not* control, only obey. It's strange, eerie. And a compulsion!

Eerie in my aerie! That is *not* a title in case you were nervous.

Speaking of aeries. It needed a name, a designation of distinction. I christened it — briefly. Briefly, because "Eagle's Nest" has been usurped by that Austrian monster! For a moment I forgot. But only a moment. That beast looking toward the city I once loved: Salzburg! But I doubt I shall ever love anything Austrian again. Do you know how many of the most vicious Nazis are Austrian? Under all that baroque gold leaf is a land of full-blown anti-Semitism. And I never noticed!

So my aerie up here in the clouds will have to be content with "it" until I come up with something appropriate. Why don't you try? Imagine being above everything. Even pain. I leave that below. Imagine looking toward Spain or near there. Imagine a killer reef and surf on one side, but on the other a gently curving Bay — Half Moon. (That's where we have the Beach House. Quite private, it is. But I haven't been down there for years.) I do miss walking on the white sand and scaring seagulls. Carniverous caterwaulers! Imagine watching great thunderclouds build, or dawn break all gold and red. Imagine a whole world spread out — and above — the universe!

So name it.

Buffy

Damn! damn! damn!

That Winsor woman, that upstart! She stole my idea!

No, she didn't. Bursting bodices may make the best-seller list, but they have no class. No class *whatsoever.*

I shall persevere midst all the uproar with my well-bred heroine — intelligent, independent, not gorgeous, middling attractive and probably as flat as fried eggs. But who said tits maketh the woman?

And Amber? Lordy, Lordy. Thought the stuff was good only for imprisoning old insects.

I see Winsor doing sequels to sequels. The succeeding succulent females will include: Ruby (good name for a tart!); Sapphire (Greek chorus girl?); Opal (the milksop variety — or the one glittering with fiery depths?). How about Lapis? (blueblood with bastard streaks.) Diamond? (a girl's best friend. Now that can be taken *several* ways. Most of them unmentionable!) Pearl? Shimmering white purity layered round *grit!*

Yes, ma'am, you've guessed it. I am Jade (the green kind) with envy. But I shall best her yet. Wait and see!

I shall send you home again, Kathleen. Forever!

Buffy

BORMANN
BERLIN
JANUARY

I am in a foul mood, Schmidt! The first two weeks of January have been the worst of my life. A crappy, fucking, endless two weeks!

Just back from Führer headquarters on the Western Front. The Ardennes maneuver ended in fiasco. The Russians are massing before Warsaw and our Vengeance weapons designed to strike fear into the hearts of the British have done nothing but doodle, dropping randomly — the V-ls, that is. The damned Englanders have nicknamed them "doodlebugs." Reprisal rockets only strengthen their resolve! The V-2s with more firepower are truly *space* weapons, but we have too few, and every ramp faces west. West! When our enemy to the east threatens Silesia!

Schmidt, for shit's sake, pour it on that cocksucker Jew. Grade fast, you Yid! And whip our Kapos to four-quarter time. Flood that camp — Stutthof — with every stone that rolls down the pipe — now! Tomorrow may be too late!

At least I'm out of that bunker in the Eiler!

Bormann

Warsaw has fallen and the Führer is underground!

I tried to persuade him that he (and we!) would be safer in the Obersalzburg. I used every argument in the book and some I made up on the spur of the moment. Nothing sways him. *Nothing!* He has sunk into the bunker under the Chancellery and intends to stay there.

A stinking hole, that's what it is. Cramped and foul and the communications setup is worse than an erector set by Märklin. A child could construct a better system!

The situation demands action on my part. The dispersal of the diamonds has become FIRST PRIORITY. Diamonds can buy and sustain life, right, Schmidt? Whose life? Ask another time, Willi. A life on a continent free of Reds, that is clear.

The means to an end is with us every day. Supreme Headquarters (that's a laugh!) is crawling with brass — and I mean crawling. The corridors are so narrow in this fucking place you have to crawl around each other in order to pass.

Which leads me to Dönitz. The Admiral is in on the Führer's conferences almost daily now. Dönitz owes me one. The convoy, remember? But I won't even have to use up my IOU for this favor. I save it. Might come in handy — later.

As soon as I get the go-ahead, I'll notify you to get on the ball. Details, arrangements, etc.

Bormann

Caught Dönitz popping out after another briefing. Pinned him to the wall! "Grand Admiral," I said, "the Führer has ordered me orally" (sounds obscene, no?) "to acquire a U-boat for a secret mission of the *utmost* importance."

Now the last thing Dönitz wants to be at this stage is defeatist, right? So he says quick as a flash, "No problem. Set it up with my adjutant."

Then I corner Himmler (who's more than a little shaky right now as a general) and I say that I need one of those English-speaking SS people *his* man Skorzeny used in the Ardennes counteroffensive. Now Uncle Heinrich isn't about to quibble about this small request from me, knowing I am, of course, speaking for the Führer, so he says that *his* adjutant, Rudy Brandt, will hop to it, contact Skorzeny, and have a list for us of the best that survived Operation Greif.

The adjutants are busy and I'm cooking with possibilities!

Bormann

P.S. Speaking of possibilities. What do you know about Stalags in the U.S.? POW camps, they call them. I know that remnants of the Afrika Korps are interned there plus sissies who surrendered from the Wehrmacht. And there are tales of escapes from these camps — and what is even more intriguing, successful escapes. Seems those who break out melt into the populace — aided by citizens!

The American government which blares news of captured "spies" keeps a lid on "disappearances."

In the last month many Waffen SS have been captured by the Americans. Where are they? Find out:

1. If there are any camps in the USA *strictly* for the SS or those considered "unredeemable," shall we say?

2. If #1 is so, have there been any escapes? And where are they hiding? Because — contact with the SS *in America* could be most profitable.

Get Midas on this. But also get the word out to other contacts that there are large rewards for information about "loyal" types on the loose.

HENRY
CAPE CHARLOTTE
JANUARY

I was handed a smaller envelope this morning which did not contain filthy pictures. Instead, there was a coded message within, a rather lengthy one. Still no sign of Lowell. I will decode this evening while Evelyn bangs away up in that beastly place.

Madrid (Berlin) announces that they will be contacting me almost daily via a new method. It appears they have much to tell me. And from the almost frantic message, it would also appear there is a bit of a flap at control. I should imagine so. Berlin is taking a pasting. What luck if a blockbuster should land on the record office and wipe out the dossier on my activities! In fact, I consider this happenstance to be just that: unlikely. Pity.

No doubt all such documents are kept underground. I imagine they do have bunkers in Berlin.

* * *

I am almost finished decoding and the new form of communication is intriguing. I will be contacted by mail. Which means my treks to the grocery have been curtailed (for the present, at least). I cannot say that this is a disappointment, seeing as my taste for Italian cooking waned some time ago. In fact, I fear my stomach juices have been irrevocably damaged, as has, indeed, my palate!

Scrod, that most delectable fruit from the sea, has lost its grandeur. What was once Boston's gift to international cuisine, nay, to the world, the young and delicious codfish, has become to me only a bland, uninteresting dish. I blame my misfortune entirely on hot peppers!

I have finished the laborious task of decoding and now I perceive why an innocuous typewritten letter accompanied the message. The letter is bogus! It is camouflage! It covers a secret which cannot be discerned with the naked eye. *Under the type* is the actual message penned with invisible writing, and the instructions for reading this secret *and* for accomplishing another like it have been spelled out in coded detail.

Secret writing! As boys we used to do it with lemon juice, but as I recall, there was always a visible residue. Perhaps we did not strain out enough of the pulp.

As I have oft repeated, the simplest methods are best. After modest research, it appears that most secret writing is done with formulae — that is — some compound or mixture, paste, if you will, as the medium. But if the materials are not on hand in an emergency, then where is one?

I shall outline the procedure I am to follow. A simple procedure which produces uncanny results:

I used Evelyn's paper; she will not miss a few sheets. I soaked one piece in the kitchen sink, let it drip briefly, and then carried it to the library, where I placed it on the glass top of the desk: an exquisite example of early Hepplewhite inlaid with satinwood.

Indeed. I place the damp paper on the glass top and over it I add a new, dry sheet. Then, with a #2 Ticonderoga, I write a message on the top paper, adding just enough force so that the pressure of the writing reaches the underlying, that is to say the soaked, sheet.

The next logical step is one I fear too many illogical types fail to remember. That is: *destroy* the top sheet! Carelessness paves the way to incarceration.

Two final steps. First, dry the underpage most carefully. And then, when it is crisp as bone, type a fake letter upon it. The camouflage. Now it is ready to be sent off to the appropriate party, who will, *after immersing it in water,* watch the true message jump out boldly, jauntily! I must add a forewarning here: do not attempt to hasten the drying process by artificial means; that is to say, note carefully all gauges. The burning point of paper, as I have just discovered to my chagrin, is *451* degrees Fahrenheit.

I have been receiving mail at *home.* And all of it similar: pleading letters for a charitable donation to — of all places — The Home for Aged Seamen!

Of course, hidden beneath the sentimental supplications are messages of a less appealing nature. They wish weather data for the month of March. What nonsense! The month of March is entirely unpredictable and follows no pattern, save that much of it is foul! No one and no thing can predict the weather two months hence, not even *The Old Farmer's Almanac,* which, for some obscure reason known only to those idiots in government who seem to believe in witches and crystals, has been confiscated. Result: *The Almanac* is unavailable to the general public. Utter rot!

Also, I am ordered (the threat, still implicit) to furnish further information — namely: the list of all operating beacons and the frequency of their signals within an area 25 miles north to 25 miles south of Jamesport. And — I must peruse the latest coastal chart for any changes or discoveries made since 1940: depth of water, hidden reefs and the like.

Once I considered myself only a small cog in a mammoth machine which, by all accounts, is now grinding to a halt. Yet Berlin sees fit to use me more than ever. For reasons I cannot fathom, they place upon my shoulders some large enterprise, the details of which I am not apprised.

I ponder the implications. What grandiose scheme is being plotted? And why am I, so far away from the seat of War, involved?

I have just sent off all information, gathered, I must state, at great expense: sleep and currency. Invisible writings via Airmail Special Delivery. Addressed per order to a Mr. L. Alvirez in Arlington, Virginia. (Lowell?) Regular three-cent mail is transported rapidly. Why go to the expense of extra postage? Two deliveries a day are as sure as the sun rising.

EMMA
CAPE CHARLOTTE
JANUARY

Peter says there's a lot to be learned from the beach, even the flotsam. That's all the stuff that washes in and doesn't look too good but was once — at least some of it.

It's very cold, but I'm all bundled up. I have my ski pants on and long winter underwear! Daddy bought me a hood for Christmas like the skiers in North Conway wear. It's soft blue wool and only a little of your face shows and no hair. It certainly does keep the sea wind out.

Today I have my paper with me because I am studying barnacle colonies. They live and die on the rocks or on old wrecks and things. Barnacles are whitish and they have round rims that are very sharp. They're sort of like tiny volcanoes because there is a slit across the center and sometimes out pops a feathery plume that is the barnacle's tongue, but looks like steam from an eruption.

Nothing is happening. I rapped on the rock, but not one barnacle has stuck its tongue out at me. It's awfully cold. Maybe they hibernate until spring.

Today was Religious Education day. All the Catholic children leave when Mr. Davey comes in. I wish I could too. I wish I wasn't a Congregationalist. Sometimes I think I'll raise my hand and tell Mr. Davey I'm a Boodist and can I go too? Mr. Davey is dumb enough to believe me, but he would tell Miss Munroe, and she would *not!*

When Mr. Davey talks, he puts me to sleep. It's hot in the class and his voice is so boring! The only thing that helps is scratching my itches. I have to wear awful knee socks that Mummy makes. She knits them by the dozens. From "sheep's wool, unprocessed, rich in lanolin, warm and waterproof." That's what she keeps telling me, *all the time.* They are sure unprocessed because they are full of burrs that *bite* me! When I scratch I do it in long sweeping scratches which feels the best, but then my legs look like a barber pole.

Well, I was sort of sleeping and sort of scratching when Mr. Davey started talking about "Evil." I perked up because I thought he was going to talk about the War or the Nazis. But he didn't. Instead, his voice got a lot louder until he was practically yelling about the devil in young bodies and unhealthy appetites. I don't know where evil and the devil come in, but I do have a very healthy appetite. I eat all I can that is healthy, except cookies and Milky

Ways — and cream horns when I can get them. So — I didn't get much out of Mr. Davey today except that he can yell. The rest of the period I went back to scratching.

I am sitting under my favorite juniper tree and rubbing my back against the bark. It's rough enough to scratch nicely. I seem to do a lot of scratching. Well, so do cats, and someday, maybe I'll turn into a cat!

I'm not going to use those little diaries anymore. There just isn't enough room to write all I want to say, so I have a big notebook with lined pages and three holes like high school kids have. I spent two hours last night sticking those round white doughnuts around each paper hole so the paper won't tear out.

My house is staring at me. The shades are up. And the picture window looks like a wide-open mouth. The house looks sort of bare from the front without shutters, like Mummy does before she puts on mascara.

I don't know why we don't have shutters on the front windows. We only have them on the side people see when they drive up the road.

It's an ordinary white house, nothing fancy, sort of summer cottagy looking. Some of the paint is peeling on the seaward side and Daddy wants me to help him scrape. We are always scraping. We have never had a whole house painted new at the same time! The shutters that are up are a pretty dark peacock blue, but they're always being taken down and put to bed in the garage to be scraped and painted all over again!

There is a wide porch that runs around the three sides of the house that look to the knoll and the sea. The porch sags a bit here and there. Part of the porch has screens, the side toward the lighthouse — James Head light. In the summer I sleep out there on a cot. It gets cold at night, even in the summer except for a few nights. But when you're lying there in the dark you can hear the waves lapping and slapping. It's a nice sound and it never stops. You can also hear the foghorn, if there's a fog, which there always is in August. Last August we had *three weeks* of fog and Mummy was sure the sun had died. The foghorn at James Head light moos and then groans. Mrs. Thurston says it sounds like a moose in heat. But she didn't see the moose and I did and it didn't say *one thing!*

I was awfully glad to see Peter today because usually on weekends he works for his father mending nets and patching the dragger. That old boat has more patches than boat. Peter let Apricot run. He chased a seagull, who screamed at him. Apricot better not hurt one. He'll get fined.

We went to one of the tidepools to see what was in it. Not much. So we sat down on rock that didn't have ice on it and popped bladders. Wet seaweed is more fun to pop than the dry wrack up at the tideline. Seaweed spit comes out, and once in a while there's a really loud snap. Sometimes we'll sit by a pool and wiggle our fingers in the water. You have to wiggle fast or your fingers will fall off, it's that cold. We sit and wiggle our fingers and don't say anything. Not talking is as good as talking, sometimes.

I watched Peter go home. I can't *really* see him a mile away because the rocks and ledges stick up between each cove. But every once in a while a yellow mackinaw climbs up and over and then does it again farther away, until it is out of sight around the big bend in the shore toward James Head light and the Fort.

Next to our house is a stone wall. Daddy and some other men helped build it one summer. It was a hot day, so they drank beer. That part of the wall looks like a snake. The part they finished on a cold day is straight.

Between the house and the knoll is the lawn. Daddy likes it to look like velvet, but it usually doesn't. I'm supposed to mow it, but I keep forgetting. The lawn mower is very heavy to push for a little kid, and the blades need sharpening and it's boring and I forget to overlap so I have to go back extra.

Poor Daddy. After an enormous storm, the lawn looks like a beach. That's because half the beach is on the lawn. Giant rocks and logs and wheelbarrows full of shale and pebbles and shells.

There are some low-growing junipers just where the lawn and the beach meet. (That's where Tortoise is.)

You know, if you think about it, Miss Munroe is the funniest-looking teacher anyone ever had. Her hair is carrot-colored and curly like Shirley Temple's. Maybe it's a wig. Maybe she's bald! Her teeth stick out on the top and her slip hangs out on the bottom because her dresses have very wavy hems.

When we do think about it, we laugh at her in the girls' room, but we wouldn't dare in class. She is *so* fierce!

But when she reads about snowy evenings or birches or stone walls, everybody stops whispering and starts listening. Maybe it's because when she's reading a poem or a short story, she loves it so much, you can tell — and if you close your eyes, you'd think she was beautiful. And by the time she's done, everybody in the room thinks the piece is beautiful. Even Hunka Haddock gets all quiet listening to Miss Munroe read Robert Frost.

They were in a box under a lot of other things in my closet and I couldn't wait for the new one to come in! I have *every single one* — up to 1940. But since this year and Miss Munroe reading to us, I decided I was too old for them. Funny books are for kids who don't like to read much. So goodbye *Superman.* Goodbye *Action Comics.* Into the rubbish with a single bound!

IZAAK
STUTTHOF
JANUARY

Ah, Izaak, you are a genius. I was rousted out and led to work as usual this morning. In this cold, even the walk across the compound nearly fells me. My usual attire is striped and thin. And my lungs are not what they used to be. However, before the jaunt, my warder met a comrade and they stopped to trade the latest vulgarism. Right outside my wall, they stopped! The chance of a lifetime. I leaned against the wall with the usual hangdog expression, patiently waiting, while all the while I wished to be the nonchalant Gabin, arrogantly smoking the cigarette with the ash that never drips. I was not Jean Gabin taunting his keepers, but I was a hero! They jawed interminably, but I needed time. Time to push the knot *in* so that later, after work and shut in my room, I would be able to pull it toward me. Leaning against the wall with a quivering finger behind my back, I pushed slightly — and it moved — inward!

It was dark when I got back to my little room. But I knew where to feel. And I felt it. And I grasped it. And it came. Right in my hand! And through the small round hole I could see the beams of light on the watchtowers and the glow of lamps from several guards' barracks — and a star!

Just after dawn, I looked again through my window on the world. A window on *my* world. And I could not get enough.

My wheel is covered with dust. Diamond dust. Perhaps my lungs are weak from breathing in a quarter century of powder. Imagine dying from a disease caused by such a coveted substance!

Brown Mouse remains. Perhaps because of me. Probably because of her litter. Her young are growing to be fine replicas of their mother. But they insist on milk at all times of the day and night. Brown Mouse is tired and needs a respite from motherhood. For this she relies on me, so I am of use to her, after all. When there is enough daylight slanting in from the chinks in the roof, I write. And Brown Mouse climbs up my arm and sleeps in the hollow of my neck. She sleeps deeply, breathing rapidly. Away from her insatiable brood.

They came in to inspect my room. They did not discover my pages. They did discover my companions. With boots and butts of rifles, they stamped out the vermin. Small bodies lay inert. But there was one missing. Brown Mouse. Will she ever return? Will she ever trust me again?

I am weaker. My breathing is labored. It rasps when I lie down. When I sit or stand, my lungs feel like those of a dying man.

The pallet has seen better days. My blanket does not cover the toes. I am not fond of my blanket. The lice seem to love it.

The Russian offensive began yesterday! I listened at the wall because the noise in there was overwhelming. The guardroom was buzzing. I shall listen more often. There is always room for hope. And I can still hear with my right ear.

Work faster! There is much to be finished. And in a short time. Idiots! One does not hurry up the faceting of a stone. The work must be done precisely.

Ah! The hurry is panic. There are cracks in the Thousand Year Reich. The walls may come tumbling down. From Russian artillery, perhaps?

The advance is swift. The flashes are visible. I put my good ear to the partition. The news gets worse; the orgies at night increase. SS office and now SS brothel. Snatches of information interspersed with women's cries.

Now they bring me cut gems by the bagful. To grade. They only want to know the best stones. Enough stones have passed through here to cause a panic on the Exchange.

I shall examine each stone from this new shipment under the loupe. Most are small, worthless. I don't know where they were obtained. Inferior work on inferior diamonds . . .

Say it, Izaak! Write it! They came from the rings worn by the women selected for the ovens! SAY IT! Treasured diamonds, not worth a tenth of what they cost. But treasured.

They sparkle in my palm. Careful, diamonds scratch diamonds. I hold a handful and see a hundred severed fingers.

You see too much! Get out the loupe and work.

I took my fine etching tool with the diamond point and made some scratches. They are not visible to the naked eye. I could barely do them with the loupe. It is a small thing, but I feel better. Small scratches.

They are late today. I look through my hole, ready to plug it at the sound of boots.

The sun shines brightly and there are some bare patches in the compound.

I see a little bird! Brown-flecked. A sparrow? I was never one to notice ordinary creatures. Birds were birds unless one had a stork on one's roof. That was luck!

This bird pecks busily at a bare spot. What can it find? I doubt there are crumbs in the compound. There are *no* crumbs in the compound, for they have been lapped up by human skeletons.

It is quiet in the compound save for the sparrow. It has become a sparrow. It pecks away happily. Perhaps ants? But why would ants inhabit a dead place? No crumbs for them either. Ah, Izaak, you have forgotten. Ants go to sleep in the winter. Deep down in their labyrinth they are drowsing, warm. What I would give for just one leg of just one labyrinth. From my dirt floor, under the compound, under the wire! Tales of tunnels I have heard. But done by stronger men than I.

The sparrow continues pecking. There must be something there. What? A puzzle to ponder.

In the spring Hetty and I went to Aalsmeer, the flower auction. We could not bid, but only look. Hetty dragged me to see *her* "jewels." In time I came to look forward to the outing.

Blinding yellow daffodils, a sea of violet hyacinths and scilla, the cobalt blue of an autumn sky. Rows of tulips like ripe apricots. I learned not to compare the colors to gems and Hetty was delighted.

* * *

It was cold in our flat at home — in Amsterdam. The damp and the wind always blowing. A satchel of coal was a satchel of gold!

Hetty piled sweaters and mufflers over and around me, sometimes adding some of hers if she thought I might not notice. She worried endlessly about her bulbs. Would they survive the cold? And I wondered whether we would.

Water in the drinking glass would film with ice. Then they turned the water off. The stove grew cold. No coal for Jews. We lit a candle, a precious candle, for an hour to eat tinned food, shivering, to sleep the night and dark away.

Suppose that for every act of horror there is one of kindness — somewhere else — a kind of balancing. Does that fact, if it is indeed a fact, make horror less?

The Amsterdammers were kind to us. Always, in spite of the star. To the end I was Mijnheer Broekman. Never Izaak, Jew. We were Hollanders first, professionals second. And there was no third.

I find solitude a lonely state. Strange not to speak for weeks on end, save to myself. Is a dialogue with oneself the beginning of madness? The beginning of the end?

I find I think of Brown Mouse often. As much as Hetty. Perhaps she has become Brown Mouse. If Brown Mouse lives, so Hetty lives?

My camp is becoming a ghost. An insignificant camp as camps go. At one time those that came here were meant to live, to labor for the Reich. Then stuffing mattresses became priority. When did a kind of panic set in? When was it decided that Stutthof should become like all the others? That crematoria be created to make this just another disposal dump? That mattresses required human hair?

Now even this is over. The crematoria are cold. The death camp has turned into a ghost camp. How appropriate. There are many ghosts here. They will always inhabit this ground.

It is so cold. The Ice Age has come to Stutthof. And my sparrow has gone. South, I hope, where snow does not cover whatever it pecked at so happily.

The Soviets continue to advance. Sometimes I can hear the rumble of heavy guns, like an approaching storm.

Today was a new experience. I sat and waited in an office somewhere. I think they forgot me. There was a wood stove in the room, and for a time I felt warmth, up close. If I could store up that heat, I could live off it for weeks. I stood up and moved around, first cautiously, then with more confidence. Old Izaak did not creak.

I glanced out the window, for I have not seen through one for how long? Years. The wire was close. Beyond, there was little but snow. A great expanse of white crust, with a wavering black line. Small specks broke out, dropped, and stayed still. But the line continued. On to the sea, beyond my vision.

Was this an evacuation? Where did they go? On to the ice? For what purpose? They need no purpose.

Someone remembered me. I sat down and looked compliant. I witnessed nothing on the snow. I was not a hero, today.

I dwell on myself. That line to the sea did not bring tears to my eyes. Maybe there are none to flow.

What I remember as vividly is a glimpse of Izaak Broekman. As he is. That reflection in the windowpane. I did not recognize you, Izaak. You were the patriarch in a portrait by Rembrandt van Rijn. Even the muted earthen colors were the same. The face was lit for an instant with that light he made so famous. I remember the pride I felt that one so great would buy a house in the Jodenbuurt, the Jewish quarter. He must have loved the Jews, for he painted so many of us. There are not many who love us now.

We are encircled. The Russian offensive has rushed south of us, toward Danzig. We have been bypassed. We are of no account. They have forgotten Stutthof. So, Izaak, you are not to be free just yet. Waiting for a rainbow? They are rare and only happen in the afternoon. What are you scribbling? Nonsense. Dreams.

BUFFY
CAPE CHARLOTTE
FEBRUARY

"Squash the buggers!" That's what I yell every morning now as I listen to the news, Meg. Adrenaline flows and I feel marvelous at the thought that soon, SOON, they will bow down in defeat, vanquished, for all time!

Can you tell that I am not a passive onlooker of world events? Can't stand pacifists, that's what. Hate is a necessary emotion and gets the juices going and keeps the arteries supple!

Do you know that I once met a woman (an idiot woman!) married to an academic. With two tiny babes, she was about to accompany said academic into the bush. What is "bush" anyway? She told me with stars in her eyes and a voice ringing with religious fervor of her devout belief in pacifism. She goaded me into bringing up a hypothetical example. Suppose, I said, you ran into an ambush, and the lives of your children were at stake. What would you do then? Without batting an eye (those stars made this maneuver impossible!), she told me, smiling sweetly, that there could be no choice. She would have to sacrifice the lives of her children rather than cause the death of their killer! I wanted to slap her. I wanted to *kill* her, right there, that bitch of a fanatic!

Well, that's off my chest, although, inside right now, my heart is behaving erratically at the reminder of fools who float above reality.

Speaking of floating. The snow was doing that an hour ago. Floating down. Now it's dropping in sheets, ruining my view. I cannot pick up the beam of James Head light, which is only a few miles north of me (as the crow flies — but I never saw a crow flying from here to there!).

Back to the snow. It's so heavy now that even Porpoise Light, which I look down upon and is only about a thousand feet from us out on the tip of the promontory, Porpoise Light is only a faint glow, that's how dense the snow is.

At least we'll be plowed out, free. The Coast Guard has a cute little jeep and it removes the snow from the entrance of the road down to the Light. The road begins at the Coast Road, curls around Half Moon Bay above the highest tideline and scoots out to Porpoise Light. The road's our only means of getting in and out, so the Service plows our driveway while they are about it. Sweet of them.

Pudge seems to be zipping in and out. When he's in, he's engrossed. Writing his history of the waterfront, I suppose. We are like ships that pass in the night — and don't bump! Don't even brush! Well, I get my jollies vicariously. My body may not be fertile, but my mind produces an immense population. Copulation rhymes with the latter, doesn't it? Wait till you read my fantasy!

At least Pudge has *stopped* warming things up in the oven. The result of a desire for who knows what food was a nasty little fire in the stove! A lot of soot on the ceiling

Spring in less than a month. That's what the calendar says. *Never* believe the written word. Spring doesn't. It will arrive when it's damn well ready to — which may be the middle of June.

Much love,
Buffy

IZAAK
STUTTHOF
FEBRUARY

The stones come in, the stones go out. I am to be finished by tomorrow. What is tomorrow? What day? What month?

I feared the end would come because my eyes would fail. They are still trying. The end will come because the job is done. I will have to work through the night. The night does not lend itself to detailed work. At forty-two you are in your ninth decade. Ancient, venerable, but failing.

What do the guards say? "There's *no* Jew like an old Jew." They put the emphasis on "no." Clever. The Death's Head makes sure we do *not* attain a ripe old age. The old ones go quickly. The young ones take a bit longer.

I heard that a visitor would come. He came today. The Black and Silver one. In a touring car for country outings. I doubt if he broke through the Russian lines, however. Perhaps the car belongs to the commandant. I write about anything!

The Black one made a special point to commend me on my work. Most correct. He even clicked his heels. And smiled. A winning smile. A boyish grin. Does he know he was courteous to a Jew?

The time was brief. He turned away and I was forgotten. Diamonds are more important than life. He left and took my work. A bit of me went with him. My spirit. There will be no more work.

I peer through the knothole. My guard walks toward the office. I do not know his name. I do not *wish* to know it. My keeper's stride is hesitant. His tunic is unbuttoned and unpressed. His boots are dusty and cracked. What has happened to discipline — held in such esteem by killers? Is fear a replacement for discipline? They should fear. Their Wehrmacht is going the wrong way. Back to its spawning place.

The list of infirmities grows. Why do I catalogue them? I catalogue them to fill in the time. I have much time. Or do I have only a few moments? You are muddled and maudlin! Stop it!

There is no work. I see no one. My liquid diet is shoved in rudely. And I am alone.

I shall never practice my trade again. Fact. The eyes have almost gone. Thank Jehovah who does not exist that I was able to add my etchings.

When does the body give up? When it loses hair and teeth? When pustules burst, scale over, and one resembles a fish? That has happened, and I still exist. When the rations do not stay in the stomach, but pass through in one continuous flood? That happens, and I am still here. When the lungs fill up with greenish slime? When every breath is as painful as a blow? So many blows and I still write.

BORMANN
BERLIN
FEBRUARY

Ley and Goebbels and I meet with him every evening for a couple of hours. I can't wait to get out of there and up above!

To have come to this! Of all the bunkers at the Führer's disposal, we use this one! He loves bunkers. He loves stale air (for fresh air carries infections and God knows what else. He is convinced of this!).

Do you know, Schmidt, the Führer has either lived in or visited *all thirteen* of his bunkers. Now that I think of it, he has spent a goodly portion of the war underground. Rastenburg, mostly. Those thirteen were spread from the Belgian border to Vinnitsa FHQ in the Ukraine. Vinnitsa's was 200 kilometers *closer to Istanbul than to Berlin!*

Our field operations have shrunk! And the Reds have crossed the Oder. Christ — there's not much left between them and Berlin. Less than a hundred open miles!

Like the sound of our man. The perfect courier. And perfect for America. Has performed distasteful tasks well, efficiently. And does not suffer from doubt. I think we shall give him the little pat on the back that you feel he aches for. The medal should stimulate his sense of blind loyalty and spur him on to do another distasteful job for us.

Now — about Midas. First, from him I want the names and addresses of *all* of his best and dependable contacts in Mexico and the United States. The faithful. I want that list *before* our courier reaches the Eastern Seaboard because after our man has had a quick contact with Majorca, he will be in Midas' hands. An apprentice, so to speak, in the running of a continuing operation. The diamonds will pay for the operation. But — an apprentice can rise to greater heights and displace the teacher. And that is exactly what our man will do. Eliminate Midas. My gut tells me to get rid of that Romanian.

Our courier should only be informed of this part of the mission after he boards, via sealed orders. Think our man will get a kick out of the award, though the signature be shaky.

The Führer has aged a decade in these last months. His eyesight is going and his arm is palsied. I am amazed at the ease with which I can get him to sign — anything! I pile papers in front of him, hold the pen and he signs. Trusts my judgment. Doesn't bother to read, barely glances at the documents. Some of my, shall we say sensitive material is positioned so that only the place for a signature is visible. Mostly, I tell him, the documents have to do with personal matters — estates and such. Mundane stuff.

Now — about our courier-agent. He needs a good code name and none of that insipid Spanish junk. So I change our method! Tough titty.

We shall inform Midas and Majorca of the code name. Our man hereafter shall be designated "Minsk." Inform him of this before he leaves for Stutthof, please.

Minsk. Believe our young ally conducted a number of open-air operations in that area. Minsk it shall be.

Bormann

EMMA
CAPE CHARLOTTE
FEBRUARY

Today was not a very good day. The sea air got into my flannel sheets through the holes that the moths ate in my Hudson's Bay blanket. Mummy says it's a filagreed blanket. I should sleep in my mukluks! The floors were so cold I stayed in the bathroom a long time because the only warm place in the *whole* house was the toilet seat!

My red plaid skirt was on the floor of the closet all squashed, so right then and there I wanted to skip school and be sick and listen to "My Gal Sunday" and have Bean and Bacon soup for lunch and then reread all the Oz books, which maybe are for kids, but I still like them. They were Daddy's and he gave me *every one.* I even have *The Patchwork Girl of Oz!* (which is not in such good condition as it was before Daddy gave it to me. It slipped once when I was reading it in the bathtub.)

But then I remembered Peter, so I decided to go downstairs for breakfast, but we were out of Maltex, and then Peter wasn't even on the bus!

So then we had a taste of beginning algebra, and I don't understand *why* we have to change the signs when we move X to the other side. Miss Munroe says just do it and don't ask.

And then we had to go down to the high school for Home Ec. This semester we aren't cooking, we're sewing. I've been making a shoebag *forever,* but until *all* the seams are straight, I can't graduate to the ruffled apron.

The only reason I went to school today anyway was because there was a chance that if I *did* go to Home Ec I might see Peter in the high school halls. But I didn't and it was a wasted day!

For a while Who Me didn't even notice Apricot. Or pretended not to. But now he does! I am very cross with Who Me. In fact I got really mad at him and spanked him. So Who Me looked up at me with that "Who Me?" expression and I couldn't help it. I told him I forgave him this time, but that he had been a VERY BAD CAT.

I'm not sure he thinks so. In fact I *know* he doesn't think so. He likes chasing Apricot. He likes it so much I think he dreams about it at night. At least I can see his legs moving. He's running in his sleep and I know who he's chasing!

Peter likes Who Me, but he loves Apricot. And I know he's a little embarrassed when Apricot runs away. I think he would feel better if Apricot would growl or bark or something. But Apricot just takes off, yelping. That's the worst part — to see a little black cat chase a big curly dog over the lawn and the beach and up and down the rocks, and Apricot howling the whole time.

Who Me doesn't chase other dogs. He ignores them. Just Apricot. This week I've tried to keep the kitty inside when I am going down to the beach, but he's very smart. He knows when I'm going and he waits. I think he waits under the couch, but I'm not sure. Anyway, I open the front door just a crack and look around. No Who Me. So I open it a tiny bit more. No Who Me. Then I open it just enough to squeeze out fast and who zips out ahead? Who Me!

Poor Apricot. I told him Who Me was only playing and to act fierce and it would surprise Who Me so much he might decide to go and play with other cats instead. But Apricot won't listen.

And now Who Me has made up another game. He pretends to go off by himself, sniffing everything on the beach. You'd think the only thing on his mind was smelly seaweed. Pretty soon he's out of sight and *not* following us, so Peter and Apricot and I go walking or climbing and feeling a lot better. But Who Me is thinking of something else besides seaweed. He's deciding where the best hiding place is. That's so as we go by he can leap out looking like a Hallowe'en cat, spitting and yowling and scaring Apricot to death. He is an AWFUL cat!

I think we're going to have a storm tonight. The barometer says we are. And I can feel one coming.

Mummy says she can tell what the weather's going to be by watching me. She doesn't have to look at the barometer (which doesn't always work). She says, "Emma, you get skittish just before a low-pressure system arrives, and positively manic in a major blow." Mummy is very scientific.

I love storms. I'm afraid of a lot of things like drowning and polio, but not storms.

I love the summer storms when the dark green and purple clouds move in over the sea and start to whack each other. When they meet, Wow!

We get hurricanes, too. They are pretty fierce. The rain is warm and goes sideways and I can go out and lean right against the wind. Lean right against it and *not* fall over! Of course, this is when Daddy's lawn gets messed up and all the fishermen out on the sea have an awful time, so I really shouldn't love them. One minute the ocean's so innocent and blue and the next it's a frothing monster.

Once the radio predicted a tidal wave, so Mummy got really scared because all the seagulls went miles inland. Usually they go inland just a little. Mummy believes that animals know more than we think they do. Anyway, we boarded up the picture window and packed some clothes and food and *evacuated,* just up to the Walkers', who live on a hill across the Coast Road. We *didn't* have a tidal wave, so the seagulls were crazy!

I guess I love the winter blizzards best — when we can get them. Once in a while we get a real doozy. Like the time the wind blew so hard we had drifts as tall as my bedroom window and Daddy had to go to the store on skis and we didn't have school for four days!

I assessed myself today. I borrowed a ladies' magazine from Amy that had an article in it about Personal Assessment.

First, I took off all my clothes and stood in front of Mummy's long mirror.

From the neck down:

Bad — My hipbones stick out, my stomach sticks in, my bottom is beginning to stick out — a lot. My shoulderblades do too, and my bosom doesn't do anything. And on my left foot, the second toe is longer than my big toe!

Good — I have long legs and a long waist (I don't know why that's supposed to be good).

From the neck up:

Good — My neck is long (like a swan's!). My nose is smallish and only has one pimple today, which I popped. My eyes are a pretty color of blue. My eyelashes are medium OK. My hair is light brown (but it would look much better with a permanent!)

Bad — My eyelashes haven't grown even though I put baby oil on them. My eyebrows are too thick and there are some in the middle. I wish my mouth was bigger and — this should have gone in below the neck — my hair has hardly sprouted under my arms when I use Arrid all the time!

Besides that I'm *too* thin and *too* tall and my feet are *too* BIG!!!

(Under Bad—I have braces on my top teeth and I have to wear a pink retainer for my bottom ones. Mummy can always tell when it's NOT in. This morning I wasted precious minutes getting to school looking for it. I found it under the radiator covered with dust kitties. I don't know how it got there! The little rubber bands were behind the Milk of Magnesia. Anyway, maybe in two years I can put my teeth under Good.)

Even when we weren't speaking Amy was still sort of my best friend underneath, but now I don't think so.

It's because of Peter. I'm not going to tell her how much I like him because she would blab it all over and then make some nasty remark about fishermen. I know she would because she's mean to Gilbert and his father's a lobsterman.

A best friend is someone you can talk to about *anything*. I sure can't do that with Amy! So I'm going to make Peter my best friend.

Peter and I have been going down to Steeple Rock, which still has ice on her. We have to climb high and Peter keeps telling me to BE CAREFUL. About slipping into the waves. The currents around here are crazy. The ocean doesn't pay attention to wind, so the currents go every which way and the undertow can carry you far out in a flash. If it wants to, the sea will throw you around for a while and then smash you back on the rocks. It likes to do that.

So I'm careful even though I do slip a little bit sometimes because my Bean's boots are still too big. But I love them!

Anyway, I'm not worried. Peter is a terrific swimmer. Last year he won a race around Bottlenose Island. And that's ocean swimming. He promised to teach me how to swim better this summer.

BE CAREFUL, he says, because the water temperature could freeze me in a minute even if I was just floating, not being smashed on the rocks or the reefs. He said I could even get frostbite if I got wet feet and didn't do too much about it for a while.

But nothing like that seems to bother Apricot. We throw chunks of ice from the top of Steeple Rock into the ocean and that nutty dog dives in, flat out like a bat, grabs the ice and paddles around until he can touch the rock. Then he scratches around with his toenails until he's got a hold and heaves himself aboard with an icecake in his teeth. Apricot is so proud of himself, and all he wants to do is to belly-flop right back in for another piece — after he has shaken ice water all over me!

HENRY
CAPE CHARLOTTE
FEBRUARY

The mystery deepens. Now Berlin (via Lowell) wants the tide tables for these shores: high tide, low tide, for the month of March. And particularly for the middle of the month.

The tides of March. The Ides of March. They obviously do not believe in the omens of entrails. That is, if they are planning — what? — for the 15th.

At this last date, the "what" is the conundrum.

A brief glimpse of the area shows that the Fleet is *not* in Baleen Bay. And there are not enough merchant vessels steaming to and fro the harbor to warrant an expedition of extermination. Since they blundered so badly in the past re the landing of saboteurs — the last mishap having taken place in the Gulf of Maine in November, as I recall — I do not foresee another attempt. In point of fact, to be successful for the Huns' War Effort, any sabotage now would be too little, too late. A year or two ago, the target might have been the Shipyard or, conceivably, the Naval Air Station. But not now. Not in March of 1945.

Do they intend a last grand gesture? Or will it be more of a last gasp?

Tide tables? The inference — of course — a ship!

Tide tables. I need *The Almanac!* Unavailable! The powers that be so decree: Roosevelt — and his crowd. That man is *not* a fair son of Harvard. Not only is he a traitor to his class, he is a smiling saboteur, a dangerous revolutionary! How appalling for that great lady, Sara Delano, to have brought forth upon this planet a male child destined to become a devious dictator. What agonies she must have endured watching the values of class distinction that she had instilled in him as a lad crumble into communistic concepts! Her public façade was most correct, but in her private moments she must have wept. Thank God she is not alive to witness the monstrous harm done to our great nation. A nation of massive doles! Socialism at its worst. Even the Nazis have an order about them. There is no order in welfare. Giveaways such as the Social Security System weaken the very fabric of free enterprise. There have always been "the poor." There always will be "the poor." And meek shall they stay. They shalt *not inherit* the riches of our country!

Tides. I was discussing tides and the lack of *The Old Farmer's Almanac,* the perusal of which is necessary to find the highs and the lows for given ports on the Eastern Coast. Ah, could this be the reason for pulling all copies out of circulation?

At any rate, *The Almanac*'s tables are most accurate. Given the times of high and low tide at Boston's Commonwealth Pier for a given date, one extrapolates +/− X minutes, depending on the location. Normally, as I recall, the tides in the vicinity of Jamesport are somewhere between 10 and 15 minutes *earlier* than those of Boston. But — at the moment the unknown, the X is Boston!

Oh my! How dense am I. I admit it. All the while, the information for today, for next summer, for *the month of March,* was almost at my fingertips, being, as I am, in the business, so to speak. I shall acquire and have available all necessary tables from the office tomorrow!

As for the currents, I have emphasized that they follow no discernible pattern; they are erratic. This knowledge had been gleaned from scuttlebutt (a word, which, when first spat from the mouths of seafarers, could only have been a vulgarism. But upon learning its derivation, that of a cask of drinking water on board ship, scuttlebutt became a useful word and a most usable one. It behooves me to learn the lexicon of the sea).

As for beacons, I have indicated the locations of those that seem of most importance. The large beacons, such as lighthouses, have had their lighting diminished since the outbreak of hostilities. This situation of half-light remains even though the Huns no longer skulk along our shores. Save *one,* of course. I *am* forgetting that which may do so within a month.

However, warned of diminished lighting — and the sequence of flashes — each beacon flashing its own pattern (the one with which I am most familiar will remain imprinted on my mind for all time! I see it even winking in the daylight hours, with my eyes closed tightly) — warned of the idiosyncrasies of each, the ship should be well prepared to recognize the pattern, and by so doing, identify the beacon.

I knew this respite would not last forever! I had vague hopes that he might disappear, by design, by accident, by Satan calling him to the fires of purgatory. In any event, I wished him loosed from mortal coils to mold. No, preferably to burn! But the Deity did not see fit to grant me this one wish. He did not see fit to answer my plea. And I, a *deacon!*

I loathe the man! I cannot abide being next to him. He appears to be harmless, a cherub, but I know better.

He did not use the message, that which I had almost managed to put out of mind, namely: "The capital of . . ." Need I continue? He accosted me outside the firm. Just walked up and in a supercilious tone *commanded* me to take the noonday meal with him. Luncheon with Lowell!! I lost my appetite.

Over a malodorous dish of corned beef and cabbage he outlined a preposterous undertaking. (All the while he shoveled in his portion, talking rapidly as he masticated, savoring a meal fit only for the Irish. The Papal enclaves of Dorchester and Charlestown fairly reek of the disgusting combination!)

The undertaking is preposterous! They plan to land a man (a spy, a saboteur?) on this coast from a U-boat! His mission is of the utmost urgency. And I, *I* am to tell them the ideal landing place, *and* be responsible for his well-being for a *very short* time. Of this they assure me. And a name. They wish a good Anglo name acceptable in better circles.

All this they want by tomorrow. I must give Lowell the answers at another luncheon (I will be ill!) about noon — 12:30, to be precise.

I shall be up the night, I fear. Into the dawning. At least Evelyn will be occupied till then, also.

* * *

The solution was under my very nose. I did not recognize it at first. But quiet, patience and the passage of time allow the brain to meander, trying multitudes of possibilities. When that which has the greatest potential for success emerges, a small charge of neuronic activity signals: follow this path, and this path only.

Therefore, I meet Lowell with my head held high, for I have proved myself under fire, so to speak, to be equal to the burdensome task! Lowell shall have all the information he desires: landing place, hiding place. I have even proposed a name to be used as a pseudonym. The *Harvard Alumni Directory* gave me direction, I confess.

I so much preferred our previous method of communication. If they cannot trust those intrepid laborers, those in the service of the United States Mail, whom can they trust, I ask you?

HANNES
BERLIN
FEBRUARY

So much to think about, to do — and so little time! An operation of this magnitude requires painstaking planning, months of it. I have less than two weeks to rendezvous!

Briefings from an officer named Schmidt. A forgettable name; a forgettable face. Not at headquarters. The place (Gestapo-RSHA) was flattened two days ago. They operate out of the cellar, I gather, and Schmidt seems to feel it better we meet away from the confusion.

Every day the American bombers appear just before lunch; the British attack around midnight. So in the early morning hours we walk in the Tiergarten.

This great park is treeless now, plowed up for crops to feed a starving populace. What trees were spared have since toppled, gouged out of the earth by concussion. Their roots like crooked fingers point skyward, accusingly. We walk along frozen furrows, hard and still covered from the great blizzard that hit the city in January. Dust from the rubble mixes its mustard-colored powder with the snow, and the result is like gazing at an expanse of vomit.

There is much to learn about this operation. Schmidt appears nervous, and makes me repeat the instructions over and over as though he is afraid I will forget some detail. I am not a schoolboy!

I suggest certain procedures and various items I will need. He agrees readily and produces enough paper and passes, so sternly official they seem to designate me God in black tunic. Orders signed by the Reichsführer himself! Orders stiff enough to make the SS turn handstands.

Ten days to go. Ten days in which I must close every loophole, triple-check that *nothing* has been overlooked or left to chance.

So I must cease these entries for a time. In this, my last from Berlin, I pledge that this ruined city will rise again to become the Rome of the Western World.

Here too, I pledge that with utmost honor and loyalty I shall undertake and fulfill the mission bestowed on me. I further pledge that I shall render any and all service to those who lead Germany in her hour of peril. Unto death if need be, so help me God.

STEINER
BERGEN, NORWAY
FEBRUARY

For ILSE: To be opened immediately upon receipt.

My dearest girl,

Deiter delivers this letter. Please do not mention his eyes. They are clouded with cataracts and he sees badly. He tried to hide his infirmity from me, for he is loyal unto death. But I ordered him invalided out. I have lost my oldest friend, but he gains new life.

Please offer him some Schnapps. I have told him to toast the three of us. Do it with a full heart and in happiness. And when the festivities are over, read the rest of this letter.

Prosit!

By the time you read this we will be at sea, my boat journeying on a voyage that is almost routine. Our mission is not one of striking; in fact, it does not involve engaging the enemy *in any way.* So do not fear.

... The first order, from Dönitz: Make ready to sail within a week. New fittings required. A snorkel, no less. *Now,* I have a snorkel!

Round up the crew ashore. Find them stuporous or in the arms of whores. They've had only a brief respite and need whatever warmth they can scrounge. It is not easy to find warmth in Norway. My men are stared at with loathing, hatred. Norwegians are a silent lot at best. But this silence is so heavy one can hear it, feel it like a bullet in the brain.

Berthed in Bergen, soon to slip out, past the fjords into the wintry North Sea . . .

. . . New crewmen added. Some are needed to service this breathing device. But the others, replacements for some of my best. The best burn out, giving all they have until there is nothing more to give. I do not feel comfortable with strangers, now. And have not the energy to win them over — as friends. Indeed, I do not have to bother. I doubt these new ones and I will become close. They are mostly young and swagger. Eager cadets who live War vicariously and have not tasted the bitterness. I do believe they have steadfast faith in Victory. Let them keep their dreams, for now . . .

. . . The final orders have arrived. The last batch.

They are top drawer! Signed by Dönitz (a mass of nautical details!) of course and Himmler and — My God! Adolf Hitler himself! At least, I believe it is his signature. The writing is hard to decipher, a shaky signature as though a feeble hand has penned it. Is this scratch a sign of senility? And there is another. An M. Bormann. Bormann? I know no one of that name. Perhaps he is an aide, a petty functionary in the Office of Deputy Führer.

I have enough bedtime reading to last a lifetime. And enough nautical charts to cruise the world three times over.

Just thinking about my Elsbeth, and about you, my love, will carry me through the months ahead. Knowing you are safe high in the Valley of the Ötztal has lifted such a burden from me! Within months, I *shall* be with you — and summer will be there, also.

I give you something to ponder. What shall I be after the War? A farmer? A brewer? Ach! No! A poet? (I try my hand when no one sees. But is it good enough for the masses?) Perhaps we two can open a Gasthaus in Obergurgl? And call it The Poet's Corner?! Think about it. As I shall.

Until summer (and ever after) I am your devoted, besotted,

Rudi

AT SEA

Dearest one,

Here begins another travelogue, a continuing letter, for you only.

I shall add to it day by day as we progress, and — as always — it will be as though we talk to each across the miles. This is the log of a beginning and an end. The last voyage of Rudolph Steiner, who prefers the warmth of his wife over the glory of all medals bestowed upon him. Who prefers love in the afternoon over promotion to Gross Admiral! The beginning is yet to come, but come, it will! . . .

. . . The engines shudder, come awake and under cover of darkness we slide from the berth and proceed to our first rendezvous. . .

. . . We navigate carefully through the Kattegat. Sweden to port. Neutral, untouched. Strange to see the lights of cities. Strange but hopeful to know that lights and lamps have not all died. . .

. . .Weather improving. The seas were heavy as we entered the Baltic and the overcast gave us protection from the hunters — British, American, Russian? One does not care what language the bombardier speaks. His actions have more force than words . . .

. . .Weather clear. The Baltic not our sea. It belongs mainly to the Soviets now. The cold blue Baltic, laced with whitecaps. We do not pause to admire the view, but proceed submerged to the Bay of Danzig. To wait for the signal . . .

HANNES
AT SEA
FEBRUARY

I left that Godforsaken place in the fog. Stutthof: a place that should be nameless and will soon be emptied; its tenants walk in ever-increasing batches to the sea.

The old Jew seemed reluctant to part with his stones. They have been the only bright things in these last three days of misery!

The misery began on the launch. I puked over the side with each swell until nothing came but bile.

I remember getting in the U-boat and tumbling down a ladder and then dry heaves and water, a bit of water that stayed down at least five minutes. A bunk, a blanket and rolling, rolling . . . a log rolling, a coffin rolling, a steel coffin spiraling.

I saw Billie Joe Campbell laughing . . . I was entombed and there was no air.

* * *

The spasms have lessened. Some seaman has informed me that we are under the sea and the surface motion will remain above. Why then does it continue in my gut? I do not heave, I just revolve. And my head — it blows up with pain and will surely burst. The air is foul. I cannot breathe! I cannot get out!

I cannot maneuver in this nightmare, this tub of nightmares! It was made for midgets! I cracked my head on a lamp and the light fluttered like an imprisoned bird, caged in like me. I hit the same tender spot going through an entryway — so damned low! and nearly fell in grease! The crew scurries by me, pushing me out of the way, brushing the legs of mutton that hang and swing and kick back as though alive. There is no space to store — anything. There is no place to exist!

There *is* a Captain. He exists and I am to meet him. For tea. Ha! He hides behind amenities. Why doesn't he come right out and say "Schnapps!" God! I need two doubles!

STEINER
AT SEA
FEBRUARY

... The signal was answered; the rendezvous completed. And the reason for all the preparation, the reason for the voyage that now commences, is on board. One man. One man to ferry across the sea. One man I am to land safely on the enemy's shores. More about this operation later.

At the moment my passenger (who is important — so state the orders) is feeling most insignificant. A worm, perhaps. He lies green and groaning on a bunk, ready to reward anyone who would put him out of his misery ...

... We pick our way cautiously back through the mouth, the esophagus, the belly, the anus, to the open sea: through the inlet of the Danes, the Kattegat, the Skagerrak and into the North Sea. I have not had time to chat with the seasick one. He remains a lump under a blanket. And I am busy ...

... I *am* busy, Ilse — to a degree. But to be totally honest, I am not that occupied. I would prefer that the officer remain a lump, that he would pass the entire voyage covered. For you see, when he rises, I must gaze upon the black uniform of the SS. Why he wore it aboard I can only surmise: to impress. Who? Me? The crew possibly, for they whisper about the "black one." I do not wish to have a meeting or engage in conversation with him. Why can't we stay apart, aloof from one another? . . .

You chide me. I hear you question my inhospitableness. Perhaps you are right. I shall extend to him an invitation for tea . . .

. . . The invitation was tendered and the Lieutenant arrived, a bit taken aback at the lack of privacy in my cabin — and the limited amount of space, having to sit beside me, the makings of tea on my tiny desk. I mentioned that tea settles the stomach and he seemed, albeit fleetingly, disappointed. Apparently he was expecting something stronger, that "tea" was code for cognac? Tea — with canned milk! How I yearn for one thin slice of lemon studded with cloves. I haven't smelled a lemon for almost two years! But I find tea calming, as you know, even without the trimmings. A ritual, preparing tea. Brings a little civilization to undersea life.

The Lieutenant — Henkel is his name — arrived in a leather greatcoat smelling like a library. Such leather, Ilse. So soft and supple. The Kriegsmarine has never seen such stuff!

We sipped and parried, each wary of the other. Courteous though circumspect. I did not ask him of his mission. I do not want to know! So our conversation was inconsequential.

I suspect he is not fond of U-boats. Many find life under the sea fraught with panic, mounting claustrophobia.

To put him at ease, I made light of his malady, mentioning that many seamen never have a stable stomach at sea. This last was a mistake as Henkel turned pale — with remembrance, I wager. Although he said not a word, it was clear I had hit a nerve and he was furious. I suspect his insides resumed their churning.

He hitched his greatcoat closer round him. I forgot to tell you that he appeared for our tête-à-tête with the coat slung insouciantly — no, arrogantly — from his shoulders so that most of his uniform was visible.

Oh, Ilse, you would like him at first. I know you would, regardless of the color he wears. Take away the uniform and he is a big, gangly farmboy, fair, with high color. He would charm you with his smile, which is innocence itself. He has all his teeth!

I can see you blushing now as he kisses your hand, sending you little sexual messages as he raises his eyes to yours.

He could be a deceiver, I suspect, but good at the art, bringing out the mother in the woman — and the woman in the female!

So we had tea and I was not too ungracious (although I might have stayed away from discussions of discomfort. You think so?). As he left, I handed him a small parcel, most intriguing, done up tightly and sealed with red wax. "To be delivered on board" the order stated.

Feeling that I had indeed been petty, I suggested that he return. At first he looked at me with coldness, but when I mentioned Slivowitz, his eyes lit up in anticipation. Now I have to find it! One bottle somewhere in the muddle of my belongings . . .

HANNES
AT SEA
FEBRUARY

. . . The shit! We had tea! TEA. And vapid conversation, mostly about mal de mer. Which only made me replay my malaise. The Kapitanleutnant was condescending. I have no doubt on this score. I think he played upon my weakness and enjoyed my discomfort. I think he does not care for the color black!

But he pretended courtesy and has invited me to share a bottle with him soon. A bottle of Slivowitz . . . Warsaw . . . Schwoermer . . . Belorussia . . . Winter. If I could pass out on Slivowitz, I could pass the entire journey unconscious!

I have just opened the package Steiner gave me and sit on my bunk stunned. The tears are falling, and I let them. The Führer, Adolf Hitler, has seen fit to award me the Iron Cross *First* Class, the decoration he holds also! I hold in my hands an executive order that *he* once held, that *he* has signed! The Führer asks me to fulfill the mission upon which he so depends. He asks, not orders.

I have new resolve and purpose! And I am humble in the presence of one so great. He is with me! He is with me.

Who designed this craft? I have tried to follow just one cable to discover its purpose and cannot. It disappears. There is a canopy of cables, some as thick as a man's wrist, snaking in colonies over and under and behind each other. Great pipes and ducts and hoses layered with countless slatherings of shiny paint meander through the tangle leading into — nowhere; there are gauges and switches and valves and wheels. The whole mess is an engineer's fuckup put together by a maniac!

Who designed the bedding? An admiral's wife? Blue and white gingham, for Christ's sake! Checks for little girls!

I wear the decoration proudly on my uniform. I wear the uniform proudly. I *will* wear the uniform — to spite them all!

Yesterday, on the catwalk, I slipped and barely managed to keep from falling into the bilge swill. I cannot wear the uniform without the boots, and jackboots were not fashioned for the metal plates of raised squares that pass for pathways!

Steiner has jacked up the heat in here to smother me, I know it. Humidity like a suffocating blanket! Beads of moisture collect and drip down my neck — slimy, oily drops slide down my tunic. I sweat diesel!

Slivowitz time. About time. I sponge my uniform as best I can, spit on my boots. No sheen. But I will present myself as polished as is possible, under these conditions. (The tunic is stiff under the arms and there is grease on the breeches. But Steiner may not notice.)

It began with Slivowitz and ended when I awoke in underwear. My uniform was missing! So are many hours. I know we drank — at least I did. Why not? My sole purpose for sharing his cramped quarters was to get blind — fast! What did we talk about? I may have mentioned the fucking Jews. I don't remember. Passing out, that's nothing to have guilt over. Where's the uniform? Did I puke all over it? Is it being cleaned and pressed? I *need* it.

That traitorous son of a bitch! That madman! He shredded it! My uniform. His country's symbol in tatters! Wait, wait. Steiner wants to unhinge you, make you fear him. Show you who has the upper hand, who's in command. Outsmart him, pretend, bluff, play the game — up to a point. After all, Henkel has been seen. What I was and still am. There was curiosity, fear and awe in their eyes, for I represent a strength of purpose that is the sun to the pitiful firefly that calls himself Captain. So no outbursts. Just quiet acquiescence — and a few simple sailors who worship suns.

STEINER
AT SEA
FEBRUARY

. . . We are on course and now I shall tell you where it will lead us: out of the North Sea into the one they call the Norwegian; north of the Shetlands, the Faeroes, then on, skimming the southern tip of Iceland; more steaming, and Greenland to starboard. South past Labrador, Newfoundland, Cape Race. Avoid the Grand Banks: full of fish. Also full of fishers. South of Nova Scotia: Sable Island. A lovely name. I always picture it as a home for sleek, furry animals, their coats glistening in the sun, running rampant, chasing each other over the rocks like seals.

Now we veer west, heading for America. Yes, Ilse. America! In years past I have been close, but not quite close enough to see her. This time I will almost touch her. Perhaps I can catch a glimpse of the shore, though it be dark. It *must* be dark to complete the mission safely. But even in the blackest night, the breakers glow with their own light. And seeing them, I can shout, "I saw America!" . . .

. . . He came — for Slivowitz. Still in uniform, the preening bastard! The black is turning gray under the armpits. And he smells worse than we do! But he had to show off his medal. A new one, I surmise, since he was not wearing it when he boarded. 1st Class.

Before he became roaring drunk, I told him the uniform must go — be changed for garb more suitable for U-boats — that we were all alike under the sea. No glory boys on my boat. (I did not add that he unsettles the crew.)

And then we drank. Or rather he drank. I sipped one small glass.

He is ugly when drunk. He is the Devil, drunk or sober. He talked . . . of things so secret, so vile, I will not tell you. He speaks of murder in the same caressing tone one would use to a beloved. He was an overseer of a hundred open-air charnel houses, who boasted of his numbers, his *quota.* And his country (not mine, not yours!) spurs him on, *rewards* him.

The camps about which we only heard in whispers — exist! They exist solely for murder. The SS is a murder machine. *A murder machine.* And millions, *millions* have been reduced to smoke!

I had him dragged out, a babbling, slobbering beast of a boy. He has fallen into that oblivion that drunks seek and is again a lump. And I ordered his uniform to be stripped from him and torn to shreds.

I thought of passing him out of a torpedo tube. Instead I vomited . . .

. . . I have a puzzle for you, Ilse. It has always been my notion, gleaned from writers more knowledgeable than I, that the face shows not only the passage of time, but records each moment of emotion — be it fear or envy, happiness or hate: that the face of an old man is the log of his life.

I saw my face in the glass this morning. Really saw it. Around my eyes are hen's tracks from squinting in the sun (and laughing at you). But the rest of my countenance is spotted with brown patches and the furrows are fathoms deep. There are satchels under my eyes and my whiskers are whitening. It is the ravaged face of a man who has seen a hundred years of agony compressed into five.

Yet beside me on my bunk sat a man who has seen death and caused agony a thousand, thousand times. A man almost four years my junior. Only four years! And he could be a lad of twelve — a rosy-cheeked, smiling boy with nary a rut nor wrinkle. A countenance so bland you could believe he had set his mind on the priesthood. What do you make of that, Ilse? . . .

HANNES
AT SEA
FEBRUARY

I saw the old man today. He *is* old — maybe forty — too old to command. Dressed in seaman's clothes and properly humble, I asked for a key to lock my storage area. That I must have a secure area, one that cannot be searched while I am on the can! (I have displaced a petty officer. I have his bunk, and for this voyage he sleeps among the torpedoes in the aft torpedo room like an ordinary seaman.)

I learn nautical terms with reluctance which I shall forget immediately upon landing. I shall never sail again. I shall never *look* upon the sea again!

Aft and forward are not difficult, but starboard and port are easy to reverse. I use a simple system: Slivowitz is good; right is good. Therefore, right is starboard. The Poles are piss; left is bad. Voilà! Port is left.

Back to the key, for it was the key that led to several interesting discoveries about Steiner. Apparently, he keeps everything of importance in a roll-up storage arrangement similar to mine. Varnished oak slats. He seemed puzzled by my insistence on security, saying that no one ever locks up on his boats. *Boats.* So this is not his first. How many has he lost? How many men? How many replacements are now on board? Interesting questions with intriguing possibilities.

The key: Steiner muttered something about there having been a key once, and perhaps, if he could find his, it might fit my lock. He shoved the cover up with a snap and rummaged around. On the inner shelf, I could not help but notice a volume displayed prominently, with slips stuck in, marking passages. So Steiner reads Heine, does he?

He got nowhere pawing through the sheaves of paper piled helter-skelter. A mind in disorder. He passed over a packet of what appeared to be letters tied with *pink* ribbon, well read by the looks of the envelopes. They hardly held together.

Ultimately, he unearthed an ugly clay pot, the color of crap, with PAPA scratched on it, and dumped the contents on the bunk between us. Odds and ends, I thought at first. But the *Knight's Cross* does not belong in a pile of junk. Not one with oak leaves on a red necklet! (At least it does not have oak leaves *and* swords.) Why does he not wear it? He squirrels it away as though he wishes to forget its existence!

Steiner discovered a key, a rather simple one, and handed it to me wordlessly. He then swept the entire mess back into the pot, rubbed his finger once gently over PAPA, and back onto the shelf. Slam! Down went the top. Like an order of dismissal.

We avoid each other like the plague. But there is more aboard this boat than two officers who hate. I have heard that submariners become a family, tight-knit. This is not a close family. There is something not right here, something in the air.

There *is* something in the air! Exhaust from engines, exhaust from lungs. Foul, filthy, thick cloying air! If this is all a snorkel can do, it is an abysmal failure! The stench of the unwashed, the stench of diesel — Oh, Christ! The drinking water tastes like piss. Who pissed in it?!

STEINER
AT SEA
FEBRUARY

. . . He demanded. With a great show of humility, he *demanded* a key to the roll-up locker above his bunk. We have never used keys. Until now, there was no need to. I found one after much poking about.

I could have dismissed him; I could have ignored him. But I gave in. Anything to keep him off my neck and out of sight!

I found the key in the vase made by Elsbeth. It was with other trivia I store there. In searching, I noticed the volume of Heine, which I have not read for a time. (Henkel, with his lightning antennae, spotted it immediately.)

I have reread "Sea Greeting" and also "Seraphine." The poems seem written for me. They soothe a troubled soul.

> Hail to thee, Sea, ageless and eternal!
> The whisper of your waters is as the speech
> of my own land . . .
> Oh, how I have suffered in strange places! . . .
> And now, with great breath, I greet it,
> The long-loved, rescuing sea . . .

and this:

> Night has come with silent footsteps,
> On the beaches by the ocean;
> And the waves, with curious whispers,
> Ask the moon, "Have you a notion
>
> "Who that man is? Is he foolish,
> Or with love is he demented?
> For he seems so sad and cheerful,
> So cast down yet so contented."
>
> And the moon, with shining laughter,
> Answers them, "If you must know it,
> He is both in love *and* foolish;
> And, besides that, he's a poet!"

I see now that the few lines I have written from "Sea Greeting" could sound ominous to you. They are not meant to be so. I only enclose them because the words are so beautiful. And look at the other. Is this a poem of sadness? It is me. It is us!

Heine was a great man. A great poet; a great German. And, oh yes, we must not forget: a Jew! Therefore in the logic of the times thought up by men devoid of reason, Heine is a nonperson. He does not exist!

I believe I shall read Heine more often. And — if I were a Landsmann right now in Berlin or Bremen, I would have a shelf of Heine in my house, *not hidden.* Bravado, eh, Ilse? . . .

. . . We travel slowly, submerged. The snorkel has cut down our speed, but on the other hand, we run unseen — or almost unseen — beneath the surface, only a feather trail visible.

I will take her up once or twice just to assure the crew the sky still exists.

Ah, yes. The snorkel. It is a great honor to have been selected to command a boat with such a life-saving device. Oh, so secret! Oh, such horseshit! You know why we have it? For the protection of one man — solely for one man. Our fifty were never so important before, but at least they now have the same protection *he* has.

It breathes for us. Do you know what it is to have fresh air circulating constantly? To have the exhaust pulled out? To take a deep breath and not choke on air fouled with diesel? To have the CO_2 and the filthy exhaust expelled by a *machine?* To ventilate below, out of harm's way?

And we can run on diesel while submerged, not using our batteries but recharging them. Running on the surface took seven hours to replenish the cells. Seven hours to wonder what vessel had picked us up. Seven hours of scanning the sky for approaching specks carrying depth bombs, scanning until specks danced before our eyes and we could not distinguish the real from the hallucinations.

Surfacing at night was little protection. We could be found, and you know too well my scream, "Dive! Crash dive!" I screamed it in your ears, lying in your arms . . . the waiting and the silence, fathoms deep . . . the absolute silence and the sweat of fear and the ping of the Asdic off the hull and the depth cans and the knowing that there was no knowing . . .

I should not have remembered. My darling, I promise you, we shall not replay those times. This voyage *will not* be a repeat of those others.

Because — we have the "snort." Notice, I learn the lingo. A little late, but so be it. The *secret* weapon that wins the War — again. We keep coming up with a new such weapon every other week, but we are not winning. There is a flaw in the equation, somewhere . . .

. . . The crew worries me . . . their attitude. I know so few well. There is little comradeship aboard. Is it me? The new ones — inexperienced and young, novices — fill the places of men who were my friends. Others are seasoned seamen, but I feel . . . something. Resentment? Do they dream of other boats and other captains?

Why am I so tense? I miss your fingers kneading the knots and ropes from my shoulders. Do it now. Oh, yes, I can feel your fingers. I can feel your fingers! My God, Ilse, you are really here! . . .

HANNES
AT SEA
FEBRUARY

The crew is sloppy, dirty. The officers emulate them. Tunics unbuttoned, no ties. Some have even shed their tunics. The Captain's cap is dingy white now; the band on the visor, cracked and peeling. And they do not shave! Bristly facial hair. There is no order when men are allowed such freedom with their water ration.

I *shall* shave and forgo the pleasure of brewed sawdust. I have *always* shaved.

I do not choose to mingle in the wardroom. The officers are ordinary and jabber about sex and food endlessly. The fresh vegetables are finished, leaving tasteless tinned stuff — unless some asshole dripped sweat on it — in which case it is briny enough to have been steeped in the deep.

The men listen intently to old records on a Victrola which seems to have only one needle: blunt. The music is bourgeois and does not blend with throbbing engines. The beats are out of whack!

The noise! The *noise!* I can see those pistons driving up and down, like pop-eyed locusts, stomping, driving, boring into my *brain.*

I cannot sleep for the noise. It seems to grow louder and all the other sounds chime in and all is magnified. The klaxon wails and who knows whether or not in alarm. The echo sounder sends out pings — torture, water torture — drip, drip, drip into a pool and lonely echoes cry back from the void. There is no quiet! There is no peace!

I slept last night. Was it night or light? How do I know it was night? I cannot keep track of time. I slept because I wore my wool cap — and earplugs. The latter I fashioned out of bread, kneaded to paste. So I slept and dreamed — of all things — of a steaming cup of bitter coffee! I awoke in a sweat with an aching in my belly for coffee, even ersatz.

The crew now have respectable beards. Perhaps I shall join them. A beard *would* change my appearance. And add maturity.

He took her up today. To survey his domain. A tiny man in a great big pond. He makes better time on the surface, so it is said. I think he took her up so his men could crawl out of their lairs.

Everyone is the color of mushrooms. Not surprising. Mushrooms grow in dank, dark cellars!

I was issued an oilskin slicker and hat that could have come straight out of "The Wreck of the Hesperus." Christ! I haven't thought of Longfellow since — Jesus! — Bussett. I never owned a raincoat then. What the hell use would it have been in Bussett!

It would seem that Steiner surfaces *only* on days when the clouds hang low. Even here, somewhere between Iceland and Greenland, there is danger from enemy scouts. Clear skies mean search planes. But clear skies mean calm seas. *Calm.*

I needed to ventilate the fucking fumes from lungs that are probably already carbonized. And check that there was more to the world than a flooded burrow.

"I joined the Navy to see the world and what did I see? I saw the SEA!"

The view was superlative. Gray clouds, gray sea, gray boat, gray faces. And then she rolled and heaved and I puked and heaved.

MARCH 1945

EMMA

CAPE CHARLOTTE

I'm sick of winter and I'm sick of school and I wish Peter would come.

I'm up on the knoll. If Mummy wants me, she'll holler out their bedroom window and I'll have to come in and help with housework. Saturday should be a day off for kids (teenagers!) and anyway, housework doesn't stay done — ever! You could do it all day and all night and by the time you've finished, what you started is dirty again. I like to do things that stay done!

I'm sitting on the *other* side of the juniper looking straight out to Portugal. Maybe Mummy can't see me. I can't see Portugal, but the sun makes a dancing path of sparkles to the horizon and way beyond. Sometimes I feel I can walk on that path straight across the ocean. Today would be a good day to do that!

I don't feel like doing homework either, so I'll draw my map of Cape Charlotte and maybe a bit of Jamesport. But I'll put down things that are interesting to *me!*

Cape Charlotte has a lot of coves! I'm only going to name some of them. If you were up high enough you would think a shark the size of King Kong had gone nibbling along the coast!

I've put in everything about Porpoise Point now. I've printed *very* carefully, but my drawing isn't so good.

There's the Thurstons' Big House and Porpoise Point Lighthouse and the cliffs where the waves smash. And that awful reef, Snaggletooth, sits off the Point just waiting to grab a ship. The reef's covered at high tide but when it's low, you can just see the tip. Looks more like a shark's fin, I think. But it's OK because there's a buoy bell that ding-dongs "Reef!" Half Moon Beach is on the other side of Porpoise Point — curvy and white like the moon, half full. I've been swimming there a couple of times and the breakers are gentle, but the water is *cold!* Mr. Thurston let us use the Beach House to change in.

The Jamesport Lightship is off the Point a bit. At night it shines a nice beam to tell boats where they are. Now it looks like it's floating above the ocean — like a mirage that wiggles in the sun. But it is *on* the water and *stays* there always because it has a special anchor to hold it. Daddy says that even in hurricanes, that boat never moves!

Mummy is calling me. Which means she wants me to do something. But I will be back!

I am back. I helped her wash the kitchen floor. I guess it needed it because there was a lot of dirty water, but in two days it will be all gucky again!

I've drawn some more. If you come on the Coast Road from the Point you go past my school, and then if you go on a bit more you'll come to Loch Cove which is *my* cove, and then there's *my* house and *my* knoll and juniper and cave and my favorite rock, Kala Nag! There isn't enough room to put in the six neighbors' houses! Amy's lucky I put in hers!

The Wileys' summer cottage is past Steeple Rock and Mussel Cove. Then comes my Easter Egg Cove and *Peter's* house. And up above is James Headland where the Fort is and James Head light watching over one side of the channel. Sometimes we just call the lighthouse James Head. A little while ago there was a party at the house here and everybody said the names had to be changed. They were going to christen the lighthouse Charles' Head, and the headland it was sitting on was going to be Cromwell's Point. Then they all howled. I looked up Cromwell in *A Child's History of England* and I guess it's sort of funny — Charles' Head because he lost it. Cromwell's Point because that's *how* he lost it. I think that when you're a little drunk everything seems FUNNY FUNNY.

I guess I'd better mention that Cape Charlotte is *not* called Charlotte. I mean, it's not pronounced the way it looks. It's pronounced Sha-*lot.* I don't know why, it just is. You can always tell a tourist. He says the name wrong and we have to explain and that takes awhile. Charlotte was King George's wife and I don't know how she pronounced it.

I like Bottlenose for the name of an island because it guards the other side of the channel. Bottlenose whales stand by guarding and trying to help their brother and sister whales if they are hurt. Baleen Bay, where the big Navy ships anchor in deep water, was named for

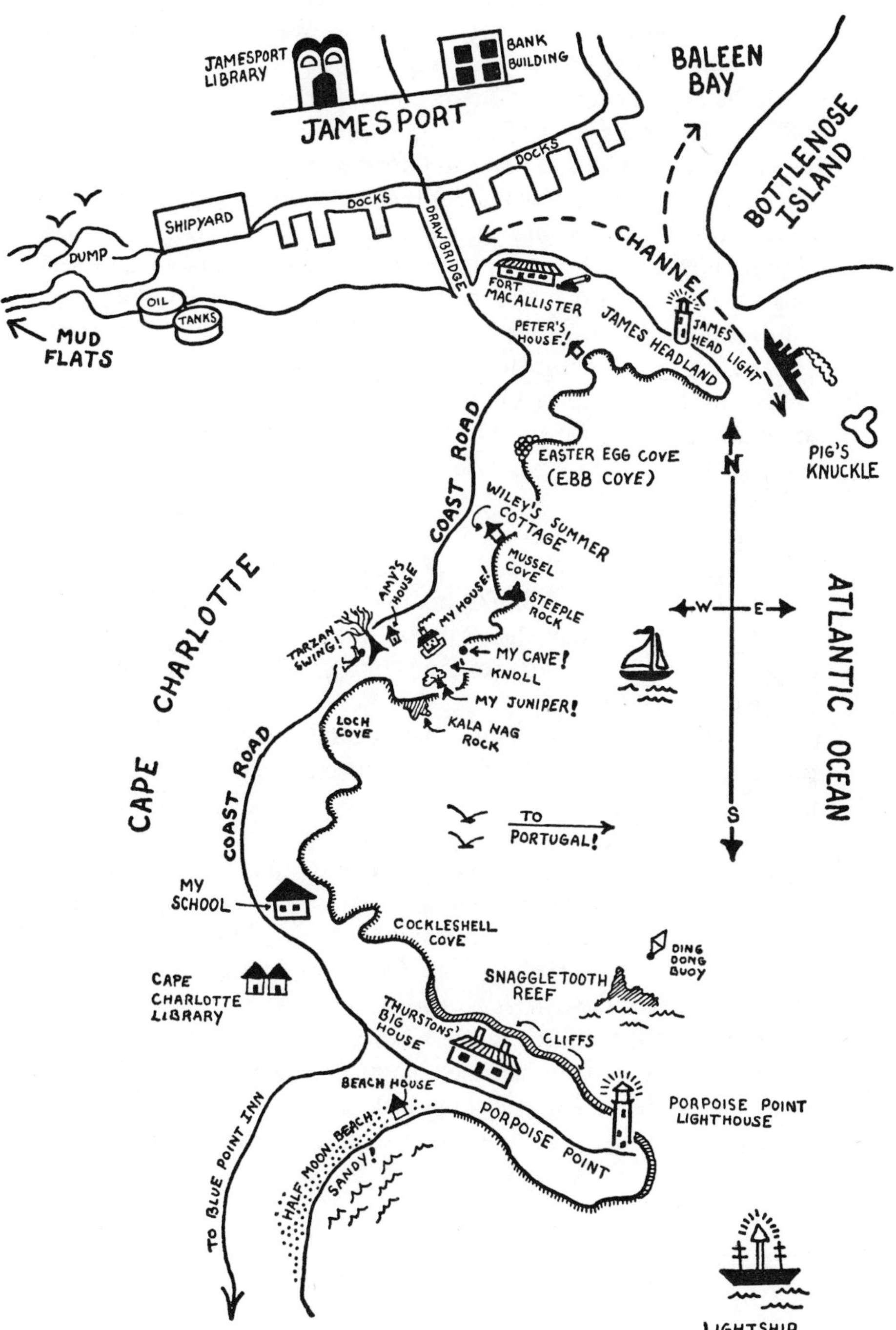

JAMESPORT LIBRARY
BANK BUILDING
JAMESPORT
BALEEN BAY
BOTTLENOSE ISLAND
DOCKS
DOCKS
SHIPYARD
DUMP
DRAWBRIDGE
CHANNEL
OIL
TANKS
MUD FLATS
FORT MACALLISTER
PETER'S HOUSE!
JAMES HEADLAND
JAMES HEAD LIGHT
EASTER EGG COVE
(EBB COVE)
PIG'S KNUCKLE
N
COAST ROAD
WILEY'S SUMMER COTTAGE
MUSSEL COVE
STEEPLE ROCK
AMY'S HOUSE
MY HOUSE!
W
E
ATLANTIC OCEAN
CAPE CHARLOTTE
TARZAN SWING!
MY CAVE!
KNOLL
MY JUNIPER!
KALA NAG ROCK
LOCH COVE
COAST ROAD
TO PORTUGAL!
S
MY SCHOOL
COCKLESHELL COVE
DING DONG BUOY
SNAGGLETOOTH REEF
CAPE CHARLOTTE LIBRARY
THURSTONS' BIG HOUSE
CLIFFS
BEACH HOUSE
PORPOISE POINT LIGHTHOUSE
TO BLUE POINT INN
HALF MOON BEACH
SANDY!
PORPOISE POINT
LIGHTSHIP

the part of a whale that filters food. Baleen also means "whalebone," and on the map the bay is roundish. Whalebone makes hoop skirts hoop. So Baleen Bay makes me think of *Gone With the Wind!*

All the ships go through the channel. (I didn't forget to draw in Pig's Knuckle near there!) The freighters and fishing boats go to the docks, but the tankers have to go past the Shipyard to the oil tanks. That means they have to go under the drawbridge. That bridge is always up, which either means there are a lot of tankers going under or the bridge is stuck. It usually *is* stuck, so a lot of cars sit for a very long time and then they get mad and then they start honking.

Beyond the Shipyard the harbor gets low and the mud flats stink, and the big city dump is there, and that stinks too.

I put in the Jamesport Library because I go there sometimes and the Bank Building because Daddy sat there a lot of nights once!

It's a pretty good map if I do say so myself!

If I could do a map in color I'd paint in the big rocks. Usually they're gray-black shale and not very pretty. But when the sun shines just right they look like big hunks of petrified wood! Iron is mixed in, sort of orangy. Pieces of rock are always falling off in rusty dribbles, then the tide breaks them into smaller pieces, and that's how beaches are made.

Last week we had a little thaw and I came down on the knoll and pretended it was spring. I scrunched down and let the sun shine on me and stayed out of the sea breeze and went to sleep thinking of summer. Well, when I woke up I knew it was still winter, because the ice on the north side of the big rocks was still there, sort of waxy. It had dripped down from the ledges and looked like saltwater taffy stalactites. I think those are the ones that hang down. Well, on Kala Nag, my special rock which is in front of the knoll, there was some ice that wasn't yellowish. It was something! A waterfall of ice that was so beautiful I wanted it to stay forever. It looked like someone had melted all the aquamarines in the world, poured them down Kala Nag's side, and frozen them instanter!

I looked for it today, my aquamarine waterfall. But it's gone, melted. Back to the tidepool, back to the sea.

STEINER

IN THE NORTH ATLANTIC

. . . I looked in the glass again. It was a mistake. Your pretty Rudi is not pretty. I doubt you could say with honesty that any remnant of a distingué demeanor remains. The husband that stands before you in the photo, the one with the arrogant eye, was 24. 1941, the day I was decorated by the Führer. I glowed with arrogance. Yes, Ilse? And I screwed you that night time after time after time until you screamed. A celebration of torpedoes.

These monsters that I carry everywhere with me — phallic symbols of rape. Long, stiff, iron-hard monsters, tips of red. Tips that explode on contact with the females of the sea. They search out their victim, homing in, and then shove their members in, erupting with orgiastic fury.

I was a monster that night. I wanted to rape. I did not mean to be so cruel. I only want to love you and hold you gently.

Forgive me my depression. But you said, "Write everything. Tell me *all* your thoughts, your worries. Write me when despair is blackest and all of life is a late November day."

Today is the second week of December, I think . . .

. . . Henkel closets himself behind his curtain. He insists on privacy; he has it. Perhaps he masturbates thinking of torpedoes! At least it keeps him busy, out of sight, out of my hair!

Speaking of hair: Henkel gave in a while back. Coffee or shaving, not both. The aroma of what passes for coffee defeated him and he began to grow a beard! But not until his face grew red and angry from shaving in salt water. We warned him, but Henkel does not take advice gladly . . .

. . . Henkel has to do without coffee! The reason: the mustache, if you can call it that, consisted of a few silky hairs, sprouting randomly. And his chin? Uneven clumps, surrounded by *many* bare patches.

Maybe it is a sin to feel such elation at his defeat. Then I have sinned! . . .

. . . I review the directives. They repeat themselves: "Proceed to landing point with all due caution. Radio silence is to be strictly observed until mission accomplished . . ."

What a reversal for the Grand Admiral, Ilse! Dönitz lives for contact with his wolf packs. He's chattering all the time — receiving, sending. The Atlantic reverberates with sound!

". . . Steer a random zigzag course out of normal shipping lanes. Do *not* engage the enemy. Do *not,* repeat, do *not* fire on any vessel for any reason, no matter how ripe . . ."

A lesson learned, love. On a previous mission such as ours, the boat captain dallied to stalk a lone freighter, anxious to chalk up extra tonnage. And thereby delayed the landing.

". . . Repeating: Radio silence to be observed until out of enemy waters. And — *No* hunting. Repeat. *No* hunting."

Ilse, I think they have made their point, don't you?

HANNES
AT SEA

I will not eat in the Officers' Wardroom. Steiner nibbles there. I get what passes for meals from the galley and take them behind my curtain.

I check and double-check and check some more — the most important thing I bring to America. Of my own design and fashioned in ten days by a craftsman: a body belt invisible under the bulk of layers I will wear.

It is wider than a money belt for it carries more than currency! Much more. One foot wide, it fits tightly around my waist and chest: canvas lined with rubber; spring seals for each pocket. And for extra protection, each section contains individual sheets of oilskin which I will wrap around the contents. The belt, secured with brass clasps, will not loosen. I have tested their strength under strenuous conditions.

I passed Steiner in a passageway. His cap gets filthier and the once-gleaming eagle on it has dulled. Tarnished like the Captain's thoughts?

Steiner sees the enemy in visions so constant, they reek of paranoia! When he gets one of his neurotic delusions we go deeper, below periscope depth, below the reach of the snorkel's tubes. Its hoses are shut off, the valves sealed, and we are *entombed.* And my ears burst and the air is canned and the chemical does not absorb enough carbon dioxide and I grow faint and cannot think. We are sealed in a bunker like rats! Rats!

There is nothing to do. My mind wanders back to inner memories that should lie buried. The dead rise up. Awake, they rise and stare at me. They stare and I am not asleep. I do not dream. I have not dreamed for months, so now they come to torment my waking hours.

He could have added that something extra! A second of his time and he could have done it. With a stroke of the pen, a promotion: Hauptsturmführer. Eye to eye, Steiner. Captain to Captain, so to speak. The Führer tried to bribe me with sweet words and a token. A lousy tin medal! I deserve more recognition! What was '44 all about? Flushing out Maquisards? Having to consort with Barbie? Top kommando in Operation Greif? Was that sitting on my ass? I started the lousy year as a 1st Lt. and ended it a 1st Lt.! I want the rank due me. Even if the Reich goes under, *I want that rank!*

How goes the War? I forgot the War.

I grow old behind the curtain. Time passes . . . nothing is accomplished. I cannot plan for land, for now the mind is fuzzy and forgetful. I am weak and flabby and my blood, what is left of it, pours into my backside. The legs are rubber. Each step is like sinking into unknown depths in slow motion, bouncing in a place of 0 gravity.

The crew avoids me. At least most of them. There must be some who cling to dreams of Victory. There must be some who still have hope and *loyalty*. There must be a few who see Steiner as a morbid defeatist!

A little exercise today. I began to shave again. The beard was unbecoming and the coffee truly stinks!

I think there are some possibles among the ordinary seamen, the raw recruits. I notice several who shoot me shy glances. They remember the uniform. They are the ones to work on. A little mingling, a little probing. A new occupation will revive my sluggishness.

I have two recruits of sorts. One from Franconia, the other from Linz. We play a game for dummies and they are dumb, but malleable. Rummy is the game. I don't think they are up to Whist. The cards are battered — chewed and peeling. I know at least twelve from the distinctive creases on their backs. The Austrian is the best bet, still full of faith and youthful exuberance. He asks me about my service. The SS carries an élan. We are the high players in the game of War. And he is a boy who wants to be a high player. He cheats. I let him. I let him win and tell him softly about Steiner. Tell him how even captains can lose confidence in themselves, *in their country,* and thereby become a danger to those they command. The Austrian nods. I have sewn some seeds. Dragon seeds.

HENRY

CAPE CHARLOTTE

I worked frantically preparing. I have been *promised* what I have worked for, these long years: negatives and the bloody confession! I had not meant to use that obscene British term, but as I glance at it, the word *does* seem appropriate in my case.

This endeavor must and *will* be my last for them. None of us can continue the charade, seeing the progress of the War. Once I am rid of my March visitor, I am done, finished, relieved of all responsibility!

I had a nightmare so fiendish I sat bolt upright in bed, droplets of fluid dotting my brow. I dreamt that the Bolsheviks had captured Berlin and in ransacking it had uncovered the extant documents — my documents: intact. The horror continued. In my dream (Thank God, it was only such), I was now made to pay tribute to *them,* to the Godless Communists!

But then I awoke and remembered that the documents are on their way. Somewhere in the North Atlantic, safe from Russian invaders!

In working out the details, I prepared a secondary rendezvous point, just in case. What that case could be, I cannot foresee. I do not wish to dwell on mishaps.

So now the waiting time has begun. Waiting is always difficult. And wasteful, for the mind is consumed with the end result and cannot function well during such periods.

BUFFY

CAPE CHARLOTTE

Dear Meg,

March creeps along, reluctant to give us April. She blows like a dragon, spitting sleet and vowing to sweep everything off the land into the sea.

Now there is a lull and the heavy overcast has given way to

patches of blue. I can see a fishing boat struggling into the harbor, weighted down with ice. She is almost lost in the whitecaps, but heroically fights her way through heavy seas to the channel and safety.

What she must have endured out there!

It becomes more and more clear to me that after this War is finished I *cannot* go back to fashioning yachts for summer people. I feel as though in doing so, I would be committing a sin. It doesn't make sense, and I don't know if I understand what has driven me to this decision — or if I can explain it.

I think it is the sea. It lives — and feels — and then rebels. These summer sailors take her for granted, use her, revel in the guileless blue, skipping over her face on sparkling July days. They dare the sea with their willfulness, and then, untouched, they depart in September, leaving behind an irritant that festers. But others will pay. With the bitter cold of winter, the sea's dark side emerges, and she takes revenge against all who sail on her — the fisherfolk, the merchant seamen.

You think I am a mystic, a kook. Then I am. But I believe with all my heart that the sea has pride — and scorned, lashes out to drown the innocent.

Therefore, be it resolved that Sinclair and Sons will, after hostilities have ceased (and the contracts run out), become a Shipyard noted for the finest, sturdiest and *cheapest* fishing boats on the Eastern Coast. And be it further resolved that only bona fide fishermen can purchase them! *There.* It is in writing and you have witnessed what? A will? I guess it is a will *and* a contract to myself, not to be broken.

Thanks for being my audience. Writing to you helps me collect my myriad misgivings into a cohesive statement of purpose.

Much love,
Buffy

P.S. My old darling has been all of a twitter lately. Goes in and out at odd times. His demeanor does not betray him. Sphinxlike, as usual. But I can tell he's twittering under that calm. And he paces. Never used to. Every night during the last week he has gone out somewhere. Thinks I can't hear the back door closing. Ha! I can hear a cricket chirp in China!

If I didn't know him so well, I'd say he was meeting some young thing on the sly. But not my Pudge. I don't think he could get it up for La Turner! That *was* beastly, wasn't it?

EMMA
CAPE CHARLOTTE

Mummy is really mad at me. She said I'm sloppy and forgetful and I don't help when I should and other things I can't remember. So then I got mad and stomped upstairs and slammed my door, and then Mummy came up and said while I was about it, why didn't I take up all my stuff which has been lying in piles for weeks on the stairs. I kept quiet because I couldn't think why. So when I came out a little later I was all ready to carry my piles to my room, but they weren't there! You know where they were? Down in a barrel at the bottom of the cellar stairs. Mummy threw every living thing wham! down there. And she's still mad.

I took in the laundry today. Mummy was very pleased and surprised because I did it without her asking ten times. The laundry was so stiff and cold that when I folded it, it was like folding icy cardboard and my fingers froze! Now I know why parts of the ends of Mummy's fingers are greenish white. They have been frostbitten!

Mummy asked what happened to all my good intentions about housework. I don't know. I did have them, but they just don't seem to last very long.

HENRY
JAMESPORT

Today, in Jamesport, I completed preparations in the unlikely event anything should go awry.

Although this precautionary stratagem was spelled out and sent off before the U-boat embarked, I did not complete the arrangements until this morning. My timing seems appropriate — one week before the first possible date of arrival.

Surprisingly, the arrangements were speedily concluded. The rooming house was necessary in either case. The second I accomplished with aplomb, and whilst there, succeeded in gathering more reference material for my history of the waterfront.

I feel a certain tenseness as this final week of waiting ticks by with agonizing nonchalance. All is in readiness; the place of refuge: secluded, safe. I attribute my case of nerves as akin to that suffered by actors waiting in the wings for the curtain to rise.

I must put my playlet in proper perspective — and out of mind! Attempting to do so, I shall write of the whale, leviathan of the seas, and its contribution to commerce.

EMMA
CAPE CHARLOTTE

I think I am growing bosoms! They are only little bumps but they hurt! *It's about time.* I hate my cotton undershirts. Amy's had her bosoms for a year and a half. Of course, she's almost six months older than I am, but that's still a year she's ahead of me. She let me try on her bra, but it wasn't any good. The bumps got lost in there somewhere.

Now if I could get hair under my arms and more below my stomach and on my legs — AND get the CURSE, I would really be on my way to being grown up. I'm 13 and a quarter and I *still* haven't got the Curse! I won't tell you that Amy's got it because she has. So what! She can't stand her mother and I can stand mine — most of the time, so I'm luckier than she is, I guess.

The other day I really thought I had it. The Curse, I mean. I ached way down low in my stomach, and it wasn't near where my appendix is and it wasn't that funny feeling, the sick one you get before you upchuck. It was a different pain. Mummy thought I was getting it too, so she gave me some gin in ginger ale. She said gin helps. I guess it does because the pain went away. But I still *do not* have the Curse yet!

Today was *definitely* not a good day! I shouldn't have asked the question, but I had to know and now I do and I wish I didn't! Valerie is (was — I don't know!) Peter's girlfriend! I asked him right out if he had a girl, and I was waiting for him to say No, but instead he said *sort of!* My stomach got sick and I felt awful, so I ran as fast as I could even though he was hollering at me. I flew up the stairs and locked my door and wouldn't come down for supper. I still feel awful. Valerie is a stinker, and how anybody like Peter could like her, I don't know! She rides on the school bus, and because she thinks she's so great and a junior in high school, she's mean to all the littler kids and everybody hates her, including ME!!! I'm not going to waste any more time talking about Valerie. I'M GOING UNDER THE COVERS!! And I'm not hungry, either!

* * *

Well, I saw Peter today and I *didn't mention* Valerie, so after a while he did. He brought her up. He *says* she's really not his girl anymore. He says he named his dory for her, but he got mad at her and painted the name out. So I asked why he got mad at her because I really wanted to know this part. Peter told me Valerie had pestered him to take her to the Junior Prom, so he said OK and he got two gallons of gas which he wasn't allowed, but when he went to her house she wouldn't go with him. She took one look at his dirty old pickup and said she wouldn't be caught dead in the thing. That everybody would laugh at her coming to a dance with somebody who drove a scrap heap! That did it, Peter says. And he's fed up with her! I hope you keep right on thinking that way, Valerie! I hope you never *ever* decide to ride in Peter's pickup!!!

I'm sitting on my bed and boiling so much I can't breathe. Mummy and I had another fight and I hurt. All I wanted was to have Millicent over for the night and Mummy said no, she was too tired. So then I got mad, really mad, and I wanted to explode so I did. I called Mummy awful names like lazy and cruel and whatever else I could think of. And then I ran out of the kitchen, upstairs. So did Daddy, three steps at a time. He grabbed me and whaled my bottom and said never ever talk to your mother like that again. And go down and apologize. Well, I said I wouldn't ever, and he said OK, stay here until you change your mind. And he clomped downstairs. I've never seen Daddy so mad. Mummy and I yell at each other a lot. And we've been fighting for a couple of months. I don't know why, but we do and we yell. So I hollered down the stairs that I was going to kill myself — I was going to jump off the rocks. But there wasn't a sound from the kitchen. I'm *not* going to apologize and maybe I *will* kill myself. But I've got to think up a better way than jumping off the rocks. I'm too scared of the deep dark water. Peter is the only person in the whole world who's not mean to me!!

I sort of apologized today. I vacuumed the whole living room and the front hall. And Mummy and I didn't fight. She even smiled at me. Maybe she doesn't hate me.

I was thinking how to really fix Valerie. I could stick pins in my cloth Greek doll that looks like a grown-up lady and name her Valerie. I don't want her to get *too* hurt, just enough to fix her for a while. Maybe instead of pins I'll put a witch's curse on her. I can't remember where I heard this, but I think it's a witch's curse.

Wire, briar, limerlock
Four geese in a flock
One flew east and one flew west
And one flew over the cuckoo's nest.

Now that I've said it, I don't think it sounds so witchy. And what happened to the other goose? Maybe it's Valerie!!

I'm worried about Who Me. He's at the vet's and he's really sick. We took him yesterday and the vet says he's got blood poisoning and he's using some sulfa stuff that might fight the poison. Maybe if I had noticed that his foot was cut, Who Me would be home and not sick. But he didn't start to limp until his foot got sore, which took a couple of days, the vet says. He probably cut it on some old rusty metal that's all over the beach and didn't notice it because he was so busy chasing Apricot and laughing to himself, watching Apricot slide all over the icy rocks. Who Me never slips, even on the iciest rock. Who Me, please get better! I miss you very much. If you get better, you can chase Apricot for a whole day if you want to. I'll even open the door for you!

STEINER
IN THE NORTH ATLANTIC

... I know I should trust the snorkel, but I am sure the feather trail gives us away as easily as the bubbling wake of the periscope, so we unflex the hoses now as often as possible. We are in range of aircraft. Better to breathe old air than none at all ...

... There is evil aboard. It walks the boat. The men sense it. Conversation is muted. Morale is low ...

... My men are robots. Awake they perform assigned tasks with glazed eyes. Those who sleep on off shifts do so fitfully ...

... I fell into an exhausted sleep so deep that dream after dream could not wake me. And Ilse, Ilse, they were dreams of horror. I dreamt that Henkel had taken over the boat. He wore black — not the uniform, but some sort of diaphanous tunic that reached to the floor and swirled around him like fog. Around his neck on a red ribbon hung a life-sized skull whose bleached jaws clattered as though it were trying to speak, but no sound came.

I shouted commands, yet I was as silent as the skull. And the men obeyed him, not me. The engines stopped and the crew moved lethargically, dreamily, opening the sea strainer.

I screamed a warning, but no one heard.

We sank sluggishly, to settle on the bottom, and the boat filled I was floating with them, but alive. And so was Henkel, still. But all at once his flowing cloak spread out in the water like the wings of a monstrous bat and slowly began to disintegrate until it was an inky stain. And then Henkel disintegrated. His flesh peeled off, leaving only a wavering skeleton. My men floated by, still clothed in seamen's garb, but around each neck now hung a tiny skull. I looked down to see the same around my neck and then I began to suffocate — to drown and suffocate. The process was endless. I wanted to die and I could not . . .

. . . The panic has passed. I am better just telling you about the nightmare. Henkel has no power here. He is a fanatic, though he would dispute the word. I think his eyes betray him. They glitter with a sort of madness.

Soon — soon he leaves my boat and takes his demons with him. He makes me see demons everywhere . . .

. . . The gramophone has been silent now for days, the records forgotten. Zombies do not play music. They do not play at anything . . .

. . . We are deaf and dumb and blind down here. At periscope depth of 20 meters or so, I have only a couple of meters of antenna above the surface. And I am not receiving well . . .

. . . We steam slowly and I have no weather reports. None. One picket U-boat with meteorological gear is operating in the area. I cannot pick her up! . . .

HANNES
AT SEA

Pigboat! *Pigboat!* The swine *stink.* They all stink. The crap tanks stink. The stink stinks!

The Austrian is a loser. He will never be a leader! It was a waste of time. But I had time. Time! Time! Time!

Creak, you bloody boat. Creak and groan and drip, you crud-infested stinking lousy vile madhouse and the green mold sprouts and feeds and grows — to eat *us!*

Blackness over everyone. No smart talk. No sex talk. Palpable blackness. Contagious blackness.

I can't . . . the pressure . . . the hull will buckle and crush us . . . thin skin ruptures and we will all die in agony and drown and our chests will explode and our eyes will pop out. Oh God, I can't scream I can't breathe . . . trapped. Steiner kills me slowly. He put me in the closet and locked me in and he is laughing outside . . . I can hear him. And he will take her so deep the hull will close in, and he will kill us to kill me, and the metal screams, moves, meets, and my bones crack and my head bursts, squeezed to pulp thin as paper, smothered, squashed, and Steiner laughs.

Steiner knows. Steiner knows. I know he knows! I made it to the can and couldn't get off. I stayed a lifetime and all the water in the world came out . . . shitters and shitters and juices and blood and pink water and clear water and still it poured.

Canvas curtain to hide behind, railing to hold on to to grip to grab. I break my hands to keep from screaming. I rock and weep and clench my teeth and bite my cheeks and they run with blood. I swallow blood, drool blood and I will yell soon, I will. I will whimper and howl and shriek and crawl under and die and die crapping. I cannot hold it. I crapped in my pants I crapped in my pants and the shit pours out and the puke and the blood pours out and the sweat pours out and I dry up and die.

A few more days, oh God. Hang on for a few more days. Steiner is the Devil. Hang on and Satan will float away and drown.

* * *

A nightmare. After all these months, a dream at night to add to days of uninterrupted horror. A nightmare with a twist, Steiner is with me.

The people stand in rows like stalks of corn, and as I approach, it is as though a great wave of heat blows through the field. The stalks wither and die, but do not fall.

In their midst is a stake set in stagnant water. On the stake is a figure, floppy like a rag doll. No, not a doll, a scarecrow. But as I come nearer, I can see the figure is that of a man tied to a rough wooden cross, his hands and feet nailed and bleeding. A crucifixion in a cornfield. The man is still alive, but dying.

And now the pool of water grows, expands, moving out to drown the stalks, and the man on the cross is Steiner. His head lolls against, not wood, but a cool brass cylinder. His arms flop over the folded-out arms of the instrument that supports his limp body. His legs have buckled. And now the water rises rapidly to engulf Steiner, to engulf the cross: his periscope.

The nightmare has become a soothing dream, for I am not involved. I am only an observer.

HENRY

CAPE CHARLOTTE

It is now 4 A.M. Eastern Wartime, Sunday. Three days have passed since the 15th and nothing! No sign of my visitor. The food and fresh warm clothing are undisturbed. The wood stove is cold. Last evening would have been the obvious time for landing a rubber raft. Ideal conditions. Clear and calm.

It's a weather breeder, Evelyn sniffs. She instinctively distrusts a lovely day, declaring that under the cover of beauty lurks violence. I do not believe that this phenomenon has been sufficiently studied. But Evelyn remains peevishly indomitable and will not be swayed by reason.

At least this time her prognostications are in error (which I shall not point out to her, savoring the victory in secret), for still the stars are out, twinkling happily before the dawn overpowers their brilliance.

Now I must sleep, for the late hours are telling. I am afraid I must miss church today, but shall erase my tardiness with extra prayer.

* * *

The stars are *not* out! I have just journeyed to the place of refuge, *still undisturbed.* I am reaching the end of my tether! This ceaseless nightlife combined with unceasing emotional letdown are wreaking havoc with my digestive system, being, as I am, not in the first flush of manhood.

The stars are *not out* and this Sabbath has seen a steady procession of clouds cluster, group and multiply until they now threaten to suffocate the sky. An ominous portent of things to come? I shall not dwell on mishap!

And — henceforth, I resolve *not* to discuss the vagaries of weather with Evelyn — never again, from this day forward!

STEINER

IN THE NORTH ATLANTIC

. . . Oh Ilse, wrap your arms around me. I am shaking and afraid. I want to be sane and human and alive with you. I want to come home so much that I think I will not. Wanting too badly is tempting Fate. And Fate is the demon who spits curses and wears the Death's Head. I see behind his mask. He wills us to perish . . .

. . . I had to take her up. Very close to the coast of the New World, we were. But I had to chance it. Nova Scotia to starboard.

I had to take her up to see the sky. I had to see for myself through eyes that are not glass lenses.

Even on the surface with antenna high, we could not rouse U-1230. She is not transmitting. Not even bursts.

What could she tell me that I do not already know? That the pressure falls? That the sky sends messages? That the air and the sea cannot keep a secret?

Ilse, you would look at the sky and see wisps of cloud strung out and liken them to wedding veils of chiffon. You would sail the sea and notice only pretty whitecaps and marvel at the gentle, dewy breeze. You would say the day was fine. And I, I would say the day was ominous.

I see storm. I smell storm.

The wisps above are tangling and multiplying. The breeze will be a gale before too long and the small chop will churn into seas so heavy they will be black water mountains. And that breeze contains more than damp. There will be much moisture in the air to ride the gale as frozen particles: sleet or snow.

We head for storm. We race to meet each other. Perhaps we can land the Devil before the worst of it. Perhaps . . . with luck . . .

HANNES

AT SEA

He's taken her up again! And, Oh Christ, I put it out of my mind that soon I will have to bob in on a balloon, a thin-skinned balloon, a black balloon that calls itself a raft — a pin might pop it. He's down from the bridge. He says nothing at first. His face is grayer than gray, but his eyes are bright; they glitter with a sort of madness. But he doesn't look at me; he's plotting something. "36 hours," he says — to no one in particular.

Think only of land, think only of rendezvous and sand and a cottage on a lonely beach. No welcome candle burning — blackout still — but fresh food and clothing — *fresh, fresh* — fresh and clean and wholesome and new, and a bed that does not rock. Think of rendezvous and Midas. Midas. Learn from him, learn all his tricks . . . then dead, Midas, and I have your secrets.

Twelve hours to freedom. Free to walk on land again; wobbly legs, bandy legs, bouncing on *land* — flat land, cracked land, swampland, *any* land — back in my beloved country again. "Oh beautiful for spacious skies that do not stink of seas." Away from salt and stink and oil, canned like a sardine. *Free* and breathing! Free of thee, Steiner! Free of sailors who are mad. I curse this boat and all who sail on her!

EMMA

CAPE CHARLOTTE

Yesterday was a weather breeder, which means it was absolutely beautiful — not a cloud in the sky and clear as clear as clear can be. Which means — we are going to have a storm, probably tomorrow.

It's gray today and there's a mackerel sky and I'm waiting — AS USUAL! — for Peter. I never know and I'm always waiting and I know he knows I do, and I wish just once he had to wait for me! If he *would* wait, which I won't ever know, because as soon as I get home from school I run down here to the knoll and hope. Saturdays and Sundays, too.

I think I see his mackinaw! *I do.* Boy! It's the only bright thing in this whole day. Such a gray day, but yellow is a happy color — at least for me. I've got to go!

It's night now, and I'm staying up way past the time I'm supposed to be asleep writing this with a flashlight because I have a lot I want to write about.

Peter came and I told him about Who Me. He really was very sad and said to tell Who Me even Apricot missed him (which I don't think is true, but I'll tell Who Me anyway). Then Peter looked funny — funny peculiar — and I asked what's wrong and he said a lot of things were wrong, so naturally I asked what? Well, then he said he couldn't explain it exactly and pulled out an envelope and said it's in here, all of it. And then he said the letter inside was for me and not to read it until I couldn't see him anymore on the beach. And he just left.

I didn't even wait to watch him go. I had to read the letter! So I zipped along the beach, practically not touching the rocks, and I flew (almost) up to my room and I locked the door and then I sat on my bed and took a lot of breaths because I was scared to read what he had written to me. I thought he was going to tell me that he liked Valerie again and I didn't want to know!

I don't care if this takes ten pages in my notebook diary! I don't care if I have to stay up till morning to write everything because it's the best day I have ever had! The really best day in my whole life!

BECAUSE Peter's letter is the nicest letter I have ever gotten. Ever! So I'm going to copy it down and I'll bet anyone would say it is something special. So here goes. It's sad in places, but it's wonderful!

Dear Emma,

I don't say things very well. At least out loud. Something clogs up and all the things I'm thinking stay inside. So I'm writing this to try and tell you what's bothering me, what's been bothering me for a very long time. Maybe after you've read this we can talk about it. Soon, I hope.

Sometimes you seem afraid that I will think you're a pest. You're *not* a pest. I love to listen to you chatter. I've had a lot of fun roaming the beaches and the rocks with you. You make me forget problems and laugh. I know I clam up at times but only because I'm afraid I can't express what's inside. You bring me out of myself more than anyone else I've ever known. You're a wonderful nut which is a compliment! Really!

Emma, I don't want to finish school. I want to go to sea now — join the Merchant Marine before the War's over. I'll work my way up. Stay in and get my master's papers and someday take command of my own ship — a tanker, maybe. I'm 17, old enough to go. If I wait to be drafted, which is sure to happen, who knows where I'll end up? The government is stupid enough to take someone who knows the sea and put him in the Army. And the Army is stupid enough to take a fisherman and send him to Kansas. I'd die in Kansas! I'd die there as quick as I would in combat. Maybe quicker!

I want more out of life than being a fisherman. If I stay here and don't try now, I'll be a fisherman all my life. And I'll hate knowing the only things in life are a leaky boat I can't afford to fix and nets that tangle and fish that stink and a house that leaks and smells of fish stink. And I'll start to hate the sea because I can't make a living off of her. I don't want to hate the sea.

My father's forty and he's old and tired, but he keeps going out. And my mother worries she'll never see him again and then he makes it back to port with the boat all white with ice from the storms and the spray — and no catch. Two weeks out and nothing to show for it.

It's a rotten life. I've watched my mother die a thousand times waiting, waiting, worrying sick. How many times have we gone down to the docks when the dragger's overdue? And then when it finally chugs into harbor, we live a little and then we die a little, knowing it's going to happen all over again. And someday there'll be the time when they're way overdue. And we wait. And the boat doesn't come in, and everybody — the fisherfolk are kind, but sort of quiet. And then the boat is listed: "Missing and presumed lost." And it finally hits. There's nobody to bury, nobody to say goodbye to. A husband, a father is out there, caught in the damned weed, floating forever.

Oh, Emma, I've *got* to go and enlist. I'm going to talk to my parents and ask for their blessing but I won't get it. I want your blessing, too. I want you to understand.

Emma, once I thought you were like a little sister. But you're more.

Love,
Peter

HENRY
CAPE CHARLOTTE

I cannot monitor tonight. I cannot open the door! The wind began this morning, picked up velocity by afternoon, and became a full-blown gale by evening. But worse, those evil clouds, furrowed like beached and bloated whales, poured out putrescence as though pricked with a pin. Like a white precipitate of pus, the showering flakes of snow have mounted into drifts whose depth exceeds my height!

I was so confident that this would be the night! With absolute certainty I pictured greeting my visitor, recovering my dossier, and at first light spiriting him into town to the next way-station on his journey: the rooming house I secured last week. And once accomplished, I could wash my hands of him and *any* further intrigue. Spying has lost all semblance of provocative pleasure! Indeed, intrigue and its consequences are wearing, wearying, totally all-consuming — a punishment of mind and body, so punishing I want to weep! But that venting, allowed to the child, is denied the grown man. Still, I want to!

Somewhere, out there beyond the breakers, under an angry sea, safe and quiet, lies a submarine — waiting until the weather clears and the surf subsides.

And so, with them, I must bide my time. I must hold on one more day!

EMMA

CAPE CHARLOTTE

Holy Hannah! It's really kicking up. It started before we left school and it's been building ever since. I got right into bed after supper where I'm safe and warm and cozy. First the wind scratched and whined at the windows trying to get in, but I wouldn't let it. Now it's screaming and clawing and I'm *very sure* I won't let it.

When it snows at night, I can always tell because the foghorns tell me. Moaning means snow. I don't even have to open the window to know. But I just peeked out, and the wind rushed in and so did half the snow in Cape Charlotte, which is a lot! It's snowing like HELL out there, and I can't hear the horns because the wind is making such a racket. Now it's stomping at the window because I shut it out. Just like a bratty little child kicking his mother. Usually I love storms, but I don't like this one. I'm glad I'm inside!

I've got your letter, Peter, under my pillow. Oh, Peter! I'm so glad you're inside too, and not in the Merchant Marine yet. The ocean's wild and mean tonight.

STEINER
OFF THE COAST

... You were singing, Ilse. I heard you as clearly as I hear my own heart. All night you crooned the same, almost tuneless song. I did not close my eyes for fear of missing it, yet I feel more rested than if I had slept for half a day.

Come to me again, tonight. I shall will the hours to pass until you whisper melodies to me once more. I can survive without sleep forever when you are with me ...

... Only twelve hours to rendezvous — more or less. Less if I push her. My boat could fly if I asked her to. *I* could fly, for your lullabies have energized me to the heights. My mind is at its peak ... I have never felt so much in command of my faculties. I need never sleep again ...

... I wonder what the whales think. Do they think we are one of them? Or do they know we are steel intruders — a deadly species? Do they have a past handed down by song when the depths were theirs? Heine says the German is like a slave who obeys the mere nod or word of his master, and needs neither whips nor chains. Servility is inherent in him, in his soul. I want to pick strawberries with you ... field strawberries, the little ones that sparkle like jewels, tiny strawberries that ripen, regardless of War and Death, so apart from Death ...

... I told you of a storm. I am a prognosticator, I am. I should get a meteorological medal, I should, one with lightning streaks — no, not that one, the SS has it. We roll at 20 meters below, which means, my love, that on the surface we pitch. I have to come up to check the bearings, to find the Lightship ...

... Nature plays with me. She thinks she can outwit me with her monstrous seas. She does not know I can outride anything afloat! She also sends heavy snow to blot my vision — clotted cream, the snow ... save some to put on my strawberries. But the Lightship beam, constant, is visible ... just. She is close to us. Seas too high to launch the black one. We wait, submerged again. A few hours ... the wind may lessen ...

... The wind has lowered. We creep in ... land beacon barely discernible ... snow massively thick and mixed with flying spume from cresting waves . . . beacon's pattern obscured, but Lightship guides the way. Direction finder operating . . . position noted . . . angle checks . . . almost . . . seas still heavy. He *must* go, but he will capsize in seconds, drown in minutes. No! he cannot die! He is Death! I am *not* a murderer! He tried to trick me but I have found him out. Of course, he is Death and Death cannot be killed! He wails in feigned fright but I know his secret. Over the side, Death . . . take your omens of doom and your evil into dark water. The albatross goes overboard . . . the boat is secure . . .

. . . We outshout the wind. We wallow in the seas and scream with relief. The Devil has left us and we are coming home, Ilse. LEFT FULL RUDDER! PREPARE TO DIVE! WE'RE COMING HOME! . . .

WJAM RADIO
JAMESPORT

Good Tuesday morning, everyone! In spite of yesterday's, shall we say intemperate, weather, today will be clear, with temperatures climbing to the forties! How's that, Spring hopefuls?

To all you kiddies out there — sorry, the roads are being plowed and school officials have said that school *will* keep. I repeat. There *will* be school!

It is now 7:02, March 20th, and this is your newsman, Larry Litchfield, with the local stories:

The late winter storm which battered the coast yesterday afternoon and continued throughout much of the night has left one person missing, scores of homes without power, and dragged the Lightship, the SS *Jamesport,* several miles off course.

The snow, which at times fell at the rate of 2 inches an hour, was blown into drifts as high as 6 feet by a wind which peaked at a velocity of more than 60 miles per hour.

Peter Trefethen, 17, of Cape Charlotte was reported missing by his parents late last night. The youth was said to have left the house after an argument. A rowboat belonging to the boy and usually tied up to a dock below the Trefethen residence was also missing. Mr. Trefethen told WJAM that his son frequently rowed to a small island at the outer neck of the channel where he was building a cabin. Mr. Trefethen added that the Coast Guard and Army personnel from Fort MacAllister were instituting a search of the channel and coastal beaches beginning at dawn. That would be about 10 minutes ago. Mr. Trefethen asked that all residents of the coastal area be on the lookout for the boy, who was wearing a heavy yellow plaid jacket when last seen.

WJAM contacted spokesmen from both Services, who confirmed that at first light they had sent up a scout plane to aid in the search.

Another casualty of the high winds was the Lightship, the SS *Jamesport,* which was driven northeasterly from her normal position, slightly south of Porpoise Point.

WJAM managed to talk with Captain Elias Daggert, master of the Lightship, just after the boat made port about an hour ago. Here are his comments:

"I can't explain the shift. This is the first time in my memory that the ship has moved from her fixed position. We must have dragged anchor for nearly two hours. The auxiliary anchor, which is set to drop at the first sign of trouble, did not function. I have no explanation for the failure at this time."

WJAM then asked Captain Daggert what the conditions were during the height of the storm.

"The wind was whole gale force, gusting up to 63 knots. Sometime between 7 and 9 P.M., when the wind was at its highest velocity, we must have started our drift.

"The seas were very heavy, but it was the snow — so thick it was like trying to see through cottage cheese — which caused us to lose our bearings. Visibility was nigh unto zero. The watch crew noticed no wake, which would have alerted us to movement. A wake is always observed when the ship is under power, even at Dead Slow.

"We were pitching so that the drift, which took place over a period of two hours, we estimate, was not noticed."

We asked the Captain why he lost his bearings. This is his reply:

"We had no bearings! Our radio antenna was blown to [bleeped] and all land beacons were blotted out. The first we learned of the shift was at 4 A.M. this morning, when the snow let up. That's when we found out that we were way out of position. Our normal beacon is Porpoise Light, north northwest of us. Now we found James Head light north northwest of us!

"After we rigged up a makeshift antenna, we immediately radioed the Port, informing them of our dilemma and also reporting some structural damage. In turn, they ordered us to come in for repairs.

"May I add that we have been advised that during the darkness no ships were due in, bound for harbor. For this I am thankful, being, as we are, a sure beacon on which all ships at sea fix their position."

This has been an exclusive interview with Captain Elias Daggert of the Lightship SS *Jamesport.*

WJAM has just learned that port authorities have announced an investigation of the incident, commencing shortly.

Now, news on the world front, coming up after these messages . . .

STEINER

ON SNAGGLETOOTH REEF

. . . It is really very amusing, quite laughable. We are atop a reef . . . I think it is a reef, or perhaps a shark's fin sliced below the waterline into our outer skin. We lose blood from the bunkers. Whatever stabbed us won't take out the knife. Navigator reports it appeared from nowhere, helmsman reports no reef in vicinity . . .

. . . I think we may have to rest here a bit, for though the tide is at its height it does not cooperate . . . it will not pull us off the beast . . .

. . . Boat moans in pain . . . no, the sound comes from above . . . a stricken animal. They have strange beasts here . . .

. . . A foghorn where there should *not be one.* The fog is snow. The horn outmoans the wind, a lesser wind . . . she is dying and the snow dies, too. The tide, however, sinks and we are atop a mountain, I think — so much for charts and beacons. Listing to starboard . . . screws out of water . . . the rudder moves only air . . . bow partially submerged in diving mode, but we do not dive. Instead we are like the arm of a sluggish windmill pushed to and fro and sometimes around by a current that has no pattern . . . and the wound tears. I hear the sound of a mountain meadow, the tinkling of a cowbell . . . no, the bell does not tinkle, it clangs a warning too late . . . cling clang clang . . . a buoy in a meadow . . . a reef in the grass . . . a cow in the corn . . .

TELEPHONE CONVERSATION

LIEUTENANT JG HORACE DECKER AND

CAPTAIN EMERSON WIDGERY, COMMANDING OFFICER

ARUNDEL NAVAL AIR STATION

0737, TUESDAY, MARCH 20

"Widgery here . . . dammit!"

"Sir, this is Lieutenant Decker."

"Make it good, Lieutenant. I now have soft-boiled egg dripping down my robe!"

"Yes, sir. Sorry, sir. Coast Guard reports U-boat off Cape Charlotte."

"Good God in hell! You're sure? This is confirmed?"

"Yes, sir. She was spotted by the crew who service Porpoise Light. They were plowing just before dawn and —"

"Shut up, Lieutenant! What's her status?"

"Sir. She's on a reef, sir. Snaggletooth Reef. She's not going anywhere, Captain. And Coast Guard reports she's losing diesel pretty fast."

"Holy shit!"

"Yes, sir."

"Position, Lieutenant! Position!"

"Sir, the U-boat is situated just north of Porpoise Point. And sir, she's really stuck. Like a pig on a spit."

"OK, Lieutenant. There's a cutter monitoring?"

"Yes, sir."

"Then hold tight, Mr. Decker. Maybe we got ourselves a pigboat! I'll send a PB2Y and contact the Port Commander for surface craft. We'll need a couple of subchasers as backup, just in case she wants to start a little war . . . and Lieutenant . . ."

"Sir?"

"Notify Naval Command in Washington what's up. And tell them we have the situation well in hand."

"Aye-aye, sir."

"Mr. Decker. I want a lid on this. *No one,* I mean *no one,* is to get out on that Point. All we need is a mob of gawking sightseers. They'd be sitting ducks in a shooting gallery if that bastard decides to use her deck guns. Understand? Now hop to it!"

"Yes, sir. Understood, *sir.*"

"I want that pigboat, Decker!"

"Yes, *sir!*"

BUFFY

CAPE CHARLOTTE

Meg, you stalwart one,

I have promised to tell you of my great plans to enhance the aerie — unnamed still, poor thing — but I must wait awhile longer until the improvements are definitely and *finally* OK'd. Think I have enough clout to pull it off, but I'm superstitious enough to wait a bit before boring you with what may be a first!

God, outside there's been a bitch of a storm! A No'easter to whip the pants off. I told you March was devious. Couldn't see a thing, not even our Porpoise Light! That's a first, believe me!

Made me uneasy — me — who loves the Wrath of God (read Nature). Maybe it was the wind. A screeching devil of a wind, almost alive, most unGodlike. Blew the bloody snow sideways, and then a warm front must have moved in, for the wind let up but the snow continued, obliterating everything. Enormous flakes like eiderdown. Spring snow. Sugar snow.

I don't feel in the mood to write of damsels in distress, so I'll tell you about Coleen, who isn't in distress. She's just dumb! Coleen is the upstairs maid. I have been trying her out. She's willing enough, but has no initiative — and *no* taste.

I am not one to stick my staff into dirty garrets or cold dungeons, but at the moment *I* am in a dudgeon! That just came out — honest and true! So where was I? Yes. The lady of the manor is bountiful. My staff has rooms that are large and comfortable and airy, and I personally decorated each, even to the art on their walls.

Daddy loved collecting manly paintings of men-of-war under full sail — colors soaring, guns bristling, cannon smoking — you know the kind. Then for some reason he softened and his tastes changed. He became entranced by those more benign things of Lane's. Well, I know they are not in style — too romantic. But they're nice in an insipid way. Even his shipwrecks on foaming reefs aren't threatening. So I picked one of those for Coleen. The witless girl has turned it to the wall — really! She looks at brown paper backing rather than a gentle shipwreck!

(Took time out to breakfast leisurely. Am back feeling out of sorts — and woozy.)

The storm has blown itself out to sea. And I do believe the sun is trying. Yes. It's out! The day will be clear, and just watch the snow melt in the warmth! Spring snow has a short lifetime.

I should go into the Yard. Pudge, ever faithful to his accounts — and to his employer, me — left for the firm as soon as the road was plowed. I heard the put-put-putting of his old heap going down the drive just after dawn. I *always* go in, but this morning I think the grippe has gripped me.

I shall order hot tea with a healthy slug of bourbon, then close my eyes for a bit. Wait a minute . . . there's a racket outside . . .

CONVERSATION ON A NAVY PB2Y

OVER CAPE CHARLOTTE

MARCH 20

0841–0910

Captain: Captain to crew. There she is. Straight ahead at twelve o'clock. Take a good look, boys. This is probably the first and last U-boat you'll see in your young lives. She seems to be very popular. There's a convention of our boats down there. Copilot, what's our fuel situation?

Copilot: Good, Captain. Three-quarters on the button.

Captain: Full . . . or empty?

Copilot: Fun-eee! You're feeling mighty chipper after five boilermakers!

Captain: The chippies were chipper! My secret to the morning after is four aspirins and a quart of water.

Copilot: Thought water never passed your lips . . .

Captain: Only in dire emergencies like dawn patrol. Duty calls for extreme measures!

Copilot: What's on for tonight?

Captain: Tonight we get soused and screwed and sleep it off. What the hell, we're both off tomorrow. And I want to make sure we don't miss any bar in this burg.

Copilot: Friend, this burg is dead!

Captain: So we resurrect it!

Copilot: Ah, My Heavenly Father, so we will!

STEINER

ON THE REEF

. . . Dawn soon, discovery soon. Ah, Ilse, I join a band of brothers who belong to a most exclusive club. One comrade saw Wolf Rock up close, very close, aground he was, off Land's End. I think we should name our association "The Beached Club." Lots of sunning on the strand. If this is a pun then I could write more, but I won't bore you with them . . . my mind is racing with puns . . .

. . . I am giddy. I can see the American shore — by daylight . . .

. . . The United States Navy is here . . . we are surrounded by curious craft and they fly above us . . .

* * *

. . . Now the Kriegsmarine would have us scuttle — yes it would. I have enough explosive stored beneath my bunk to blow her out of the water — what about that? I hear you. Yes, yes, I hear you. "Disobey," you whisper. Don't whisper, shout it, "DISOBEY!" . . .

. . . The men are restless . . . what will the Captain do? The Captain will say "Good morning" to the Americans and then he will bargain one well-used boat for fifty lives . . .

. . . The men are mustered on deck and I must go to the bridge and do this surrender business properly, correctly . . . pull the War flag down, but Dönitz has not provided a white replacement. Sloppy of him . . . what to use? You say a bunk sheet. Oh no, Ilse, not gingham checks, they wouldn't take us seriously. I have it in my drawer — I have the flag of surrender — the perfect one! — and with it I can bare my ass to the Führer! . . .

. . . I go topside to sleep for eons . . . I am so tired, suddenly . . . Sing me to sleep, Ilse . . .

DECKER TO WIDGERY

VIA TELEPHONE TO ARUNDEL NAVAL AIR STATION

0905

"Widgery!"

"Lieutenant Decker, reporting, sir."

"What ya got?"

"Well, sir, the PB2Y is circling and we have a subchaser and a frigate standing by and a couple of fishing boats have joined the party —"

"AND?"

"Sir, the Coast Guard cutter is exchanging messages with the U-boat. Seems she wants to surrender."

"Holy Mother of God! Not even a little skirmish! By the way, what's her heading?"

"No way to tell, sir. She's turning round and round all the time. Current's mean out there."

"Just wondering, Decker. Just wondering what she was doing in so close. Probably prowling farther out and got pulled in by the storm. Bad time for boats last night. Theirs *and* ours. Well, we'll soon find out, won't we Lieutenant?"

"Sure hope so, sir."

"I'll fly down forthwith in scout. Want to watch those Krauts cry!"

PB2Y

ABOVE SNAGGLETOOTH REEF

Captain: How the hell long have we been up here, for Chrissake?

Copilot: Forever! More like twenty minutes, Jimmy. Just seems longer, goin' around and around in the same damn circle. The guys are gettin' itchy. Can't understand what we're doin', babysittin' the enemy.

Captain: Orders are orders are orders. What the hell? The crew's on deck and the flag's coming down! I do believe we have ourselves a prisoner. Yes, indeedy! She's surrendering. Captain to crew: U-boat is surrendering! Repeat: U-boat is surrendering! . . . Keep it down! My ears, for God's sake!

Copilot: Well, my bucko, what d'ya think of the ferocious sea wolf now?

Captain: Isure. Nothing to bite with.

Copilot: What the hell's that white thing goin' up? It sure ain't no white flag . . . I'll bust my gut! It's somebody's Doctor Denton's for God's sake! Oh, beauti——

Captain: Oh Jesus *God! Oh Jesus God.* Captain to crew! We've been hit! *We've been hit.* And — Oh Christ, there's blood all over the cockpit! The copilot's been hit — blood gushing all over — throat torn out — those fuckin' bastards — goddamn fuckin' bastards. You hear me, you fuckin' bastards, you killed him! *You killed him!* Captain to crew! Captain to crew! We've taken a hit! Copilot — Oh Rusty! Copilot dead. We're going in. We're going in. Prepare for bombing run. Blow her out of the water!

Bombardier: Sir! The orders!

Captain: Fuck the orders! Get your babies ready . . . *NOW!* We're going in!

Bombardier: Wilco, sir. Set, sir!

Captain: Do it! Do it! Kill her! Fry the bastards! Burn, baby, *burn!*

BUFFY
CAPE CHARLOTTE

I have been delayed by a War. An honest-to-God naval battle which we won — I guess.

Seeing death close up is not the same as watching selected short newsreels by Movietone. Believe me.

I realize you don't know what in hell I'm talking about. I don't know either. I just saw the destruction of a German submarine, and instead of shouting "Bad luck, you bastards!" I felt the fire and the concussion and screamed — for them! For the damned bloody Nazis, I screamed.

I think I'm sick and not just grippy. I *am* . . .

Sorry. A bit of retching. I write better on an empty stomach, anyway.

Oh God. There they were, helpless, snagged by Old Snaggletooth. Well, not completely helpless. They had a gun and they used it — or one of them did. And we retaliated. And there's nothing left but flotsam. Bits and pieces.

And Jesus! I just noticed — a leg on the lawn. With a boot still attached — Oh Meg . . .

I don't seem to write well about this — or talk about it. The newspaper and the radio station and INS — everybody's been badgering me. The phone's been ringing all morning. I *will not* describe the "scene" for avid listeners or readers — or those reporters who drink blood for breakfast. Ghouls, all of them.

Pudge had left for the firm before Dante's *Inferno,* for which I am grateful in a way. I phoned the office with the news. Seems they had just heard a radio bulletin and informed Pudge, who left soon after. Not home? they asked. No, dammit! An extraordinary incident in his own backyard. So where is he?

Gather everything around here's cordoned off. Good! Keep the gore-seekers away. They're as bad as summer people — almost!

The stupid Navy won't confirm anything. If they think they can keep a lid on this, they're nuts! (Probably embarrassed as hell that a U-boat could get in this close without detection.) Wonder why she *was* in this close? Well, we'll never know now.

Wish Pudge would call. I need *someone* right now!

Think I will have several shots of bourbon and pull the covers over my head. And sleep away this day.

B.

HENRY
CAPE CHARLOTTE

The events of this day are too horrendous even to contemplate. And to record them will take more effort than I am able to muster as persistent somnolence o'ertakes me. I am, as it were, beyond the pale.

At last I am in control of my faculties and able to deal at length with the extraordinary happenings of the past several days, happenings of such an intricate nature that they have involved my every fibre of intellect.

It all began with the snow. I have mentioned previously, I am certain, that the weather was most atypical. March means *Spring,* no matter what ignorant pessimists (of which there seem to be thousands) hiss. The 21st of March bodes happy tidings of warmth to come.

This year, however, Winter gasped loudly and spit an inordinate amount of moisture, greatly overacting her farewell. The consequences of her unnecessary nastiness have been unduly unkind: mainly to me.

As I say, it all began with the snow — and the wind, of course — unattractive flakes, clumped together and borne on the gale, rapidly mounted against the door, effectively imprisoning me.

I could not sleep for worry, and as soon as I heard the Coast Guard plow (which never fails its mission of freeing the way to the Lighthouse) go by, I roused our resident idiot to shovel me and the Studebaker out of its heavy white mantle. A vague foreboding swirled about me, telling me to hasten into town.

Muttering that he was now too old to wield a shovel, he winced when I informed him that unless he got on with the task, he would receive no more gifts from me. Namely: my used copies of *Country Gentleman.* Servant he is; squire he wishes to be!

I had hoped to be at the office before dawn, but found myself trailing a sluggish snowplow and hence was delayed.

I crossed the drawbridge, turned left, passed the wharves, the fishing fleet — those that had managed to make it to harbor to ride out the storm. The sun greeted me as I walked into the firm and my foreboding dissipated. In the lovely light, a visit to the grocery — for reassurance — seemed quite unnecessary.

So I plunged into my accounts and, to my delight, felt not the least trace of exhaustion. Indeed, work of a meticulous nature is most refreshing. And at such an early hour peacefully soothing, for I do prefer the pen over those clanking adding machines. However, I disdain the fountain pen, which, at odd times, does just what it is advertised *not* to. To wit: gush all over my columns! Therefore, I cling to the nib.

My only regret at my early arrival was the absence of tea. Ginny always had a fresh cup brewed and waiting — with milk. But Ginny was not in, and I have no idea *how* to make tea, or even if I did, where Ginny puts the milk. She secretes it, of that I am certain. No! I meant to say she hides it. Hides!

As the morning wore on the staff dribbled in. Each arrived with a new story of near collisions. I had no skidding narrative to relate, but did hold them enthralled with descriptions of the mountainous seas which bashed at our seawall.

Ginny finally remembered my need and dutifully presented me with a hot cup, which I was about to sip when the "office boy" burst in. He is neither a boy nor observed much in the office. He blared news (gleaned from a radio he was listening to on company time, the burbling, inarticulate fool!) — news of a U-boat *aground!* All turned in my direction as if I owned the vessel, being, as I am, the nearest neighbor — to the Reef!

I had barely repaired to my office when Ginny rushed in. Breathlessly, she informed me of total destruction: bits of debris — all that remained of an enemy intruder.

Stunned, I felt torn to bits, also. My stalwart demeanor could not hold up much longer. Yet I forced myself to sip the tea leisurely, bringing the steaming cup to my lips by sheer force of will. Even so, milky copper droplets found their way downward to soil the sheen of my silk club tie. Good manners were waning by a laxity I could not control.

Hurriedly I left the premises, giving the impression that my wife needed me at home during this trying time. With absolute certainty, I knew I must be gone before Evelyn called, which would happen momentarily — of that, I had an unerring instinct — demanding that I be with her! I had more important matters to attend to!

As I walked to my auto, I reflected on the storm just past and on the stupidity of the entire Germanic race. I pictured an attempted landing in broad daylight with a broad audience looking on. And the spot this put me in. A spotlight, more likely.

I also reflected on trickery. Were the rascals really eradicated? Were the documents — my dossier — now only undecipherable floating flotsam?

Could all of this mean that I had loosened the bonds of entanglement? That I was free?

This possibility was heady stuff and nearly obscured the fact that I needed some confirmation before proceeding further.

I drove at once to the dismal area wherein the grocery squats. A young Latin woman, comely now, but with the ripeness that bloats in a decade, was in attendance. I asked for the owner. She pierced me with black, angry eyes, announcing that he was unavailable.

The "unavailable" Wop poured out from the back to confront me, his normally dark and greasy face now drawn, ashen. It resembled the silvery underside of a fish, the tautness revealing black specks of whiskers sprinkled o'er all like poppy seeds on a white belly.

Our conversation was one-sided. He whispered that the storm had caused *much* damage and *no* fishermen had survived. With that, he exited rapidly, leaving me with the thread of an answer but a thousand questions still to be unraveled.

I had to establish with certainty the ramifications of his oblique message combined with the public pronouncements of a disaster.

I drove in the opposite direction and parked on a side street, walking leisurely (even as I wanted to move with haste) the short distance to that splendid example of Romanesque sandstone: the Jamesport Public Library. The purpose? A swift retrieval.

The Library: a place of contemplation. The repository of culture. Also the unknowing repository of a set of instructions to the alternate rendezvous point *and* a key to a room of safety.

I forced myself not to race up the steps with abandon, not to make a spectacle of myself. Impatience is not a virtue even in extremis.

I strode purposefully but lightly through the hush and dimness. Libraries delight in dimness, a half-light which inspires serenity.

The Reading Room was situated at the eastern end of the main lobby and I entered it, glancing about to note the few inhabitants. All appeared immersed in literary pursuits, oblivious to my presence.

The immense mahogany table (early Victorian, I judged), centrally placed, was occupied by one female — an elderly spinster. My goal, the northern end of the table, was empty. I said several huzzas silently as I crossed to its companion chair. For moments I did nothing, gathering strength, collecting my wits. Then I picked up the nearest reading material, a copy of *PM,* a newspaper of pro-liberal, pro-labor propaganda which I am glad to say I have *never* set eyes on. With complete honesty, I can still state that I have never so much as read a *single* word of its polluted prose, for although I studiously pretended to peruse it, *nothing* on those pages entered my conscious mind.

Under cover of the newspaper I reached, stealthily and unobtrusively, to the nether reaches of the table's underside. And my hand felt it. Touched it! The envelope with the key inside still taped, undisturbed! My heart leapt and with great effort I managed to stifle the immense murmur of relief which threatened to erupt and burst the heavy silence enveloping the room.

At that moment all manner of pictures flooded my brain. Marvelous sights: bits of charred metal sinking into the foam. Gluts of oil staining the surface of the sea. And a courier with his damning documents lying torn on the bottom. I wanted to shout, "The courier is dead! Long live Henry!"

I felt exquisite release, the sudden alleviation of long-submerged anxiety that accompanied the discovery of the cache. The sweet air of freedom flowed over and through me at that instant.

I undid the tape which adhered the envelope to the unsanded underside. (Sloppy work!) I crushed my prize into a ball, aware that sudden pressure might cause a crackling, which in this room would have resembled a cannon shot.

And then, with an appearance of unstudied nonchalance, I exited, the paper ball with the key at its center resting secure in my right-hand trouser pocket.

I do not remember reaching the sidewalk. I do remember a cold chill and a swift glance behind — to the heavy oaken doors. For what was I alert? What did I sense? Or fear? A courier's ghost vaporizing through them?

The coldness passed as abruptly as it had arrived. And the sun warmed my being as I journeyed back to the auto. My mind had settled into thoughts of new beginnings. And I was at peace.

All at once, my arm was jostled. Beside me, a denizen of the docks had sidled up, smelling of fish and filth and, doubtless, rotgut rye. He staggered and I pulled away, loath to touch the creature let alone part with any currency.

He whispered in a whining rasp words I could not make out, did not wish to make out. I only desired to be rid of him, but he persisted.

Then out of this wreckage came the dread word: "Minsk!" The impact of the word had not yet made the connection when he added, in short wheezing bursts, "The capital of Spain"!

Brittle and crumbling, I only wished to blow away. "You're dead!" I wanted to cry out. Yet even as I was drained of life, I knew he lived.

He lived, but barely. His gait was uneven; he stumbled at times and was in obvious pain. I let him follow me, but strode ahead. I could not be seen aiding his progress. One does not assist a derelict in public.

THE JAMESPORT TIMES-GAZETTE
EARLY AFTERNOON EDITION

U-BOAT DOWN OFF CAPE CHARLOTTE?
Stranded Sub Bombed by Navy?

Cape Charlotte — March 20, 1945. Efforts to confirm the reported bombing and subsequent sinking of a stranded German U-boat were rebuffed this morning by a terse "No comment" from Port and military personnel.

But several eyewitnesses report watching a naval engagement in which the Nazi submarine was hit squarely by a depth bomb dropped from a U.S. Navy reconnaissance plane.

Although this reporter was prevented by authorities from entering the area, at least three residents of Cape Charlotte have given on-the-scene accounts of the incident.

One of these, Phineas T. Jordan, 56, a lobsterman, described the events:

"It was a U-boat, alright. No American sub flies a flag with one of them broken crosses on it. (Swastika — Ed.) Must have been pulled in by the storm and the tide. Wicked tide, she was. No ways that boat coulda heard the buoy in the gale. There she was stuck on Snaggletooth (Reef — Ed.) like a spoke on a spindle, twistin' and turnin' in the current. You could hear the metal bein' torn apart. It was near low tide and she weren't gettin' off!"

When asked the sequence of events, Mr. Jordan replied, "As near as I can recollect, there was a big fat plane, one of ours, just goin' around and around in a great big circle, sorta keepin' an eye on things. The cutter was standin' by, off southeast, about 500 yards or so. There was some blinkin' goin' on between the cutter and the U-boat, and all the while that oil kept bubblin' out amidships (from the U-boat — Ed.). And then that high hatch must have opened (the conning tower — Ed.) because men, sailors — they looked like little bugs — they poured out from there. And other sailors, they come up through the forward hatch. And then they all lined up on deck in a kind of squiggly line.

"And then a couple of the men run down that flag, the one with the crooked black cross in the middle. Red, white and black it was. Funny, they had a regular cross on that flag, a big one, but that other crooked one was right smack-dab in the middle of it.

"Well, then they run up what honest to ——— looked like longjohns. White longjohns!

"Well, right after that there was a commotion, it seemed like, because one of the men broke line on the forward deck and run aft. Some others took after him, but it was too late. That sailor, he grabbed the gun they have there on the fantail, a thin cannon-like gun, and he just aimed it at the plane that was mindin' its own business, he aimed that gun and let off a few rounds and the plane, she took a hit, you could see her shudder. And then she come around, all business now, she come around fast and low and just like that — she drops a bomb, a bank shot right into the pocket. The best pool playin' I ever seed! Right down that tower. And whooosh! Up she went! Pieces of her flew every which way and there was an awful smell of oil and burnin'. And then what was left of her went straight down with a lot of bubblin' and gurglin'.

"She was a sittin' duck, aground like that."

Mr. Jordan did not think there were any survivors. "I can't see how. It was a ——— of a blast! I wasn't allowed to stay around and find out. The Navy, they come around with a Jeep and hustled me right out of there. But it was a ——— of a sight, I can tell you! All those people burnin'! There ain't no other smell like it. I oughta know. I was one of them that pulled those crazy people outa the water when that pleasure boat exploded in '37. Loaded to the gills with summer people, it was. Never listen. Think they know the sea. Don't know nothin'! Gasoline engine and all. ——— fools! They was charcoal broiled, they was. That smell'll stay with me, I can tell you!"

The coastal area around Porpoise Point has been designated Off Limits to all sightseers *and* the press. The order is being reinforced by military personnel.

Questions about the incident have been put by this newspaper to the Port Authority, the First Naval District, and to the War Department.

We await a reply.

HENRY

CAPE CHARLOTTE

Images of photos exposed for all the world to gape at snapped within my head. Hurriedly, I tipped him into the rear seat, where he sank down with a sigh. After more than a cursory survey of the side street, I retrieved a tarpaulin from the boot and covered him securely. The doors were locked, the engine sparked to life, purring — as always.

Shaken to the very core, my first thought — to deposit him at his next way-station — became impossible. He held my future life. On him? Or placed in safekeeping elsewhere? Until I recovered the documents, he would be my prisoner. A docile, ill, almost uncomprehending prisoner.

Discontinuing all thought, I drove without seeing. Habit took over. All the fuss that must have been generated by the sinking completely slipped my mind, for I was astounded to be halted by a roadblock — two Naval vehicles, positioned just off the Coast Road. They barred the way to my home!

In seconds, from a wellspring of assurance born and bred and carefully nurtured, I reduced the two uniformed lads to servile boys. After only a brief examination of my driver's license they waved me on, then came to attention, giving the salute due me.

All activity was centered on the north side of the Point. My goal, however, was the southern edge. Half Moon Beach was deserted; the Beach House empty — the House I had so carefully prepared.

The drifts were decaying rapidly. I drove round to the door, which is invisible from the Big House, and, with great effort, pulled and tugged until I managed to maneuver the weight inside.

I could not possibly move him farther, so he lay in a heap on the braided rug.

I stood watching, pondering procedure, when all at once he half-rose to a sitting position and attempted to tear off his boots. He muttered incomprehensible words, his speech slurred, his jaws chattered, as though with intense cold. The exertion was too much, and he collapsed in a stupor.

Seeing that he was unconscious and therefore no match for me, I took the opportunity to search his person. He smelled vile: of decayed fish and wet dog.

He was dressed inconspicuously, perhaps intending to pass for a merchant seaman: dark wool cap, Navy pea jacket, a fisherman's sweater still oily and rough from the lanolin and burrs woven therein. Under these he wore a flannel shirt of indiscriminate taste. Umbre, shabby corduroys completed the outfit. Attached to the belt was a hunting knife in a scabbard, which I immediately put away, out of reach. A cheap wallet reposed in the trouser pocket and that I set aside for later perusal.

Now down to a singlet, drawers, and footgear, it was painfully clear that he carried *nothing* as bulky as a dossier on his person!

I was submerged in disappointment and despair. And full of disgust for this foul-smelling creature lying on the floor.

To be utterly certain that nothing was taped to his clammy skin, I removed his still-damp singlet and drawers. A distasteful task. Even in college, we were modest about our private parts and did not flaunt nakedness. Father never appeared in anything less than an evening robe, brocaded round the collar, as I recall. As children, I do not believe we ever thought of Father as having skin at all. He was so impeccably turned out.

I let him lie there, sucking in his own fetid fumes! Fumes that nearly felled *me.* For propriety's sake, and to protect my lungs, I threw an afghan over him, and thence proceeded to peruse the contents of the wallet.

It included: three hundred and twenty-two dollars in American currency, no bill being larger than a twenty; Social Security card, draft card, United States medical discharge papers for a wound suffered in 1944 (extent or type of wound not given); a valid driver's license for the state of Nebraska; one unclear photograph of a young woman (face squinting at the sun. Presumably posed in front of some cathedral specifically for inclusion in a spy's collection of trivia); one chewing gum wrapper, wedged deeply: Wrigley's Spearmint; and — one negative, slightly puckered from moisture. *One* negative belonging to me! Only one from many!

I noted with satisfaction that Berlin had used the name I had suggested, the Anglo name. I could not, in good conscience, bestow upon a blackguard any surname from Harvard, so I conferred upon him a surname well known in less well thought of circles. To wit: a name so connected to that institution that immediately all would state, "Ah-ha! A Blue!" Therefore, within minutes I postulated the perfect pseudonym: "Sheffield." To most, it would designate England; to Elis, a solid, stolid Yale fellow!

Cabot, Peabody, Warren, et al. The reputations of Harvard's cream redeemed again!

However, the sacred name of Lowell has been sullied forever. By that *odious* one. He intrudes upon my thoughts like a discordant theme, stirring me to speculate on his whereabouts. He has not shown himself. Will he ever, now that — oh my! How marvelous! — now that he believes his man to be *dead?*

The boy, for that is what he is, age given: twenty, lay on the floor unconscious still, but twitching. In repose, "Sheffield" appeared to be that young; yet I could not imagine entrusting a mission, whatever it might be, to one as immature as he.

I settled into my Queen Anne, upholstered in quaint calico, and studied the shivering mound under the afghan.

I let reason, logic, work their magic.

Knowing now that "Sheffield" carried nothing pertaining to me save one negative, I posited numerous possibilities which I have narrowed to the following three:

1. The documents did not leave the submarine, and are, therefore, destroyed.
2. The documents went with the courier and he has hidden them, safely, in a yet-to-be-named spot.
3. The documents *never left* Germany. (I have always had a niggling fear that this circumstance could occur, being that the word of bourgeois warriors should not be taken as a contract.)

As I sat meditating, sipping a glass of Plessis, which had aged many years in the cask before being bottled, the form on the floor gesticulated wildly in delirium, throwing off his blanket. I knelt to cover the nakedness when the odor rose again, assaulting my nasal passages.

It came from the one area untouched — *and* unsearched. His booted feet! With alacrity, and a certainty that I had almost missed the hiding place, I tore at the boots. They would not budge! It was as though they were welded on, an outer skin, so to speak. In haste, I cut them off, slicing the leather, peeling it down in snakelike strips. The feet were enormous, bloated. And there was nothing hidden. Nothing!

Yet I had not reached his skin. Disgusting stockings blocked the way. I cut those off as well and wanted to retch, for the one on his left foot pulled away small pieces of tissue!

Now certain that something was amiss, I glanced more closely (after first placing a handkerchief over my nose). Both calves down to the ankles still showed a faint flush of life, but his feet, his feet seemed to be dying. His left in particular, the skin an ochre-gray, glossy, shiny; the toes, blistered, hard and cold. So cold. Those blisters broken now, their coverings a film of tissue stuck like adhesive to the stockings.

I diagnosed immediately: frostbite of a deadly nature.

Aware that dead, this boy would be of no use whatsoever (and where would I dispose of his mortal remains?), I acted. My mind was nimble. One more competent than I would have to be responsible for his well-being. A physician. And I knew of one who *could* not, *would* not, ask questions, now or later.

Accordingly, I prepared "Minsk" for travel. (I shall not refer to him again by that term. "Minsk" brings to mind some cheap vaudeville act and this is no laughing matter.)

The matter of clothing him was a problem, seeing that all his former apparel was ocean-damp. And I was not about to lend him anything of mine. In his state he might foul it. Therefore I wrapped the afghan around him once again and found two pillow casings (percale), securing them to his legs with elastic bands. With him so covered, I dragged him through the slush to the Studebaker, his feet bounding along the way, sending up small fountains of water. The exertion was enormous, causing me to sit for a time and recover my equanimity.

No pausing for the two on duty; I sailed through with a sharp salute, which was returned.

Turned south and thought of St. John. Only those with a fine education slanted toward the history and culture of our English cousins pronounce his name correctly. It is, of course: Sin Gin. How apt. How apt, indeed. A physician with no license to practice. An alcoholic. An abortionist, now. Nefariously, of course.

We were roommates, once — so long ago. His dreams of medicine came true, only to dissolve in the spirit. Spirits. How far he has fallen, but when sober, he has good hands. And a surgery in his house.

I view with distaste his need for alcohol, but feel his newly found endeavor does a much-needed service to mankind: ridding it of mongrels and other life of lowly nature that should never be added to the already burgeoning mass of mental incompetents.

St. John will keep silent. The Hypocratic Oath coupled with that special bond that exists between Men of Harvard ensures complete secrecy. I did not, of course, meander in details, only stating succinctly that the young man *was not* to be treated in hospital.

I must say that St. John greeted me with a notable lack of enthusiasm which I can only attribute to the ravages of rum. In fact, I suspect he wished me gone! I, who have kept his secret from curious classmates these many years. I, who still consider him a good fellow in spite of his woeful lack of will. I, who, knowing of his unfortunate state, have never tendered to him an invitation for dinner, lest it cause him embarrassment.

St. John ministered to the patient and confirmed my suspicions of frostbite. He was absurdly upset at the coverings which I had so carefully prepared. Said, unnecessarily, that they were inadequate, even for a corpse.

He was particularly worried about the left foot, which he said was severely damaged. "Looks like he froze it, rubbed it hard to thaw it, then froze it again. Bad. Very bad. Those toes will die."

He turned to me, swaying slightly, and slurred, "Who's he running from?"

His sobriety was no longer a question. He was under the influence! Never would an educated man use the colloquialism "who's"! So utterly common, so utterly *wrong.*

After treating great gashes on both palms, wounds I had not observed previously, he warmed and bathed the patient, then rubbed him dry, those parts not affected. He made me touch the shoulder to feel for myself the disappearance of the clamminess. I did so with reluctance.

St. John prepared for surgery — and extreme measures. He amputated all five digits on the left foot, muttering all the while about tissue death, necrosis, gangrene; "open" versus "closed" procedures: terms and procedures that did not interest me in the least. I, of course, did not watch the operation, preferring to avert my eyes. He packed the open wounds with what he termed "Vaseline gauze" and inserted a needle into the patient's fanny — "Good stuff," he said. "From mold, a miracle. New and hard to get, but I have my sources. You'll have to continue the injections, of course." I was nonplused at the thought but St. John was adamant!

We practiced on a pillow which St. John noted did not have the resilience of flesh. Soon, a tirade poured forth directed at my attempts — at my failure to master the simple, nay small, maneuver: forcing out a small stream of yellow liquid before the actual injection. It seemed such a waste of precious medicine!

Accusations flowed from his lips: I took immediate umbrage at his innuendo, nay his actual intimation of insidious intent on my part.

"You fool! There goes a deadly little air bubble — an embolus straight to the heart — or are you planning to kill him!

"If you want him alive, learn! And while you're about it, a dose of compassion wouldn't hurt!" With that upbraiding, I resolved never again to nod to St. John in passing. Never!

He continued, harshly: "Penicillin in the buttocks. Four times a day. Don't forget! I have the schedule written out. Keep the stuff cool — and squirt the needle first!"

Since I had so forcefully stated that recuperation could *not* occur in hospital, it appeared that *I* must be the nursemaid!

St. John then proceeded to acquaint me with the ritual of bandaging and unbandaging, regaling me all the while with the horrid sights I might encounter: sloughing tissue, pus, delirium, impaired judgment and the like.

Looking about for suitable dress, St. John sniffed — at me? No, more likely at the odor — and disappeared, reappearing with a set of clothing from his own collection (shabby, but still of good quality and quite serviceable). Clad now from head to one foot (the other was swathed), we made ready to move the patient.

Back to the auto. I had wished not to be involved with transporting "Minsk" (I must not think that *again!* A tawdry act and so *foreign*), but St. John was firm, and so I found myself assisting in a kind of human chair. Once in the rear seat, Sheffield was wrapped in blankets from St. John's own supply. He offered me the afghan, which I refused, seeing as it carried a stench that would cling for eons. My nose is a delicate instrument and picks up scents that most cannot discern. I now caught traces of wood smoke. In fact, Sheffield's hands carried the aroma of a Sunday morning brunch. Thick, sizzling slabs of frying bacon.

I was handed a bag, containing, I was informed, syringes, medicine for injection, pills for pain, pills for sleep, quantities of sterile bandages, alcohol, cotton balls, adhesive, salves — a veritable dispensary!

Nurse I was to be! I had little choice in the matter.

Of course, St. John received no recompense from me. His parting words: "He's not a slab of meat, you know. Keep him warm!" were quite unkind.

On the journey back, some thirty miles, Sheffield slipped in and out of consciousness, groaning with new pain. I, on the other hand, was surprisingly fit, considering the anxiety and pain *I* had endured.

By the time we reached the Beach House, I had formulated a plan that would calm Evelyn and see me through the next week. Or weeks? I sincerely pray for the former.

Meanwhile, Sheffield tosses in the Beach House as I prepare for the luxury of linen sheets.

DATE: MARCH 22, 1945

TO: COLONEL FRANKLIN L. HARRIS III
COMMANDANT, FORT MACALLISTER
CAPE CHARLOTTE

FROM: MASTER SERGEANT JOSEPH BRENDAN GILHOOLEY
STATUS REPORT RE AWOL PRIVATE JAMIE ELWELL DECATUR AND CIRCUMSTANCES SURROUNDING THE SEARCH AND SUBSEQUENT APPREHENSION OF SAID JAMIE E. DECATUR

Sir:

The alarm was sounded at 0005 hours on the morning of Tuesday, the 20th of March of this year. I received your call three minutes later and immediately roused myself. (*Oh, Christ — I was already aroused. A dusky maiden whose sarong was slipping was fingering my crotch!*)

I then alerted Cpl. Rubin Deveraux, who collected his K-9 dog, an expert in tracking, to aid in the search. The weather was inclement. (*You lousy bastard, you pansy in uniform. You made me go out in that Siberian Shit to hunt up one more poor freezing southern draftee whose only mistake was to trust the army which shouldn't be trusted as far as you can throw it! I'd like to throw up on you and your lady at least once an hour. What the Hell, you lying in that warm bed of yours and picking up the phone and out goes Yours Truly, pretty as you please, and all the while that old bag of yours snoring up a storm. She could snore through typhoons, you said. Remember? Manila '37? Or have you forgotten your evening maneuvers during our tour at Fort Santiago? That was when you was sucking Filipino titty and I caught you. Drunk out of your eyes, and I was your buddy for life and don't tell my wife! The Colonel's Lady don't know to this day. I'm saving that little nugget for a special occasion. All she thinks I'm good for is to move the furniture around. In her sweetest Miss Prim and Proper voice she calls, "Oh Sergeant. I've changed my mind. Do come over and let's rearrange again." She needs to rearrange her brains. They're all screwed up. I'm all screwed up being posted under you again. What a lousy rotten throw of the dice. Loaded, that's what they were. Against me! Fuck you!*)

Cpl. Deveraux and I proceeded to follow the route that 90% of all the deserters take. That is, south along the shoreline, away from the Fort and Jamesport. The going was treacherous, due to the heavy snow which made for poor visibility and the ice which covered the rocks with a thin film. However, we monitored the route as best we could and gave the dog a good lead. We had, of course, given her a piece of Pvt. Decatur's clothing to sniff before leaving. (*His jock-strap, you fart. Gave her a hell of a smell. Jolted her, I can tell you! Hell, I didn't mention the wind which was screaming up our cans!*)

In spite of the weather, which showed no signs of improving, we continued our search. The flashlight was almost useless — the beam only cut through a foot or two since the snow was so thick. Blotted out even James Head light, right behind us.

Our only hope was the dog, being deprived of any visual sighting. (*We were getting panicky. Couldn't see the rocks for the sea!*) We shouted again and again and received no answer. (*I yelled you poor bastard at least twice!*)

We proceeded cautiously and let the dog off her leash, thinking her ability to track and her surefootedness would be an asset. (*The hell we did. That dog is dumb! A real bitch. Rubin calls her Honey in a voice that's so thick with syrup, it drools. Honey, shit. I told him, Rubin, that dog's an Alsatian. You call her HUN. Dumb HUN. You let her off her leash and she'll go off and fraternize with the enemy! So he kept her on a short one and all the while she's trying to outbark the wind.*)

We waited, hoping to hear her bark, but she made no noise to indicate a find. Presently she reappeared and sat down awaiting further orders. (*Hey — that sounds good. Can see the old fart picturing a real patriotic war dog saluting with a paw. "What's next, sir?" The HUN hasn't sat in her life. She flops and then she rolls and then she slobbers!*)

By now the weather had closed in so much that we surmised any further searching to be unduly hazardous. (*We were pissing scared out of our minds, hearing the waves like to roar in and grab us!*) We continued on to Ebb Cove where I made the decision to turn back, for I noticed the Cpl. was having difficulty gripping the leash and I feared he might be suffering from frostbite. (*He had trouble all right. HUN the dumb decided snowflakes were bugs and was leaping out of her mind trying to catch them!*)

After regretfully turning back (*You lie, Gilhooley, you lie in your teeth. We were racing for the Fort's gate, that's what!*), we concluded that a more thorough search should wait until daylight.

If that other missing person, the Trefethen boy, was on any of the beaches we went over, we had no indication either from cries for help or from the dog. (*So the dog heard something. So I heard something — maybe a scream — and I yelled. I wasn't about to get near that wild water or fall down on those damned stones that rolled around like eggs! How could I know the kid was on the beach? Deveraux hasn't brought it up so it's like a secret between us without exactly putting it into words. You learn in this man's army not to volunteer. Nothing!*

What the hell. The dog did hear something. Barked a couple of times. I wasn't about to risk my neck for some southern bastard who by now might be bait for the fishes or frozen into a khaki statue. Jesus, why is a fort on the New England coast full of y'all southern rednecks who all get shipped north equipped with tropical gear in the middle of winter? Same reason every Yankee gets shipped down to 'bama in the middle of malaria land all decked out in fur to go fight a war in Eskimo land, that's why!)

Subsequently, at 1400 hours on March 20th Private J. E. Decatur was apprehended at the railroad station in Jamesport attempting to board a train to Boston. (*He was dry! Dry, not a drop on him. And warm. Got a lift right away into town, the fink!*)

Private Decatur was taken into custody and returned to Fort MacAllister by Naval Shore Patrol, who asked for his Identification Papers. (*Goddamned Navy. Think they own the town. They* do *own the town, what there is of it. We army types get dumped right and left when the Navy comes in. Goddamn Gunga Dins, that's what they are — water boys! May it please the Colonel, SIR, I'm in artillery, not bounty hunting. Do you plan to put me on KP next, SIR? Because if you do, I'll spill the beans about your bimbos, you can bet your ass on that as sure as God made little apples!*)

Private Decatur is now in the stockade awaiting the Colonel's decision re punishment.

May I point out, sir (*Listen you brainless eunuch!*), that the facilities for holding prisoners are strained to the limit. (*How can you hold ninety-two AWOLs, all of 'em homesick, shivering southern boys? This Goddamned Fort was built during the Civil War to keep the Rebs* out! *It sure as hell is doing that, but good!*

When this war's over, I'm getting out. We cream 'em and then I'm out! This man's army is not this *man's army. It's Colonel pee-in-your-pants Franklin L. Harris III's army and I've had you up to here! I'm getting as far away from you as ever I can. Half a world away. From you and your pea brain and your orders interrupting my dreams and your making me an MP when I'm an expert artilleryman. I'll use you for gunnery practice, you windbag. I'll fill you so full of holes, the wind will whistle through your drawers like water through a sieve!*

Hot shit! I got it! The South China Sea. I'll land on Luzon and open a tavern for native types. Just me and a nipa hut and two brown bargirls all my own. And at night when it pours and the customers don't come, we'll snuggle all together and listen to the rain roll off the roof of nipa palms and nary a drop will touch us. And we'll roll on the wooden floors and drink and fuck and sing to hell with snow and Colonel Harris!)

I suggest that the records of all prisoners be reviewed in the interest of the army and of you, sir. The War Department has expressed interest in the inordinate number of desertions. (*This is crap! They ain't interested in anything except division strength and body counts.*)

With regards to your wife, I am,
Joseph Brendan Gilhooley
Master Sergeant
2nd Artillery Bat.

HENRY
CAPE CHARLOTTE

I knew nothing of the Lightship's misadventure until the following day when a startling headline apprised me to read further. The Lightship changed position! The ensuing events were the direct results of this dereliction of duty. It is clear that the crew (and the Captain) of said Lightship were irresponsible. If the Lightship had held, there would have been *no* catastrophe and *I* would long since have been rid of responsibility!

Concurrently I considered the conundrum. I had sent all relevant information needed: the position of the Lightship, the position of Porpoise Light, and the distance between. By reading the chart (and I assumed a U-boat Captain had passed the test on navigation!), he could find his *own* position by using simple calculations. Even a half-witted schoolboy can master trigonometry!

But Fate blew in, and even trigonometry fails when one of the points changes position!

I have pieced together what I believe to be a plausible explanation for the subsequent events.

Captain Daggert testified that his Lightship drifted northeasterly for at least two hours. Soon after, I surmise, the U-boat surfaced, found the Lightship in her *new* position and took a bearing. According to the map drawn in the newspaper, the *new* position was near a certain land beacon. The Captain determined his position from the beacon and the Lightship. But the beacon was *not* Porpoise Light. It was James Head light. Given that the snow was a curtain through which the exact pattern of the beacon was not easily discernible, it behooves me to ascertain that the U-boat Captain assumed only that he was not reading the pattern of Porpoise Light accurately. He thought that he was off Half Moon Beach when *in reality* he was off some cove just south of James Head light. His passenger (and now my bird of passage, his stay of short duration, I trust) came ashore somewhere north of Porpoise Light and south of James Head light. It is not clear where he landed, given the churning sea and errant currents. Most probably he landed nearer James Head light. That would explain the hand gashes — crawling up on a shale beach.

One aspect of the affair puzzles me: the grounding. If the vessel came in unscathed, as I assume it did, why did it not *leave* via the same arc I drew out so carefully?

I believe there is one explanation: there are no reefs or shoals in Half Moon Bay. And the Bay is deep. Did, perhaps, the Captain, after loosing his passenger and assuming he was still *in* Half Moon Bay, widen his arc in a southerly direction toward the open sea, intending to swing around later to a northeasterly heading, thereby avoiding all radar detection and other antisubmarine devices? Detecting devices which he chanced, heading in, so as to fulfill his mission rapidly?

I believe I shall indulge in more novellas of the detecting genre. Those I have read seemed to have sharpened my intuitive powers.

BORMANN

BERLIN

The blind fool! The blind fucking asshole shit! Caught on the rocks like a crapping cadet! Smashed to hell and back!

Jesus fucking Christ!

The whole thing down the drain and *that* was not meant to be funny, Schmidt!

All those diamonds scattered on the ocean floor like little seashells for the fishes to play with.

I hope that whole U-boat crew was *nibbled to bits* — those that went under still breathing.

Oh Jesus! I'm getting out of this hole. I'm going up to the Great Hall of the Chancellery and get pissing, puking, bombed out, flat-out drunk — to my eyes. And then I'm going to smash what has eluded those flying fuckers! I'll crack that marble floor till the white chips fly!

B!

Demolition is pure pleasure! Pure, marvelous, satisfying wrecking!

Midas doesn't know how lucky he is! A stay of execution because his executioner *died.*

Midas is to stay put and keep us posted. We might need him again. We *will* need him again!

Bormann

HENRY

CAPE CHARLOTTE

Five days have passed and the first of several hurdles has been overcome: Evelyn. Evelyn's wonderment, nay wrath, at my whereabouts during the day of destruction.

I spun her a tale to which she gives complete credence: a tale so sentimental and full of pathos that no one with an ounce of compassion could fail to be moved by it.

My mind is a fertile field of germinating seedlings which swell with each retelling to become tall tales rooted in the truth — or what I have almost come to see as the truth.

I told Evelyn of a homeless War veteran, the son of an old classmate (since deceased, of course), an orphan even, who lies ill and despondent in a government hospital.

Two events occurred almost simultaneously, I informed her. Just before I heard of the engagement on the Reef, I had slit open a Special Delivery letter (I can say it arrived *before* Ginny so she cannot state there was no letter!). The letter, I felt, precluded all else, knowing, as I did from the reports, that Evelyn was in no danger.

I admitted it was a painful choice, but that in a moment she would understand why I had chosen as I had.

A nurse at the government hospital, feeling pity for this "boy" with no immediate family, took it upon herself to read everything in the boy's possession. Included were several letters, one of which announced the death of his father, and another, an earlier one *from* the father (my classmate!), apologizing for his *dependence on spirits,* and further stating that though he was beyond help now, unable to be a good and stalwart father when the boy needed one, a friend from College days, a good and true friend, would always be available in time of trial.

Evelyn was now intricately involved in the story and the touching embellishments I added as I became caught up in the narrative.

The address in the letter: *My own,* of course. *I* am that tried and true comrade! And, as I told Evelyn, touched by the faith old "Sheff" had in me, my heart went out to the lonely boy lying, forgotten, in hospital.

So, after ascertaining that there was indeed a C. Sheffield there, I drove *to* and *from* the hospital *that day.*

By now Evelyn was intrigued in spite of herself and had quite forgotten her charge of desertion and her unhappiness at having to bear the burden of death on the doorstep alone.

I am preparing her. Better to prepare her with a woeful tale than spring a house guest on her without warning. A pitiful sight he will be, guaranteed to melt even Evelyn's gruff demeanor.

Sheffield still sleeps restlessly and cries out — in pain or dread? During the few times he is vaguely awake, I pop pills into his mouth and make him sip liquids, a goodly portion of which dribble down his chin, but St. John impressed upon me the importance of liquids in the system, as dehydration is a silent killer.

Since I am unable to alter my normal routine without arousing suspicion in many quarters, he remains alone much of the time.

I shall move him to the Big House where the staff can care for him. But not yet. I cannot have him cry out in German!

EDWARD PICKERING

CAPE CHARLOTTE

Dear Mother,

I know I was rambling and incoherent on the phone. To watch our child trying to will a dead boy back to life was a ghastly sight.

A week has passed and Emma does not see or hear us. Her love for Peter was a tightly held secret, protected by layers and layers of practiced indifference. I doubt she told a soul. But now the layers have ripped apart and she is shattered. We ache to help her, but can't get through. We can't cure the pain.

Every time she glances out a window in this house, she sees the ocean and the rocks — and death. Her depression is so deep she cannot even cry.

Will you and Father take her for a couple of weeks? She adores you both. And Pick's Crossing is a gentle, woodsy New England village without a vista of whitecaps to smack the eyes.

Don't fuss. Why did I write that? You never fuss! Is that wild animal farm still there? The place where you can pat the animals? Emma's kitty has been at the vet's for three weeks. She needs to love and hold on to something right now. She needs to cry in warm fur.

That morning, still stultified with sleep, we sipped coffee and vaguely thought of rousing Emma. Then the 7:30 news blared out the bulletin of a missing boy.

In an instant we noticed a half-eaten bowl of cereal, a child who had been there and now was not. Without a word we headed for the shore.

We found her tracks veering toward James Head light. It was often hard to follow the prints, for the snow was melting rapidly.

We searched every cove in turn, as she must have been doing ahead of us. It was so clear as it often is after a storm. But the sea was still surging, as though in remembrance of the gale, and even though it was dead low tide, the water was very high. Cold and dangerous. It was impossible for any human being to have survived in it for long. Yet a spark must have flared for Emma. It did for us. Each of us looked for a yellow mackinaw.

At one point Emma turned and went up from the beach to a small bluff, toward a summer cottage, empty since September. We believe she went into the cottage, found nothing, and left. *Someone* had clearly been there during the night, for there was a lingering trace of wood smoke in the air. An odor, too, of soaked, then steamed wool. (Probably another deserter — one from our weekly quota of AWOLs that flee the Fort.) But the cottage was empty.

I rushed ahead, convinced that in her search Emma had slipped from some rocky crevice into the sea. I became a maniac, clambering over ledges, falling, pulling myself up to go on, driven by utter terror.

And then there she was. Quite far away. On the beach of Easter Egg Cove (Emma's name for it). A gentle name for a resting place. A final one, for there he was, a yellow blotch, stretched out. She was holding him, rocking him. I ran toward them, tears of relief stinging my eyes. I thought of warm blankets and miracles. But there was no miracle. He was stiff. Quite dead. But Emma didn't know.

She held the boy's head and wiped the frozen hair from his eyes. He had a deep hole in his head, a dreadful wound, and his clothes were icy tatters. The sea and the rocks had been brutal.

We watched our daughter look on the boy, Peter, with such an outpouring of love that we were embarrassed to witness such a private moment. Emma stared into his eyes, his very dead eyes, that stared only at the sky. But she believed he was looking at her.

We only managed to budge Emma after the Coast Guard had come and covered him. It was as though she couldn't leave until she was sure he was warm.

Back home, Emma wandered through the rooms as though she had never seen them before. Then, like a zombie muttering an incantation, she said she had to go down to the knoll.

I let her go but watched from the picture window, not sure whether her utter calm was masking some inner bent for self-destruction. I know this sounds unduly morbid, but in the last few months, Emma has gone through other tortures of the damned — awful adolescence.

When she reached the top of the knoll, she lay down in the snow and began moving her arms and legs back and forth until she reached the edge. Her arms were out of sight, but she was obviously working very hard. Then she brushed the snow off and came back to us.

Her face, which is normally so alive with *some* emotion, was absolutely blank. There were no tears. But there was an air about her that seemed to signal a job done. Finished.

And there it stands. She is silent as the grave and we don't know what to do. She needs help. And time. And to be away from this place. She needs to grieve. She *needs* to cry. She hasn't shed a tear because, I think, crying would be an acknowledgment of reality.

It's strange that this one tragedy overshadows the death of dozens that occurred on the same day only a few miles away. But it does. The sinking of that U-boat could have happened in Africa as far as I am concerned. It has nothing to do with us!

My love,
Ted

HENRY
CAPE CHARLOTTE

Keeping the Beach House at a comfortable temperature is beyond me, seeing as the wood stove gives off less energy than is expended stoking it! Not insulated, the Beach House is reminiscent of English cottages. The dampness does penetrate the bone.

Satisfied that Sheffield is surviving, I have discontinued the series of injections. Bare flanks are abhorrent!

Today, in desperation, I rang up St. John: What to do about the residue of liquid? That is to say, the liquid which, not being absorbed, passes through? St. John, rather vulgarly, I thought (tippling again?), laughed, saying, "Do you mean he is a bad boy and is wetting the bed?" Well, of course I meant that, but would not have put it so coarsely.

He suggested everything from milk bottles to diapers! I do *not* wish to be Nanny or a laundress! And I shall *not* sit there coaxing a half-demented creature to please fill my bottle! Oh, yes. St. John also inquired of the patient's progress. I replied neutrally — for Sheffield does not appear to be worsening.

I *have* dressed his foot twice and do not relish the task. And so far, thankfully, there seem to be no red streaks of infection or any sign of gangrene, although there are fetid fumes emanating from the bed. Does this odor rise from the wound or from the sheets? Does decay blend in with ammonia? The sheets will not be changed! Newspapers, perhaps?

I *am* bothered by the foot. A foot without toes is an unpleasant sight — as though God forgot.

Each day Sheffield improves. Just an iota; but there is improvement. And each day he is lucid for periods ranging from one to five minutes. At first I used these lucid periods for a single purpose only: he held his own milk bottle! But now we have begun to converse enough to convince me that once he is ensconced in the Big House, he will pose no problem re language, for his English is remarkably good — American combined with several other strains: strangely flat, even harsh.

He has asked few questions, as have I. It seems wise not to know of his past — or his future after leaving Cape Charlotte. I am only interested in the present (and recent past-present). He does not mention the submarine, and may not remember the events leading up to and including his injuries. In time, I will draw on the memories that reside within his mind, but which at the moment are forgotten, cloaked, perhaps, by pain.

I will now have to fabricate War Service. The Army: infantry. It would not do to make him an officer. He is too young. The wound, not specified on his medical discharge papers, is now *most* specific! And could easily have occurred in combat. How fortunate! I will have to coach Sheffield carefully.

Yesterday I measured his length from armpit to floor and today I obtained a pair of crutches. I purchased them from a supply house rather than the pharmacy in town, which carries this type of convalescent equipment. I also purchased a bedpan, for he is eating a few solids now. There being no WC, the means of disposal is all about me. The bare spring ground. One might think a dog passed by — often.

For a brief period only, he *must* be able to maneuver the crutches. Twice now he has attempted to do so and failed miserably. He will have only to go up a few steps, just a few, and hobble to the elevator (Evelyn's Folly!).

Perhaps tomorrow Sheffield will be ready. Ready to be driven from hospital (Beach House) a long journey of one-half mile by road to the Big House. (I have not so much as hinted to Evelyn the hospital's location. Nonexistent, it remains only "the government hospital for wounded veterans.") I have impressed upon the patient the necessity of remaining awake and alert enough to greet Evelyn. But only that.

Today was one of great accomplishment. No, two. I completed two tasks and succeeded superbly at both!

Today was the day I informed Evelyn I would drive to hospital and return with the son of Sheff.

Instead, I first drove into town, and since my destination was in the East End, out of habit — and perhaps curiosity — I chanced to pass the grocery. I did not stop, for a large, poorly lettered sign caught my eye. Even through the greasy film and from a distance I could read the misspelled: CLOSED INDEFINATELY.

Ah-ha, I thought to myself: the plotters scatter. There is no work for them now, no reason for being. The explosion shattered their duties and, it seems, their livelihood.

The next stop was at a rooming house, a rundown affair, the one I had reserved as the alternate rendezvous point. I now sought out the landlord and with an apologetic air explained that "my nephew" would not be coming after all, that the room in his name would not be needed. And I returned the key I had retrieved from the library. Having already paid through the end of the month, I was loath to add to the landlord's coffers, but decided extra currency would dispose of any questions, now or later. He fetched the still-locked valise that I had stored in anticipation of a guest's arrival, handing it back and adding, almost as an afterthought, "An old guy came here awhile back, wanting to see the roomer. I told him, he ain't come in yet."

My heart plummeted! Lowell!

"What day?" I asked brightly. I hoped brightly.

"Lessee. I think i'twas the day after the howler. Ayuh. Know i'twas 'cause that'd be the day the power come back. The front doorbell worked again and I was surprised, you can bet."

So Lowell only checked the day *after.* Was he delayed? Fuming with impatience, perhaps even then, hearing about obliteration from wagging tongues, yet not totally believing the tale until he could read press reports on arrival at Jamesport? He must have stopped by the grocery, and to be quite certain, at the rooming house, the place where the two of them would meet, and thence go on to further adventures in skulduggery!

And then the pieces came together in a wave of understanding: all the participants were convinced the affair was *over.* Over! The mission was "scrubbed," as they say — because the courier shared the fate of all aboard: blown to smithereens!

Lowell did not attempt to contact *me.* Why? Why? Because he wanted me to dangle and drown in anxiety! He was sending me a silent message: "You do not know, for sure. And I will not enlighten you. Wait and worry and wait some more. I keep you choking on a string of hope that the dossier will be returned! delivered by — who knows?"

If that despicable person ever *does* contact me, I shall play the trapped mouse squealing for release. Lowell must not suspect that I shelter Sheffield, an addition to the household.

Leaving the rooming house, the landlord content, I carried with me the valise containing an extra set of "town" apparel for the courier. The clothing will come into use when Sheffield recovers, as recover he must! Only he knows the secret: the dossier's disposition.

Thence back to the Beach House. To dress Sheffield. This procedure took time, as the boy was in agony. But after much futile coaxing I tried a different tack. I *ordered* him to get hold of himself, for the next few minutes he would have to limp. It worked! He jumped and his head cleared and he followed my instructions. It would appear that he *has seen* some military service at one time.

We rounded the drive to the Big House and I stopped precisely in front of the steps, not the ramp, for reasons of which I shall write in a moment.

I disengaged myself from behind the wheel and straightened up in a manner which bespoke of a long, tiring journey.

Evelyn was waiting just inside the open door, and although she offered immediate assistance from the staff for Sheffield, I waved them away, saying to her quietly that the boy must enter on his own to save any shred of dignity left him. Rot! I wanted him to fall. And he did. Nearly toppling Evelyn and her conveyance in the process.

And that endeared him instantly — to Evelyn! She became Mother hen, Mother Earth, for that matter. And from now to doomsday, Sheffield will be the "brave boy" and I, I will be a samaritan, nay, a savior, qualities Evelyn has not endowed me with in the past.

The Big House is obviously unclean! Within a day of Sheffield's arrival, all the signs that St. John had warned me of were startingly apparent: red-purple lines radiating upward on his leg; a fever of quite high proportions and dreadful, dreadful pus! Also, there was a rather harsh, rasping sound emanating from the chest area.

All in all, it seemed quite reasonable to ring St. John again. When he learned that there were seven bottles of the medicine left and that I had stored the entire lot near the stove, I thought he would have an apoplectic fit. When asked a question, I answer truthfully. I do not lie!

He ranted. I did not bother to listen to his discourse until he uttered a phrase which contained the word "nurse." His nurse. His trusted, most capable nurse.

At last!

The responsibility for recovery has been lifted from my shoulders. No one has the capacity for understanding how much I have suffered during this entire sorry business!

IZAAK
STUTTHOF

It cannot be. Yet it must! I was sleeping. I seem to be drowsy much of the time. I awoke to feel a delicious warmth which I have not had since the beginning of time.

Nestled in the hollow of my neck was a furry creature, radiating heat and hope. It can only be she! Why, after so long? Do not try to fathom mysteries. Revel in them.

I can talk again. Try to. My voice squeaks as hers does. I can caress her. Love her.

I cannot feed her crumbs. There is no bread.

Why does she stay? I have no presents. And she has no young to care for. Maybe she stays to keep *me.*

The days go on and I do not die. The slops are warm water now. A bit of meat floats on top. Maggots. Each day four maggots. No more. No less. What tortured mind places these worms in my water? I chew them. Swallow them. I drink the water. A little protein. And one can survive on water only — for a time.

I think I do not want to survive. Yes, Izaak, you have said it. It is on your paper. This is not survival, what you endure. Death is only a moment away from life. And this is not life.

They will not mark your death with ritual. Why waste a bullet when neglect does the job? They will drag old Izaak out and throw him on the trash. Pile his tools and wheel on top. All will sink and disappear. Perhaps the glass in the loupe will catch the sun to wink briefly. But only briefly. A boot will crush it.

We are together, we two . . . no one has come . . . no water . . . nothing . . .

APRIL-JULY 1945

HENRY
CAPE CHARLOTTE
APRIL

I am fatigued, worn to a frazzle playing this game which is *not* a game!

Sheffield assures me he has the documents of my episode in Berlin safely hidden and will release them at an appropriate time. He intimates that that time draws nearer. But for what nefarious purpose does he still withhold them from me? I have kept my part of the bargain, performed all tasks, gone far beyond that which was asked of me!

Yet this villain withholds my promised payment!

And stays *far* beyond his welcome!

Where in the Name of the Almighty could he have secreted them? On the strands? *No!* Too much chance of disintegration from the roiling surf!

He spent the night — somewhere. Whither? Sheffield cannot remember, or so asserts. Am I to trust his word?

I do believe he delayed the disposition until the following morning — in a *logical, safe* place. Did he arrive at the Jamesport Library before me? If so, even in his stuporous state, he had ample time to slip the papers and negatives into a volume, an esoteric work, one which would not be in demand by the masses. But which one? Must I search the entire collection?

HANNES
CAPE CHARLOTTE
APRIL

Oh to be somewhere now that April's here . . . somewhere else. What a fuckup! What a goddamn fuckup! And I can't remember what happened! Not a bloody thing except what the contact tells me and he tells me little . . . except to keep my mouth shut and act sick. Not difficult. I feel like crap and my toes ache. My toes that are in some trash pile or being chewed by hogs. An old battleax wants to comfort me. I just want to sleep.

I had a mission! Important, important, and . . . a belt a belt a belt, strapped to me, with all my life inside. *Gone.* The old man doesn't have it. He's so worried about the negatives he's near to pissing every time he brings them up. Thinks I've hidden them on purpose. Nothing I've done since I've set foot in this lousy country was on purpose . . . I can't remember! Fucking Steiner got me into this mess. I've lost time, *time!* And he's sailing merrily home on the bounding main!

What about the War? I have to ask him what about the War. Far away from a wildflower garden. Across the sea from bedroom wallpaper strewn with flowers, wildflowers on everything like the feed sacks — the Bussett female uniform, flowered sacks for skirts and blouses . . . Mama made me a shirt with buttercups and they called me "Hanky" and I tore it, ripped it off. I can see a bit of the ocean and a bit of the sky and the ugly puss of a nurse who missed her calling — she belongs with those kind doctors at Auschwitz. Sadist! She jabs me with a spike dipped in yellow venom!

I had journals once. I have scraps of paper now. Back full circle. I hide them under the mattress. I try to push the fog away . . . write it down as it comes. Pull the remembering out of the mist.

Awful cold and a child's face and cobblestones. I can see the face in shadow and feel the cobblestones . . . and . . . the cold. It disappears back into the fog. The picture . . . don't push . . . it will come.

First time out of bed. Hobbled to window. The sea, the vile sea below me. And a nasty piece of work sticking out of it like the fin of a shark.

* * *

The old man came — to chat, to pry. I have nothing to tell him. Pretended about the belt, about its hiding place, that I know. When I can walk some, I will retrieve it . . . when I remember.

Steiner is dead! *Drowned. Blown to bits!* The old man just told me the tale of the U-boat and the aftermath. The shark *was* a killer — the fin impaled them! In a million pieces you are now, Steiner, with all your crew. Tender, chewable morsels, savored by crabs. I can see them tearing, I can hear their jaws chomping!

And *I* am dead! To the world *I* am dead as a doornail! To Berlin I am on the ocean floor with Steiner. Hannes Henkel is *dead!* A new man lives — as Sheffield until I recover and then as — who knows? Find the belt! Find the belt! Blow away the fog!

HENRY
CAPE CHARLOTTE
APRIL

The cad lies in his catafalque; the measured cadence, the cries of sorrow, the cannon boom, are like an opiate to me. I slumbered deeply, the first restful sleep I have enjoyed for weeks, drugged with delight, satiated with satisfaction, blissfully dreaming of new beginnings, new directions!

Roosevelt is dead! In his place that *most* ordinary — person, that — pipsqueak! Momentarily he will be crushed under the heavy weight of the office, to rise no more.

Now is the time for all stouthearted men to come to the aid of the Republic.

Now is the time to grasp opportunity and bend it to our will.

Now is the time for our great minds to plan with diligence, to recapture, once and for all, the Presidency of our sovereign states!

1948: The Year of the Tory!

And ever after shall we reign!

HANNES
CAPE CHARLOTTE
APRIL

The War is *over* and still we fight. Berlin lies ruined, smoking — dead. And the Führer — where is *he?*

* * *

The old bat asks, "Would you like to keep a diary of your new life?"

Lady, what would happen if you read the journals of my old life? Pop off, that's what! Fall out of your chair, gasping for air like a fish out of water!

A kid's diary! For Chrissakes — a kid's cute little leatherette book mit key! And not enough room on one page to record even a good shit! To hell with dated pages! And what do I do? Wear the key around my neck?

Where to hide them? That bitch of a nurse turns the mattress! Under the chair cushion? She'll probably wash the cover!

The bookcase — behind old books, selected light reading for weekend guests. Mary Roberts Rinehart; cartoons by Hokinson and Arno. Up, higher, as high as I can reach — but not too high. I need it every day.

Light reading? Thackeray's *Henry Esmond.* Cobwebs up here. No one's browsed — or dusted — for years. Which means no one *touches.*

Perfect! Behind *Eve's Diary.*

My mind is clearing. I can see through the fog. Images that don't connect. Write it. The sea boils . . . it boiled that night . . . it roared and screamed and frothed and tried to kill me . . . it tries to climb the cliff, the seawall, in frustration now . . . it knows I'm here . . . but I'm out of reach . . . I climbed a cliff! That night *I climbed a cliff* . . . I remember! Terrible cold . . . wet and freezing scrabbling up a beach of rolling stones . . . a something . . . someone . . . and I hit out with a rock . . . smashed its head . . . and then moaning began . . . a demon sound out of the past . . . a beast in agony and I ran and the dead white bodies followed with their dogs barking and they shouted for me to stop but to stop was death and the moan rose and fell and I was suffocating snowflakes white moths fluttering in my mouth gasping a blind man caught in a maze of black rock and I was hugging the sides of the cliffs and blundering into them like a crippled crab and I slammed into a rock with no beginning and no end and I climbed and they were nearer and I climbed handholes footholes where there were none I was a limpet I was glue the dogs were panting to reach me I felt their hot breath panting rasping lungs my own hot breath an eye for an eye they'd tear my eyes out and feed them to the dogs and they would feast their eyes on the diamonds their eyes beaming through the snow they would not have them I tore the belt from my body and shoved it into a crevice a cave and the top I was at the top and they could not reach me wandering an alien on a frozen planet lost in blankness and the moan was all around me but the beasts had gone struggling through drifts and falling a cocoon of down warm enveloping sleep you sleep into death arms out stiff searching circles around circles splinters wood a wall a door a room metal cold metal ashes dead matches searching wood piled up wood burning heat heat toes and fingers dying sticks suck and bite and rub and slap and heat your frozen body burning heat huddle there and live huddle there and live . . .

BUFFY
CAPE CHARLOTTE
APRIL

Meg!

You'll never guess my latest. The Big House is a Convalescent Home! No, not for me, you idiot! For a house guest. For a boy — a boy-man, to be accurate.

He's about twenty or so, I would guess, the son of a friend of Pudge's — from Harvard, I think. Pudge never does make things crystal clear.

What's relevant is that the poor kid's been wounded — shot up on D-Day, no less — and for the last nine months or so has been shipped hither and yon, from one government hospital to another. At each, it seems, the resident surgeon, eager to slice, did so, taking yet another piece from the boy's foot. Even then, 'twouldn't heal, so Pudge says.

Why do we have him? Because the boy's all alone in the world — no family whatsoever. Pudge was notified as *the* family friend and drove — somewhere — to bring him here.

Although I was prepared a bit ahead of time, I was *not* happy. I like my privacy, I *cherish* solitude — and I *hate* the smell of disinfectant. Reminds me of hospitals . . . sickness, death.

However, the boy — Christopher — gamely tried to walk into the House unaided — and promptly tumbled, right at my feet. Didn't moan or cry. Just smiled a sad little smile. And that was it. Of course, I was won over, instantly!

Pudge arranged for a practical nurse to do the chores. A homely thing! She changes dressings and sticks poor Christopher with a syringe as big as an icepick! The medicine is some miracle stuff we have to keep in the icebox, but it seems to be doing the trick.

When Christopher improves as he seems to be doing, I'll have a long talk with him. But only when he's ready. At the moment he's shy and speaks only in monosyll*a*bles. Love that word!

About the U-boat. Have gotten over the first shock. But it is impossible *not* to watch the Navy busily sending down divers and cranes and grappling stuff each day. Their salvage attempts seem fruitless, for all they have brought up so far are mangled bits of metal and . . . other things. This continued activity does not help to erase the image of *that* day. Oh, God — did she blow!

Our 25th next year. I can't, I *won't* believe it!!

Buffy

P.S. Confession time. I now confess to you after all these years that the sole reason I went to Smith was because of a rumor. Someone — I suspect a Smithie — told me solemnly that *all Wellesley gals had monstrous legs* — the result of daily rowing. I believed — oh did I, and crossed poor Wellesley off my list. What a laugh! *I* should care about legs?

BORMANN
BERLIN
MAY

TOP SECRET! VIA OFFICER

This is my final communication, Willi. By the time it reaches you I will be on my way out of an inferno, reaching for tranquillity in the cool beech forests and lakes of Schleswig-Holstein. Plön, to be specific. War (in the form of the British) has not intruded there. And there, too, is Dönitz. Dönitz, the heir apparent. Dönitz, the unknown — to the Party. Dönitz who cannot possibly operate without my know-how. He doesn't understand the first thing about intrigue and politics, two things I am well versed in!

Yes, the Führer is gone. Killed himself yesterday along with his *wife.* Little Eva made it after all. Both dead and burning.

But — I am alive and intend to remain so — as Party Minister to help with negotiations (although, to be brutally honest, Schmidt, at such a late date, that unconditional surrender ultimatum may make any demands or even requests null and void).

So, I carry the Führer's Testament to Dönitz at Plön.

But from there — who knows?

You will know and you are the only living soul who will — for now. Remember the IOU I hold, the one from the Grand Admiral? It appears that the time has come to collect it: one nicely outfitted U-boat. A fast one. A new one. One that cruises to places I have never seen.

I shall elaborate where *after* I tell you your future.

You will be the recipient of my "largesse." (That's a French word, Willi, in case you do not recognize it!) I could have you shot in an instant. Right now! Shot! But I won't, Willi, because I hold your life with me forever.

You are free to start over — with the diamonds I assume you skimmed from those you delivered to me. Of course you skimmed, you turd! Think I didn't know of your thievery? Only a fool would keep his hands clean, and you are not quite a fool. I respect your ingenuity. And I can afford to respect it since I am about to be loaded down with stones!

Now to my magnanimous present to you, my gift. It is the gift of continuing life. (I do not count the 11 years of life already presented to you. By me.) New life, Willi. All documents relating to your association with Röhm and your service with the SA were destroyed long ago. Nothing remains of Schmidt the stormtrooper, no evidence of the Putsch-plotter. And yesterday I had your SS dossier excised from RSHA.

Open the enclosed. It is your current identity. As of this moment you are a member of the Volkssturm. My creation, the Volkssturm. SS Hauptsturmführer Schmidt becomes Schmidt, a 58-year-old Home Guardist — one of a million I envisaged would rise up to save the Reich. They barely got to their knees! So — put on rags and shuffle. Be subservient to the conquerors and you will survive.

I expect that you will not only survive, but prosper. With diamonds one can invest in the future. In ten years I may read about the millionaire industrialist (bona fide anti-Nazi, of course!) — the tractor king of Düsseldorf! Or go with the big boys — Krupp, Bayer, IG Farben. They too will survive. In ten years no one will remember or *wish* to remember that the big three fed and thrived on the bones of the dead.

But be warned, Schmidt, while you luxuriate in your villa and contemplate the good life — five years hence, a decade hence — remember that I too will exist — somewhere. I am in the prime of life, not yet 45. For all time I shall stay thirteen years younger than you. And, for all time, I shall control the strings and the mouth of the puppet Schmidt. Insurance against slips of the tongue regarding the whereabouts and status of Martin Bormann. My security? The fingerprints of Wilhelm Schmidt and correspondence between said W. Schmidt and Reichsleiter M. Bormann — all nicely, clearly photographed and reduced to a compact size for transport. One roll of microfilm.

For weeks now this place has been a madhouse. It reeks of wretches scrambling to get out. Vermin conspiring, fleeing the Führer bunker, squealing in fear. The SS has taken off the mask, and what is underneath snivels with cowardice. They plot — escape. There are rumors of well-financed safe routes and gold is the currency. Stories circulate of hidden hoards — roofs in Bad Ausee are not what they appear. Scratch a shingle and it gleams!

I have no friends in the top ranks of the Schutzstaffel. I go my own route.

Which means, Willi, that South America is out. The SS, conniving bastards, believe that there lies freedom, a new beginning, *a base of power.* That a Fourth Reich can rise gorging on the instability of countries that stage a coup a week! They have absolute faith that the large and seemingly sympathetic German populace — the émigrés — will follow them blindly. They *assume* they will be welcomed into positions of importance by military dictators.

They are dead wrong. They dream fantasies. Reality, Schmidt: groups of aging officers scratching for power, hiding from seekers of vengeance, stuck together in the wilderness, remembering glory and breathing stale air at a flame that only flickers.

I deal in reality. And reality is settling in a place where no one expects me: America. To America with a fortune. And an idea.

I shall start life anew. A life without boundaries. A life without the burdens I have shouldered for so long. A life without family. (I assume they live in the bunker at Berchtesgaden — or have died, for I ordered them to take poison. In either case, they are nothing to me now.)

How alike are the American and the German peoples. How alike. Industrious, cultured, patriotic, impatient with shoddiness. We envy the British snobs and hate the Frogs. And we wish to rid ourselves of pollutants — all coloreds, Catholics and Jew lice.

I will have the good life in America, perhaps becoming a businessman myself. Having been compared to a bourgeois butcher (the comparison, of course, refers only to my build!), I might go into the meat business — meat packing.

Whatever life I choose for myself will not make headlines. I do not wish to stand out in the crowd. Rather, I plan to stay in the shadows, manipulating behind a curtain of anonymity. No power plays of grand proportions. But politicians can be bought and judges bribed and my own small fiefdom will flourish on greed. And — in time — from little acorns, mighty oaks?

One thing is sure. I will not atrophy as those who venture to the Latin states are destined to. I shall not dissolve in the sun, raise steins to the old days, and then waddle out to tend the marigolds!

I have *good* contacts in America. Midas was most helpful. (Where *is* the bastard?) I plan to learn the language — enough to pass. I shall visit a hospital and come out with a new jaw, a new face. A precaution, only — for my image is not graven on the minds of the masses. And, Willi, unlike you, my fingerprints were never — fingerprints! Fucking fingerprints! 1923! The Freikorps! The murder frameup! Parchim! They *inked me.* So long ago I *forgot.* Do they still exist? Enough . . .

I must reach the airfield at Rechlin. Baur has a Junker waiting. If we can slip through the encirclement of Berlin (no safe conduct from the Bolshies!) the route to Rechlin is still open. From there, Plön is only a short hop.

Time out for a party. We prepare for breakout with the aid of bottles . . . many bottles . . . so many bottles . . . my spirits are high the spirits are low . . . hardly a drop left!

Have disposed of all the top traitors in my own way. Goebbels made it easy — crunch! Whole family gone. Göring, Himmler disgraced. I am the top!

Not many of us left in this stinking hole. They watch me fill my oilskin bag full of stuff like my Obergruppenführer insignia, the Führer's last will and his Testament. What they don't see are the pockets sewn into my overcoat lining — nice fat quilting, stuffed to the gills with glitter. Let others go first, see the lay of the land. Will they get picked off or will they find a breach? We follow . . . have a map of stars to guide me.

Baur and Stumpfegger and I go soon, in the darkness. I carry a small vial, glass; with a snap of jaws all is over. But I shall make it! I think I shall make it, Schmidt. If only I had invested time in what has suddenly taken on great importance. Think of all the thought I invested in the People's Militia — and no return for the investment. The million shrank, slunk away and they are useless to me now. I should have fed and nurtured kids! *Kids.* A squadron of Kellerkinder. My own little guides: dirty brats who live like rats in the sewers, who know every passageway under Berlin better than the faces of their own mothers, underneath where all is cold and quiet and safe, under the guns, under the fire and rubble and *out.*

I don't know them . . . I have no Kellerkinder.

More Schnapps . . . a last swallow.

I don't know that I will survive.

What a laugh! What a funny fucking end! I become part of the rubble . . . bones to dust. Those filthy kids will kick a mound of rags, scoop up the pretty stones, and like packrats scurry to their holes with them. Play a game . . . play toss with the pretty stones . . . play something else . . . this game is boring. Fling the things away, heave them into the river of crap that flows beneath Berlin.

Ah Willi, what I would give for a tank right now . . . or the hand of a child . . .

M.B.

EMMA
CAPE CHARLOTTE
MAY

I haven't done much for a long time. I didn't even do my May baskets yesterday. Last year I worked hard on them, putting colored paper around in a ruffle and looking for wildflowers, which is a waste of time on the last day of April unless we're lucky with the weather. So I used Necco wafers and candy hearts and pieces of licorice rope cut up. And then I put them on everybody's porch. I was too tired to do them this year.

Today was V-E Day. Victory in Europe Day. Germany gave up and we had a special assembly in school. It didn't feel that special . . .

I don't see Apricot anymore because Mummy said he was given away to a family with lots of children down east somewhere. I think if I saw him bouncing along the beach right now, I would lie down and die.

I feel sleepy in school all the time, and then when I go to bed I can't sleep for a long time, and then when I do go to sleep I have bad dreams.

* * *

A couple of times on the morning school bus I saw him. I really saw Peter. He was sitting way in the back of the bus. Just for an instant. But when I blinked and looked again, the seat was empty . . .

HENRY
CAPE CHARLOTTE
MAY

Researching my history of the port of Jamesport is immensely soothing, particularly during these trying times. The waiting, the lack of a decision on Sheffield's part, the expectation of one, would prostrate another man. Indeed, it would so do to me were it not for my scholarly enterprise. This work impels me to transport and immerse my being into the world of yore.

Upon the undertaking of this project, I, of course, applauded the resolute whalers, those intrepid types who braved the elements, risking their very lives in the hunt for the great beasts, those leviathans, kings of the deep. But at the risk of sounding Socialist, which Mercy, I am not, I have come to the reluctant but inevitable conclusion that needless slaughter, nay great butchery, was committed in the name of Commerce.

The Great ——— Whale, particularly, has been decimated to a point that will endanger the propagation of future generations. Prized for the oil contained in the casement of its head (its name, unfortunately arose from a resemblance to certain . . . seminal fluids, shall we say), the Great ——— Whale is destined to disappear. A most unfortunate occurrence which continues to this day.

HANNES
CAPE CHARLOTTE
MAY

The Führer did *not* die fighting to the end in a firestorm. No, *he cowered in a rathole to the last.* Dreams die and heroes fall and Gods become cowards and nothing lasts.

I have begun to move about more—just in my room. But I move. My limbs are flabby and there is a softness over my gut. More exercise each day and I soon shall start to search. I was fast becoming an old fart with gout, my foot propped up on pillows. At least sadistic

Sadie has departed! So now the crippled bitch clucks over me. I can't decide whether she wants me as a son or a stud. Maybe both.

I am dead and free and resurrected! As of today the Third Reich is history and I died with it, to rise, unfettered. A free man with no obligations save to myself. The good life. I want that. I deserve it.

My life, my past, my accomplishments, are in that belt. And Christ! My ID! My paybook with picture!

And my future is in it. My whole future is cradled in chamois bags surrounded by oilskin and canvas. In a cave. Where? Where? *Where?!*

Go back. Go back and read the entry. It's a stream of nonsense yet it makes sense. I can feel the cliff, pitted and slimy. And near the top, a crevice, a place to hide secrets. The belt is there, I know it — and not far away.

A fog, not of the mind, has rolled in. A real fog and I am awake and Oh God! the howling, the moaning. My dream creatures howl and moan. I ran from the beast and it is with me. It is with me and I am awake!

My beast is a foghorn — a *foghorn!* The Lady of the House looked in to find me in a sweat. Assumed I was feverish. And apologized for the noise! Says the horn here on Porpoise Point is much worse than James Head! *Two* foghorns . . . both were chasing me that night. I heard *two* foghorns. So I was somewhere in between. Miles of coastline to scour.

My first outing. Old Henry dropped me off at a beach. I am exhausted but managed to hop and hobble alone along a cove: the name given to an indentation along the shore. I did not come ashore here, for the beach is shale: sharp pieces of rock. I landed on a beach of stones — rounded, rolling stones. Which proves — nothing! Because I wandered. I know I wandered. Straight as an arrow? Or around, in circles?

Second outing. A bit stronger this time. I have added muscles in my biceps.

But I cannot climb — and I must!

Another cove. Nothing looks familiar. The ledges rise and the crevices are too high. I need a monkey!

It was Siberia that night and I wandered in ice.

EMMA
CAPE CHARLOTTE
MAY

I woke up this morning already thinking about the poem I was going to write because it was in me. It's about a storm coming and a seagull who loves to play his game, diving at the big waves long after the other seagulls have flown inland. I think it will be a sad poem.

All the kids are pretty excited about graduating from grammar school. Particularly Eddie, who will be sixteen and isn't going back in the fall. I was excited too, way back, but I really don't care now. The summer is coming up and I don't think I can stand it. It will just be three months of trying not to think about things and waking up early thinking about them. I am so lonesome.

Mrs. Roosevelt must be lonesome. Her husband, President Roosevelt, died last month. I didn't write about it then, because . . . well, I just didn't write about it. He has been President all my life. When we heard the news on the radio, Daddy cried. I know how he feels.

HANNES
CAPE CHARLOTTE
MAY

I shall try each cove in turn. Each one between the two foghorns. Between the two lighthouses. *Lighthouses!* The *eyes!* The snow was still thick but not too thick for eyes to burn through, wavering beams. *Eyes!* I am not mad!

The old man is beside himself with joy to see me on my feet — or foot. He twitters with expectation.

He's about as subtle as a rolling cannon. Drops hints as heavy as cannonballs.

Suggests I might want to visit the Jamesport Library. Why, for Chrissake?! You old fool! *What I want is not there.* But for some curious reason you think it is, don't you?

Just keep your mind on town and off the beaches.

But keep on hoping, you henpecked boob. I need you to chauffeur me.

I walked too far and slipped on rocks. My shoulders ache and I banged my foot — what's left of it. So today I did not search but stayed in bed, recovering, eating *bananas* in cream, *yellow cream.* And listened to the radio.

What slop! Fifteen-minute slots of whining agony. They don't know shit about *real* agony. *Real* agony is listening — all afternoon!

EMMA
CAPE CHARLOTTE
MAY

I went down to Loch Cove after school. I've found a good rock to lean against. And it's a good place to think when the sun has warmed it. I don't think on the knoll anymore. The juniper hasn't felt my back for a long time. And it won't again ever.

I met a boy down at the Cove today. He's not really a boy because he's been in the War and was wounded landing in France. But he's not terribly old either. He started talking to me while I was skipping stones. At first I didn't want to talk to anyone, but he tried to skip stones too and he was awful. So I showed him how, and pretty soon I just started talking.

At low tide Loch Cove looks just like a peaceful pond, which is how it got its name, I guess. It's peaceful because there's a pebbly bar that keeps the ocean out. The Cove is perfect for skipping, and the water warms up a little bit in the summer when the tide's out because it's shallow. You can wade in and not freeze your legs off in two seconds. And if you can stand it for about fifteen minutes you might get up enough courage to duck a couple of times before you turn to ice.

I forgot to say that Christopher, that's his name, was shot in the foot. He has a big bandage on it and he limps on his crutches and I know it hurts, but he is very brave and doesn't cry.

HANNES
CAPE CHARLOTTE
MAY

Third time never fails. On the first two outings, the beaches were deserted. Today, in a new cove, Loch Cove (seems the bloody Scots were here, too!), I met a girl. Young, but not a child. Skinny. Braids. Outspoken, yet withdrawn. For some reason she seems familiar. But I have not met her before.

I shall work on the friendship; I have figured out how to use her.

I dredge up images that swim before me. If I can grasp them, hold them, put them together. It is not night, but dawn . . . the small figure silhouetted against the new sun . . . a sexless child bundled against the cold, a hood around the face . . . the face unseen. I reached for my knife then . . . my knife! The old goat has it now! . . . I reached and the child told me to take a bus, go into town, get away from the fort and the MPs and the dogs! Dogs! A deserter. I am a deserter and the child thinks I look sick! Get to the Coast Road. And a mittened finger points the direction — away from the sun . . . There *were* dogs!

Why to town?

My feet are pulp. I have no feet . . . I walk on nothing across a field of melting snow . . . Dead brown stalks like sabers lash me . . .

A bus. The bus for shipyard workers to the docks. A rotting place stinking of fish . . . greasy planks with holes to fall through . . . filthy people — fishermen and whores, whining whores and cobblestones . . . an undulating ribbon of slippery stones, and I fell and the boats bobbed up and down in green slime . . . small boats and I was on them and I puked and lay in it. Tea . . . hot tea . . . I asked for tea and she told me this was a saloon for *men,* and she brought me glasses, dozens, and smirked and I drank glass after glass and heaved it up and found the money, wet with brine and mashed it into the puke and laughed thinking of the greedy cunt fishing out five dollars . . .

And . . . the Lightship . . . the Lorelei laughs . . . and I passed out.

Himmler's gone. Another leader bites the capsule and finds Valhalla. I feel nothing. Only boredom, and think of Heydrich, who could have made all the difference . . .

EMMA
CAPE CHARLOTTE
MAY

I started down to the Cove today right from the school bus, so that's how I happened to notice the man in the car. He was parked behind some bushes right near the bridge where the water from the Cove runs inland under the Coast Road. He was just sitting there looking out at Loch Cove, so I snuck up on him and he couldn't see me because the sea roses were in the way and anyway he wasn't looking in my direction.

For a little while I pretended that I was Judith. Judith is my friend, and one day back in the War, she had to walk home because she missed the bus. And there was another man sitting in a car just about where this man was and the other man was writing stuff down in a notebook. We were all scared of spies then, particularly because everybody said they had found one with a big radio transmitter behind his bookcase — a German person who lived in a house near the channel. Well, as soon as Judith saw the man writing and staring out to sea, she thought about spies. So she memorized the license plate and so she wouldn't forget it, she broke a branch off and kept saying the number over and over and writing it in the sand beside the road as she walked. She must have written it a million times! When she got home she told her father and he called the FBI. The FBI never said boo! to them, never told them *anything!* But the man never came back, either!

So I snuck up on this man and was I disappointed! He was old and looked like a jolly elf — one of Santa Claus's helpers! And then I remembered he couldn't be a spy anyway because the Germans are all finished. They gave up!

Christopher was down in the Cove again today. He must have been there awhile because he had had a picnic, it looked like. I went down after school to study my part for graduation but I don't want to. Miss Munroe says Archibald MacLeish is a great poet and I will love reading him. Well, A.M. will just have to wait. I decided I was not in the mood.

I said Hi to Christopher and he said Hi and then I went off and climbed my cliff to get to my rock and sat there and thought. After a while Christopher came and sat down below me and told me I was quite a climber and he missed not being able to climb like he had once. I said he would when his foot got better, and then I decided not to say anything more because I didn't feel like talking.

BUFFY
CAPE CHARLOTTE
MAY

They are *finished,* Meg! Kaput! Good word, kaput! Put in the can? Anyway, as you have no doubt noticed, I have regained my equilibrium (as far as hating is concerned!) and revel in the knowledge that the Nazis are squealing in defeat. Something new for them — although they were always rats. Mustn't let one of them wriggle free! Hope we plow over the whole Goddamned country and issue them plowshares. Back to the fields, boys!

Which leaves the Japs. Unpleasant business, that. We can island-hop, take coral reef after coral reef, and yet what looms up? The Big Island. The Empire of Japan. Before they bow in abject surrender we have to storm the mainland. And that last push will be so costly. Those buggers will fight to the last man, die in their holes before they give up an inch. Much blood is yet to spill — and thousands upon thousands of our boys will die. Two more years, at least.

Speaking of American boys, we still have ours — Christopher. Coming along nicely. What's left of his foot is cushioned with bandages. Still tender, the foot, but he hobbles about on crutches and has even gotten out of the House a few times, now. Expresses an interest in the shore and environs, so Pudge drives him down to a cove and leaves him alone to explore for a couple of hours.

Chris has discovered a new world and is as excited as a youngster hunting for buried treasure. He proudly offers me shells — common periwinkles — handing them to me as though they were diamonds. And from him — they are!

So I ply the dear boy with books about his "new world" which he reads voraciously. Being from that Godforsaken area — the heartland of America, which by all rights should be termed "heartless land" — the rocky coast and the creatures of the sea are a revelation to him.

Speaking of shells, Christopher is withdrawing from his. Talks a bit, now, instead of the nod and the infrequent "yes" and "no." He was more attractive mute! (Did I tell you he has a smile one would like to bottle?) It's the accent — enough to curl the hair! A scratchy whine plus something like a gargle plus — who knows? God! He needs speech lessons! I shall institute them presently. Take the edge off his voice, replace it with the softness of pure pear tones, and he'll be a winner!

Speaking of winners, maybe *I* have one. My opus. My BOOK, Meg! Remember? That mess that was once a pile of scribblings and typed hunks lying helter-skelter has now been fashioned into a second draft. A coherent story. Yes, I know most people would call it a *first* draft, but I am *not* most people. Anyway, I have sent it to a publisher *out* of New England, a publisher who hasn't passed out at the *vivid,* shall we say, imagery. I know, because an editor did not send it back! Instead, he sent a letter *praising the forthrightness* of the book! And — can we talk contract. Which means, love, they want to publish!!

All for now — until new happenings. The daffodils are happening which should mean spring — but may mean nothing.

From your possibly *published* friend,
Buffy

P.S. I tell you most everything, but I will *not* tell you the title. Because, my sweet, you would scream!

HENRY
CAPE CHARLOTTE
MAY

Sheffield's affinity for the strands is puzzling. Why the consuming interest in Loch Cove? He shows no interest in visiting the Jamesport Library — not one whit. Yet, I still surmise that it became the repository of his cache, *my* cache.

So I pose the question: What is his intent and why his lengthy stay? He is presumed dead by his former employers; he has a fresh and well-prepared identity. Therefore, he need not hibernate. Does he tarry until his foot has clearly healed and he can, once more, walk with normal gait?

Until he hands me all that I am due, I am unable to slumber peacefully. I dream of the ax above me, quivering, ready to fall. I see it gleaming with razor edge, beveled, bloody from repeated use. At times I have awakened, tasting fear.

EMMA
CAPE CHARLOTTE
MAY

I finally decided to read A.M. The long poem is "America Was Promises." We are going to have a patriotic graduation. At first I said so what, but then I started to read it out loud and I felt as though I was singing — I mean the poem was singing and I got goosepimples. Then I went back and read the sentences that Miss Munroe marked, which are the pieces I will say, and I burst out crying. I don't know why.

So I went down to the Cove and leaned against my rock and started to write my own poem. I talked out loud to myself and wrote down what I said as fast as I could. I thought of singing and that helped my writing. But when I was done I read it over, and I saw I had written about not having anyone to love you and I cried again.

Christopher was there on the beach looking in the seaweed, but I ignored him.

BUFFY
CAPE CHARLOTTE
MAY

Meg!

It just came — the contract! I am to be published — really *published!* Won't our social set die, just die! Not out of envy, my dear. Oh, no. From *mortification.* They will throw up their hands in horror, expunge me from the Blue Book (or is it Green? I never can remember), and pretend I never existed. But I shall whoop in their faces! Oh glorious thought!

My mate knows not *what* I have written — but — he has a good idea; I have dropped enough hints. Poor Pudge will palpitate and avert his face in shame. And whinny.

On the other hand, *his* literary effort is a distorted perception of documented history! He goes on and on about the whaling industry, which along with the China Trade *made* Jamesport. Pudge has plunged into a late-life love affair with whales. So here he is, full of moral rectitude about the beastly whalers, the depletion of the species, disgusted that blubber and bone and sperm (The prig! He avoids *that* word!) oil built great mansions. Yet in his thin little treatise he mentions briefly, only *briefly,* the Slave Trade. He refuses to acknowledge that Bostonians had anything to do with slavery. They did! Almost in an aside, Pudge does admit that many a New England carpenter or farmer made his fortune sailing the Triangular Slave Route — but — to justify the whole sorry chapter of American history — greed and cruelty! he states that "whilst the Slave Trade might be viewed as discomforting to those in bondage, it must also be viewed as justly rewarding those daring men who sailed their brigs to hostile shores, thereby enriching the economy of New England and also that of the eastern coastal states, in turn adding to the coffers of *this land of liberty* (My emphasis!); the bravery of such heroes is part of the fabric of which the free enterprise system of this great land is woven."

God! What a sentence! God! What a pea brain!

If he publishes this, *I* shall weep with embarrassment — and shame! Just quoting Pudge gives me a pain, so I will refrain from any more sludge. There's a poem in there somewhere, but I shan't search!

To brighter things. Christopher is opening up. Talking a bit about his earlier life — just a bit. I gather Father did not go the route of the typical Harvard grad — i.e., into investments, banking, the professions. Seems he fancied himself a pioneer, went west to carve out a life from the land. Had it made until the dust wiped out his dream. Thence to drink, ruin — the old story. Mother dead, I guess from anguish — or something. Father went a few months ago, a corroded liver, probably. Chris says little about his last years. They are painful for him, I can tell. And of course, I know more about his desolate background than I let on.

On other things he is more open. Beginning to talk about the dreary life of a wounded veteran — and it's disgraceful! Peeling walls, lousy care — no one cares. Little to read but magazines way out of date and comic books. We send the boys over, throw them against the guns, and then ship back the pieces to molder in prisons disguised as hospitals!

I am composing a letter of outrage. Heated. To Washington! Wish Franklin was alive. I'm going to miss that old reprobate! He wheeled around with gusto. And had class. And was *not* a traitor to his class!

I don't know this Truman so won't write to him. Can't imagine what Franklin was thinking of at the '44 convention. Harry — a *President?* With a squeaky southern twang? I'm afraid no one will hear him and he'll melt into obscurity.

Will keep you informed about our boy and book.

Much love, dear,
Buffy

EMMA
CAPE CHARLOTTE
JUNE

Graduation is in two weeks, so I finally decided to learn my part. I practiced down on my rock. Today I was saying the poem out loud and Christopher came limping along. He asked me what I was saying so I recited a bit to him. When I told him the name of the poem was "America Was Promises," he smiled in a funny way. I can't describe it exactly, but it looked like he didn't believe it — for a little bit anyway. And then he said something like "it just may be." I think that's what he said, but it doesn't make any sense. Probably his foot hurts.

That man in the car keeps coming. And he always parks *after* Christopher is on the beach. It's as though he waits for Mr. Thurston to drop Christopher off and then comes out of nowhere and just sits, staring. I don't think Christopher notices and I haven't said anything. And the man isn't bothering anybody.

Christopher says he used to climb all over the seashore before he got drafted, but since he's been shot he can only hobble along on the ground. When he gets better, he's going back to college and finish studying oceanography. He loves the cliffs and the caves — finding what's in them. Now he can only collect the stuff like old seaweed in the caves he can reach from the ground.

I told him a little bit about graduation and he told me a lot about seaweed. I thought I knew about seaweed, but Christopher knows everything! I mean, he can tell the name of *any* kind just from a speck of a little piece!

I don't know whether I suggested it or he suggested it but whatever — I promised him I'd be his legs and climb for him sometime after graduation. He seemed so pleased! He doesn't have any friends and I guess he's lonesome just like me.

HANNES
CAPE CHARLOTTE
JUNE

Emma Pickering: Thirteen years of age. Underage. But vulnerable. Christopher, you who drifted almost unconsciously through your 25th birthday have become such a sympathetic character! And brilliant. Now only a 20-year-old boy — just two years out of high school. And wounded to boot. So innocent and unsuspicious!

I should have made me 21. I cannot drink in a public place!

The weather is foul; the sea churns and I cannot go out. I continue to read up on the years I have missed — *Collier's, Look* — piles of print that she plies me with. The Forties from the American point of view. The War from another slant. Pragmatism.

There is something black out there. The sea will swallow it. It tried to capsize me . . . the raft so flimsy . . . only canvas between the sea and me . . . crests and valleys and swooping down, then up . . . slammed from swell to swell and ice water sloshing around my feet . . . paddling a frenzy of breaking arms . . . the beam to starboard . . . keep the beam to starboard . . . thrown on stones . . . *stones,* not sand! The Captain threw me off to drown . . . keep alive . . . stand up . . . knife the raft . . . shred it . . . move . . . move!

I dreamed I could not move and was being shaved by a French maid. Boar bristle brush and soap from a jar. A spicy scent and the maid smelled of musk and I was being seduced. Her hand held a blade which scraped my cheek, but the other hand — Oh lovely! the other circled my cock, teasing, enticing it. Helpless, I had to submit.

I am going to *buy* a French maid and dress her up in a tiny skirt and ruffled apron, encase her long legs in black. Jesus! I need a woman!

In these few weeks, Henry the Hen has aged noticeably. And tonight at dinner he was positively ashen. Twitched — quivered in his chair — as much movement as he allows himself. It would not be *proper* to bounce! As soon as the cow left, so did he. Out the door.

HENRY
CAPE CHARLOTTE
JUNE

The affair is concluded, a frightful affair. Caught in a maelstrom I could not foresee, I acted instinctively. Now the deed is done and the dastardly demon inhabits other spheres.

The doing was so unlike me — a man of quietude. A man of peaceful nature, content only to balance the books and in my free moments pursue the high road of a scholar. Since rediscovering the lure of history and following this academic bent, I wanted only to contribute a new nugget of knowledge to the world.

Yet my self-determination was shadowed by a cloak of blackmail. Nigh unto a decade I was made to bend under the yoke of tyranny, and when the moment of freedom was surely in my grasp, I took it and struck!

The affair which I am about to unfold began with harshness: the frantic jangling of the telephone, which by good chance I picked up first.

The voice on the line spoke with a silky softness redolent with menace. It enquired after my health and that of my "house guest"!

Lowell!

Lowell, who had vanished after ascertaining that demolition bombs had rendered his raison d'être obsolete, useless.

Lowell, whom I had put out of my mind as one forgets a dark cloud that briefly obliterates the sun.

Lowell was back laden with doom and he would not let me go!

He whispered demands of a nature that would bind me to him for life. My service was not enough, now. My information, my sources, were of no use. That facet of his life was over. Instead, his wishes were those of simple greed.

Sums of money. Large sums of money. I had access to wealth and he expected me to accommodate his wishes.

Knowing, as I did, and as he no doubt had discovered, that my inheritance was meager, he meant the accounts. *Altering* the accounts. Embezzlement! Thievery! Lawlessness!

He would be on my hands forever, clinging like a leech, sucking me dry, insatiable for more!

My silence must have signaled shock, for he blandly offered his payment — his sop — for my acquiescence: papers denoting the true identity of my house guest. Papers, which if revealed to the authorities, would brand me a traitor for eternity!

Vivid, horrid pictures: a drumming out from the Newtonian! Shunned in Boston — a Boston forever stunned!

He would, however, hand over some papers as evidence of his good faith at a meeting to be agreed upon.

With a rapidity which astonished me, I set the time — and the place — a place each of us knew well, and he concurred to both.

And so, at the conclusion of dinner, and after Evelyn had departed for the heights, there to continue her *most unacademic* endeavor, I set out for the rendezvous.

Immediately it was apparent that the omens were not favorable: the Studebaker refused to idle. Indeed, it would not even turn over. Consequently, I was forced by time constraints to borrow Evelyn's vehicle — an ostentatious elephant.

I had no conscious plan of action, but a plethora of possibilities paraded before me as I wrestled the beast forward to the appointed place.

Only three minutes tardy. The grocery was dark, and darker still the cul-de-sac beside it. But in the shadows, Lowell lurked. I could feel his evil presence.

By skillful maneuvering and strength of arm, I managed to best the wheel and slip into the narrow passage.

All was silent; the neighborhood seemed to have died. All was silent save my heart, which pulsed at an accelerated beat, pounding louder than the drum of Harvard.

Suddenly, I was not alone. Adroitly, he had opened the passenger door and, like a puff of smoke, slid in beside me.

Without delay he began to blather, neglecting even the common courteous greeting. He went on blathering; I heard nothing.

The night had settled in, but even darkness has its remembered light, and in the dimness I saw his face grow clearer with each interminable minute. Suffice it to say, my anger increased proportionately.

He leaned over and patted me. Patted me! A snake slithering on my arm. Instinctively, I pulled the limb away in utter disgust, bouncing it against my side, where it encountered an object which I had forgotten momentarily, having slipped it into my pocket earlier for . . . protection, of course.

With infinite grace, seeing that it was my left hand, I withdrew it, using the cover of my hacking jacket. I withdrew the knife, Sheffield's knife, intending only to prick him if he dared to touch me further!

Lowell, feeling he had me suitably cowed, sidled closer, so close I could smell his rancid breath.

He put his arm around me! A comradely "we are two brothers" gesture! Lowell, a *brother?*

And then the unthinkable: "You supply me with money and I'll supply the young boys."

With all the force I could muster, seeing as I am not ambidextrous, I thrust the knife forward — into a soft belly. Blood poured forth quite freely. He gurgled a bit, attempting to extract the blade, which only intensified the bleeding. With the small beam from a flashlight, I chanced a glance at my nemesis. I watched his arms flail feebly, saw blood trickle from his mouth. And then his eyes, popping with fear and realization, suddenly rolled up, the whites quite glassy.

I pushed the loathsome thing away from me — to the farthest corner of the seat — and sat in a state of detachment. It was done.

What blood had escaped (and there seemed to be little beyond that which soaked his trousers) was absorbed instantly into the upholstery. Fortunately, the hues matched perfectly.

The body — for he was quite dead — posed a problem. I must be rid of it — yet where should the disposition be? The sea?

I pondered the ramifications if he were found shortly, washed up on shore. Not only murder most foul, but worse — a description. On numerous occasions he had been in the area and seen by some — including Ginny. Whilst I doubted that an attempt at identification was probable, considering that Lowell was an elusive nonentity to the American authorities — if they knew of him at all — it remained a remote possibility.

I knew then what I had to do. Distasteful as it may have seemed, it was imperative to remove any distinguishable traces. My mind swept to the grocery, closed and abandoned. If I could gain entrance, it would be there I could begin the task.

There was one door on the side; one door shut tightly. I pulled with all my might and it would not budge. But not willing to give up without a struggle, I pulled again, finding strength I knew not existed — and lo and behold — the door gave an inch, two inches and then creaked open!

Lowell, small and rotund, now became a weight of enormous proportions: a walrus. His limbs flapped like flippers and I tugged; the exertion on my part was immense. Dragging and puffing, I managed to deliver his lifeless body to the entrance and with a final burst of energy heaved him inside. He promptly bounced downwards: stairs. It was well he went first! Most carefully I negotiated the stairway, knowing to avoid the pile at the bottom.

After what seemed like an age of exploration, I discovered a switch. And with faint hope that it would work since, no doubt, the electricity had been severed long ago (bills not paid), I flicked it.

One large swinging lamp illuminated all! Quickly, I examined the room (for it was more than a cellar), and finding no windows to betray me, set about my repugnant task — one which must be completed quickly, else the chance that a most unordinary auto parked in such a lowly, unsavory neighborhood might be discovered and remarked upon.

First, I scrutinized my clothing for bloodstains. Relieved at finding none, I now examined the room more fully. I had stumbled on an *abattoir!*

Under the lamp, which was swinging as though in glee, was a heavy table, maple perhaps, whose many marks indicated that its surface had felt the chops of years. In slots at one end were utensils for butchering. I chose carefully.

But first the knife; it must be removed. I drew it forth, a disagreeable task, as more blood burbled out. But I cautioned myself not to become squeamish, for there was nastier work ahead. I wiped the steel back and forth across the back of his coat until it shone and then replaced it in my pocket. Soon, Sheffield would have his knife back. Rather his than mine! After this night, I would have no fear of it — nor him.

Swiftly, I stripped Lowell of all clothing, relieving him of papers meant for me, breast pocket wallet and gold watch (rather fine. Swiss: an antique I presumed from a cursory examination). The clothing I kept separate, piling it neatly next to the cache.

Naked, Lowell appeared to be but a grown baby, not a man. In fact, his private parts were obscured by gross corpulence, for which I was most grateful.

Hanging on the farther wall were several white aprons smeared with rusty stains. I used two, after removing my trousers and jacket. (I was particularly pleased to note that the latter had not absorbed a single spot, it being an iron-hard Harris tweed of a heather shade, one of which I am most fond.)

Now to the chore, which I found to be exceedingly difficult, being, as I am, not a physician, not knowing the fine points of anatomy, points which would have served me well, since being acquainted with bone structure and joinings would have made the task child's play. It was not for me! Using a large cleaver, I chopped and hacked, and finding that the pieces still clung tenaciously to the body, resorted to a meat saw, which finally did the trick.

What remained of Lowell would have to be hidden for a time, at least until it decomposed — or did it have to? My first consideration was to drive with the torso and bury it under a layer of garbage.

The area christened by the city fathers a "landfill" is in actuality a dumping ground. A dump, to put it crudely, where the debris of the city is thrown out, gnawed on and finally compressed. But in its raw state from that flotsam floats a stench that reaches even to my working chambers!

The gulls who flock there could do my work: pick clean the body until only a bleached skeleton remained. Bones that would have no discernible history. Date of death: unknown. Identity of person: unknown. Motive: one of revenge, perhaps. A gangland slaying, as it were: a Capone-style killing?

I mulled on this possibility and discarded it for reasons that should be apparent. Driving to the dump meant driving with a body. And that body would have to be removed from the auto — by me. I might be under surveillance by anyone at any time: seen and remembered.

I formed a more practical idea, one which, besides its pragmatism, contained a bit of whimsy.

Lowell's resting place — for a time, at least — is in a barrel. Upstairs, alone in splendor, sits the barrel of brine. If anyone ever comes to fetch a cucumber, they will instead grasp Lowell, pickled!

With Lowell safely salted away, I made final preparations.

I would have to carry home a number of bundles. His clothing, the papers, watch, etc. — and several pieces of *him.* Namely: his head and hands. Any butcher shop worth its salt has wrapping paper, the coated kind. And there remained a partial roll!

But before touching any more surfaces, I surveyed the scene. It resembled a charnel house, which it was and had been. A butcher shop "butchers," and consequently is a tacky place. Coagulating blood is tacky, sticky, and there was much around, pools of it — splatters here and there, made by my inept dissection. Twisting a head, hacking at it, does spread gore.

But it was not the blood which worried me. It was that which coated my hands. I knew intuitively that no water would be forthcoming from the tap (the Water Company, of which I am a Director, would have long since shut it off! No payment; no water. We are in business for profit! Which is more than can be said for that utility providing power. Knowing some of *their* Directors, I expect that deficits are staring them in the face!), so I searched the room for a suitable cleansing method. And there, nearly hidden under the table, was a pail half filled with brackish, brownish water. For my purposes, it sufficed, despite being somewhat viscous. But patient scrubbing removed most of the mess, and the outer apron, used as a towel, absorbed the remainder.

Now I was prepared to wrap. The clean objects — the watch, wallet, papers — were done first. Then came the clothing, which I handled gingerly, for it was rather soaked. Finally in two separate bundles went Lowell — those parts of him I planned to carry home — the head and hands. The latter I centered on the paper with the aid of one apron as protection from further fouling. All objects now were wrapped and tied and ready to be transported.

Removing the second apron — which was cleaner, being under the first — I used it to wipe any surfaces I had touched knowingly. The light switch, the cleaver, saw, etc.

Then, to be doubly sure — one cannot be too careful — I wiped and swiped at any place I might have touched — and to my chagrin, neglected to remember the floor. My footprint! A reddish footprint! The offending shoes were removed and dabbled in the now-disgusting water.

I squelched my way upward in the darkness to the landing, toting one load after another until all were ready for their trip. Then, most cautiously, I pushed open the door — just a crack. Hearing nothing, I moved it outward ever so slightly until I could just slip through with my parcels. Each was deposited on the seat and I turned to close the door of the shop. In my haste to leave, I am afraid I used more force than necessary, for the door moved, groaning on hinges I had presumed to be rusted, and slammed suddenly with a clap that seemed to shatter the night. I waited, not daring to draw a breath, but all remained quiet. No dog barked; no window was thrown open in alarm. No one heard.

Silently, I slid inside the mammoth vehicle. Wearily, yet gratefully, I filled my lungs to capacity with fresh clean air. I was free! Free of tyranny! Don't tread on me!

On the way home I hummed — perhaps a snatch of "Yankee Doodle Dandy"? — as I contemplated what story I would fabricate for Evelyn this time.

HANNES
CAPE CHARLOTTE
JUNE

What a difference a day makes. Henry the Hen doesn't cluck today. He purrs. In fact, he smiles — like a satisfied cat. What canary did he eat? Must have had rejuvenating powers. The cat has shed years.

For the time being I am confining myself to the one cove — Loch Cove. There are endless and fruitful possibilities in Loch Cove.

Henry the Tiger has regressed. He is a wary kitten. Wary of me, ever since my hunting knife mysteriously turned up. He continues to ferry me to the Cove, but he keeps his distance now, as though I smelled!

But I have an admirer. For I am a natural teacher and she delights in learning. And wants to help me. Legs for lessons, Emma.

Slimy stuff, seaweed. But I am an expert seaweed man!

He wishes I would go away, poof! Reward him and leave. I have outstayed my welcome. But not his mate. That lovesick sow would have me forever!

BUFFY
CAPE CHARLOTTE
JUNE

Dear Meg,

Lord, what will I ever do with Pudge? Help!

This last week he has been impossible. And throughout — ebullient, even *forceful!* He must be ill!

Several days ago, he took the Packard. Took *my* car! Without asking! And messed it up! I have told him time after time *not* to use it because he is not the most careful of drivers. His mind wanders and it wanders — right off the road.

Well, after Pudge's sojourn to who knows where, Alfred came to me the next morning most upset, which is par for Alfred (I swear he only rows with one oar!), but then Cook waddled in wiping off tears and muttering about leaving. Cook! Cook never mutters, never weeps, and has been my confidante (as much as servants can be) since my prep school days. Cook upset meant the Apocalypse was upon us! And who was the cause of all this misery? Pudge, the oaf!

To return to the Packard. Alfred, as I have stated, was in a tizzy, which at first I did not take seriously. But after seeing why, I was ready to scream. Pudge had *soiled* the upholstery! A dark stain on the passenger side. Burgundy on burgundy. The place smelled strangely sweet, almost gacky. And I suspected the worst. Pudge had tippled from a cheap pint of muscatel! That smell was terribly reminiscent of ragged types reclining under the Third Ave. El!

I sent Alfred out with a bottle of seltzer water instanter. And spent the rest of the morning deciding that the world was going to hell in a hack if Pudge was reduced to guzzling bum's nectar.

Finally I tackled Cook's woes, which included — 1. Rusty footprints on the kitchen floor leading in from the back door. 2. Strange parcels in the icebox leaking red with "DO NOT TOUCH!" inked upon! 3. Pudge's fury at Cook when she asked him the contents. He raised his voice to her — the first time, *ever!* telling poor Cook it was none of her business — but when it was time to *roast,* he would tell her. Until then, he said, he actually said, in a tone of authority tinged with rudeness, to keep her *sticky fingers off his mutton!*

Pudge believes that mutton is the king of lamb. It is the ram of lamb, that's certain. I *hate* it. Tough and old and reeking. And I vowed that right then and there I would confront Pudge and lay down the law. No more Packard! Re servants: noblesse oblige and — no roast mutton *in my House!*

I caught him that afternoon and did just that — and more. I was furious — and a little worried about the wine episode. He took the parts about the car and the mutton with equanimity, and when I came to the stain (I put that rather delicately, I thought), he laughed. He laughed!

The mutton was the culprit, not wine, he countered! How could I think that he, of all people, would drink anything, even Moxie, in a moving car? It was the mutton, the cause of all the troubles, leaking blood through the wrappings — and he only used the Packard because his old thing, that prehistoric put-put, wouldn't start. Pudge said he had to go into town to pick up the meat — a gift from an acquaintance who supplies the big boats — before it spoiled. As for Cook, he swore she embroidered the whole incident, although he *had* trod in the drippings. He then agreed to remove the parcels, saying the meat was going bad and would be disposed of.

My God! Was I relieved. (I was gearing up for my Carrie Nation sermon!) All my doubts evaporated. And Pudge was smiling! It was odd, seeing the corners of his mouth turn up. Must have hurt. Those minuscule muscles have not been used for years! He *seemed* a new man.

He *was* a new man!

Three days later, I awoke to hear a ghastly churning outside. Down below were three laborers, laboring — on the seawall — as a cement mixer merrily churned away!

I had ordered nothing of the sort. But Pudge had! Without asking me, *without permission,* he had contracted with a firm to "restore" the seawall. Murmured about damage — storm damage — in March. Bullshit! Excuse me. Double shit! That wall has outlasted four hurricanes!

Last night I discovered Pudge's purpose. So sly, he is. The moon was nearly full and some noise made me glance down. There, in the silver light, was my idiot husband lugging something — rocks presumably. There he was, pretending to be a stonemason and cementing his burden into the wall. I have unearthed his secret! The only reason he made up a story about deterioration was to practice rebuilding a wall by the light of the moon!

I think he's nuts. Don't you think he's nuts? Only lunatics practice vices on a full moon!

Maybe men do get menopause or something. Who knows, since no one dares write about what's really underneath our uncrackable façades — except me!

I guess Pudge is bored with whales.

Much, much love, lambie — whoops! Mutton on my mind!

Buffy

EMMA
CAPE CHARLOTTE
JUNE

Graduation was wonderful, beautiful, marvelous — *perfect!* I wish Peter had seen it . . . I mean maybe he can . . . maybe . . . Christopher did! He came, which was terribly nice of him and I didn't even mention it — the date, I mean. He sat in the back.

Everybody was really good. And I was too. I said ". . . Promises" all alone on the stage. Most of the graduation was about the Civil War and slavery and Lincoln and a better country, and we did it all in poetry or song — "Nancy Hanks" and "The Blue and the Gray" and "John Brown's Body."

We sure did a lot on slavery, but you know, I haven't ever even seen a Negro.

We were all, the girls, I mean, supposed to wear white dresses. Well, I didn't own a white dress, so Daddy said I could shop for one in Jamesport. Well, there wasn't one white dress I liked. They were all too ruffly, so I bought a Lanz pinafore *without* ruffles and a white blouse. And — I got the Curse on Graduation Day! *Really!* There I was just before I had to go on with *nothing!* I was terribly worried, so I stuffed a wad of toilet paper in my pants and hoped. *Not one spot on my pinafore!* It was quite a day!

HANNES
CAPE CHARLOTTE
JUNE

School is finished and now Emma will be mine *all* day.

Boring ritual, commencement. Platitudes fervently uttered. They say "Americer," "heaah"! In that white outfit she seemed older and reminded me of — a gazelle?

As of today I am proficient in two more subjects of earth-shattering importance: horseshoe crabs and seaworms. How else to woo a girl?

I shall recite the lessons tomorrow and Emma will marvel and mimic.

That night, that morning . . . I awoke screaming . . . tearing the rats from my face . . . dead stove . . . numb with cold and they were over me . . . furry things with tails . . . chittering . . . mice! The old torn sofa stuffing bursting, my bed . . . being abandoned, leaving countless litters behind . . . blind hairless litters, flattened . . . the cottage . . . I cannot picture it . . . I cannot find it . . . there are cottages and cottages and which was mine? My cottage. My beach. What do they matter? If I wandered. There is *no* relationship between them and the cliff, the crevice! Three points — all unknown!

Every sign of infection gone. The toes itch!

Emma Pickering. My little bloodhound, still a gangly puppy, but embued with a streak of mountain goat. You are my eyes, my fingers — my legs, my feet.

We have a fine time, you and I.

But the old crow is not happy. I think she is jealous of the beach!

EMMA
CAPE CHARLOTTE
JUNE

Did you know there are about eight thousand waves hitting the shore in one particular cove, any cove, every day? Did you know that horseshoe crabs aren't really crabs at all but descendants of something that I can't remember the name of that lived half a *billion* years ago and that the horseshoe crab's nearest relative is the spider? Did you know that the shipworm is a worm that uses a shell at the end of it to bore holes in ships and the only way to stop them is to coat the timbers with some chemical? I didn't know any of this, but Christopher does! I will look at a crab differently from now on. And when I hear a wave, I'll know I'll hear it again and again. A third of a million times in a year! That's when I'm home to hear. I shouldn't count schooltime. And all those little holes in driftwood were made by tiny worms eating away!!!

I haven't seen the old man in the car for quite a while. I guess he got bored staring at the sea. Maybe he's gone to look at a lake.

BUFFY
CAPE CHARLOTTE
JUNE

Oh Meg—

Whatever ails men? I allude to my editor. While on the one hand he praises the book's frankness, with the other he blue-pencils some of my more interesting passages! He really does *not* understand women, so, patiently now (the hollering comes later) I am educating him on their desires—that women are not passive creatures. Quite the contrary!

Also, I am teaching him the use of the dash. Dash—! He conceives its use as indicating a sloppy mind. I do not! I am *not* sloppy—just in a hurry. The dash connotes excitement, verve, movement!

My editor, poor man, would prefer a colon at all times. Bah! Humbug! Colons connote lower-case emotions. Colons are boring—Victorian. Colons are also lower-case bowels, good sir::::::::::::!

Christopher is *so* much better. Enjoying the good weather (summer may actually materialize) by examining our shores and tidepools. He knows the rocks and ledges better than I—and I knew them well in my walking days. He's always quizzing me on things ranging from geologic formations to whether pirates ever hid booty in the caves! God! I haven't the vaguest notion whether or not Blackbeard and his ilk ever got up this far. But Christopher pretends they might have, and I think, though he doesn't say so, that he's looking for hoards of buried treasure! If searching for gold gives him pleasure, why not?

The sun has bronzed him, handsome boy. When Chris arrived he was pale, ghastly pale, as though he had spent months underground. Of course, he had been imprisoned! The weeks with us have transformed him.

He reads—voraciously. I've taken out back issues of all the magazines—newsy ones. Christopher feels he lost part of his life in the last couple of years and has much catching up to do. Was most intrigued with my lurid tale of the U-boat and the storm. But within days of the event I heaved out all the news stories (couldn't bear the thought of saving them) and the stingy Cape Charlotte Library won't let their precious paper out — so, sometime in the future when Chris feels like seeing more than shale and sea — the outside world, Alfred will chauffeur him to our Town Repository, and there he can read about the March Massacre to his heart's content. (Wish someone would invent a way of reproducing printed matter cheaply!)

Writing this reminds me that I left out one incident in my narrative to Chris. Not important compared to the big story. Forgot to mention the death of the fisher-boy. Drowned, poor kid. Washed up on . . . can't remember the official name for the cove. Full of pastel-colored stones. Always reminded me of great big Jordan almonds.

To other news. For months I tantalized you with hints about my aerie. A new addition. Everything was set to go, and then because the War is heating up in the Pacific, my marvelous idea was put on hold for the duration. *Poop!*

I shall not be responsible for depriving a Flying Fortress or a Super Fort of its bubble. That's right, a bubble! It's that thing, maybe they call it a blister, that gunners use, the clear round thing they sit in under the belly of the bomber. I guess some planes have them on top, too. Anyway, the guns poke out and swivel and pop, pop, pop, there goes a Zero.

Well, I wanted a bubble. Made of stuff called Plexiglas, a new material out of "plastic" which is *not* celluloid. Clear, tough stuff — which I had envisioned as a dome — a DOME to roof my aerie.

Can't you just picture what the night would be under a classy glassy dome? Not to be just yet. Poop! Poop! Which will give me time to figure out how to keep from frying in the daylight.

Back to red-penciling my editor's blue. I shall fight for every phrase, nay, every word. And all my dashes — !

Chris misses his mother, though he rarely mentions her. The other day he paid me a huge compliment. Said I reminded him of her. Me? A mother? Not on your life! Maybe the Auntie type?

Love from your wishful stargazer,
Buffy

P.S. OK. I *was* touched. It might have been fun to have a kid — if he could have turned out like Chris. So I'm a bit mushy, maternally speaking. Who would have thunk it?

EMMA
CAPE CHARLOTTE
JUNE

Every day almost I've met Christopher down at some Cove and we do the cliffs. That is, I do the cliffs. Climb them, I mean. Christopher watches from way down below. He's interested in every cave, every little hole — what's in them.

So I find footholds and handholds and shinny and hoist myself up trying not to miss an opening that might have something in it. He yells up, "Make sure you don't miss one, Emma. There might be a bird's nest or an egg or a bit of sealife thrown high by the spray."

Hah! I've found three mussel shells, nine periwinkles, some bits of brittle seaweed and a whole mess of pebbles so far. I haven't even found a cracked eggshell yet!

But Christopher says you never know what treasure you might stumble across. Stumble! I nearly stumble and tumble — straight down! Like the time it was so foggy and we couldn't see the tops of the ledges sticking out into Cockleshell Cove and I decided they were too slippery. When fog settles for a bit, the rocks feel like somebody sprayed oil on them. But Christopher dared me to try, and there was such a cute twinkle in his eye I just had to. I know I was showing off, but I just had to. Didn't fall. Didn't find a thing!

I think we've done every possible cliff from Loch Cove south almost to Porpoise Point. Christopher doesn't think there's anything too interesting near the Thurstons', and besides, he says, the cliffs are too high, even for me. He wouldn't want to be the cause of an accident. Boy, am I glad. Those cliffs are mountains!

What I'm afraid of is that he'll want me to start climbing the other way — toward James Head light. I can't do it. I just can't. I don't ever want to go that way again. I don't want to see those rocks and beaches . . . ever. I see them all the time in my dreams still. If he asks me I've got to tell him why, and I don't want to talk about it to anybody — even Christopher.

Maybe he'll get bored with holes. I sure am! I'd much rather be down on the ground talking to Christopher!!!

HANNES
CAPE CHARLOTTE
JUNE

Nothing! Not a damned thing! And June is nearly over!

* * *

A thunderstorm: no hunting. The ocean fumes. The gods of the sea are angry . . . the god . . . the God of the Sea! . . . gold, pure gold . . . yellow and shimmering under the water. I stabbed him . . . in the gut and diamonds . . . diamonds poured out . . . and the Golden King . . . Midas . . . Midas! I have to meet Midas . . . I *had* to reach Midas . . . and kill him . . .

Pictures . . . flashing . . . hobbling on stumps . . . up from the docks . . . it was crouching a reptile a toad angry . . . ugly . . . unblinking oval eyes . . . the library . . . my life began with a library . . . this one my salvation . . . under the table, instructions. The Reading Room . . . the table a monstrosity . . . the north end . . . occupied! By a . . . bum! . . . a shabby old geezer gnawing on a picnic lunch . . . slurping . . . an angular woman looks daggers at him. I spin and want to faint . . . the woman gestures furiously . . . the bag of bones wheezes into his paper bag . . . wheezes until it is full . . . one fist and Big Bertha explodes . . . he cackles . . . the space is empty. I lurch to the table . . . I feel . . . underneath . . . tape . . . it is there! I am going to faint . . . into the stacks . . . I lean my head against cool shelves . . . the waves pass . . .

Another sits at my place . . . a familiar face . . . I have seen that face — older than in photographs . . . the man leaves . . . and there is nothing under the table . . . only stickiness!

He has taken it! . . . and I have no place to go. I stagger after him, this traitor! The door so heavy . . . sunlight and slush . . . my feet are burning freezing . . . down stairs on stumps . . . I float after him . . . I bump him and whisper . . .

Henry would have me dead! Thought I was . . . and now — he would do me in. Henry, you first. An accident — like falling from a cliff one day? And Christopher will live to comfort the old broad.

HENRY
CAPE CHARLOTTE
JUNE

I become wearier. Each day brings with it the expectation of release, but sundown sees only disillusion once again.

My home is alien to me for he is *there*, always *there*. And he exhibits not one sign of leaving. Indeed, in Evelyn's mind, I fear, he becomes more of a fixture with each passing hour. It is painful to see her positively gush over her "boy" whilst I must keep silent, hold in the searing truth about the blackguard.

I have tried everything I can possibly conceive of to tempt him into town. I have dropped hints, most subtly of course, but he does not bite. Subtlety is the watchword. I am a master at understatement. He does not suspect a particle!

Can the attraction of the beach be the Pickering child: Emma? A fine old name, Pickering. I believe there was a Pickering among the first selectmen down in 17th-Century Portsmouth — Strawbery Banke. Ah, yes, a fine old name until the brash outburst from Mrs. Pickering sullied it with her ultra-liberal views on equality. But then, she only married *into* the family.

At first blush, there appears no evil intent on Sheffield's part. Rather, he and the girl are often separated. He, hobbling along on his crutch; she, perched on a ledge, calling, laughing down to him.

Evelyn is noticeably peeved. Does she believe she has a female rival for his time — and perhaps for his affection?

I, too, wonder . . . about the relationship.

EMMA
CAPE CHARLOTTE
JUNE

I went to the Cape Charlotte Library today and took out all the books they had on the ocean and the seashore, which weren't a whole lot. You'd think they'd have more, considering we live by the sea! Christopher knows so much and I don't and I live here. I am going to surprise him with how much I have learned, not just from him. I am going to do *research.*

It's funny. The last person to take out these books was Mrs. Thurston. Now if anybody else knows about the ocean, she does. Maybe she just wants to learn more the way I do so she can be more knowledgeable with Christopher.

I am reading these books and it's almost like listening to Christopher. Like listening to him tell me about shells or crabs or seaweed. He uses the same words to describe things. The *same* words. It's almost like he learned the stuff just before I did! And he hasn't told me *one thing* that isn't in these books. Not one extra thing!

HENRY
CAPE CHARLOTTE
JUNE

It was a mistake, a grave mistake, to return the knife to Sheffield. I wished to be rid of it so heartily, that much too hastily, I deposited the weapon upon his bed whilst he was down by the tide.

I can be excused for this precipitate action, seeing as my mind was elsewhere: in the fridge with two meat parcels; their ultimate disposition required complete concentration. I had no time, engrossed as I was with removing and thence "replanting" said parcels, to peruse other matters — until today, oh awful day! I neglected to examine the papers I took from Lowell that night — papers relating to the previous life of the man called Sheffield. A man Evelyn dotes on, a man she thinks of as a boy.

I am between a rock and a hard place!

Any exultation I may have experienced after Lowell's resolution evaporated speedily upon the scrutinization of Sheffield's dossier. The content therein gave me quite a turn, and — I hasten to add — was swiftly dispatched to licking flames, destroyed for all time.

Ah, Evelyn. You are so taken with an SS *Leutnant!* In this instance your intuition has grievously failed you. You pride yourself on your ability to separate wheat from chaff, living by the adage: "Beware of charmers; distrust smoothness."

Evelyn, your "child" is most clever — positively brilliant. That boyish charm radiates innocence. A winsome lad, isn't he, Evelyn. He teases you, knowing just when to cease. And you gulp in all his attentiveness. I did not know you had the capacity to be wooed.

My dear, you are consorting with your pet hate. A consummate Nazi, he is. And I have rearmed him!

HANNES
CAPE CHARLOTTE
JULY

She scampers up and down. She hangs on to cliffs like a fly and throws down *junk!* The same damned stuff! Bloody beaches, empty cliffs and the sea always churning. The waves slapping the rocks as though there's a bug to be swatted. Missing the bug and swatting till the end of time!

I am stuck in this fucking place!

I am stuck on this stinking lousy coast for as long as it takes and I can't take it much longer!

What have we missed? We have done all the coves and cliffs from Loch Cove almost to Porpoise Point and Snaggletooth. Emma's idea. She pointed the way and I agreed — to keep her on my leash.

Emma, why not go in the opposite direction — toward James Head light? Emma, why don't you ever play on your own beach?

Emma dear, tomorrow night I will sweet-talk you into going my way. I will play a game with you. After tomorrow night, with the fire of celebration all around, I think you will heed *my* directions, without question. Your eyes give you away. You need, you want, to grow up. And be taught how nice it is by one who is such a fine teacher.

Tonight. I feel that tonight is the turning point. I feel the belt in my hands already — damp but intact.

Soon, I will buy a mountain as far away from the sea as I can get, and build a chalet. Never look on the sea again. A sumptuous chalet on top of the world. A lifetime of peace and luxury. A lifetime of ease and comfort to look forward to. The past is past and my service and distinction exist only in my journals — and my mind.

Tonight — Loch Cove — and Emma — and lobster — Oh Christ! Lobster!

EMMA
CAPE CHARLOTTE
JULY

Two wonderful days in three weeks! First Graduation and then tonight — the Fourth of July!

Everybody came, including CHRISTOPHER. I asked him. I told Mummy could I please invite him and she didn't say anything for a while. Just pursed her lips and sniffed. When Mummy doesn't like something, she usually doesn't yell (except at me). Instead she swears a little or snorts a little, but most of the time she purses her lips and sniffs. That's what she did when I asked her. She's only met him once but she doesn't like Christopher. I don't know why and I don't think *she* knows why. So I invited him to come to the party down at the Cove in spite of sniffs.

The whole neighborhood came, and we chipped in and bought cherry bombs and snakes and sparklers, and then Daddy and Mr.

Armstrong set off rocket after rocket — so many that there wasn't a blank place in the sky. Liquid fire in all colors of the rainbow poured down into the sea, so we got double our money's worth with the reflection!

We said to hell with the blackout (dimout) because the Japs can't see the Atlantic Coast and the Germans are dead and buried and surrendered.

Nobody had seen fireworks since the summer of '41. I was only nine years old then! And we had a lobster bake just before it got dark, which we haven't had since then either.

You dig a big pit, not you but the fathers, and pile a lot of wood and big stones in it and then set the wood afire and wait. When the coals are red hot and the stones could fry an egg, you add a layer of wet seaweed, then potatoes, then another layer of seaweed, then lobsters, and so forth until you're steaming those things plus corn in the husk and clams, and eggs which get hard-boiled and have a smoky sea taste. Then you wait forever until everything is cooked. But it's worth it!

I haven't eaten so much since last Christmas, but that's because there was lobster, which is my favorite food and which I think I would eat on my deathbed!

Christopher wasn't sure he wanted to try a lobster. He said he was from the Plains and they didn't grow ugly things like that out there. But I made him try a piece and he liked it. Or else he's good at pretending.

And then — Christopher took my hand and pulled me behind a rock and gave me a hug and said he was looking forward to tomorrow, when we would start climbing near the knoll and maybe even find a cove with round stones, and I was about to say No! I can't! when he kissed me! It wasn't a big one, more like a peck, but it was a kiss! I was so surprised I jumped and ran, which was pretty stupid. He must think I'm awfully stupid! I wish I hadn't run but I was a little scared. And happy!

Now I can add a star to today. It's my first *real* star, but you have to start somewhere!

I just thought. How come Christopher has climbed all over the seashore the way he says he has if he's from the Plains? Maybe he means during summer vacations. But then he must have seen lobsters if he knows so much. But what does he know? Exactly what's in those books, that's what. Oh well . . . it's not important what he knows about anything. What *is* important is his *star!*

JULY 5

I just woke up and I was ready to be happy and I'm not. Last night seemed so wonderful — last night. Now it's early morning, and for some reason it seems more like a bad dream. I'm going down to my juniper tree. That was where I was really happy . . .

Oh, Peter. I'm so sorry. I'm writing on the knoll under my tree and I can almost see you. It's summer now, Peter, and I've missed you so that I guess I thought Christopher was you. He seemed to be so much like you, I got you mixed up with him. But you're not the same . . .

I haven't forgotten it! I know what I'm going to do right now!

HANNES
CAPE CHARLOTTE
JULY 5

What the hell went wrong? The moment was ideal. A soft summer night. My simple request for changing our search direction and the query I should have mentioned long ago — where is the beach with the round rolling stones? Just the two of us — quite alone — and she was aching to be kissed. I know she's infatuated and she wanted it. And then — the stupid girl ran like a frightened fawn!

Must not frighten her. I shall be gentle, chagrined . . . and hurt — yes, hurt, that I imposed. And she will feel guilt and want to comfort me. And the only comfort she can give will be to begin searching toward James Head light.

Young, vulnerable Christopher will limp in that direction and she will have no option but to follow.

I will wait for her in Loch Cove.

She did not come! Where the hell is she? I can't understand it! I waited most of the day at the Cove, expecting any moment to see her running toward me, plaits swinging, bursting with enthusiasm for another day of adventure!

She did not come! Is she ill? Or embarrassed to face me? That's it. She must be timid after the kiss.

Emma, my sweet, if you persist in avoiding me, I will have to come and find you!

HENRY
CAPE CHARLOTTE
JULY 5

Last night was one of celebration — a blazing patriotic night, but my mind was not with Our Forefathers.

Rather, it was toting up the eternity I have been saddled with misfortune: misfortune in the guise of one Christopher Sheffield, deadly behind his mask! I do believe it to be so!

It will be four long months less a fortnight plus since he arrived, and in all that time he has never intimated a particle of interest in the Jamesport Library. Not once.

Yet he has spent day after day trudging along the shore, shouting up to little Emma. He has inspected more coves than I would care to see in several lifetimes.

But he cares. And he has acquired knowledge of the seashore through avaricious reading. Reading for a purpose. He does nothing without a purpose, a scheme, this Henkel.

But his scheme has nothing to do with me! He doesn't care a tinker's damn about me, about trust, about contracts. This niggling suspicion which I harbored deep within me has surfaced and is as clear as crystal!

Henkel *does not* tramp the beaches, frequently in pain, for love of the seashore. Henkel *does not* go into town to visit the Jamesport Library, for there is *nothing* of interest to him there. *Nothing!* There never was!

He searches along the shore for that which is *his and his alone.* That something possesses him, is precious to him. Exceedingly precious. Not hidden — *lost.* Lost on a storm-tossed night. Lost in a moment of panic, insanity.

And that child is involved — innocently — but involved.

I must take action. I must gird my loins for confrontation. I must beard the lion in his lair. (H.H. is *not* a lion; he more closely resembles a monster. And "lair" is inappropriate considering I confront him outdoors in broad daylight. However, the metaphor will have to suffice.) Therefore, to continue, I shall not be at our *assigned* meeting place, but rather challenge him where and when he least expects me.

I must know! Tomorrow, I *shall* know his secret!

BUFFY
CAPE CHARLOTTE
JULY 9

Meg, Meg —

I can't bear it! The two people I love most in the world gone in an instant. My world destroyed in an instant —

Pudge is dead and I'm dead — no I'm not, I'm in a stupor — and the boy — they brought his broken body up — that handsome, brave boy — *smashed.* Pudge's body — Oh Jesus God, washed up on Mussel Cove — the sea could not have him! I hope, I pray to that Vile Creature that calls Himself Compassionate, that Pudge did not suffer long —

I'm stricken with guilt — awful guilt. I can't sleep thinking how badly I treated him. He's a hero. My Pudge is a hero — tried to save a child who was slipping from a rock — fearful undertow. Chris saw them sliding and went to help in spite of his foot. Both men heroes — grappling to save a child who had no business being in such a dangerous place! And she caused death!

Someone saw the ending — the three wildly holding on to each other, and then Pudge went over, to be carried out by the current, and Chris fell trying to grab Pudge and was smashed on the rock below, and the girl — the girl — that little bitch! is safe and my men — Oh God, Meg — I am stricken —

Pudge is the last person you would ever tag as a hero. His obit was spare just like he was — I tried to pad it, but there it is — Henry Everett Thurston really didn't do too much in life — just plodded. Had no excitement. No fears. Just was — and I miss him awfully — *awfully* —

1955

SUSAN PICKERING
CAPE CHARLOTTE
APRIL

Emma dear,

Couldn't get you on the phone. Are you home and not answering or out on a story?

Anyway, couldn't wait, so one of my few letters. The art of letter writing vanished with the rise of Mr. Bell's infernal machine. Why does one feel a ringing phone *must* be answered? I can see you don't, but I have stress pangs when the thing shrieks. On the other hand, telephones have advantages: I don't have to write — usually.

I have news. *Incredible* news. While others might not find the stuff front-page, you will.

It is your father. No! Not a heart attack! *A change of heart.*

After years of staying put because he had this preposterous idea that traveling was tiring, guess what he proposed? A trip — and not a short one to Champlain or Willoughby, either.

More like Lake Louise and vicinity! He actually wants to go clear cross-country (well, across Canada) and visit scenes from his youth. Perhaps it's age or something, but he is nostalgic for Jasper Nat'l. Park.

You can't possibly forget his talking about that summer during college when he was a cowboy and rode a horse. I think he rode a horse. I *know* he rode a horse, because he used to ride up and check on some old prospector — bring him supplies and such.

He has a thing about mountains. You must remember his making you read *Scrambles Among the Alps.* I doubt that we will ever see the Matterhorn, *but* he wants to see Mt. Edith Cavell again.

Your father is still rather proud of the fact that he, along with a few crazy Yalies, holds the record for the fastest *descent* ever recorded on Cavell. The rapidity was dictated by absolute necessity, not bravado. They were outrunning a storm!

All this preamble is to tell you that he has actually talked to a travel agent and arrangements are being made for a leisurely trip on the Canadian Pacific to Banff and Jasper *this* summer. One month — all of June, my darling — I can't believe it!

But the house is a problem. I don't want to rent it. I'd have to clean the damn thing, and can you see your father tackling the garage? So — how would you like to house-sit for a month? Put up with the mess. No house cleaning involved!

Surely the paper would give you a month's leave and maybe you could write some pieces for them here. I don't know — silly stuff, columns, think pieces, satire — whatever. Or just muse.

Please call and let's discuss the idea.

Much love from your soon-to-be-much-traveled,
Mother

P.S. All right, Emma. Let's talk frankly.

Yes, I could rent the house. A month on the coast — in June. We could ask a fortune! No, it wouldn't kill me to swipe some dust around. Using the excuse that picking up would waste my energies convinced your father that we should *not* rent. He wants me fresh as a daisy. God help me if he envisions my trekking up that damned mountain!

Ever since that summer you've hardly been inside this house. I think I can count the visits on one hand. And never once would you go outside, or acknowledge *anything* you associated with that period.

Private school that fall. Even at that late date, the sympathetic admissions office found a place. And it was right that you get away from an area where you witnessed such trauma: two awful accidents in four months are more than anyone should have to bear — for a time. But it's now ten years and still you will not face it.

Your father understood why you wouldn't come back — perhaps more than I. You two are on the same wavelength.

But at the same time he hurts inside. All those excuses: visits to roommates; jobs as a counselor in countless camps; the Experiment in International Living, abroad. I swear you experimented with every available job.

Now you're a grown woman with a career and a place of your own. And a life of your own which excludes us. Oh, I know we see each other, but always on your turf.

Your father hurts and so do I. *We* love you very much. *We*— *I*— love you, my dear, although at times it was hard for you (and for me) to understand that — or each other.

Much of our hurt is knowing that we have not helped you. Those childhood horrors haven't faded; rather, they've grown like some malignancy, stifling a spirit that was you.

I want you to take a chance. Confront the ghosts head-on — now, while you're still young. Not for us. For you. Dredge up dark memories, free that space they control, and let in some light!

Whatever kind of exorcism it takes, *do it.* Lay the ghosts to rest once and for all.

Come back to a lovely place that still loves you as we do. Have courage and resolution — and come home, Emma.

Mummy

EMMA
CAPE CHARLOTTE
JUNE

I want to chuck the whole idea! Just hit the outskirts of Jamesport and sucked in a good whiff of mudflats: the sea's residue, dying in the sun. Rotting flotsam!

But if I stop, park the car, rest a bit, I'll lose my nerve. Keep driving. The sun pours through the windshield. Forgot my sunglasses. Squint against the light. Forgot how clear and bright the air is here. The sun scorches the wheel. Steer with fingertips; a light touch, only. The gearshift knob is molten fire. Baking bakelite! My Jeep does not respond to the gentle touch; dinosaurs require strength of arm and brute force to direct them. Grab the wheel and show who's master! To the victor: burned palms.

At least there's a breeze. There's always *some* breeze since I removed the canvas door. Meant to hinge it back. Couldn't find the damned door!

Closer now. Unadulterated sea air a jolt. Fresh and briny.

Can I stay here? Can I really see this thing through? All those times I zipped in and out, never letting down my guard, never admitting reality, never sure what reality was. Can I stay here for weeks, sorting things out, when I barely made it through a couple of days before I was off to — somewhere. Summer jobs were plentiful; roommates had room. Can I go home again and feel it's home?

Off the Coast Road, now. Up the hill. And there it is. No old blue

Chevy parked in the driveway. And the garage door is closed! Can't remember a time it was closed — ever. Things *have* changed.

Not so much, after all. The door is heavy and squeaks and says quite plainly that it prefers the upright position. God! The garage is still jampacked. Everywhere — stuff! Sidestep between *six* sawhorses and 12 shutters waiting to be scraped. No change. Daddy's the same, it seems.

The kitchen door won't unlock! Did Mummy send me the wrong key? Push the door, wrestle the key. Won't budge! Curses! Push! Damn it to hell! I went through hellfire to gear myself up to come — and now I can't get in! Start over. Start over and stay coolly calm. Rattle the doorknob. It turns — easily, very easily. Very easily because the bloody door was unlocked in the first place! Mummy has not changed one iota!

Went back for the suitcases. Plunked them down in the kitchen. Back to close the garage door and lock the kitchen door. I lock doors.

The kitchen, the room most used. Looks out on the backyard and the clothesline, which I barely knew. The lattice up the side of the garage. Rungs for raccoons. How long did they sit and wait patiently for me on the garage roof? How long does it take a raccoon to know that its food supply has dried up, gone away? Hope someone became a sucker for pleading eyes.

Confine myself to the kitchen. Don't feel like wandering. Found a bottle of mediocre sherry and a mashed pack of those Marlboros — the ones with the cork on the end. Saves losing pieces of lip. Sip sherry and smoke. Should stop puffing but not just yet. Not a propitious time. I need to think; I need my wits. Rationalization. I love to smoke.

This old oak table — round, ugly and comfortably familiar. It has heard a lot of talk. Literary, historical — and bawdy. Tales of war and woe; tales of sieges and school. Adolescent outbursts — and much laughter. Not the Algonquin's. But a good round table.

What for dinner? I brought nothing. Maybe some cheese if there's some — and more sherry. With each glass the flavor improves. Dinner in the living room when it gets dark. Don't want to look out at the view just yet. Stretch out in front of a driftwood fire and feel crackling heat. It may be June, but the evening smacks of October.

* * *

I relegated him to the past, put him out of mind almost, yet I knew he was here. A thud, then a soft patter down the stairs. I waited for him to announce himself; instead he sat on the threshold and said nothing. He stared at me unblinking, appearing to be more than a little bored with the company. He would not open the conversation, quite content to bide his time until I was forced to speak.

Okay, Who Me. I'm sorry. I'm sorry I ran away and left you. I'm sorry that not even you could keep me here. I'm sorry for all the nights you had to sleep alone.

For all of that you look exceptionally well for a man your age. I mean, you are nearly eleven and still a handsome tomcat. Black satin coat gleaming and you have all your whiskers. The notches in your ears: Are they a count, a tote of battles won and enemies vanquished?

You seem a bit more dignified. A little more weight around the middle, perhaps? Oh, no! Not fat, just amply padded. I didn't mean to imply a paunch!

Let's have a general conversation. I don't want to discuss dogs with you right now. So please don't bring up the subject, okay?

How about making up, Who Me? There's a piece of an avocado in the icebox — all right, refrigerator. A rather dark half, but delicious still. It used to be your favorite, once. In fact, you usually ate them before we did. Mummy had to ripen avocados in the cupboard to foil you. A piece for a rub — bargain? . . . That wasn't much of a rub; more a flick of tail against my leg. Will you condescend to sit in my lap? Not yet? All right. I'm here for a while. Think it over.

My room. Why hasn't Mummy repainted it! My wild pink stage lingers and now is dusty rose. I loathe pink!

My bedroom, so small, yet it has a fireplace, never used, never seen. The bed blocks it off. How mightily I wished that somehow, magically, the room would expand and I could sit in bed and have a real fire. A driftwood fire on a snowy night and guess which mineral in the driftwood would burn next. Would the flame be blue or teal or purple?

This bed was a haven. I slept and wrote and read and ate in this bed. It was a nest, I guess. And full of crumbs. Scratchy, but very cozy.

I dreamt I was suffocating. Drowning! Water, heavy over my nose. No air! Crabs on my head, pulling me down. Going down!

God! Not water! Who Me! On my face. Not crabs. Claws in my hair, kneading. And I hear you purring, Who Me. Can't control that, can you, you great big enormous mush!

I rolled you off so I could open the window. Odd not to have to worry about blackout curtains. Closed the window. The waves are lapping and I don't need that sound just yet.

Slept soundly and didn't expect to. I don't know what I expected. Certainly not a dreamless night. Maybe the warm motor beside me helped.

Bathroom hasn't changed. Still the warmest place in the house. Toilet seat needs sanding! Table in front of it loaded with *Saturday Reviews*. Ah, that day, long ago, when Mummy heaved out the pile that had become old hat — and forgot to replenish. Diarrhea struck with a vengeance and she was stuck — reading the instructions on old pill bottles for half a day. As ever, the bathtub plug doesn't fit.

How strange to be alone in this house. Mummy and Daddy not home for supper. No one to bother me. No interruptions. No friendly visits from neighbors. Thank God I don't know them anymore; new people. The ones I knew as a child have moved away.

I need this solitude. I need time and quiet to go back. One by one. I'll take things one by one. If I can do the first, then maybe I can do the second — and the third. I have a month to try.

Into town — Jamesport — for supplies. The old town has a new face — at least the waterfront does. Somebody decided the place had some charm buried under the neglect of years. All done over, refurbished. Probably used some exterior decorator who had two courses in art history. The wharfs can't claim kinship to the Leaning Tower anymore; new pilings and . . . The Clamshell and The Denizen of the Deep! Lordy! Eat and hear the water slurp!

The old brick row all clean and stable. Housing lawyers and architects and — shops! Art galleries and clothing boutiques selling cutesy nautical wear. I might drop in sometime and inspect the store with carvings: ducks and terns and Canada geese and seagulls. Eck! The old Porthole, once a drunkards' lair, is now respectable and shipshape. Exit Mizzentop under full sail.

At least they saved the rosy brick. And the cobblestones survive.

How small the house is, really. Not a new discovery. Writers write of it; every memoir mentions the phenomenon. The large house of childhood becomes tiny and cramped to the grownup. But I wasn't a midget child when I left — nearly the height I am now. Why does this house seem so small?

First step. I've managed to go into the living room in daylight — and pull the curtains open. How innocent the view! Blue ocean, rounded knoll, postcard juniper — and rocks.

Otherwise, the room is almost the same. New cover on the living-room couch. Lots more books. But the carved Victorian desk chair still has the same cut-velvet upholstery and is still damned uncomfortable!

The guest room. Why the name I haven't the foggiest. It's storage for Mummy. Or rather, Mummy's clippings. Scrapbooks filled with Arno and Addams and all the "Annals of Crime and Medicine" going back to their beginnings. And Hokinson. At least the bed is clear if some poor soul wants to flop. No wonder Daddy called this room the *Hotel New Yorker!*

The kitchen is now graced with a dishwasher/washing machine. Didn't have one when I lived here. Still don't. Damn thing's on the fritz. Back to washing in the slate sink on the scrubboard. And where the hell's the wringer?

They were all together in a box labeled "Emma's Diaries." Up in the attic with the heat and the dust and the trapped flies buzzing in the eaves.

Somewhere in them must be the reason I had to leave this house. Somewhere I must have written what drove me away. Some awful thing. I seem to remember I wrote of things I would never say out loud. Would die rather than mention. Somewhere near the end. But I'll begin at the beginning . . .

I've almost finished and there's no clue yet. Am into March 1945. What a secretive, brooding child you were, Emma. The entries are funny and sad and sometimes quite irrelevant to the times. And the language. Did you really have only a vocabulary of 1000 words! Probably, but why? You read — everything. Didn't some of it rub off then? It was Miss Munroe who opened up the world of poetry, and that helped. But you did not help Miss Munroe! Poor woman, how she growled that she'd go blind trying to decipher i's dotted with circles! I was furious. At 13, circles seemed the height of sophistication.

Compared to the young teenagers of this decade, you were not only a late bloomer, Emma, you were a baby!

This house, this coast, frightened me; I left, terrified, and I can't remember why. I couldn't talk about it; I couldn't articulate the fear, even to myself. Underneath, underneath, somewhere — oh, how the mind protects — is a horror story, a Hallowe'en nightmare that goes boo in the dark. Under layers of forgetfulness lies something — evil. I am evil. I was evil. And there's evil here — all around me.

What did I do that was so awful I couldn't come to Mummy and Daddy and say "help!"?

I savor guilt. I know I do and I can't help it. I wanted more than love from them, I wanted respect. I felt diminished in their eyes each time I strayed from the perfect path, even innocently. Insidious guilt. Is it inbred, seeping down through generations, delightful, awful Puritan guilt? The destructive, overactive conscience?

Reread the diaries. What went so terribly wrong? Reread them.

But I can't bear to read far into March. Later. I'll tackle the second half of March — later.

MURIEL DOUGHERTY, R.N.
CAPE CHARLOTTE
JUNE

Dear Alma,

Another job another dollar, so they say. And well, I've been busy, so am sorry I haven't written you since I moved here, which is almost two months. Time just seems to fly by because the routine is the same day after day — keeping somebody alive who should by all rights be wearing wings. But there's money, all the money in the world pouring in to buy the latest equipment, the machine monitors and such, and who am I to say whether it's right or wrong. And I'd be out of a job right quick if they decided to pull the plug, that's for sure!

The man from the bank was just here — again! Checking up. I think he's even counting the silverware — making sure I haven't pinched some. Alma, you oughta know I'm not pure for God's sake, but I draw the line at pinching what's not mine!

One, sometimes two doctors are in a couple, three times a week to examine the patient, regulating the flow of the saline and glucose, looking at the respirator close, making notes and peering into the eyes to see if there is any reaction — which there isn't which there never is which I could have told them in the first place. Then they go away and say please continue the good work, Miss Dougherty and let us know immediately of any change — so I go on doing what I've always been doing. But you know doctors! Well, you don't know doctors like I know doctors and that's pretty good, Alma. What they aren't is gods. I could tell you some stories that would curl your hair about those high and mighty doctors that would pull a lot of them down to *my* level if I chose to tell them — which I won't. Aren't no flies on me, Alma.

Sometimes it gets kinda lonely in my work, seeing as though my patient never says nothing. I mean, it would be a nice change to have someone to talk to. And this place here is kinda lonely anyway, perched up on a cliff and the ocean looking like a bubble bath, but mean and talking to me sometimes like it wants to drown me. I sure don't go near it! And there's the foghorn, which I know is a foghorn because everybody tells me it is and we've been having fog for a week now and it just cleared off today, thank the Merciful Virgin, but that horn at night sounds, it really sounds like someone is dying, and I go in to check my patient and everything's OK, but I can't get the sound out of my mind and I haven't slept too well lately.

I forgot to tell you this house here is the Thurston house, which wouldn't make no nevermind to you except that Mrs. Thurston is *Buffy Sinclair. The* Buffy Sinclair. The one that wrote all those dirty books! Like *Dark Pulse of Passion.* Oh I loved that one! That was her first. *Dark Pool of Love* was pretty good too and *Lust into Darkness* — Whew! Her so grand and all and underneath — Well! No more books, poor lady.

You know Alma, if I gave a personality to my patient I'd go stark raving loony I would. Right up the wall. So I just think of each new one as a great big squash or something — a lump. I wash that lump like it was a helpless baby, which it is. I turn it over all the time so it won't get bedsores, which isn't hard on my back because it weighs *nothing,* and I do the usual — take the blood pressure, monitor the paper feed with the pen squiggles and look for a change — which I have told you never happens. Oh — and I check the temps and put eye drops in cause the eyes can't blink and would dry out — and if I could I'd put diapers on . . . yes really! They don't make catheters the way they used to and sometimes these new ones leak . . . Well — you get the picture . . .

EMMA
CAPE CHARLOTTE
JUNE

It's going to be hot. There's no breeze off the sea today. There's no horizon; the sea becomes the sky and the sun is hazy with heat.

I'm going back to March 1945. I am walking the route I ran that March morning. Skirting the knoll, taking the path to the beach. The mind is wondrous. Already I am pulling in cold air.

There's snow — quite heavy in places where the wind has whipped it. Other patches of beach are bare except for icy spots. Bright snow, dark rocks and seaweed. White on black.

The sun is out, a spring sun that will melt the snow soon. I must hurry. I have to look and there isn't much time. I have to search every crevice and depression that would give shelter.

There are tracks in the snow. Up to the Wileys' cottage! And wood smoke. The smell of wood smoke! And Peter is there! He made it and is drying out and my stomach is sick and drops a mile and I open the door and start to call . . . and it isn't Peter! It isn't Peter. *Just a face with a wool hat pulled down and funny eyes. I can't quite see his face but he is scared and limps a little and . . . he's only another* deserter!

So I tell him fast they'll be looking for him and to get into town. To flag down the Coast Road bus that takes the shipyard workers into Jamesport. It always runs because they work shifts — all day and all night — and I won't tell. I never tell. And I've got to go!

Did I tell him that I've sent an awful lot of cold soldiers into Jamesport and that I'm very friendly with the MPs? They know me, and they talk to me when they search the beaches with their dogs, and they never think to ask me whether I've seen a deserter. And if they did I'd probably lie, because all those poor soldiers are freezing and homesick. And the MPs can't figure out whether I'm a boy or a girl with my special ski hood on, which Daddy gave me. I keep my braids inside, curled around to keep my ears warm.

— Emma. Where are you? That's trivia. You're back too far. Replay only what you must. Continue along the beach.

I run down from the cottage and slip on the beaches and almost slide into the sea from the ledges, and I try first one cove and then the next and then the channel is straight ahead — and so is Pig's Knuckle. Pig's Knuckle! I can see it clearly and that's where he is — *safe and in his hut — waiting until the rough seas go down and he only has to row through chop! He'll row back soon. Already the ocean's getting tired.*

The sea reached deep down last night and brought in a bundle!

Flotsam, flotsam everywhere. Old timbers and strips of black rubber and piles of fresh seaweed. Long dark lines of it. It's all right. He's not in there. Or in the spume on the beach whipped to a froth, quivering, shaking like mounds of egg whites — half-beaten dirty old egg whites.

Easter Egg Cove is next. Over that high outcropping of gray ledge. I'm tired and I can't run so fast. I'm at the top and I can see the whole Cove and my special beach of Easter Eggs, which the ocean made just for me. All the colors of the rainbow, but today they are iced with a sugar frosting. The beach rattles as the tide pulls and pushes.

There's one spot where the ice has melted and the yellow eggs are brighter. I don't remember so many yellow eggs all in one spot before. Maybe the sun is hitting the place just right.

It's not the sun. I'm closer and it's not the sun. It's Peter's yellow mackinaw! It's Peter, and he's trying to crawl up the beach, and I can see his hands stretched out! His fingers — now I can see. They are digging into the stones . . .

I rubbed your arms so stiff. I rubbed your legs so cold. I tried to warm you. As long as I held you, you would live. I knew that. Couldn't anyone see the tears in your eyes?

Over and over I said don't cry. I'm here, and if they took you away you would die, so I held you and I rocked you and I brushed the rime ice from your hair, which made you look so old. I'd never touched your hair before and I pushed it back, and my hand bumped something sharp that stuck out. A piece of your skull, white and shiny, and the hole was pink and puckered and I could see deep into your head . . .

The first hurdle. I managed it without crumpling. "Who Me! Dinner will be served at six. It is now only one-thirty! Leave me be, please. I have a letter to reread. I haven't looked at it since that night — the night of the storm. I retrieved it today in spite of your help — if one considers a yowling cat who is treading out a nest on my back while that back is hanging straight down a help! That cave is *hell* to get to."

The letter seems in good shape. I must notify the Cut-Rite Company that their product protects more than sandwiches.

"Hush, cat! I'm concentrating . . ."

Oh, Peter! I endowed you with such saintly qualities they would fell an ordinary saint!

How hard I tried — to be feminine, but I wasn't sure how. To be sexy when I didn't even know the word.

So I used every trick in my repertoire. I ran faster, climbed higher, jumped farther than any boy.

Be a tomboy; snare a boy. And I did — in a way.

Toward the end you needed me more than anyone else. This letter, this kind, loving, trusting letter . . .

Oh God. You *are* dead. You died on the beach. You were dead long before I found you.

Such a waste — to die so young. Only 17 and so special. For months you were my life and you still haunt me. I judge all men in your image. There are very few of them. Very few.

Holding this paper makes you very real. You are talking to me — and saying more — more than in the letter.

Your spirit's here. In this kitchen. A troubled spirit and I don't know why!

— Emma. Look back. You remember some of it. The morning after the storm. Today, ten years later, you went down to the knoll and pulled out the letter, so you remember putting it in the cave after you found his body. You remember coming home, going upstairs, getting the letter, and then going to the kitchen drawer for the wax paper. Out the door past your father, down to the knoll, squirming in the snow to get to the cave. Remember, you left a trail like angels in the snow. And then you put the letter in on top of your treasures and *sealed* the hole with a big rock. You remember all this. And you did all of this because Peter was dead. Dead! And you knew it.

— But Emma, today you said that this is the first time you have reread the letter since that morning in March. It isn't the first time. You've forgotten. You took out that letter later — the same year. In July. The day after the Fourth.

No! It's been in there since the storm! I haven't looked at it . . . I haven't . . . touched it since!

— What does your diary say, Emma? You wrote about the letter in July.

I don't know what it says. I stopped reading it. I stopped . . . after that March night.

— July, Emma. Go to July. You came here to be honest with yourself. To find the truth. Now what does the entry say — the one on the fifth of July?

It says: "I haven't forgotten it. I know what I'm going to do right now!"

— "It" must be the letter, I presume. Why did you suddenly decide to take it out?

Dammit, Who Me! That's my leg! Go scratch the couch!

— Cats are hard to ignore.

Especially ones that need to sharpen claws on flesh! Where were we?

— You took out Peter's letter on the fifth of July, the day after the beach party with all the fireworks. What made you do it?

I had to. I was afraid of forgetting him — Peter. I wanted — needed — to make him real again. Make that letter a wall between me and . . .

— And what?

Christopher.

— Why?

I forget why.

— You were doing fine, Emma. Now don't withdraw on me. Think how far you've gone already. Across the beach to the cove of Easter Eggs and down to the knoll for Peter's letter. Now why don't you go back down to the knoll again and take out something else.

Look. I'm grown up! I don't need my treasures anymore! They were for a child, a secretive child — silly things, glass and marbles and shells and things!

— There's more in your cave besides *your* treasures, Emma — and you know it.

MURIEL

CAPE CHARLOTTE

JUNE

I've got a lot of time on my hands, Alma, not to say that I don't work hard which I do, but a comatose patient just isn't as demanding as a live one . . . well, not dead exactly, but it sure isn't alive either — more like an unborn baby if you know what I mean. Fetus is the word, if you didn't know. Curls up like a fetus. So as I was saying I've got all the time in the world — well, not quite. I have to check all the tubes in a while and there sure are a lot. In and out of every hole, sucking and dripping. Well, as I said, until I have to go in again I thought I'd write you about this house.

It's something. It's called the Big House which makes sense, because it's enormous, but you know, if it was my house I'd call it Cliff Manor or something classy. Maybe Seaview.

You could call it a palace except that people like the Thurstons didn't show off their money. They'd hide it in the bank so no one would know! Now if I had the money she made offen them books,

I'd have green marble floors and white marble bathrooms and gold ceilings and shandeleers with all those crystal doodads swinging and tinkling and heavy red plush drapes and thick velvet carpets and silk pillows on sofas you could sink in and die in. You can bet, Alma, I'd fix this place up till it looked spiffy enough for the Queen if she happened to be passing through.

Not that I'm complaining. The house is comfortable enough. The outside goes on forever. Some of it is stone — beach stone, I guess and the rest — most of it is shingle but not your ordinary shingle. This stuff just gets grayer the older it gets. So would you if you sat in the salt air for a hundred years.

There are porches all around the house with wicker rocking chairs. *And* there is kind of a swimming pool which is dug out of the rock down below and fills up when the tide is full, which is every 12 hours so they tell me. Anyway, I haven't tried the pool because the water is not your lake water. First of all it's salty, and second of all it's colder than a witch's . . . well you know how cold.

There's a seawall too, which is supposed to keep the ocean away from the house, and since the house is still standing I guess it's done the job, though I can't see how it'll last too much longer seeing as bits of it are falling down.

Some of the floors are great big slate blocks. Store up cold even in the summer. Must be wicked cold in the winter! And all around are those rugs with the little patterns in them and such with fringe — they're slippery I can tell you! The living room is filled with leather sofas and chairs, sort of cracked. Boy, would I heave those — first thing. Some of the furniture is carved and you can tell the wood is very old, and the backs of some chairs have little lions on them and they are uncomfortable, but uncomfortable! And everywhere there's brass and copper, so much you could open a shop and have some left over. And bone — I guess — figures, little ones of mice and fat Chinks. I don't know why somebody would want to ruin them punching holes in them, but they did. Oh, and there's a heavy thing that looks like a man with a beer belly except he's not like anyone *we* know, Alma! This one's got four arms and an elephant's head. With a trunk.

There's a cabinet that's locked — I know because I tried it — just a mite — and oh! It has the prettiest little colored bottles in it. I wouldn't mind having just one of those! Having, *not* swiping, Alma!

And there are real painted pictures of boats — a lot of boats with sails and a lot of old people with sour pusses.

Oh, and there's a black screen in pieces that's taller than me that has Chinks all over it. At least they have slit eyes. Maybe they're Japs. Anyway it's kind of pretty with all the people wearing long bathrobes, and there are trees and birds and mountains and streams and flowers all painted in between the little raised edges. Guess they're there so the artist wouldn't go outside the lines.

Anyway Alma, as you can see, there's a lot of stuff in this house, but not what I'd put in a palace! . . . .

EMMA
CAPE CHARLOTTE
JUNE

I have to go down to the knoll again. The trip back in time is almost over. It's a gray day for June. Clouds low and heavy like sick seals. I really don't want to be here. I could cut out right now and go back to Pick's Crossing and my job and the house that Nana left me and say that I've done it. I've set a troubled spirit free and I am free.

— Not yet, Emma. It's not June. It's July 5. And it was gray that day, too.

Yes, gray. But it's not going to pour and the sun is pushing the seals away. They're glowing around the edges — and moving. The sun has revived them and they are swimming down the sky to the horizon line and the sea.

How peaceful it is here. My juniper will never die. I know it. Bayberry smells so nice, spicy nice. Perky. It takes a mass of berries to make one candle. Boil and skim. Boil and skim. Blueberries green still. Another couple of weeks. How anyone can eat high bush is beyond me.

Almost four months ago I came down here with his letter wrapped so carefully. The day he died. And I buried it for all time along with him. The snow had crusted in the sun and I needed a rock to seal his tomb, and I squirmed and dug and got a rock finally, and I put the letter in the cave on top of my treasures. There was loose shale around the opening. The storm the night before must have loosened some. And then I got the rock to the edge. It was so heavy. And I was digging in with my boots and pushed that rock with all my might. Hard. Wedged it in. I moved some old brown turf which would turn green in the spring and pushed it around to cover the rock. To seal it forever. In time the bayberry and the blueberry will grow here. In time I will forget the cave.

— But it's summer now, Emma! Not that March morning!

Which summer? Now or then?

— Both. But go back to the summer of '45 first. What did you do here?

I forget.

— You must try. Go back to July 5, 1945. Remember? You went down to the juniper tree because, as you wrote in your diary, "That's where I was really happy." You felt guilty.

I didn't feel guilty! There was nothing to feel guilty about.

— Don't quibble. You opened the cave to take out Peter's letter, the one you were never going to look at again. You took it out to recapture the magic and to apologize in your own way for —

I couldn't help it! He was alive and Peter was dead. Truly dead! And he was like Peter — not exactly — but sort of and he liked me and he made me laugh and he wanted to be with me . . . and it wasn't until I woke up that morning that I realized I didn't love him, that Peter was . . . was . . .

— Yes, I know. Now open your cave. That's why you came down to the knoll. Don't dawdle anymore.

Where am I again?

— It is morning, July 5, 1945.

Oh, yes. I get confused. I move back and forth in time. Too fast.

I have to tear the turf away. It clings to the rock like a baby to its mother. Fiercely. And it's only four months old. I can just move the rock a bit at a time. It's hard being here and doing everything hanging upside down.

— You can do it. You have all day. And tomorrow and the day after that.

No I don't. If I don't go to the Cove to tell Christopher that I can't search, he'll wonder.

— Yes. You're right. I almost forgot we're back in 1945.

I've got the rock . . . oh! It fell down to the beach and smashed!

— It doesn't matter. Reach in and get Peter's letter.

Yes. I can. I think I can feel it, but the adhesive tape has stuck to something else. It got sticky from the damp and won't let go.

— Pull them both out, Emma. The letter and what it's stuck to.

I've got them. The letter's OK. I can see through the wax paper . . . but what's the other thing? I didn't put anything like this in here!

— It's like a moneybelt, Emma. The kind of flat, safe belt one wears around the waist.

This one's kind of bulgy.

— That's because it has a lot in it. What's that piece of yellow caught in the clasp, Emma?

I don't know!

— Yes. Yes you do. Tell me.

It's . . . it looks like . . . it looks like a piece of Peter's jacket. I know because the wool is heavy like a horse blanket and nobody in the whole world has a mackinaw like his.

— Why do you suppose the plaid is on the clasp?

Because the belt is Peter's. That's why! He must have put the belt in here to hide it. And he tore his mackinaw on the clasp — see, it's sharp — and didn't notice.

— Why don't you open the belt? Look, it has pockets that snap open and close tightly like a lady's pocketbook. If you open it, you can tell who owns it, can't you?

I don't think I will right now.

— Emma, it isn't fair to the owner. He must be worried that it's missing. Don't procrastinate. Put Peter's letter aside for the moment and open one of the pockets.

All right. This one has a book, it looks like . . . leather . . . and a couple of streaks of lightning. And it was wrapped very carefully. *Not wax paper. Darkish funny stuff. Same thing in the next pocket. Black leather it looks like — the book.*

— Put them on the ground and open another pocket. Tell me what you find.

It's an envelope, and there's a piece of paper inside wrapped around . . . those things that you make pictures from — negatives. I can't tell what's going on in them.

— Now . . . another pocket.

Well, this one's got a soft bag, soft leather bag and — oops! rhinestones, I guess. Like in Mummy's evening necklace. All the stones in her necklace have gold paint on the backs.

— Do these?

No. Same bag in the next pocket and the next. Someone must have collected shiny rhinestones!

— Do you think the belt was Peter's?

No.

— Why?

Well . . . he would have told me. He told me everything. I know he would have.

— That's correct. Go on. What's in the last pocket?

I don't care. I've opened enough.

— There's one more pocket you should see, Emma.

Why, if I don't care?

— It's necessary to complete the puzzle.

I don't want to complete the puzzle. There isn't any puzzle!

— Just this last one and then you're done — almost.

Really done.

— Almost.

Well . . . first there's a piece of paper and — I can't read it — it's in . . . it's in German, I think . . . and a wad of money — a lot of it! and then there's one, no two metal things . . . medals, they're medals for something . . . and there's a small . . . a cardboard book it looks like.

— What's the symbol on it?

I'm not sure. It's those lightning streaks again.

— What else is on the cover?

A word — Soldbuch.

— That's German and means literally "Soldier Book," Emma. Soldbuch is the paybook for a German soldier, which serves both as a record of his pay and his *identification.* Don't you want to know whose paybook this is? The name might not mean anything to you, but the picture would. The picture right inside the front cover. Open it. It's a picture of someone you know.

It could be . . . anyone. I don't know the picture! I don't know it! Please! I'm tired! I've looked at enough stuff and I'm tired!

— Emma. Stop it! Look at the picture!

It . . . it might . . . it could be — Christopher. The man in the picture looks a little like him. But lots of people look like other people!

— Turn to page 2, Emma. What is that circle, the one with the eagle? What is in that wreath that the eagle is holding?

It's that Nazi sign. The — you know — the swastika.

— Now Emma. Listen to me. Christopher is the soldier in the picture. Christopher the charmer. Christopher the choirboy. Christopher with the sad-sweet smile. He's fooled everyone. But mostly you, Emma. Go read the leather books, Emma, and learn about your Christopher. *It's still July 5th, 1945,* and you have a *lot* of reading to do . . .

I read them. All of them. All day and all night. I wanted to throw up!

— Now have you put the pieces together? Christopher was landed by the submarine he wrote about the night of the storm. He found Peter on the beach. Peter was still alive. He had to be, for he crawled *above* the high tide line. That hole in Peter's head was too deep to have been caused by the sea and the rocks. Was it caused by a rock smashing down, a rock held by a man? In the struggle, a bit of yellow plaid mackinaw snagged on the clasp of the moneybelt — but it was dark and Christopher didn't notice. He murdered him, Emma.

What happened the next day? *Emma, what happened on July 6th?*

I stuffed the moneybelt with everything I had taken out — the awful diaries — everything — and wrapped the belt tight in a poncho.

— Did you put it back in the cave?

Yes.

— Then what happened?

I . . . I . . .

— Look at Kala Nag. Look at your big rock and remember. You were frightened.

Yes. I started to get up and run back to the house but I couldn't.

— Why not?

Because I bumped into Christopher.

— What was he doing?

Just standing there. He must have come up behind me. He'd never been to the top of the knoll before.

— Did he say anything to you?

Not at first.

— What did you do?

I wanted to run. I wanted to run so fast but I couldn't move, so I just stood there and tried not to look at him.

— Did you say anything?

I tried to act natural. I did try to say something, but my voice sort of squawked . . .

— What did Christopher do?

He watched me. He squinted like he was looking through binoculars and then said, "Where are your merry eyes, Emma? You look like you've seen a ghost. Has someone died?"

And then I said — I tried to stop saying it — but I said right out: "You!" And then I tried to run again, but he grabbed me and held my wrist so tight I thought he would snap it.

— What else happened, Emma?

So then he said, "Why were you hanging upside down a minute ago? Were you playing monkey with something down there? . . . Something you haven't told me about?" And I started to say "No," but I stopped myself and didn't peep. But he wouldn't let go of my wrist and it hurt!

— And then?

And then he said, "You've found it! And you forgot to tell me. You found it right down there and you looked inside, you read things, didn't you, *Emma?" And he crushed my wrist so hard I wanted to die so I nodded.*

— Go on.

I can't!

— *What did he do?*

He pushed me. Not hard. Just pushed me forward down the knoll on the easy side, down toward the lawn and the path to the beach. He said if I screamed he'd stick a knife into me. So I didn't scream. I kept hoping Mummy might be looking out their bedroom window and come and help, but the trouble was, nobody would see anything wrong. I guess it just looked like we were walking together kind of close.

— Where did he take you?

Up on Kala Nag. It took a long time . . . days it seemed . . . because he had trouble climbing, with his foot and all. But he still had a tight hold on my wrist, and all I could think of was that knife sticking into me. When we got to the top, I could see down to the sharp rocks at the bottom and the sea smashing on them . . . and then I knew what he was going to do so I started to pull and scream, but he wouldn't let go and he started to push, and there we were pushing and screaming and yelling and nobody heard us — not even Mummy —

— Don't stop, Emma!

I'm not stopping! I remember it all! Everything! I remember my feet weren't on rock anymore. They were kicking air and Christopher had his arms around my stomach and I was over the waves, and he — he was about to drop me into them when all of a sudden there was a shout: "Henkel! Stop!" And Christopher heard it too, because he turned way round and I went round with him, and then he dropped me and I saw Mr. Thurston coming like the devil after Christopher, and he — Mr. Thurston — had on his going-into-town suit and vest, and his shoes must have had leather soles because he couldn't get much footing. But he fought hard — the two of them whacking and wrestling and pushing and grunting — and I kept crawling the other way, away from the sea edge. And then — then they weren't there anymore. Just like that they disappeared, and there wasn't a sound except for the sea. After a while I crawled over to the edge and peeked down. I couldn't see Mr. Thurston but I saw Christopher, lying all deadlike, all broken, on the sharp rocks and the waves washed over his legs again and again . . .

— And then?

I must have sat there for a long time and I heard sad little squeakings. I thought they were coming from Christopher but they weren't. They were coming from deep down in me . . . and finally, I got up and began to run for home, and I bounced down Kala Nag like it was rubber, and I got to the beach and I fell and cut my leg, and . . .

— Then you started screaming.

Yes.

— You screamed for days.

Yes.

— And . . . ?

I wouldn't, I couldn't talk.

— For a long time?

For a long time.

— You forgot who Christopher was, didn't you, Emma. You put SS Obersturmführer Hannes Henkel back in the cave of your mind and sealed him there. And since he didn't exist, there was no murder of Peter or attempt on you. What was left was fear and horror — at what *you* had caused. What you *thought* you had caused. All these years you have blamed yourself for that awful day and the destruction — the death. There are just a few more ends to tie off and then you are done.

All done? Finished?

— Finished.

Then I'll go back up to the house.

— Don't forget the poncho. You have to take the poncho with you.

But I remember everything now. I know what's in it!

— Emma, there's more to do. When you do it, then you are done. Not before.

I hope it's rotted! I don't want to touch it!

— It won't burn *you* . . .

I have it. The outside is damp, but . . . the inside is dry.

— Take out a journal. Don't read it . . . now. Unwrap it and check that it's still legible.

It's in my hands. But if I unwrap it, it will be like letting out all the evil in the world. The sea didn't get it . . . the writing. I can read . . .

— Take the belt and the journals up to the house . . . and do what you know must be done.

MURIEL
CAPE CHARLOTTE
JUNE

After Mrs. Thurston (can't help thinking of her as Buffy S.!), after she had her first stroke or maybe it was her second, anyway, she put in an elevator. Saves my legs, you bet. You just close an elegant door and whoosh! you're at the second floor, and then Alma, if you can believe it, you're right up with the birds. Really! There's this crazy plastic roof — a round thing you can see right through! But one of the lawyers told me he went up once and there she was, wheeling around and swearing and thumping on the plastic with a big broom because the seagulls would sun themselves on the top, which was OK. What pissed her off — and I don't mean to be funny although it is sort of hilarious when you think about it — was because while the seagulls sat on top, they *piddled and pooped on the top!* Well, even so she liked it — seeing all the stars and the moon and being up in the clouds. Poor thing, she can't look at them sights anymore.

As I've said it's kinda lonely here. The light that goes round and round from the lighthouse's sort of a cozy feeling, though. Nice thinking about all the ships it's saved ... Just checked the brainwave monitor on the paper roll. Brain still working. That's something.

I guess I haven't mentioned that there are some people living here. They don't exactly do much or say much, except sometimes they tell me stories about the house and all the people — that's when they remember what they were going to say, which practically all the time they forget.

One of the people is Cook — who doesn't! She's obese (which is fat *fat,* Alma) and her feet hurt and she slops around in carpet slippers she's run over because the heels go one way and her heels go another. Well, Cook can't do much in the kitchen because she can't remember how to cook! She forgets what goes in what, like last week she decided to make a strawberry pie which sounded real good. Well, she put the strawberries in but when she came to give me a slice — well! have you ever seen pie crust without flour? That poor woman was knifing up the shortening but she didn't have any flour in the bowl! Weird, huh? That pie! Mushy strawberries and Crisco — all melted. Yuk!

Then there's Alfred. I think Alfred used to drive the car. A big purplish-plumy one. They took away his license which is a good thing cause he can't see further than his nose, but he seems happy enough polishing the silver (which if any is missing they can blame on him!). The funny thing is that he does it from morning till night, the same damn silver *every day,* and singing at the top of his lungs "Rule Britannia!" Drive anybody stark raving nuts — but for an Irish lass like me it makes me want to shoot him! Old Black and Tan, that's what he is! I won't shoot him — but I'd sure like to gag him!

So as you can see my company isn't much. But they're here — forever! Or as long as they live. That's what Buffy — Mrs. Thurston — made sure of. No matter what happened to her, they would be taken care of. Boy, they live the life of Reilly if they knew it!

There's sort of a museum here. Sets down a mite on a bluff above a white sandy beach in what they called the Beach House once. It's called the Henry Everett Thurston Maritime Museum, which is a fancy name, but the things in it are about the sea. Buffy — damn it! I'm going to call her Buffy. She can't hear me! Buffy must have loved her husband an awful lot to build that thing for him. He died in an accident.

There's a lot on building boats. Mr. Thurston worked at the Shipyard. He was a big bug there, I guess, and he must have loved boats because there are a lot around — models — like freighters and yachts for posh people and an awful lot of fishing boats, and some olden boats — ones with sails like clouds. They are the best!

There's a whole big tank that shows you what a tidepool has in it like seaweed, which isn't so interesting although I never knew there was so many kinds. It's called "Christopher's Pool." I'll tell you why in a minute. And there are crabs and shells (with live things in them because they move) and barnacles on rocks and Chink caps and sea urches. Well, you get the picture.

And then there's tusks from seals' husbands — those big fat blubbers — walruses — with ink drawings all over them. I don't think they're so hot.

I like the whale things best — except that part about skinning them — when they was still living! Jawbone so big you can walk through. And thick yellow oil in glass jars and pictures of big whales and little baby whales — although the babies aren't so little! I guess Mr. Thurston liked whales because there's cards round telling about not killing them anymore.

Then there are small models of the waterfront in Jamesport. The first one shows how it looked in the olden days. *Beautiful* houses with green lawns and statues yet, going right down to the harbor where the clipper ships anchored.

The next model shows what it looked like around the War. Pretty crummy!

And then the last part shows what it looks like today. The brick houses look beautiful again and the wharfs don't tip and all those sleezy saloons are gone. The whole new thing is dedicated to Mr. Thurston too, because he thought up the idea.

Lots of stuff for the museum keeps coming in, so the Big House is slowly becoming a storing place for it. Why not? Most of the rooms never see a face from one month to tother. Course they won't put anything into Buffy's room — that's the sickroom, big as a dance hall with all them machines around, buzzing and whirring and scratching . . .

EMMA
CAPE CHARLOTTE
JUNE

Mummy and Daddy just called from Banff! And it was as though all the years apart hadn't happened. I think we three felt a new sense of — love, and it sparked across the line both ways. They sound younger and full of spirit and adventure. And I, I told them the truth — that I was finding out a lot about myself, that the sea air was good and calming — and what the hell were two rock-hard jelly beans doing behind the clock on the mantelpiece? Mummy said to save them — they were antiques — and who dusts *behind* clocks!

I have been up all night feeding the fire. One page at a time — pages that I read with horror another night — so long ago. Nothing must remain to give away your connections to America. Bussett goes. Steiner, you were probably a good man, but I'm absolutely sure your boat has been identified. There must be *no* connection to Cape Charlotte. His journal on you goes — and I'm sorry. There must be nothing about a landing — no connection to a submarine.

The fire is hotter. Hot enough to melt metal? Yes. The ribbons flare and the enamel scorches and the crosses fuse into blobs on the coals below.

Mr. Thurston flames up — a confession to heinous crimes signed and countersigned and stamped with that splintered cross. You saved my life, Mr. Thurston, and so in go the negatives which held up to the light show a mélange of arms and legs. The negatives explode in the heat.

Hitler Jugend stays. You were still cynical then. SS Officers' training stays — but no place names. What hope you had to serve the Fatherland with distinction. To look back on those days with pride!

Paybook with picture and lightning streaks. Two bolts. Waffen SS. Burned.

Letter in German to Lt. Hannes Henkel. Signed: A. Hitler. The signature almost indecipherable. Wonder what historians and analysts would make of this hesitant penmanship? They *will not* have it to ponder over.

The fire devours the wood and the sap boils and whistles like a steaming kettle. Sometimes I can hear the faint wheezing of lungs and shrill screams of terror. Why do the cries seem louder with each page?

The fire has burned down to glowing coals.

Einsatzgruppen and Russia are left and must remain. Two and a half years that sear my hands. But with a razor now, carefully. No names. Schwoermer goes — except the S.

Schwoermer flares up and the flames are bloody.

Stutthof shall stay — and so shall the little Jew, the nameless little Jew.

I slept for a time and the fire is out. The ashes are nearly cold. I stir them, mash them, crush everything to dust and pile fresh wood on top. For the next fire — an ordinary one. Two small clusters of unidentifiable metal will be heaved in the sea.

There was a scale around here once. One to weigh staples — flour and such. Try the cellar . . . Lord how narrow the stairs are and I forgot the dirt floor. Damp. *Damp.* Humidity hangs. Dear Helen Hokinson, you would definitely rot down here!

If I were Mummy, where would I put the scales? Not in any logical place, I can assure you! Please God! Not behind the furnace! It's dark behind there . . . with creepy, crawly things . . . I knew it! Behind the furnace. Festooned with spider webs . . . and spiders. Yes, E.B.! I *am* remembering Charlotte.

I have a solution to Mummy's storage problems. She could move

Berton Roueché to the cellar. Roueché thrives on molds and fungi and strange strains of bug. He'd feel right at home down here.

OK. The package is wrapped neatly and tied. No slipshod folding at the ends. Nice and square. Would that my Christmas presents looked like this one! Ordinary package. Hundreds, thousands like it. I have shut and roped Pandora's box.

Checklist checks: no fingerprints. Hard to block-print address in rubber gloves. Even harder to cut out words and letters from the more popular magazines. Esoteric ones were out! Glue and paper from Woolworth's.

Wrapping paper from an ancient bag, one of at least two hundred meticulously folded ones found in the cellar. Twine bought at hardware store. Not from Mummy's culch. That would have seasmell clinging to it.

Now weigh the package. The scale says 3 pounds. OK, now to deviousness. I shall make up another package that also weighs 3 pounds, address it to a nonexistent person, and take it inland to the nice man at a post office where he will tell me I owe him so much. There will be no return address on the package. It will lie on the dead package shelf until somebody decides to open it — to find a cache of marbles wrapped in cotton batting.

Knowing what 3-pound packages cost ahead of time allows me anonymity. I can stamp the thing myself and toss it casually into a mailbox and no one will associate me with the package. Nefarious types must be forgettable — or better yet, unseen.

Rats! Now Pandora weighs 3½ pounds on the scale! Maybe it's the humidity. More likely it's the scale.

More stamps! More than enough. How much is more than enough? Think simply. Think calmly. Have a cigarette and admire your nice *3-to-4*-pound package. Now get cracking!

I mailed it!

By the end of this day it will all be over. A phone call, a visit — and I am done.

I think I need a slug of so-so sherry. A large slug and ample cigarettes to give it flair . . .

She said this afternoon at three would be fine. I gather there are few visitors.

MURIEL
CAPE CHARLOTTE
JUNE

Here I've gone on and on and I forgot to tell you about my patient! The reason being it would drive me bats seeing as the person is comatose (which, for your information if I haven't told you already, means out of it, Alma).

So that hard shell I put around me usually works — except I keep looking at the picture, the one on the dresser. My poor patient was a ladykiller, that one. For sure he's changed, but he must have been *something* before the accident — the one that killed Mr. Thurston. Buffy loved him like a son, because she *adopted* him, gave him the name of Thurston. According to Cook, who was having a good day the time she told me, Mr. Thurston would have been proud to have this Chris bear his name seeing as the boy, who doesn't look young anymore more's the pity, had tried to save him. That's what happened. They both tried to keep some little girl who shouldn't have been up on that rock in the first place from falling in the ocean and they pushed her aside, but then they both began to fall trying to help each other — and the upshot is Mr. Thurston drowned but the boy, Christopher, was saved — if you can call lying completely paralyzed for ten years now saved!

He can't move, he can't see, he can't talk. I'm not sure he can hear. I did try reading to him for a bit. Not anything like the newspaper, of course. Too much killing going on. And besides, he wouldn't care about what happens in those foreign places which I can't pronounce anyhow. So as I said I read to him, but more interesting stuff from magazines. Stories — the kind I like where the girl is pretty underneath but nobody can see it, until the end when she gets the Lord of the Manor who knew it all along. Well, I read him a ton of stories, but he sure showed no signs of perking up so I quit.

I've nursed quite a few in my time, but I tell you, this one's a dud. I've seen people in comas wiggle a little finger or something. But this one is living death, believe me. Nothing.

I was thinking of that plug. It would be so easy to pull it out — just a bit, mind you — to look like I bumped it when I was sponging his face or putting drops in his eyes. Poor thing. Can't blink even. Most of the time I keep his eyes covered with special gauze to keep out the dust. Well, if that plug *did* get bumped, who's to say it wasn't an accident, I ask you.

The suction isn't working right . . .

Back again. Boy, machines — you can't trust em. I had to pull out the guck because he'd get p-neumonia quicker than a lick if it stayed down. Whacked the friggin excuse the expression pump and it behaved itself. They spend Ft. Knox on these things and I have to keep my eye on every blessed one!

Wait — that's the phone and Alfred can't hear and Cook is taking a nap.

Speaking of the devil which I just was — guess who *that* was? Miss Emma Pickering, herself. She's the little girl who caused all the trouble, the one who got saved. And she wants to come over here! To see him for a few minutes. And thank him. Says she never got a chance after it happened and then she moved away, but she's back for a few days and wanted to know if it'd be OK. So what could I say but sure — but only for ten minutes. So she's coming at three o'clock.

That's a good time because at four, the people from the little library, the one here in Cape Charlotte, are coming to take all the books — the classics they call them. Buffy willed the books to them and she died two years ago. Boy! If I got willed something, which Glory Be would strike me dead if I was, cause I don't see no rich relative on the horizon. Do you, Alma? If something was coming to me, I'd sure pick it up quick. Well anyway, they're coming to take all the books in the library and the ones in the bedrooms. Good thing too. Dusty old things! I wouldn't be caught reading such boring stuff. I remember looking around for something to read when I was out of magazines and I chanced to find myself in Mr. Thurston's study, and there — in a closet — was a box that had "Henry's things from the office" written on it. Well, I wasn't exactly prying, you understand, but I couldn't help noticing that under old maps and *Farmer's Almanacs* and that thing you slide and learn about numbers with was — guess what? *Gone With the Wind!* Mr. Thurston must have used it for doodling! A lot of words were circled. Sister always whacked us if *we* marked up books! Bet he woulda stopped if he'd had Sister do a number on *his* knuckles! Betcha!

Well, I'll stop now and have lunch.

She came — just let her in. I don't know what I expected. Yes I do — a little girl — and she's growed up. When you think about it, Alma, it was almost ten years ago it happened so I shouldn't be surprised. I'll give her a few more minutes . . .

EMMA
CAPE CHARLOTTE
JUNE

I've never seen the inside of the Big House before and it's not so scary. Always seemed so dark and gloomy from the outside— maybe because Mrs. Thurston didn't suffer children gladly ...

He's there ... behind the door and she's opening it and chattering away and I don't hear a word she's saying.

The door has closed and I'm all alone with him. I thought the room would be still, but there are all sorts of squirting, sucking, whooshing noises.

He is there ... on the bed ... he still exists ... I've known it all these years. Somewhere down deep I knew he survived. This *is* the last horror ... and I've made it to here. Can I step closer? My mouth is dry and my hands are jerking and I can't move. Evil lies there and it scares the hell out of me. I can just see tubes snaking out, a lot of tubes. I have the awful feeling he can rise up right now and shake them off. Is he pretending? He was so good at pretending ... maybe he's not an invalid but has waited all these years to rise up and destroy me.

Closer ... closer ... oh my God! He's not going to leap out and get me! He's not playing a waiting game — oh God! The boogy man is ... bald! A large shiny head, so shiny it looks like it is buffed lovingly each day. Such a large head on a shrunken body, a wasted body curled up like a baby. But a very old baby. That mouth, the mouth that could snap into a grin in a twinkling, is sucked in like a prune and the cheekbones are two cliffs, with lines cut into the face radiating down like lava trenches.

"Obersturmführer Henkel? You have a visitor. It's me, Emma. The girl from the beach. You remember me, don't you? I didn't die that day. I almost did, but Mr. Thurston came just in time and I kicked the knife away. I can still hear it clattering down the rocks before it hit the sea. You hit the rocks and they thought you would die but you didn't. These machines keep you alive.

"I don't know if you are listening, Hannes ... Christopher ... Christopher, I'll use the name you will die with.

"I can only stay a few minutes, but I wanted you to know that your journals and diamonds are safe and will be put to good use. Just this morning I finished editing the journals. I decided that some of your diary was badly written and needed cutting. So I took it upon myself to excise those pages. I burned them — along with miscellaneous medals and letters — one a commendation from your Führer. However . . . however . . . I saved certain portions of your journals, particularly one portion that was so well written, so graphically written, that I thought it should be preserved for others to marvel at.

"For a time I wondered who should have the honor of knowing Hannes Henkel at his best — although your name has been eliminated in all the passages. Too bad you will not go down in history as the author of that brilliant work. But you will speak for all those brave men, those hand-picked heroes of the SS known as the Einsatzgruppen.

"Ten years have passed. I'm twenty-three, nearly as old as you were then. I've cut off my braids. I've grown, especially in the last two weeks. Ten years have passed, and the world has changed and gone on, and new wars have broken out and new countries have started. Did you know there is a homeland for Jews now, Christopher? The new state is called Israel. You tried so hard, but you didn't get them all. Perhaps that is the place where your journals would have a wide audience. Not knowing whom to send them to there, I did what I hope is the next best thing. I bundled up the pages and put them in a box and on top I placed the chamois bags of diamonds. I wrapped the package very neatly. Oh, before I wrapped it, I enclosed a note that you would understand and I hope they do, too.

"I wrote: 'A Final Solution.'

"There are still Jews who want and need to go to Israel. The diamonds can help pay for *that* solution.

"I came here, Christopher, full of fear. And hate. And even thoughts of murder. An eye for an eye. The Old Testament. The testament of the Jews reeks with revenge and Jehovah is pointing his finger at you.

"And as I stand here, I'm stifling the beast inside me that wants to murder.

"You lie there like a white slimy slug. You can't even hear me . . . can't know how much I want to hit and stamp and smash you. I have to do something or I will scream! I . . . I . . . can only . . . *spit on you!*"

MURIEL
CAPE CHARLOTTE
JUNE

Well! She left. Just like that! Whooshed out like a whirlwind without a by-your-leave or nothing. Didn't even say thank you. No manners! These young things don't know what manners are anymore, Alma! I'll be right back. Have to check and I'll be right back.

Oh Alma! I want to bawl. I want to lie down and bawl my heart out! It's just too sad. It's a miracle is what it is. A miracle! He was crying! He was crying tears! Running down one side of his face, and I checked the EKG right away I can tell you and his pressure cuff, and there was an elevation, not a dangerous one, but a change. Do you realize what this means? He can *hear* and *feel!*

Yes I know you think I put too many drops in his eyes. Well I didn't! I know because in all the flurry of letting her in I plain forgot to put in his regular.

I washed off them tears. I hated to cause they were a sign. I know it! They were a sign. And I said to him as what he needed was more visits from that nice girl. Well, Alma, between you and I, I know he won't get none again from her because she's left for good. But she made him *feel.*

I know what I'm going to do, Alma. I've got a pile of magazines, and right now I'm going to sit by his bed and read him the best love stories I can find and that'll cheer him up, you bet!

EMMA
CAPE CHARLOTTE
JUNE

I'm going to sit under the juniper, Who Me. Will you come and keep me company? I need company . . .

You know, Who Me, I'm going to miss you when I leave. Would it be too much to ask that you accompany me back? I know it would mean a different house, but you'd like the house. It's old and has interesting smells and corners and closets to hide in. And I'd buy you an avocado a week and chicken hearts . . .

Oh, Who Me! I'm sorry . . . I'm crying all over your fur . . . I'm a coward! I couldn't do it! I couldn't! I wanted to, I got all ready to, and then . . . then I swallowed . . . and I . . . couldn't spit on him . . . I couldn't!

Epilogue

THE NEW YORK TIMES
JULY 7, 1955

UJA MYSTERY PACKAGE RESURRECTS HOLOCAUST

The United Jewish Appeal of New York announced today that an anonymous package addressed to them contained journals said to have been written by an unknown SS lieutenant involved in mass murder.

Ten years after the unconditional surrender of the Third Reich, the graphically detailed journals may rekindle the world's horror. So believes Harry Saltzman, deputy director of the UJA.

"Some of the entries written between 1941 and 1943 were . . . they were beyond belief . . . awful! But I can't go into particulars. That's up to Jerusalem."

He said that the journals had been flown to Israel for evaluation. He also said that the parcel contained about a half-kilo of diamonds in chamois bags. "Over 2000 carats. They must be worth a fortune! It is a pity that we may never know where they came from."

He explained that the New York Diamond Exchange was sending one of its best people to examine the stones.

Contacted in Jerusalem, a spokesman for Prime Minister David Ben-Gurion acknowledged the receipt of the journals last night. "We have not had time for a full examination. But they contain explosive material. Explosive! You see, over the years we recovered many SS diaries. They had a monotonous sameness, rehashing propaganda and fiery rhetoric. These journals are different — very, very personal. They chronicle a man's pathway to hell: the evolution of a killer. It would appear that there is a murderer in each of us — if the right button is pushed.

"It's too bad there isn't more. Some sections have been cut."

When asked about the diamonds, he replied, "We don't consider them of high priority. The important material is here — in Israel."

THE NEW YORK TIMES
JULY 8, 1955

REVELATION IN HOLOCAUST PACKAGE

Journals written by an unknown SS lieutenant, a member of the infamous murder squads, the Einsatzgruppen, were hailed as a major find yesterday. Today, in a bizarre and enigmatic twist, the spotlight has shifted to a cache of diamonds contained in the same package.

Irving Weiss, 72, of Brooklyn, a diamond appraiser, was reported recovering from shock and unavailable for comment.

Harry Saltzman, deputy director of the UJA, reported that the process of examination began this morning at UJA headquarters. Weiss quickly separated the diamonds into two piles. The first pile contained stones of over two carats. Although they were few in number, Weiss was impressed by their high quality.

He then turned to the large pile of smaller stones. One by one, he declared them worthless. "He called them 'trash!' I couldn't believe it," commented Mr. Saltzman.

And then, suddenly, Mr. Weiss began reciting the Hebrew prayer "Lord God of Israel," chanting it over and over. He was shaking.

According to Mr. Saltzman, the office was very hot and Mr. Weiss still wore his long woolen coat. "He was in an awful state, fumbling around in his bag. I was sure that his heart was failing and he was looking for digitalis."

Weiss, however, was searching for a jeweler's loupe of greater magnification. He looked at the small stone he'd been examining before and burst into tears.

Saltzman continued, "He couldn't talk. He just pressed the loupe and the diamond into my hands. It was a very small stone. At first I couldn't see anything, just edges and planes, and a little rainbow fire. Then I saw it. On one of the tiny facets. Sort of crude, but unmistakable. On one of the facets someone had scratched a Star of David!"